Rich Waters

An Amazon Best Book of the Month: Mystery, Thriller & Suspense

"A compelling dive into the life of a lawyer out way past his depth."
—*Kirkus Reviews*

"Small town, big story—*Rich Waters* works like magic as a mystery and a legal thriller, but what I loved best was Robert Bailey's attention to the details of character and place. I'd ride with Jason Rich to a courthouse anywhere!"
—Michael Connelly, #1 *New York Times* bestselling author

Rich Blood

An Amazon Best Book of the Month: Mystery, Thriller & Suspense

"Well-drawn characters match the surprise-filled plot. Phillip Margolin fans will be enthralled."
—*Publishers Weekly* (starred review)

"*Rich Blood* is a deliciously clever legal thriller that keeps you turning pages fast and furious. Robert Bailey's latest is wildly entertaining."
—Patricia Cornwell, #1 *New York Times* bestselling author

The Wrong Side

"Bailey expertly ratchets up the suspense as the plot builds to a surprise punch ending. Readers will impatiently await the next in the series."
—*Publishers Weekly* (starred review)

"Social tensions redoubled by race intensify a workmanlike mystery."
—*Kirkus Reviews*

Previous Praise for Robert Bailey

"*The Professor* is that rare combination of thrills, chills, and heart. Gripping from the first page to the last."
—Winston Groom, author of *Forrest Gump*

"Robert Bailey is a thriller writer to reckon with. His debut novel has a tight and twisty plot, vivid characters, and a pleasantly down-home sensibility that will remind some readers of adventures in Grisham-land. Luckily, Robert Bailey is an original, and his skill as a writer makes the Alabama setting all his own. *The Professor* marks the beginning of a very promising career."
—Mark Childress, author of *Georgia Bottoms and Crazy in Alabama*

"Taut, page turning, and smart, *The Professor* is a legal thriller that will keep readers up late as the twists and turns keep coming. Set in Alabama, it also includes that state's greatest icon, one Coach Bear Bryant. In fact, the Bear gets things going with the energy of an Alabama kickoff to Auburn. Robert Bailey knows his state, and he knows his law. He also knows how to write characters that are real, sympathetic, and surprising. If he keeps writing novels this good, he's got quite a literary career before him."

—Homer Hickam, author of *Rocket Boys/October Sky*, a *New York Times* #1 bestseller

"Bailey's solid second McMurtrie and Drake legal thriller (after 2014's *The Professor*) . . . provides enough twists and surprises to keep readers turning the pages."

—*Publishers Weekly*

"A gripping legal suspense thriller of the first order, *Between Black and White* clearly displays author Robert Bailey's impressive talents as a novelist. An absorbing and riveting read from beginning to end."

—*Midwest Book Review*

"Take a murder, a damaged woman, and a desperate daughter, and you have the recipe for *The Last Trial*, a complex and fast-paced legal thriller. Highly recommended."

—D. P. Lyle, award-winning author

"*The Final Reckoning* is explosive and displays every element of a classic thriller: fast pacing, strong narrative, fear, misery, and transcendence. Bailey proves once more that he is a fine writer with an instinct for powerful white-knuckle narrative."

—*Southern Literary Review*

"A stunning discovery, a triple twist, and dramatic courtroom scenes all make for a riveting, satisfying read in what might well be Bailey's best book to date . . . *Legacy of Lies* is a grand story with a morality-tale vibe, gripping and thrilling throughout. It showcases Bailey once more as a writer who knows how to keep the suspense high, the pacing fast, the narrative strong, the characters compellingly complex, and his plot full of white-knuckle tension and twists."

—*Southern Literary Review*

"Inspiring . . . Sharp in its dialogue, real with its relationships, and fascinating in details of the game, *The Golfer's Carol* is that rarest of books—one you will read and keep for yourself while purchasing multiple copies for friends."

—Andy Andrews, *New York Times* bestselling author of *The Noticer* and *The Traveler's Gift*

RICH
JUSTICE

ALSO BY ROBERT BAILEY

JASON RICH SERIES

Rich Waters

Rich Blood

BOCEPHUS HAYNES SERIES

The Wrong Side

Legacy of Lies

MCMURTRIE AND DRAKE LEGAL THRILLERS

The Final Reckoning

The Last Trial

Between Black and White

The Professor

OTHER BOOKS

The Golfer's Carol

RICH JUSTICE

ROBERT BAILEY

Published by Thomas & Mercer, Seattle

www.apub.com

Amazon, the Amazon logo, and Thomas & Mercer are trademarks of Amazon.com, Inc., or its affiliates.

ISBN-13: 9781662516634 (paperback)
ISBN-13: 9781662516641 (digital)

Cover design by Jarrod Taylor
Cover image: © Judy Kennamer / ArcAngel

Printed in the United States of America

For my father-in-law, Dr. Jim Davis

PROLOGUE

Albertville, Alabama, November 13, 2019

At 10:15 a.m., a black SUV pulled into the entrance of the Alder Springs Grocery. Tyson Cade opened the back passenger-side door and, without looking at the driver, said, "Fifteen minutes."

He watched the car turn onto Hustleville Road. In the distance, he saw Branner's Place, an old abandoned barn that used to be the site of many a drug deal.

But seven months ago, it had been the scene of a murder. And nothing in Tyson's operation had been the same since.

Tyson gazed past the barn to the billboard in the distance. Even from here, he could see the attorney's stubbly face.

IN AN ACCIDENT? GET RICH!

Tyson grinned, wondering when the tacky ads would be taken down. *Not too much longer,* he thought. So many people had tried to get the best of Tyson Cade over the years. Jason Rich had joined a long list of people that Tyson had chewed up and spat out.

But I'm not done, he thought. Rich and his crazy neighbors, the Tonidandel brothers, had become a huge thorn in Tyson's operation. They'd cost him his mole in the sheriff's department and had almost succeeded in putting his right-hand man in prison. It had been a long time since an adversary had hurt Tyson's methamphetamine empire, but Rich was a resourceful lawyer, and Colonel Satch Tonidandel and his two brothers, both captains themselves, had drawn blood. They needed to be eliminated.

And if Tyson's plans were carried out, all four would be dead in a few days . . .

. . . *or hours.*

He hawked a loogie on the asphalt and gazed in both directions along the road that connected Highways 227 and 75. His territory now stretched over several counties and even into Tennessee.

But home was here. He'd grown up less than a mile from where he stood.

Tyson turned and walked toward the front door with purpose. He was a busy man and had little time for a trip down memory lane. And though he made his living selling vices, he rarely enjoyed any.

But there was one particular perversion that the drug dealer would not deny himself. The door jingled when he opened it, and he saw the clerk counting bills at the cash register. She looked up at the sound, and he noticed the slightest sucking in of air before she gave him a fake smile. It was a reaction that Tyson had grown accustomed to. Not just in the women he enjoyed, but the dealers, distributors, and cooks who worked for him.

Fear.

He smiled back at her. "Slow morning?"

"Not too bad." Her voice was timid. He could tell that she knew what was coming.

He nodded toward a storage closet adjacent to the restrooms. "Let's make this quick, huh, Doob?"

Marcia "Dooby" Darnell had long red hair that she'd put up in a ponytail. She wore faded jeans and a gray hoodie over a T-shirt. Her skin was pale in the fluorescent glow of the overhead bulb, and there was a sheen of sweat on her neck. It was one of those classic fall days in Alabama where the temperature was too cold for air-conditioning but too warm for the heat to click on. The air in the store wasn't circulating. It felt muggy and uncomfortable.

Not ideal work conditions, but perfect for what they were about to do. Tyson began to walk toward the storage area but stopped when he didn't hear steps following him. "I'm in a hurry, Dooby. Let's go."

"No." Her voice escaped her mouth in a squeak, and Tyson wasn't sure he'd heard right. He turned and glared at her.

"I didn't catch that, Doob. What did you say?"

Her jaw was set, and her face had turned a ghostly white. "I said no." She bit her lip. "There's a customer outside at the pump."

Tyson squinted at Dooby. "What's gotten into you?"

She held his gaze. "I'm working."

He scoffed. "Never stopped us before."

She opened her mouth to say something, but Tyson turned his back on her. He went to the restroom and relieved himself. Then he grabbed a bottle of Sun Drop from the drink cooler and a Twinkie from the snack aisle. He put the conveniences on the counter and watched Dooby. Her hair was greasy, and her neck glowed with sweat. Her cheeks were red. She was scared, and Tyson felt himself stiffen. He leaned forward and gestured for her to do the same. He took a deep breath and exhaled into her ear, biting down on the lobe. "Nobody tells me no, Dooby."

"I'll make it up to you tonight," she whispered. "I just can't today."

He ran his hand down her arm and then her leg, and grabbed the waistband of her Levi's. He felt her stomach clench when his hand moved around to the front. As his fingers began to probe lower, she pulled back and put her palms out in front of her. "Please, Tyson. I said no."

He glared at her. Dooby Darnell had never told him no. Ever. "What's up with you?"

"Four dollars and twenty-six cents," she said, her voice quiet but firm, glancing down at the snacks he was buying.

Tyson guffawed and pulled out his wallet. He flung a twenty-dollar bill on the counter. When Dooby reached to grab it, he caught her around the neck and squeezed. "I asked you a question."

She struggled for breath, and her eyes went wide.

"I trust all is well with your momma." Tyson spat the words, running his face down her neck and breathing in the salty perspiration. "All her nursing home bills good and paid for?" He loosened his grip just enough for Dooby to nod. "We wouldn't want there to be any interruptions in her care, would we?"

Tears filled Dooby's eyes, and she shook her head.

"I didn't think so." He let go, and she fell to her knees, gasping for breath.

Tyson looked down at her and then glanced out the window. A woman was getting gas at the pump.

"I'll see you tonight, Dooby." He whistled through his teeth. "And I'll make sure this month's nursing home invoice gets paid."

She had pulled herself to her feet and was rubbing her neck with both hands.

She nodded, still not looking at him. "Thank you."

"Glad to do it." He leaned forward and grabbed her chin. "I always take care of my people, don't I?" He kissed her neck, again tasting the salt on his tongue. "See you soon."

Tyson glanced at the clock on the wall. He'd been inside exactly fifteen minutes. He winked at Dooby, took his items, and turned for the door.

At 10:30 a.m., Tyson Cade stepped out of the Alder Springs Grocery. The sun was full in the sky, and the meth king breathed in the fresh air and enjoyed the heat from the rays on his face. He carried his Twinkie in one hand and the Sun Drop in the other.

He glanced to his left and saw a car approaching. He began to walk toward the road as the car slowed its pace. As Tyson was about to get in, he heard a voice yell out from behind him.

"Tyson, wait!"

He turned and saw Dooby Darnell. Even from thirty feet away, he could see the perspiration on her neck in the glare of the sun.

"You forgot your change."

Tyson wrinkled up his face. Then, feeling his stomach tighten, he tried to duck.

He wasn't fast enough.

Gunfire erupted from behind the convenience store, and Tyson felt his chest explode. He sank to his knees.

Dooby dropped the change she was holding to the ground and covered her mouth.

Tyson Cade blinked his eyes and fell over on his back. He touched his chest and looked at his bloody hand. Then, as his pulse slowed and he began to lose consciousness, he laughed.

And the cars continued to pass on Hustleville Road.

PART ONE

1

Jason woke up when he heard the sirens. He struggled to open his eyes, which were crusted over with sleep. He was lying on his side, and his face was mashed against something rough.

His outstretched left hand was clasped around a pistol.

Jason let go of the weapon. He rolled over on his stomach and felt nauseous. Crawling forward, he saw the dark water. He turned his head and recognized his dock. The two lawn chairs behind him. The small table with the captain's chair. The empty fifth of Jack Daniel's lying on the wooden flooring, cap off, exactly where he had dropped it after finishing the last sip.

He took in a deep breath. He had no idea the time. How long had he been out here?

The sirens grew louder. Closer. Coming up Highway 79 from the direction of Guntersville. Jason gritted his teeth, trying to hold his stomach together. He coughed and could no longer control himself. He leaned over the dock and vomited into the lake.

He heaved twice more, coughing and spitting up the bile. Finally, his breathing relaxed, the fit over, and he pulled himself to his feet.

The sirens were on top of him now, and he saw blue and red lights turning down Mill Creek Road.

One squad car.

Two.

Three.

Jason stared down at the gun. It was a Glock 17. He'd bought it almost two weeks ago. He'd wanted a nine millimeter that was accurate from a longer distance than the 43X that Satch had taught him to shoot last year. During his practice sessions, he'd been accurate up to about forty yards.

He grabbed the handgun and checked the chamber. There were several bullets missing. Feeling his heart begin to race in his stomach, Jason turned and tossed the gun into Lake Guntersville.

Then, as the first police car turned in to his driveway, he sat down on the pier.

And waited.

2

Yellow crime scene tape covered the asphalt surface between the lone fuel dispenser at the Alder Springs Grocery and Hustleville Road. At least a dozen sheriff's cruisers blanketed the area around the spot where the victim still lay.

Hatty Daniels, the newly appointed sheriff of Marshall County, gazed at the body on the ground. Hatty's arms were crossed, her chin tucked low against her chest. It had been three hours since the shooting. She had walked the entire area several times and talked to both witnesses.

The checkout clerk was in shock and had been taken to Marshall Medical Center South for treatment. Based on the limited amount of information they were able to glean from her upon arrival after the 911 dispatch, she'd seen only the victim. Not the shooter.

The customer hadn't seen the murder at all. She'd been pumping gas and looking at her phone when she heard the shots. But she'd responded, calling 911 seconds after finding the victim lying on the ground. She'd knelt beside him and waited for emergency personnel to arrive.

And heard his last words . . .

Hatty continued to stare at the corpse. She had never met Tyson Kennesaw Cade, nor had she ever seen him up close. But she knew of him. Hell, everyone in Marshall County knew Tyson Cade.

His body was lying in the condition it had been found. Cade was on his back. He had a large wound in the middle of his chest. Though she would wait for the official coroner's report, Hatty knew what she was looking at.

At least three rounds directly in the center of the chest.

Whoever had shot the victim was a good marksman . . . *or a professional.*

Hatty raised her chin and moved her eyes around the gas station. The body was facing the store, so the shots had likely come from that direction. Of course, that wasn't entirely true. Cade could have turned away from the shots and fallen, which would have the rounds being fired from the road. She knew it would be unwise to make any assumptions. Especially this early.

But I've already made one, she thought, fixing her jaw as a deputy approached her.

"Our team has arrived at Rich's house," the officer said.

"And?" Hatty asked, peering down at the victim as crime scene technicians continued to work around him.

"His neighbors are making it difficult."

Hatty sighed. "The colonel?"

The officer nodded. "And both his brothers. Greta says the situation is volatile."

"OK, I'm headed there. When the CSI folks are done, call me."

"Yes, ma'am."

Hatty strode to her car and took a last look at the scene, which was pure pandemonium. Not only was there yellow tape around Tyson Cade's body, but the officers had roped off a large area around the grocery. Beyond those ropes were at least a hundred people. Some had pulled their trucks up and were sitting on tailgates. Others stared in disbelief. Across Hustleville Road, there were at least fifty others. Similar expressions. Shock. Bewilderment. A few appeared to be satisfied, as if justice had been done. Others looked angry. Most, though, gave off a vibe of curiosity.

Tyson Cade, the methamphetamine czar of Sand Mountain, was dead. Murdered on Hustleville Road. Hatty had been on the job less than a month, and she would now have to deal with the biggest murder investigation in the history of Guntersville.

To law enforcement, Cade had been the scourge of Marshall County.

But to the people in Alder Springs, Albertville, and all along that stretch of Alabama referred to as Sand Mountain, Tyson Cade had been more. Yes, some thought of him as a devil. But others saw Cade as a protector. A Robin Hood–like man-child who had risen to the top of the meth trade before he was thirty years old.

And now, like a meteor, Cade had fallen. Shot to death in the absolute heart of his territory. And, if Hatty's instincts were right, his killer might very well be the most famous, or perhaps infamous, lawyer in Guntersville. If not the whole state . . .

Hatty pulled onto Hustleville Road and passed by a large tacky billboard, one of the many that had yet to be taken down since the attorney's suspension from the practice of law. A man with thick dirty-blond hair and similarly colored stubble, wearing a navy suit, white shirt, and red tie, grinned in the advertisement, below which was written his slogan.

IN AN ACCIDENT? GET RICH!

The lawyer had cluttered up the entire Southeast with the billboards. He'd only been without a license for a few weeks—much too soon to have all the placards removed.

She took a deep breath and exhaled.

No one said being sheriff was going to be easy, she thought, flipping on her siren and headlights and pressing the accelerator to the floor.

3

Jason trudged up the slope to his house and walked around the side. He had expected the officers to come down to the dock, but they had not done so. As he rounded the corner, he saw why. He heard loud angry voices and saw three men holding off an army of deputies.

Despite his weakened condition and shock at the spectacle, Jason couldn't help but smile.

"What's going on?" Jason asked. He stepped forward, nodding at Mickey and Chuck Tonidandel before making eye contact with their older brother.

Colonel Satchel Shames Tonidandel wore a stained white tank top, jeans, and a straw cowboy hat. He stood six feet, four inches tall and had thinned down to around 235 pounds. Even slimmer, his curly brown hair and salt-and-pepper beard gave him a rugged presence, and his reptilian squint tended to scare people. As Jason looked past Satch to the officers, he could sense the tension in the air.

"These sons of bitches barged into your house without a warrant," Satch said. "I'm not a lawyer, but I know damn well that ain't legal."

"The door was open," the officer in front said. "All we were trying to do is find you. Besides . . ." She pulled a piece of paper out of her pocket and handed it to Jason. "We do have a warrant."

Jason glanced down at the document and then back up at the officer, a thin woman with brown hair. **SGT. GRETA MARTIN** was embroidered over the lapel of her uniform.

"Sergeant, what are you doing here?"

"We need to search your home and boathouse. And we'd also like you to come down to the station with us. We knocked on the door, and, when it was open, I stepped inside. All I wanted to do was locate you to explain the situation, and then these three went berserk." She paused. "They seem awful touchy."

"Colonel Tonidandel and his brothers are my security detail," Jason said. "I pay them to be touchy. And you haven't explained anything."

Sergeant Martin held up her hands. "You haven't given me much of a chance."

"OK, what do you want from me?"

"To ask you some questions and to search the premises."

Jason scratched his neck. Adrenaline was beginning to flow through his body, pushing past the fatigue. He was wide awake now and hyper-alert. He was also pissed off. "About what?"

Martin frowned. "It would be better if we went to the station."

"Better for who?" Jason asked. "Come on, Sergeant, what's this about?"

Martin cleared her throat, but the sound of another siren made her turn around. A fourth squad car had pulled onto Mill Creek Road and came to an abrupt stop in front of the house.

When Sheriff Hatty Daniels stepped out of the car, Jason's entire body tensed. He waited as she approached. Though the new sheriff had been on the opposite sides of both murder trials he'd had in Marshall County, Jason had worked with her last year on a tangential matter. He admired her, though he couldn't say he trusted her.

Jason didn't trust anyone except maybe the three brothers standing by his side.

"Sheriff?"

"Jason."

There was a pause, and Jason waited for it. Just as he was about to ask the question that hung in the air, Hatty answered it.

"Tyson Cade was shot this morning outside the Alder Springs Grocery. He's dead."

Jason couldn't believe his ears. *What?* He looked from the sheriff to Sergeant Martin. Then he glanced down at the search warrant. "And you think I did it?"

"Your SUV . . . not the Porsche . . . was seen on a traffic light video about six miles from the Alder Springs Grocery." She hesitated. "Approximately ten minutes after the shooting."

Jason said nothing, but felt cold sweat begin to percolate on his face and under his arms.

"Will you agree to come in for questioning?" Hatty asked.

"Hell, no, he won't," Satch said.

The sheriff turned toward Satch. "We'll need to talk with you, too, Colonel. And your brothers." She glanced behind him to Chuck and Mickey. "And we have a warrant to search your property as well."

Jason thought of the gun in the lake and touched Satch's shoulder, forcing a smile. "It's OK, Colonel. We're happy to accommodate, Sheriff. We have nothing to hide. But can I have a few minutes to clean up?"

"I'd rather you come with me now," Hatty said, her voice firm.

"Hatty, this is ridiculous."

"Jason, we know you blamed Cade for your investigator's murder last year. And I heard you tell me firsthand that you were going to make Tyson Cade pay for it."

"That doesn't mean I killed him."

"No, it doesn't." Hatty took a step closer and spoke in a soft voice. "Look, just come down to the station with me. Answer some questions. With Cade being killed and given the bad blood between the two of you, it may not be safe here anyway." She hesitated, glancing from Jason to the colonel. "We're concerned about the potential for retaliation from the Sand Mountain meth ring that Cade controlled . . . particularly in light of who may be in line to succeed him. Do I need to remind either of you of how dangerous Matty Dean is?"

Jason's stomach tightened. *Matty Dean* . . .

"Retaliation, hell," Satch said. "We're already on Cade's hit list, according to my Sand Mountain contacts. That's why we're so god-damned *touchy*." He glared at Sergeant Martin and then back at Hatty.

Hatty gazed down at the pavement and licked her lips. When she spoke, her tone was softer. "All the more reason for Jason to come with me, Colonel."

For several seconds, there was silence. Jason again thought of the pistol he'd thrown in the lake and the condition he'd been in when he heard the sirens.

Tyson Cade is dead . . .

"OK, Sheriff. I'll go," he said. "But I want Satch and his brothers to stay here until the searches are over. Forgive me if I don't trust the sheriff's office."

Hatty frowned, her face tense, but she finally nodded. "OK then. Come with me."

Jason was escorted into the back of the squad car. As the door closed behind him, he glanced up at Satch, who was peering hard at him.

"*It's OK*," Jason mouthed, thinking the exact opposite to himself as the car began to move forward.

It's not OK.

4

Inside the confines of the police car, Jason felt small. Weak. He took a deep breath and smelled himself. The scent was an earthy aroma layered with sweat and what he thought was a mild tinge of bourbon. *Not awful,* he thought.

"You reek," Hatty said, as if reading his erroneous thoughts. She kept her eyes locked on the road as she turned onto Highway 79.

"Thanks," Jason said, hearing the rasp in his voice. His mouth tasted like sandpaper from the vomiting episode he'd suffered on the dock.

"I'd heard you fell off the wagon," Hatty said, the disapproval palpable in her tone. "I guess I can now confirm that. You smell like a distillery." She paused, then added, "If the whiskey was being made in a locker room."

Jason managed a chuckle. "I doubt you've been in either place."

"I played four years of volleyball and basketball in high school," Hatty snapped. "And, when I worked in Pulaski, I made the trek to Lynchburg several times. I even have a bottle of single-barrel Jack at home for special occasions."

Jason scoffed. "Congrats."

Her mask finally broke, and she studied him through the rearview mirror.

"No, I mean it," Jason said. "Not just for being around whiskey and sweat during your life, but for winning the election. You made history, and you deserve it."

Hatty kept her eyes locked on his for a second, as if she were trying to determine whether he was bullshitting her or being straight.

"The first Black sheriff in Marshall County history," Jason said, glancing out the window as Lake Guntersville came into and then out of view. "And also a female. I never thought . . ." Jason paused. He wasn't bullshitting, and he wanted to make sure that Hatty understood that. "I'm proud of you, Hatty. You may not believe that, but I am."

Silence filled the squad car as Jason looked down at his hands. His fingernails were grimy with dirt from the lake. He was nasty. Actually, it was worse than that. He felt rotten. Like a piece of spoiled meat that had been sitting out on the counter too long.

"Thank you," Hatty finally said. She turned onto Highway 431, and Jason frowned at one of his billboards as they drove by it. In another month, all the highway posters would be gone. Just like his website. His offices in Guntersville and Birmingham. His law license. His family.

And all his friends except the Tonidandel brothers.

Gone.

Jason looked out the window as Hatty drove them over the Veterans Memorial Bridge. In mid-November, there were few boats on the grayish water, which almost matched the color of the cloud-filled sky. To the right, he saw Fire by the Lake restaurant. And to the left, the scenic beauty of Buck Island, where the elite of Marshall County lived and where the even wealthier had their vacation homes. A murder at a boathouse on this stretch of lakefront had brought Jason home a year and a half ago. He'd thought he was doing the right thing, but he'd since lost everything he cared about.

As they crossed over the bridge and into the quaint city of Guntersville, Jason felt a wave of depression grip him.

He closed his eyes as they passed the establishments that Jason had known most of his life. He didn't want to see his old law office, which was now boarded up. Nor did he want to observe the blank billboard just above it, which had once advertised his smiling stubble-faced mug. And he damn sure didn't want to view the courthouse, where he was no longer allowed to make a living. He sighed and leaned his head against the cold window glass.

As the car came to a stop, Jason kept his eyes shut, hoping that perhaps this whole thing was a nightmare. He rarely had a full night's sleep and, when he did go into a deep slumber, he almost always ended up in a cold sweat, opening his eyes as his past came back to him. His sister, Jana, taking a bullet that was meant for him. His niece Nola jumping into Lake Guntersville to kill herself, and Jason diving in after her and almost drowning as he pulled her back onto the dock. Finally, the one that came to him most now. The shooting a month ago at his office. Sergeant George Mitchell's head exploding like a watermelon hitting pavement from a high altitude. Jason's ears ringing as he dived on top of prosecutor Shay Lankford. Then the return fire from the woman driving him in for questioning right now.

"Jason?"

Hatty's voice. Was he back at the shooting, or was he in real time? He wasn't sure what to hope for anymore.

"Jason, look at me."

He finally opened his eyes, and he was still in the squad car. They were in a dark parking lot with room for only a few cars.

"Where are we?" he asked.

"In the basement under the sheriff's office." She cut the ignition and switched off her dispatch radio. "Jason, I've terminated the video and audio recordings to the squad car. I've got about ninety seconds before I arouse any suspicion, and I want you to listen and listen good."

Jason felt gooseflesh on his arms. "OK."

"I think you should know by now that I'm going to do my job, even if it means charging you with murder."

"Hatty—"

"Let me finish. But I'm not one to forget those who have helped me in my life. But for the Cowan case and your efforts to expose the former sheriff as dirty, I wouldn't be here right now. You helped me, and now I'm going to give you some advice. Don't talk to me. Don't talk to anyone. Hire an attorney and keep your mouth shut."

"Hatty, I'm innocent—"

"Shut up. We don't know enough right now to make an arrest, but it doesn't look good, you hear me?"

Jason blinked, again thinking of the gun he'd tossed in the lake.

"There's also something else. While I won my election, our mutual friend Shay Lankford did not win hers. There is a new district attorney, and Wish French is looking for a return to glory, you understand?"

Jason cringed. *Wish French . . .*

How many times had he heard his father say that name through clenched teeth? Of all the possible replacements for Shay, he couldn't imagine a worse choice. And while Jason could take a tiny bit of the credit for Hatty's victory, he knew he bore a large portion of the blame for Shay Lankford's loss in the DA contest. Shay would still be the head prosecutor absent Jason's victories against her in the Jana Waters and Trey Cowan murder trials.

"Damn," Jason whispered.

"Damn is right," Hatty said. "I won't pull any punches. I'll be fair. But if the evidence demonstrates that you are guilty of killing Tyson Cade, I won't hesitate to charge you. Do you understand?"

"Yes," Jason said, then swallowed and tasted acid in his throat.

"One last thing," Hatty said, turning and looking around the small basement area as a group of deputies poured out of a door in front of them. "Don't do this by yourself, Jason."

"What do you mean?" Jason asked, knowing they only had a couple more seconds before an officer would be opening the door.

"You know precisely what I mean." She glared at him, and Jason raised his eyebrows. "Hire a lawyer, Jason." She paused. Then, in a loud whisper, added, "A damn good one."

5

Mentone, Alabama, was a tiny hamlet that sat on the western tip of Lookout Mountain. Known for children's camps such as Riverview, Skyline, and Alpine, the scenic spot had been used by Tyson Cade for more sinister purposes.

Matty Dean entered the cabin at 7:30 p.m. He trudged toward a circular table and took a seat in a hard-backed wooden chair. Then he let out a deep sigh. He was tired. Physically. Mentally. But most of all . . . emotionally. Finally, he gazed across the room at the two men who'd been waiting on him. "I'm sure you've both heard," Matty said.

"Hard to believe." The voice was a deep baritone, and it belonged to Tanner Sparks, who stepped forward into the dim light given off by the fluorescent fixture above the table. Sparks had thick brown hair that he covered with a trucker's cap. He sported a long *Duck Dynasty*–style beard and wore faded jeans, a plaid flannel jacket, and shitkicker boots. His jaw worked a chaw of tobacco, and he held a Styrofoam coffee cup.

"Yeah," Matty said. Then he forced a hardness into his scratchy tone. "But the show must go on." He glared at Sparks. "How are we looking in the north?"

Sparks spat into his cup. "We're looking fine, old man. Production is on time, and distribution shouldn't miss a beat. Got a new cook in Henagar who's twice as fast, and the product is even better." He paused. "But they're all wondering."

"Wondering what?" Matty asked.

"Who's in charge." Sparks didn't say it like a question, and his blue eyes gleamed in the dim light. Matty knew that look.

Greed . . .

Tanner Sparks was responsible for DeKalb County, which encompassed Fort Payne and a dozen smaller towns, including several unincorporated, off-the-grid holes-in-the-wall. He also had eastern Jackson County, which was a similar territory. From a geographic standpoint, these areas were the largest part of Tyson's Sand Mountain meth operation.

Who's in charge? Matty thought. *That shouldn't even be a question.*

"And what about you?" Matty asked, gazing past Sparks into the darkness, where the other man in the room still stood.

"You want some flowery bullshit or the cold, hard reality?" His tone was cocky. The disrespect palpable.

"You know exactly what I want," Matty said, keeping his tone low but firm.

Reginald Strassburg stepped forward. He had a blond buzz cut and wore brown overalls over a white T-shirt. Reg oversaw meth operations in Etowah and Blount Counties and called Sardis City home. "From a business standpoint, we're fine. At least for now." He paused. "But the community is in shock, Matty. Angry too. Tyson was like a god. He was feared, but he did a lot of good. Gave money to the churches and the schools. Looked after his employees who were being investigated by the law. I'm supposed to have a meeting tomorrow night at a warehouse in Snead. All my cooks, distributors, and sales crew will be there."

"Good," Matty said. "So will I."

Reg frowned. "Sure that's a good idea? The few folks I've been able to reach have all mentioned that you might have had something to do with Tyson's death." He paused again, this time letting the silence drag. "And the thought has crossed my mind as well."

"Mine too," Sparks said.

Matty felt his neck and arms tense. He forced himself to his feet and walked toward Reg. He chuckled, glancing at Sparks before back at Reg. "It has, huh?"

"You were closest to him," Reg said. "And Marshall County is your territory. Nobody knows Alder Springs, Asbury, and Guntersville better than you."

"And there were rumors that you were upset about being busted during the Cowan trial," Sparks said, spitting into his cup, the gleam still in his eye. "As I understand it there's still a warrant out for your—"

A loud blast cut Tanner Sparks's voice off, and the top of his head exploded. He fell backward onto the hardwood. Tobacco juice oozed out of the corner of his mouth and mixed with the blood on the floor.

Reg gasped and took a reflexive step backward. He grabbed a pistol from the front pocket of his overalls and wheeled toward the hallway to the left of the table, where the shotgun blast had come from. But, like Sparks, he was a sitting duck.

Another boom echoed through the cabin, and Reg's left kneecap shattered. He fell in a heap on the floor, clutching his ruined leg, the pistol flying out of his hand. He screamed in agony and tried to crawl away toward the door, but Matty stepped around and in front of him.

"You didn't think I would suspect an ambush?" Matty asked, feeling adrenaline surge through his body as Reg tried to prop himself up. Matty brought a Ruger out of his jacket and swiped it across the young man's face. Then he kicked him in the chest and again in the side of the head.

"What? Did y'all think that you'd just team up to take old Matty down?" He spat on the ground. "Didn't think I was young enough or strong enough for the job?"

"You got this all wrong, Matty," Reg said, wheezing as he rolled over on his back. He held his hands out in front of him in desperation. "We've always worked well together."

Matty pointed the gun at his head. "I got this right, Reg, and you know it. You and Tanner were next in line . . . *behind me.* But guess what? I'm a good bit stronger and a whole hell of a lot meaner than either of you two turds thought I was." He grunted and spat again, the saliva landing on the side of Reg's face. "I'll handle the meeting in Snead. I'm taking your spot myself before I find a replacement." He glanced at Sparks's dead body. "And I've already got someone lined up to take over the north."

Matty glanced toward the hallway, and a woman stepped out of the darkness. Luann Stephens had short brown hair and a petite figure. She wore a T-shirt and camouflage pants and held a sawed-off shotgun with her right arm. Her face was stained with grease from her day job as a mechanic at Sand Mountain Motors. "Looking forward to it," she said.

"Lu?" Reg asked.

"Surprised, shit for brains?" the woman asked, pointing the weapon at his face.

"You really thought you were going to get the jump on me?" Matty asked, his tone incredulous. "*Me?* Matty fuckin' Dean." He chuckled and shook his head.

Any hope had gone out of Reginald Strassburg's eyes. "Did you kill him?" he rasped. "Did you kill Tyson?"

"You'll never know," Matty said, then pointed the pistol at the man's chest and pulled the trigger.

Reg screamed again, bringing his hands to the new wound. Then he stretched his arms out in vain supplication. Blood pooled under him.

"Well, you boys have sure made a mess of the place," Matty said, his eyes flickering to Tanner Sparks's corpse before moving back to Reg. Then he leaned down and put the barrel of the Ruger against the side of the young drug dealer's head.

"Bye, Reg."

An hour later, the cabin showed no signs of the killings.

The floor sparkled from a fresh cleaning, and the room smelled of ammonia. Lu had handled everything. Her son, Butch, who, like his mother, was a lifer in the Sand Mountain meth trade, had hauled the bodies out of the dwelling in industrial-strength trash bags and now was en route to Scottsboro. Later tonight, the bodies of Reginald Strassburg and Tanner Sparks would be unceremoniously dumped into the Tennessee River.

Meanwhile, Lu had scrubbed the floor, removing the blood before it dried and then mopping it twice. For his part, Matty had stood guard in the driveway, moving in a circle around the outside of the cabin, making sure there was no one else who wanted to take a shot at him tonight.

Matty had figured that Tanner and Reg would make a power play. They'd assumed that Matty was too old and weak to take the reins. They'd underestimated him.

He stretched his back and looked out over the mountain. He'd watched a television show recently. *Ted Lasso*. About a football coach that moved to England to coach soccer. A silly show, really, but Matty had enjoyed it. There was a great dart-throwing scene, where Ted took on a rich prick and talked about how folks had underestimated him his whole life. Ted even quoted the famous Walt Whitman line "Be curious, not judgmental" before wiping the floor with the conceited bastard by winning the game with a clutch throw.

That's me, Matty thought. Always overlooked. He'd been OK with it after King Hanson went to prison. It was obvious that Tyson Cade was a unicorn. A force of nature. Matty was self-aware enough to know that the best play for him was to help Tyson seize power. To be Tyson's right hand. And that strategy had paid off. At least . . . until a few months ago.

Matty sighed, his breath making a smoke cloud in the air. Reg had been right about one thing. Tyson *had* been like a god. Swift with his actions. Completely self-assured. He could be kind but also brutal.

But ambition had finally done the young phenom in. Tyson's desire to control the law enforcement of Marshall County and to micromanage his own operation and inside sources had stretched him thin. He'd brought too much risk to the organization.

And to me, Matty thought. He felt his eyes growing misty and swiped at them.

But it wasn't just ambition that had bitten his boss. Tyson Cade had been a man of a few ingrained habits, and that predictability had also cost him. His midmorning trek to the Alder Springs Grocery was a part of that pattern. Matty knew it . . . and so would anyone else who tracked him.

There was one other factor that had led to Tyson's downfall. Though the young meth king had run over almost everyone in Marshall County, he'd finally encountered someone who hadn't backed down.

"Jason Rich," Matty whispered. The stubborn lawyer had managed to survive the Trey Cowan murder trial, despite Tyson putting a hit on him, and now that cocky sonofabitch still lived while Tyson had breathed his last.

Matty began to walk back to the cabin. His energy was now up, sparked by adrenaline and desire.

Tyson Cade's death had been inevitable. Matty had known that for a while, but the reality of it was no less sad. Again, he sensed his eyelids growing moist, and he forced back the tears.

Matty would have been happy to play second fiddle to Tyson the rest of his life.

He opened the door and saw Lu Stephens sitting on the couch with her legs crossed. She'd taken off her T-shirt, and her chest and stomach shone with sweat.

Matty smiled at her. "Aren't you a sight?"

She stood and walked over to him. If she were ashamed or shy at being topless, she didn't show it. "Thank you for this opportunity," she said.

"You've earned it," Matty said, meaning every word.

"So we're going to Snead tomorrow night," she said.

Matty nodded. "I trust you've told the rest of the team."

She smirked. "Matty Dean and his magnificent seven. A bit cheesy, don't you think?"

Matty thought about *Ted Lasso* again. And his love of old westerns. "I am who I am."

She touched his face and ran her fingers down his neck. "What do you want, Matty?"

Matty Dean was sixty-one years old. He had a thick head of gray hair and a beard to match. His face bore a permanent sunburn, and his skin was so leathery a cobbler could probably make a nice pair of boots out of it after he died. Matty had been dealing methamphetamine his whole life. He'd cooked it. He'd sold it. He'd distributed it. He'd worked his way all the way up the chain.

What do I want? he repeated the question in his mind.

She took his hands and placed them on her breasts.

Matty rubbed his thumbs over her nipples and felt them harden.

Lu kissed his cheek. "I'm going to take a shower," she said. "Feel free to join if you want."

She pulled her jeans off and walked toward the hallway. She wasn't wearing underwear. Her legs were long and her calves were sinewy. Her butt was firm. At thirty-nine years old, Lu was an attractive, sexy woman.

Matty cleared his throat. "Lu?"

She looked at him over her shoulder. Her eyes were hard. Flat. If he gave in to her request, Matty knew he'd be giving Lu a certain power over him.

Matty Dean was too old and smart for that. "Not tonight," he said.

"Suit yourself," she said, her voice betraying nothing.

"You asked me what I wanted," Matty said and gritted his teeth.

She waited, saying nothing.

"I want Jason Rich dead."

Lu blinked, hesitating in the entrance to the hallway. Then she walked back to the couch and sat down. She was so close that Matty could smell the slightly musty scent of her pubic hair. He gazed down at the landing strip of light brown and then into her brown eyes, which were probing his. "What?" he asked.

"Rich has been arrested," she said, her voice quiet but firm. "He'll probably be charged with Tyson's murder. Why not let things play out?"

"Because that's not what Tyson wanted. His last instructions to me were to take out Rich and the three Tonidandel brothers." Matty glared at her and fought to control his emotions. "And I'm going to finish the job. Do you hear me?"

Lu held his gaze for a long second and then nodded. "I hear you."

6

The holding cell stank of urine and body odor. Jason sat on the concrete floor with his arms wrapped around his knees. He gazed across the space to the door, where a tray had been placed at least an hour ago. Meat loaf, mashed potatoes, and green beans. The aroma of the food had done nothing to mitigate the two overpowering scents that dominated everything in here. Jason moved his eyes to the far corner, where there was a commode and a roll of toilet paper. He wondered how much piss had collected on the floor over the years and how many unwashed bodies had caused the other smell.

Jason knew he wasn't doing much to help the stench. He was still wearing the clothes he'd woken up in. Golf shirt, pullover, and jeans. According to Sheriff Daniels, he reeked. And he'd relieved himself about fifteen minutes ago.

Rite of passage, he thought.

Jason heard the rattle of chains and then a key being inserted. He made no move to stand.

A guard opened the door. He filled the entryway. "Are you . . . done with your meal?"

Jason scoffed but said nothing.

"OK," the guard said, picking up the tray. "Did you want to use your phone call now?"

Jason stared blankly at the officer, not seeing him. Instead, he saw a vision of his sister, Jana.

You have no one, baby brother.

Jason shook his head.

"All right then." The guard started to go.

"Can you pass along a message for me?"

"What?"

"I've been here awhile, and there have been no questions, and I haven't been charged with anything."

"Anything else?" the guard asked.

Jason extended his middle finger. "This is just a global message. You can give it to anyone you want."

"I'll keep that in mind."

Then the door clanged shut behind him.

Jason glared at the tiny opening at the top, which was covered with iron bars. He saw a head pass by. Then there was nothing.

He sighed, gazing at the toilet again and then the cot to his left. He'd been put in a holding cell last year—a different one—but he doubted this bed would be any more comfortable than that one. He'd had a nightmare then, and he knew if he slept, he'd have another.

So he sat on the cold, hard floor. He buried his face in his knees, closed his eyes, and tried to remember.

———

He'd started drinking again two weeks ago. He'd bought a six-pack of beer on his ride home from the disciplinary committee meeting in Montgomery. He hadn't drank it the first night.

Instead, he'd jumped from the cliffs at Goat Mountain. He'd thought if he could do something as utterly crazy and terrifying as jumping from fifty feet in the air into the icy-cold lake, his desire for alcohol would subside.

It hadn't.

He had other "defusers," as he and his friend and alcohol mentor, Ashley Sullivan, called them. Lifting weights. Shooting guns at the range. Reading fiction. Watching old pro wrestling videos. Working a case. *Talking to Ashley . . .*

But he found that none of them worked without something to live for. He missed his friend and investigator, Harry Davenport, who'd been killed during the Cowan trial. His partner, Izzy Montaigne, had been in love with Harry, and she'd left Jason too in the aftermath of Harry's murder. His on-again, off-again girlfriend and lake neighbor, Chase Wittschen, was also gone. Chase had been an addict and relapsed into meth abuse last year. She'd been a central player in the Cowan case, and there had been a point where Jason had thought she might have been involved in Kelly Flowers's murder. He'd sent her to rehab and she'd gotten clean again, but the damage to their relationship was irreparable. After testifying in the Cowan trial, Chase had left Mill Creek, and Jason doubted he'd ever see her again.

Likewise, he hadn't seen either of his nieces in months. Niecy was a sophomore at Birmingham-Southern and had stayed clear of Guntersville since her mother's death and seemed distant and guarded every time Jason tried to communicate with her. She'd checked out of her former life, and who could blame her? Meanwhile, her sister, Nola, had been a senior in high school last year, and Jason had struggled in his role as guardian. Like Chase, Nola had fallen into drugs, and it was Nola's and Chase's dual addictions that had led to Jason being blackmailed by Tyson Cade into taking the Cowan case. Nola had served her own stint at a rehab center after nearly drowning in the lake. Since being discharged, she had gotten a job at the campus bookstore at Birmingham-Southern and was living with Niecy with plans to start at the University of Alabama next fall.

And she's avoided me like the plague . . . Jason sighed, knowing it was more complicated than that. Nola had thanked him for his efforts, but . . .

I'm a trigger for her . . . and for Chase. And now . . .

. . . they're both gone.

And while Satch, Mickey, and Chuck Tonidandel were his friends, they were also eccentric ex-military men who had their own demons. They couldn't solve or help with Jason's. And while he never questioned their loyalty, he knew they were more devoted to the mission than to him. He'd given them a war, as Satch had so much as admitted last year.

He thought of Ashley Sullivan. Her red hair, freckles, and green eyes. She was a lawyer in Cullman, and she'd been a good mentor for him, taking his calls and always meeting with him when he was on the verge of falling off the wagon. She'd been his best defuser.

But when he started having feelings for her, she'd been kind but firm. There could be no relationship with her or anyone else until Jason put his own oxygen mask on first.

Until he figured himself out, he'd be no good to anyone else.

Jason's suspension had broken up his mentor relationship with Ashley. Gone was the obligation for him to check in with her, and she hadn't reached out to him, either, since the disciplinary hearing.

Two nights after being informed of his suspension, Jason sat on his boat dock and drank all six beers he'd bought on the way home from Montgomery. He'd listened to music, drank the IPAs, and felt sorry for himself.

In the time since, bourbon had been his preferred poison. He got up, told Alexa to play Bob Seger's greatest hits, and drank the day away, alternating between his porch and the dock. When his favorite track, "Turn the Page," came on, he'd ask that it be repeated over and over.

The Tonidandel brothers still guarded his house as they'd done throughout the Cowan trial. Matty Dean, Tyson Cade's enforcer and the man who had killed Harry, was still out there. As was former sheriff Richard Griffith, who had killed Sergeant Kelly Flowers last year and framed Trey Cowan for it. Griffith hadn't been charged with Flowers's murder, but he likely blamed the loss of his political position on Jason.

And finally, there was Tyson Cade himself. The meth lord wasn't going anywhere, and he'd already tried to kill Jason once. Would he try again? Would he send Dean?

Satch was convinced another attempt on their lives was coming. He, Chuck, and Mickey had heard rumors through their Sand Mountain contacts that Cade had put a hit out on them. As Jason had slid into a drunken despair in the weeks after the Cowan trial, the brothers had become edgy, irritable, and paranoid.

But Jason found he didn't care.

Come and get me, he'd thought, imagining a showdown with Cade, Dean, or Griffith. At least he'd go out in a blaze of glory and not hurt anyone except maybe the Tonidandels.

But there had been no shootout, and the Tonidandels had said nothing to Jason about his drinking. Even Satch, who had never shied from giving Jason his opinion, had held his tongue. It was as if this was uncharted territory that they were unwilling to explore.

Not that Jason would have listened.

He was done. He saw no light at the end of the tunnel. No future. He had become the word his father had used for ne'er-do-wells.

A turd.

There had been no calls from his nieces. No texts from Izzy. And no check-ins from Ashley.

Earlier this morning, he'd finally had enough. Tyson Cade may have forgotten about him, but Jason's memory was clear as a bell. He'd endured another sleepless night haunted by nightmares of Harry's murder, the shooting at his office, and the loss of his family, and he was determined to do something.

If he was honest with himself, he'd been thinking about doing something ever since he'd taken his first sip of beer two weeks ago. Why else had he bought the Glock 17 that now lay on the silty bottom of the lake?

Jason had wanted a pistol with more range. He'd told the brothers he needed it for protection at the house. He'd use the 43X as his conceal carry, because it was lighter and he could put it in his pocket, and he'd keep the 17 at home in case Cade, Dean, or one of their goons attacked the house. And every night before bed, he kept the longer handgun either on the floor below him or next to him in the bed, the couch, or the cot he'd put on the sunporch.

But yesterday morning, after another sleepless night, he'd gotten tired of waiting.

He saw himself loading his Glock and then driving into Guntersville. Pulling onto Hustleville Road and passing the Alder Springs Grocery. He squeezed his right hand into a fist, remembering how the pistol had felt. Seeing the gun lying on the passenger seat of his Explorer. The same vehicle Harry had been driving the night the investigator was murdered.

An eye for an eye, Jason remembered thinking, which was odd, as he was no Bible beater. He'd sipped Jack Daniel's from the bottle and then put the whiskey in the drink console and held the weapon in his right hand.

Jason rocked his head back against the cinder block wall of the cell. His legs had begun to shake.

He remembered pulling the trigger. Once. Twice. Three times. How many shots had been left? He recalled driving back to Mill Creek. Swerving into his driveway and stumbling down to the dock, holding the gun in one hand and the bottle in the other. Jumping into the dirty lake water and then climbing up the steps of the ladder and sitting in the lawn chair. Watching cars drive by on the Highway 79 bridge. Drinking the whiskey until his body warmed and again clutching the Glock and pressing it to his own forehead.

It would have been a noble way to go.

But instead, he'd passed out with the gun in his hand.

Jason finally opened his eyes and stared up at the ceiling.

"What did I do?" he whispered, feeling his heart racing.

What did I do?

7

At ten the next morning, almost twenty-four hours since the murder of Tyson Cade, the Marshall County Sheriff's Office was hopping. The phones were ringing nonstop, as media outlets and residents pumped the department for any updates on the investigation and dispatchers scrambled to answer each call. Inside the "war room," the large conference area where meetings were held, Sheriff Hatty Daniels paced around the long rectangular table.

All chairs but the two head seats, one of which was reserved for her and the other empty, were taken. As she walked, she looked at as many of the officers as she could in the eyes, sizing them up. In the past month since being appointed sheriff, she had cleaned house in the department, firing at least fifteen deputies and all the detectives. She was determined to start with a clean slate.

Four weeks ago, her predecessor, Richard Griffith, had been revealed as an inside source to the Sand Mountain meth trade. Hatty's old partner, George Mitchell, had confessed in a come-to-Jesus meeting at Jason Rich's office at the close of the Trey Cowan murder trial. Cowan, an ex-football star and an occasional employee of Tyson Cade, had been charged with murdering Deputy Kelly Flowers at an abandoned barn off Hustleville Road. The physical evidence against Cowan was overwhelming, and he'd been seen assaulting and threatening Flowers at the Brick Bar & Grill just hours before the murder.

But during the trial, Flowers's history as a dirty cop who quashed charges against women in return for sexual favors was brought out with great effectiveness by Jason Rich. Cowan turned out to be a patsy. The true murderer, according to George Mitchell, was the high sheriff himself, who had killed Flowers because the deputy had been blackmailing him due to Griffith's illicit affair with Flowers's sister.

But Griffith never stood trial for his sin. The only witness who could place him as the killer was George, and Hatty's former partner was gunned down in front of Rich's office just minutes after his confession.

Richard Griffith was forced out of office, but because there were no other witnesses to his crime, he walked without ever being charged. Hatty didn't know where the former sheriff was now, and she didn't care. Since being appointed as his replacement and winning the uncontested election, she'd terminated any staff member who'd been directly hired by Griffith and a few others who Hatty simply didn't want working for her. It was both a statement to the public and to the department that there was, quite literally, a new sheriff in town.

Now, though, Hatty was doubting her actions. Growing pains were all but inevitable with a new staff, and they didn't have time to learn on the job now. She'd hired a lot of talented officers, but few had experience investigating murders, and none were ready to spearhead a case with this level of scrutiny.

No mistakes, she thought. *We can't afford any on this one.*

That was why, despite the fact that she was now the leader of these men and women, she would not be delegating the Tyson Cade murder investigation. She welcomed help and hoped she would get it. But at the end of the day, the buck stopped with her. And since she didn't yet trust anyone in this room, she'd have to lean on her own instincts and rely on her gut.

She'd also have to work her ass off.

"Greta, walk us through what we know," she finally said, stopping and peering down at a brown-haired woman sitting at the middle of the table.

Sergeant Greta Martin was easily the star of Hatty's new team. She'd started as a traffic cop in Boaz and worked her way up to detective in that city's police department. And while she hadn't investigated any homicides, she had led several investigations into rape and felony sex crimes. She'd jumped at the opportunity to join the sheriff's office, as she was getting a significant pay raise and was closer to her mother, who lived in Guntersville. Greta stood and spoke in a clear, confident tone. "Tyson Cade was shot outside the Alder Springs Grocery at approximately ten thirty a.m. He'd just gone inside, where he'd bought a Sun Drop soda and a Twinkie. The desk clerk, a woman named Marcia Darnell, had come outside because Cade had forgotten his change. She said she called after him, and he turned toward her. Then he was shot."

"Did Darnell see or hear anything else?"

"No, she went into shock right afterward. I was just able to interview her at the hospital about an hour ago. She did say that Cade was in the habit of visiting the store around midmorning on most days."

"Any other witnesses to the shooting?"

"Not that we've been able to track down. According to Darnell, that was a typically slow period of the day for them. There were no other customers inside the store at the time of the shooting and only one car getting gas."

"What about Cade's vehicle?"

Greta held out her palms. "Darnell didn't see one. She pretty much blacked out after the shooting. The driver of the car getting gas, a woman named Candy Atkinson, didn't see the shooting. But she did notice some type of dark SUV pulling away from the store. She couldn't pin down the make, model, or even the color of it."

Hatty groaned. "Was the SUV behind Cade or in front of him?"

"All Candy could say is that it was leaving the store. She hadn't been paying much attention before the shooting."

"What happened next?"

"Candy called 911 and walked over to the victim. She knelt beside him, and he was struggling for breath. She told him that an ambulance was on the way."

"Did she know the victim or recognize him?"

"No. Candy is from New Hope and was visiting family near Alder Springs. She wasn't familiar with Tyson Cade."

Hatty took in a deep breath. She knew all this information already but wanted the whole group to hear it. Especially this next part.

"Did the victim say anything?"

Before Greta could answer, she was interrupted by two loud knocks on the door. Irritated, Hatty turned toward the sound as a man entered the room without uttering a greeting.

"You should have waited for me," the man said, not looking at Hatty as he strode toward his seat at the end opposite the sheriff. He wore a charcoal pinstriped suit, starched white shirt, and maroon tie and carried a briefcase in his right hand. He dropped the satchel on the table and put his hands on his hips, glaring at Hatty.

Aloysius Holloway French had been the district attorney of Marshall County for almost two decades before losing the election six years ago to Shay Lankford. Because of his unusual first name, which was a Germanic word meaning "famous warrior," a fact he was quick to point out during campaign fundraisers, he'd gone by "Wish" since he was in grade school. Since being defeated in his bid for a fourth term as DA, Wish had lingered in the background, raising money and waiting for the next election. On the heels of Shay Lankford's dismissal of the claims against Trey Cowan and failure to charge anyone else with Kelly Flowers's murder, Wish was able to defeat her.

"Well? Where are we?" Wish's voice was a southern baritone that oozed good old boy charm when he wanted it to and old money arrogance when he didn't. Now would be the latter.

"Greta was walking us through the operative facts."

"Has she gotten to the point where the victim identified his killer?"

Now, Hatty glared back at the district attorney. "That's where we are."

Wish turned to Greta. "By all means, please continue, Sergeant."

Greta cleared her throat. "The victim, Mr. Cade, said something that Ms. Atkinson heard." She looked at Hatty and then Wish. The prosecutor moved his right index finger in a circle in a "move it along" gesture.

"Cade said 'I can't believe the bastard got me,'" Greta continued. "Atkinson asked, 'Who?' and Cade started coughing. She repeated the question, and Cade pointed toward the highway. Then, according to Atkinson, he kind of chuckled, and the next thing he said came out in a gasp. She barely heard it."

"A dying declaration," Wish said. "Admissible in court."

Greta shrugged.

"What did he say?" Hatty asked, speaking through clenched teeth.

"Jason Rich."

———

Thirty minutes later, Hatty and Wish French were the only ones left in the war room.

"Can I see the video from the stoplight on Hustleville Road?" Wish asked.

Hatty pulled it up on her laptop and pushed play, then stepped back so that Wish could sit in her chair and watch.

"That's Rich's vehicle?"

"Yes," Hatty said. On the screen, a maroon SUV passed under a stoplight. The time in the corner read 10:43 a.m.

"And that's him driving, right?" Wish asked, squinting at the computer.

"Yep," Hatty said. "Not the best quality . . . but it's him."

"The timing fits perfectly," Wish said. "Rich could have shot Cade, and this stoplight picks him up on Hustleville Road a little more than six miles from the murder scene within ten minutes of the shooting."

"That's correct," Hatty said.

"So he certainly had the opportunity to kill him," Wish said. "And, based on his history with Cade, there was plenty of motive."

Hatty nodded, thinking about her drive into town with Jason. Had he acted guilty? She couldn't tell. Jason Rich was hard to read. He'd been very distant, but cordial.

"Does he own a gun?"

"We found a Glock 43X at his house." Hatty paused. "We know he's a member and frequent visitor of the Tonidandels' shooting range off Highway 431, and, based on interviews we conducted this afternoon during our initial search of the property, at least one customer remembers seeing him shooting a longer-barrel pistol in recent weeks."

"Longer barrel means larger range," Wish said, and Hatty nodded. "Did we find a second gun at the house?"

Hatty paced down to the end of the table. "No."

Wish pushed his chair back and crossed his legs. He ran his hands through his thick silver hair and then placed them both on his stomach. The man had wide shoulders and a narrow waist. His skin was a pale yellowish color, and his face tended to redden when he got fired up. Now, though, the only thing red were his eyes, which betrayed the seventy-one-year-old prosecutor's fatigue. "Are we missing something here?"

Hatty sighed but said nothing.

Wish tapped his fingers on the table. "I mean, Cade was a drug dealer. He was in a dangerous line of work. I'm sure he had enemies besides Jason Rich, but—"

"But we don't have any evidence linking anyone else to the crime." Hatty finished his thought.

"What about Matty Dean?"

Hatty ground her teeth together. Dean had tried to kill her last year, and she was confident that he'd been the one who had taken down George Mitchell. "Cade's enforcer," Hatty said, remembering the man's mug shot. "Much older than Cade. We arrested him in October for meth possession and failing to register his boat, but Griff let him out on bail."

"That stupid sonofabitch," Wish whispered through his teeth.

"Griff was a lot of things, but he wasn't stupid. I suspect Cade forced his hand."

"We need to track him down and interview him. Griff didn't just lose his job in the last month. His wife filed for divorce too. He would have plenty of motive to kill Cade."

"And he's killed before," Hatty said. "George said he killed Kelly Flowers."

"And you believed him?"

"Yes, I did."

For a moment, silence filled the room. Finally, Hatty walked toward the door. "I'm going to check on where things stand with the rest of our interviews and property searches." Hatty had dispatched deputies to comb the neighborhood behind and in front of the Alder Springs Grocery for anyone who might have seen something, and she'd sent Greta Martin to talk with the Tonidandels and root around their home and gun range.

"I'll see if I can get a lead on Griff," Wish said.

"Thank you," Hatty said. "The coroner should have us a preliminary report tomorrow morning first thing. I'm meeting her at the morgue at eight a.m."

"I'll be there," Wish said. Then, he placed his hands over his head and his feet on the table. "Hatty, you saw the bullet wounds. What did they look like to you?"

"I'm no medical examiner," she said.

"But you've been the best detective in this department for over a decade, and you've seen your share of crime scenes. I want to know your thoughts."

"The wounds weren't deep or significant enough to be a rifle or a shotgun. I'm thinking multiple shots from a handgun."

Wish squinted. "A Glock 43X?"

"Could be," Hatty said. "We'll see what Emily has to say. I would think it would probably be a longer pistol, which . . ."

"Rich might also have owned or—"

"Had access to."

"Exactly. You know how this is looking," Wish said.

"I do."

"Can you be impartial if we have to charge Rich? I've heard rumors that you and he worked together behind the scenes during the Cowan trial."

"We had a common interest in bringing Matty Dean down," Hatty said. "That's all it was."

"My question stands," Wish said, dropping his hands down to his stomach and forming a tent with them. "Can you be objective?"

"I'll do my job." Hatty spoke in a low, deliberate tone. She was irritated and annoyed at being cross-examined, but she kept her face a mask of calm.

"Good," Wish said, sweeping his feet off the table and rising to his feet. "Because I have a feeling that come the end of the day tomorrow, we are going to be charging one of the most recognizable faces in the state of Alabama with murder."

Hatty said nothing as Wish brushed past her to the door. "And unlike the former district attorney," he growled, "I don't plan on losing to this prick."

"I'm sure you'll love the publicity."

Wish turned and winked at her. "I'll do my job."

8

By the time Matty Dean walked into the warehouse in Snead, word of the meeting had spread to the other territories. As he entered the rolled-up garage door, he knew that the entire Sand Mountain meth operation was here tonight. And judging by the looks of fear and apprehension in the eyes of the men and women he passed by, Matty knew that they all had grave suspicions about what had happened to Tanner Sparks and Reg Strassburg.

And he could see a question in each of their faces. *Who's next?*

Lu strode ahead of Matty with her sawed-off shotgun holstered in a leather pouch against her leg. She wore black jeans and a leather jacket over a white tank top. Combat boots covered her feet.

At the front entrance was Dexter Parrish, a fifty-six-year-old mountain of a man from Sardis City who'd fished, hunted, and sold methamphetamine his whole life. A violent man Matty dubbed "Chief," in ode to the famous Celtics center, Parrish had a talent for torturing would-be informants. Matty nodded at him and then shifted his gaze to the back exit.

Frank Crutcher had a shaved head that he covered with a faded Atlanta Braves cap. At five foot, ten inches tall and a tad over 160 pounds, he was smaller than Chief but no less dangerous. With long wiry muscles, "Crutch," as most folks in Alder Springs called him, was country strong and had served two tours in Afghanistan. He had returned home two years ago, battling PTSD and needing money to support his ailing father, who suffered from Alzheimer's. He'd found an outlet for both by dealing meth, which had kept his mind and body busy and more than paid the bills at Marshall Manor, the nursing home where his father resided. Crutch tipped his cap to Matty, who surveyed the crowd.

Matty didn't bother to sit down as he approached the large circular table. There looked to be about fifteen people in chairs and another ten or so standing in the background. Matty nodded at Lu to begin.

"You all know Matty Dean," she said, her voice rising so that it reached the far corners of the warehouse. "There is no one that Tyson trusted more than Matty."

"Where's Reg?" The voice came from a man sitting at the other end of the table. His name was Hunter, and he was known as the best meth cook in the group. He was a short man with yellowish skin who couldn't weigh much more than a hundred pounds. Hunter probably figured he was valuable enough to get away with asking the question they were all thinking.

"He's on a permanent vacation," Matty said. "And so is Tanner Sparks." He hesitated so that they could all grasp the meaning behind his words. "Chief is going to run Sardis City and Etowah County."

Hunter's eyes darted to the front of the warehouse, where "Chief" Parrish stood with his arms folded.

"And Lu's got Fort Payne and the rest of the east," Matty said, looking past Hunter to the other men and women at the table. "And she's going to assist me and Crutch with Marshall and Jackson County."

"They're saying on the news that the billboard lawyer is the one who killed Tyson," Hunter said. "That true?"

"Looks like it," Matty said.

"How could a dipshit like that get the jump on Tyson Cade?" A ponytailed woman dangling a cigarette out of the corner of her mouth hurled the question from the far end of the table. Her name was Susie

Ragland, and she'd worked with Matty for years in the Marshall and Jackson County theaters. Her specialty was making deliveries, as the police tended not to suspect a middle-aged woman driving a minivan.

Matty rubbed his chin, thinking about Susie's question and realizing that there might be one quality that he and Jason Rich had in common.

"Tyson underestimated Rich," Matty finally said.

"We can't let him get away with it," Susie said, pressing her cigarette into an ashtray and rubbing her hands on her jeans.

"No, we can't," Matty agreed. He took a step back. He wouldn't be explaining his plan for Jason Rich to the whole group. "Does anyone else have a question?" He moved his eyes around the room, seeing acceptance in all their gazes. Tyson Cade was gone. Matty was now in charge. If there were any thoughts of a coup, the killings of Reginald Strassburg and Tanner Sparks had ended them. The silence was deafening and beautiful.

"Good," Matty said, giving a final nod. "I look forward to us all making a lot of money."

9

"Three shots to the chest from a nine-millimeter pistol." For someone who had only been in office for a few weeks, Emily Carton, the newly elected coroner for Marshall County, Alabama, spoke with calm reassurance. Of course, Emily had spent much of her adult life working for her father, longtime coroner Clem Carton, and that was after she'd graduated with a PhD in forensic science from Vanderbilt. She also had extensive training in forensic ballistics and worked for several years at the DFS crime lab in Birmingham. In truth, Emily was more qualified than Clem had ever thought about being, and the county was lucky to have her.

But that's not why she won the election, Hatty thought. She won because of her last name and the thousands of voters who had supported her father. Just as Wish French had claimed victory on the backs of the good old boy network that was alive and well in this county and probably always would be.

Hatty was the oddity in this mix. A lifetime detective who just so happened to be appointed sheriff two weeks prior to the election after a shootout a block from the courthouse that made Richard Griffith, the former benefactor of the good old boys, scum—and her an unlikely hero.

I was lucky, she thought, watching Wish French pick at his teeth with a finger. "Are the wounds consistent with a Glock 43X?"

"Yes," Emily said. "And any number of other nine-millimeter handguns. We've recovered bullet fragments from the sternum and are sending them to the crime lab along with Jason Rich's 43X. I'll go to Huntsville today and conduct the ballistics analysis myself to expedite the testing. If the 43X is the actual gun, then I suspect I'll be able to make a definitive conclusion. However . . . in light of the distance of the shot . . . I would think the murder weapon is a longer-barrel handgun."

"Rich was seen practicing with a bigger pistol at the Tonidandels' gun range," Wish said, rubbing his hands together. "What you've said is definite enough for me." He stepped back from the corpse.

"Wish—" Hatty started, but the prosecutor interrupted her.

"Damnit, I don't want to wait any longer. Emily, it sounds like all you will be able to do is either rule in or rule out the 43X, right?"

"Yes," the coroner agreed.

"Hatty, where are we with the searches of Rich's home, office, and cars?"

"Done," the sheriff said. "The only thing of significance was the pistol. But Greta is out at the Tonidandels' gun range today, so perhaps something interesting will turn up there."

Wish sucked air through his teeth and scratched his neck. "Perhaps," he said, looking from Hatty to Emily and then back at the sheriff. "Listen, we have video evidence from a traffic light placing Rich's maroon SUV in close proximity to the scene of the crime at ten forty-three a.m. We have an eyewitness who puts a dark SUV in the damn parking lot of the Alder Springs Grocery. Rich is the owner of a nine-millimeter Glock 43X, which the county coroner confirms is consistent with the murder weapon, and, based on our investigation, he also either owned or had access to a bigger nine millimeter with a greater range that also would be consistent with the gun that killed Tyson Cade. Finally, because of his history with Cade, the billboard lawyer has a powerful motive. I mean, look at what we can show a jury. He's been suspended by the bar. Lost his family. His investigator was killed. His partner left him. And he blames everything on Cade. And if all that wasn't enough . . ." Wish snapped his fingers. ". . . we have a dying declaration from the victim himself that Rich did it." He scoffed. "No case is perfect, Sheriff, but the only plausible story is that Jason Rich, who, to our knowledge, had no legitimate reason to be on Hustleville Road at ten forty-three a.m., drove to the Alder Springs Grocery, knowing that Cade might be there—as it was the bastard's habit to visit the store at that time of day—and shot the drug dealer to death from some position behind the store. Rich made his getaway, was seen passing under that traffic light, and drove to his home, where he proceeded to get drunk."

Hatty knew that the evidence uncovered so far suggested everything that the district attorney had just said. "I'd still like to wait and hear from Greta and have the benefit of Emily's ballistic analysis." She cleared her throat. "Since no one saw the shooter, he was likely standing either to the side or somewhere behind the grocery store. That means a shot from at least twenty yards away." Hatty paused. "Pretty good shot."

"Rich was known to practice target shooting at the Tonidandels' range. It was broad daylight, and Cade was a sitting duck. The eyewitness, Darnell, thought she heard at least five shots, which means the shooter missed a couple times."

Hatty pursed her lips. "Not so perfect then." She knew she shouldn't be, but she was impressed with the crafty prosecutor's ability to put together a story so quickly. She'd worked cases with Wish French before Shay defeated him six years ago, and she knew that he was a resourceful, street-smart lawyer who would do anything he could to win. In three prior terms as district attorney, Wish had never lost a felony trial that he'd tried himself, while Shay had lost two in two years.

That had been his campaign theme, and it had been good enough to win.

But Wish never had to face Jason Rich . . .

"Let's do it, Hatty," Wish said. "We're wasting time, and we need to make an arrest." He nodded at the coroner. "Thank you, Emily."

"I'll call regarding the results of my ballistics testing tomorrow morning, and I'll have my full report to you by the end of the week."

But Wish was already out the door.

"Thank you, Emily," Hatty said. "Good job."

"Thank you," she said, speaking in a low voice. "Dad never liked Wish much," she added. "I think I can see why."

"He's a prima donna," Hatty said. Then she sighed. "But he's a hell of a good trial lawyer."

———

The following morning, at 8:30 a.m., they had their answer back from the coroner.

"The murder weapon is not Jason Rich's Glock 43X. The rifling is not a match." Emily's voice came from a speakerphone that had been placed in the middle of the conference table in the war room.

"Are you sure?" Wish asked, scratching his neck.

"Yes. To put it in simple terms, I fired several test shots with the 43X and compared the bullets to the ones uncovered from Tyson Cade's body. The width of the land and groove measurements on the test bullets are distinctly different from the ones that killed the victim." She paused. "I can't say I'm surprised. Like I said yesterday, based on the length of the shot, I would think the killer used a larger pistol with a greater accuracy range."

"Thank you for jumping on this, Emily," Hatty said. "Please send your report to me as soon as possible."

"Will do."

The line went dead, and Wish French stretched his arms over his head. "That changes nothing."

Hatty remained quiet. She gazed at the only other person in the room.

Sergeant Greta Martin stood at the end of the table between them. The young deputy's eyes were bloodshot red, indicative of the nonstop nature of the investigation since the discovery of Tyson Cade's body almost three days ago.

"Did the interviews turn up anything?" Hatty asked her.

"No," Greta said. "We've spoken with all the people who live within a half mile of the Alder Springs Grocery, and there were no other leads." She wiped a strand of hair out of her eyes. "The search of the Tonidandels' gun range hasn't been concluded. We are going through the paperwork and computer records first, and it's all a bit haphazard."

"What about the nine-millimeter guns on site?" Hatty asked.

"We are still doing an inventory, but a rough estimate would be around twelve new models, which are for sale, and approximately eight used."

The prosecutor hissed. "Emily will have to test every one of them. Anything else?"

Greta cleared her throat. "I tried to speak with Satch, Chuck, and Mickey Tonidandel, but as you might imagine, they weren't all that forthcoming. However . . . I suspect if they could provide Rich an alibi, they would have come forward by now."

"I agree," Wish said, rubbing his chin. "Rich would have already mentioned that as well."

For several seconds, silence filled the room. Finally, Wish broke it. "Has Rich talked at all?"

"No," Greta said. "Refuses to answer questions and hasn't hired a lawyer. He also hasn't eaten anything and has vomited several times in his cell. We've offered the jail nurse, but he's refused to see her."

"OK," Wish said, looking at Hatty. "I don't think we should delay the inevitable any longer. Do you agree, Sheriff?"

Hatty cringed, knowing that there was no going back once they crossed this bridge, but also seeing no alternative. "Yes," she said.

10

Jason had lost all track of time. He was still sitting on the floor.

Same clothes. Same stench.

He'd eaten nothing since being incarcerated and had drunk little water. His throat tasted like sandpaper. He was dehydrated and was in the midst of suffering withdrawal symptoms.

The shakes.

Sweating.

Nausea.

All were present. He was so weak that when his cell door opened, he made no move to stand. He didn't think he could.

He blinked and saw two people standing in front of him. Hatty wore a dark suit and stared down at him with her arms folded. Next to her was an older white man wearing a charcoal suit, white shirt, and red tie. He had thick gray hair and a cleanly shaven face. At six feet, two inches tall with wide shoulders and a narrow waist, the man reminded Jason of Jock Ewing from the television show *Dallas*.

Satch's favorite character . . .

Jason giggled at the absurdity of the thought and of the comparison. Wish French might look like Jock Ewing, but that was where the comparison stopped. Jock had been a powerful oil man on the show, the patriarch of the Ewing dynasty, who was a pillar of mental and physical strength. He rode horses, got in barroom brawls, and was the only person man enough to break up fights between his two sons, J. R. and Bobby. He wasn't a saint, but he stuck by his principles and loved his wife, the equally strong and no less compelling Ms. Ellie.

Wish French was nothing more than a politician. A paper tiger. Jock Ewing was the real McCoy.

"Something funny, Rich?" Wish asked, his voice deep and gravelly.

Sounds like old Jock too, Jason thought, covering his mouth to keep from full-out laughing. Satch Tonidandel watched an episode of *Dallas* on Amazon every Friday night at 8:00 p.m., as if he wanted to re-create 1982. For some reason, that's all Jason could think about. Hence, the giggles. Jason's mind was a blubbery mess, and he blinked and shook his head, wondering if he was in some kind of withdrawal-induced dream.

"I'm glad your daddy isn't alive to see this," Wish said, his voice dripping with mock sincerity.

Despite his weakened state, Jason felt a rush of adrenaline as he gazed up at the stately lawyer.

"Good old Lucas Rich," Wish continued, chuckling. "We sure had some battles. He was a fine lawyer and a decent citizen." He paused, squinting at Jason. "A far cry from the loser you've turned out to be."

Jason extended his middle finger toward the new district attorney. "Sit on it and rotate," he said, then giggled again. It was one of his sister Jana's favorite comebacks, and it was a by God good one.

"Jason, are you OK?" Hatty asked.

Jason squinched his face up as if he had tasted something sour. He held out his palms. "I mean . . . obviously . . . *not.*"

"We're wasting time," Wish said, peering at Hatty. "Get on with it."

"Jason Rich," Hatty said, her voice firm, her tone no nonsense. "You are being charged with the first-degree murder of Tyson Kennesaw Cade. You have the right to remain silent. You have the—"

"Hatty, this is ridiculous," Jason said, trying to stand as the sheriff rattled off the Miranda warning. When he finally pulled himself to his feet, he felt dizzy and the room began to spin. He leaned against the wall for balance.

"Let us know when you hire an attorney," Wish said.

"Hey, fuckface," Jason said, pointing at the district attorney, seeing his finger shake in front of him. His throat ached and his stomach rumbled. "My dad thought you were a first-class prick."

Wish grinned, showing off his pristine white teeth. "Old Lucas didn't like to lose, Jason. And that's all he ever did when he faced me." He turned for the door, looking back over his shoulder. "And soon, you'll be following in your daddy's footsteps."

The door clanged shut, and Hatty and Jason were alone in the cell.

"Have you gotten a lawyer?" Hatty whispered.

Jason squinched up his face again and pressed his thumbs into his chest. "You're looking at him."

He fell to his knees, puked first, and then slumped forward.

He was out cold before his head hit the concrete.

PART TWO

11

Matty Dean sipped Eagle Rare bourbon from a Styrofoam coffee cup. He leaned against the brick wall of the truck stop building and let out a deep breath, blowing smoke into the night air. He watched an eighteen-wheeler pass through the array of pumps and turn right out of the stop and then take another right onto I-65.

He was in Columbia, Tennessee. At least a hundred miles from the border of his Sand Mountain meth kingdom.

He drank a sip of bourbon and watched a rig move past the pumps and park in the overnight area. There were about ten long-haul trucks already parked there for the night. A man wearing a thick flannel jacket was sitting on his trailer hitch smoking a cigarette. Drinking something in a cup too. Matty had eaten dinner with him inside the diner. Country-fried steak, mashed potatoes, and sweet tea.

Matty was full . . .

. . . but he hadn't gotten his fix.

He was in a celebratory mood. An hour earlier, in the same diner, he'd made a deal that would put Jason Rich six feet under the ground. Now, he wanted a buzz. He glanced again at the man in plaid.

. . . and maybe something else.

His cell vibrated inside his pocket, and he snatched it out, then stared at the screen, which read "Lu."

"Yeah," Matty spoke into the phone.

"Just heard from my source in the clerk's office. Hearing is set for nine in the morning."

Matty took another sip of bourbon. "Is the diversion ready?"

"Yes." Her voice was firm. Confident. No hesitation. Matty had always known that Lu Stephens would be his right hand if he ever ascended to the throne of the Sand Mountain drug empire. "You still think he'll be released?" she asked.

Matty grunted. "Rich may be a mess right now, but he's too dumb to stay locked up. And he's got enough money to pay whatever bond is set regardless of how outrageous." Matty paused, peering again at the flannel-shirted man, who continued to smoke on the trailer hitch a hundred yards away. "He'll want out."

"Well, once his ass hits the sidewalk, all hell is going to break loose."

Matty rubbed his chin. "Good."

"How did it go with the sniper?"

"He'll be there. At the spot we decided."

"Kind of fitting, don't you think?"

At this, Matty smiled. "Yeah, kinda."

"All right then," Lu said. The line went silent for a few seconds. "You OK?"

"Never better," Matty said and ended the call.

He picked at the rim of his cup and exhaled. Then he sipped more bourbon. Since Tyson's death, he had made his presence felt in the organization. After the come-to-Jesus meeting in Snead, he'd been on the ground for five days straight. Fort Payne. Stevenson. Albertville. Boaz. Alder Springs. Scottsboro. In a week, he'd met with every cook on the payroll and almost all the distributors and salespeople. There'd been no further coup attempts since Tanner Sparks's and Reg Strassburg's failed try in Mentone.

Matty had known he had to send a message, and the brutality of Reg's and Tanner's deaths had reverberated through the outfit. He'd shown them all what he was capable of, and he'd assembled a team that would protect and serve him.

And tonight, he'd finalized a deal that would put an end to Jason Rich. He glanced at his watch, an old rubber Casio model he'd bought at Walmart. Matty Dean wasn't one to put on airs. It was 9:45 p.m. In approximately twelve hours, the billboard lawyer would be no more. The war between Jason Rich and the Sand Mountain meth trade would soon be over. Once Rich was eliminated, Matty would sic Chief and Lu on the Tonidandels. The brothers would be reeling from the attorney's death and more likely to make a mistake.

They'll never see it coming . . .

That had been Tyson's plan, and Matty was hell bent and determined to carry it out.

Matty leaned his face into the Styrofoam cup and breathed in the scent of bourbon.

He missed his friend.

He had never met anyone like Tyson Cade. Young. Smart. Ruthless. Completely self-assured. Tyson was a born leader. He oozed charisma and confidence. Not only did his employees worship him, but a lot of the townspeople did too. He'd heard "Robin Hood" thrown around a little in the news outlets since the murder.

But Matty knew the truth. Tyson Cade cared only for himself and his business. Creating the perception of altruism among the folks in Sand Mountain was something the young phenom had cultivated, as Tyson hoped "his people" would seek his protection. But he didn't do it to help them.

He did it *to own them.* So they'd look the other way and cower to his needs. And up until he was shot to death, the plan had been incredibly successful. Just thirty years old, Tyson Cade had been one of the most powerful people in the state.

He'd shown his power during the Cowan trial by literally orchestrating everything. He had then-sheriff Richard Griffith in his pocket.

He also had blackmailed Jason Rich into representing Cowan. It was a one-man puppet show, and Tyson was pulling all the strings. But he'd overreached. Taken on too much and tried to micromanage everything. He'd lusted for control, and that desire eventually had gotten him killed.

It was . . . inevitable, Matty thought again.

He got me arrested. He put me at risk. Took me for granted.

Tears filled Matty's eyes, and he drank another sip of bourbon. He watched the man sitting on the trailer hitch. The man crushed out his cigarette and stared at Matty across the hundred yards between them. Then he walked around to the passenger side and climbed up into the sleeper berth.

Matty hung his head and scratched the back of his neck. He'd loved Tyson. The last thing he'd wanted was for him to die. He thought of all the times they'd been together alone.

Boat rides to deliver drugs or dump a body.

Road trips to interview a new cook or distributor.

How many times had Tyson spent the night at his cabin in Polecat Hollow? Matty kept a guest room ready for him and would cook him breakfast in the morning.

Did he know? Matty wondered, drinking the last of the bourbon and wiping his eyes with his sleeve. *Did he know how I felt?* Matty gazed at the rig where the man with the flannel coat was waiting.

He had to . . .

But Tyson Cade only thought about the business and himself. And what Matty wanted would have never jived with Tyson's desires.

He used me . . .

Matty thought of Lu Stephens's invitation a week ago. Walking naked across the cabin in Mentone. He'd been right not to take part. Lu was a diamondback rattler. He couldn't afford to need her for anything, or he'd get bitten.

But that wasn't the only reason he'd said no. The truth was that he didn't want it.

Maybe Lu was playing me, he thought. He knew there were rumors about him. A sixty-one-year-old career bachelor. Perhaps her invitation was a test.

If so, did I pass . . . or fail?

"Fuck it," Matty whispered. He was tired of thinking. Tired period. He'd come here for two things. He'd made the deal with the sniper.

Now it was time to check the second box.

He walked to his car and leaned inside the open window. He grabbed a second cup and the fifth of Eagle Rare. He took a deep breath and exhaled another plume of smoke.

Then he walked toward the long-term parking area.

A minute later, he was climbing up the steps of the man in plaid's rig.

12

"ALL RISE!"

Jason had expected the familiar salutation, but the volume still startled him, and his shoulders shook as he rose to his feet. His legs were weak from his last few days as a patient at Marshall Medical Center South. He'd been fully detoxed, hydrated on IV fluids, and given the whole spiel about AA. If he wasn't being held on charges of first-degree murder, he likely would have been referred to a rehabilitation facility.

Instead he was here, wearing the orange jumpsuit of a prisoner, for the initial hearing in what would in all likelihood be the last case of his life.

My own.

As the Honorable Terry Barber strode to the bench, Jason felt a tightness in the pit of his stomach.

"Please be seated," Barber said, standing at the podium and speaking in the nasal southern voice that grated every nerve that Jason had.

Jason sat and leaned his elbows on the defense table. He fixated on the wood so he would not be tempted to glare at His Honor. He felt his shoulder being nudged.

He glanced at the woman sitting next to him. Sergeant Greta Martin wore the khaki uniform of the Marshall County Sheriff's Office. She had been assigned to watch Jason since his admission to the hospital last Saturday and had essentially been babysitting him ever since. With no one else to talk to and feeling restless and on edge, Jason had worn her out with questions about her own life. Initially, Sergeant Martin had not engaged, but after a while, boredom had set in, and she'd shared a few things. She was divorced with a young son that her mom kept a lot so she could work her job. Deadbeat ex-husband who wasn't in the picture. She loved being a detective and seemed to worship Hatty Daniels, the new sheriff, who had taught her a lot and proved that a woman could advance to the top. She also didn't seem all that angry with Jason. He'd thought about that a lot and concluded that, among some citizens and perhaps even law enforcement, too, the murder of Tyson Cade, while still a homicide, was a good thing in the long run. Something that made Guntersville safer. Even though Jason knew he was innocent, he thought he might be able to use that sentiment going forward.

"You OK?" Martin asked.

Jason smirked. "Peachy," he whispered. "No place I'd rather be."

She rolled her eyes and returned her attention to the bench, but the faintest hint of a smile played on her lips. Jason was grateful for Sergeant Martin. There were times, at least, like now, when she treated him like a person and not a prisoner. He made a mental note to thank Hatty for assigning Martin to him. But that exchange would come later.

After this torture.

He took a deep breath and exhaled. Then he looked behind his shoulder, where the courtroom was filled to capacity. He saw a smattering of media types, including his old friend Kisha Roe, the editor in chief of the *Advertiser-Gleam*, Guntersville's flagship newspaper. Kisha raised her eyebrows at him, and he did the same. He hadn't seen her since the Cowan case was dismissed. That had been a glorious day.

And every day since has been pure-grain dogshit.

Jason noticed someone else at the back of the courtroom. Colonel Satchel Shames Tonidandel wore a black button-down and jeans. Satch squinted at Jason with his reptilian eyes. The big man's arms were crossed, and his expression was tense. No nonsense. *On guard* . . . Jason figured the other two brothers, Chuck and Mickey, were outside at different locations.

Jason had finally made his one allotted phone call yesterday afternoon.

Satch had been waiting for it. "About damn time," he said. "I was close to arranging a posse to bust you out."

Jason chuckled. "Save that for tomorrow."

"First hearing is at nine a.m. We'll be there."

Jason knew not to be surprised. Gossip spread in a small town like stink on manure, and his arrest for the murder of Tyson Cade was big news. Then the colonel said something that shocked him. "The sheriff told us about it." Satch paused. "She said that we should probably plan on coming."

The revelation had sent a shiver of fear down Jason's spine. "Did she say why?"

"No, but I got the drift."

"Which was?"

"She's afraid that Cade's successor may take a shot at you."

"In broad daylight on the courthouse square?"

Satch didn't hesitate. "Yes."

"And are we thinking that the new boss is Matty Dean?"

"Don't know," Satch said. "But that's my bet."

"You heard anything?"

"Nothing I didn't already know."

"What?"

"Dean's put out a hit on you and us." He paused again. "Gonna finish what Cade started."

"Great," Jason said, chuckling and hitting his forehead with the receiver of the phone. "Any other good news to share?"

"I think it's a positive thing that the sheriff cared enough to call us."

"I guess. I wish she cared enough not to charge me with murder."

"Just doing her job. We'll talk about that when you get out."

"Talk about what?"

"Never mind. Look for Chuck when you post bond. I'll be in my Raptor. Chuck is the escort. Mickey will be doing reconnaissance and scanning the ground and roofs. Jason, I know you've been through a lot lately, but you're gonna need to wake the fuck up. Even though Cade is dead, the war isn't over."

Jason hung up the phone, feeling his heart pounding in his chest. For the first time in a while, he felt scared. But also alive.

He probably should've been grateful, but being alive brought back the pain. All the people who'd either died or left him since his return to Guntersville. If he'd had access to a drink last night, he'd have gotten drunk. But instead, he'd lain on his cot in the holding cell, his thoughts a tortured mess of regret. Because of him, so many lives had been lost, damaged, or ruined.

He'd woken in a daze and been escorted across Blount Avenue by a team of at least twenty deputies. He figured there were too many uniforms for someone to get a clean shot at him and wondered if Satch and Hatty were just being overly cautious. How in the world could someone pull off an assassination attempt with this many officers covering him up?

Now, as he turned his attention back to the bench, he wondered if he was being naive. His sister, Jana, had been gunned down right outside of this very courthouse minutes after being acquitted of murder charges. To think he couldn't meet the same fate after being released on bond was foolish.

"State of Alabama versus Jason James Rich." Judge Barber spoke in a deliberate manner, seeming to relish every syllable. He lowered his spectacles. "Will the defendant please rise?"

Jason did as he was told.

"Mr. Rich, this hearing has been called to advise you of the charges against you and to set bond." He paused. "I'm surprised that you don't have an attorney present."

"I am an attorney, Your Honor." Jason hesitated, trying to calm his nerves, as he spoke on instinct. "I'll be representing myself in this case."

Barber blinked as if he hadn't heard Jason correctly. Behind him, Jason picked up murmuring from the crowd. *Are you crazy?* Barber's irritated expression seemed to be asking. *Maybe,* Jason thought. But despite how foolish it might seem, representing himself felt . . . *right.* At least, in the current moment, it did. He couldn't think of anyone else he'd trust with his defense. Maybe Izzy, but even his former partner was lacking in criminal defense experience, and he would never put her in danger again. He gazed down at the table. But that wasn't really it, was it? It wasn't so much that he didn't trust anyone to represent him. It was . . .

"Mr. Rich, your license to practice law has been suspended by the Alabama State Bar." Barber's grating voice interrupted his thoughts. "You are *not* authorized to act as an attorney in this court."

Jason glared at Terry Barber, feeling hate oozing through his veins. How many times in his career had he encountered a smug, disapproving judge? Was it the tacky billboard campaign that had bred such disgust with him? His sophomoric behavior? Jealousy over the money he'd made?

All of the above, Jason thought, grinding his teeth. "Maybe not, Judge. But I'm the defendant in this case, and I am authorized to represent myself. Just like any other citizen in this state and in this country." Jason held eye contact until Barber broke it.

"Very well then," he said. "If you choose to do that, you'll still need to retain advisory counsel. If you were indigent, I would appoint one for you. But . . ." He shook his head, trailing off.

"I'm rich," Jason volunteered.

The courtroom, which had been silent as a church up to this point, broke out in several guffaws. Barber banged his gavel on the bench, not amused.

"You have seven days in which to retain advisory counsel, Mr. . . . *Rich*."

"Yes, Your Honor."

There was a pause, and Barber glanced at the prosecution table. Jason followed his eyes. Wish French wore his customary charcoal suit, white shirt, and burgundy power tie. He sat with his legs crossed and his hands forming a tent in his lap. The old bastard oozed confidence. He nodded at the judge, and Jason couldn't help but wonder if it was a nod of approval, as if His Honor needed the district attorney's acceptance of a ruling.

I wouldn't be surprised, Jason thought.

"All right then," Barber said, putting his glasses back on and snatching a piece of paper from the bench. "Mr. Rich, you have been charged with first-degree murder." He again eyed the prosecutor. "What is the state's position regarding bond?"

"We feel it should be denied, Your Honor." Wish remained seated. Another subtle power move. Normally, any time an attorney spoke to a judge, he or she stood.

But not this arrogant prick.

"Mr. Rich is an alcoholic. He was discharged from Marshall Medical yesterday after being treated for detoxification. As you indicated, the state bar has suspended his license. The state feels that this type of volatile behavior indicates that the defendant could be a flight risk. Given the overwhelming evidence against him, we feel Mr. Rich might use his wealth to try to escape." He paused and put his hands around the back of his neck. "Mr. Rich has an airplane."

Now it was Judge Barber who formed a tent with his hands. He leaned back in his chair, glancing up at the ceiling. He was either thinking or pretending to think, and Jason figured it was the latter. Finally, the judge stared down at Jason.

"What say you, Mr. Rich?"

Jason smirked, feeling the hate again. "Mr. French's argument is preposterous and lazy. I've never run from a fight, and I look forward to proving my innocence. His argument is pure speculation and based on stereotypes and innuendo." Jason glared across the courtroom at the district attorney. "No actual facts."

Barber peered down at Jason and then again up at the ceiling. He cleared his throat and looked at the prosecutor. "Do you have anything else concrete showing that Mr. Rich is an immediate flight risk . . . or a danger to the community?"

"He's a drunk, Your Honor. Is that not dangerous enough?"

"No," Barber said, surprising Jason. "It's not. Anything else, Wish?"

"No, Your Honor."

"Very well. The court sets bond at $5 million."

Jason almost laughed out loud. That was an outrageous amount, but the judge had wide discretion to set bond, and Jason knew he shouldn't be surprised.

"Mr. Rich, after your advisory attorney has made an appearance, I'll expect a decision about whether you desire a preliminary hearing. As you know, that is your right."

Jason did know. In the two criminal cases he'd handled in his life, he'd passed on the prelim with Jana, at her urging, and utilized it with Trey Cowan. He wasn't sure how he was going to fall with his own case.

Jason's legs began to shake. The reality of his situation was beginning to sink in.

A lawyer who represents himself has a fool for a client.

He knew it was true, but he felt he had no choice. *This is my life. How can I put it in another lawyer's hands?* Again, while the thoughts felt accurate to him and sounded good . . . they didn't seem complete. *That's not it . . .*

"Mr. Rich, do you understand?" Barber's nasal voice brought Jason back to the present.

"Yes, Your Honor."

"OK, that's it for today." Barber stood and glared at Jason. Then he shifted his focus to Sergeant Martin. "Please take the defendant away."

13

At 9:37 a.m., Matty Dean's cell phone vibrated in his pocket. He pulled it out and glanced at the screen.

"Are we ready?" he answered, forgoing pleasantries as he gazed out over his bass boat at Fire by the Lake restaurant. Before his arrest last year, he'd kept his runabout MasterCraft at the harbor in front of the seafood establishment. The boat had been his pride and joy, but it had been confiscated and was now rotting away in a slip at the harbor where the sheriff's office kept their tiny fleet. Beyond the tiny seafood establishment was Highway 69. From where Matty was sitting, he could see a blank billboard that had once been an advertisement for Jason Rich. *Gone,* he thought, working a toothpick in the corner of his mouth. *Fitting.*

"Ten-four," Lu said. "The diversion is set to occur as soon as that slimy sonofabitch exits the courthouse. And the marksman?"

"In place," Matty said.

Silence for several seconds. "You sure this is the right move, Matty?" The slightest edge of doubt in her tone.

Matty Dean ground his teeth together. Would she or anyone have ever made a comment like that to Tyson? "I'm sure as shit," he said.

Then he ended the call and let out a breath he'd been holding. He thought about the end of the movie *The Godfather*. When Michael

Corleone became his nephew's godfather. The organ music playing as all the family's enemies were gunned down.

With any luck, in the next few minutes, Matty would have accomplished the same objective. Fishing alone didn't quite match the pomp and circumstance from the movie, but, for understated, underappreciated, and perpetually underestimated Matty Dean, it was . . .

. . . *fitting*.

He cast his line.

And waited.

14

After all the spectators had exited the courtroom, Sergeant Greta Martin stood and tapped Jason's shoulder. "Ready?"

Jason sighed. After the drama of the hearing, he was exhausted. He was only a few days postdetox, and his legs still felt rubbery and weak. "I guess."

She smiled at him. "Come on. Just a short walk to the department, and then you can bond out. Five million is chump change for you, right?"

"Not exactly," Jason said, wincing at the sound of the number. "But I can swing it."

Sergeant Martin was joined by at least seven of her uniformed colleagues. "OK, Mr. Rich. Let's do this." She gently placed handcuffs back on him. "You know, I'm going to kind of miss you." She winked at him.

"Ah, Sergeant. Are you flirting with me again?" It had become part of their banter anytime she said anything remotely nice to him. Jason winked back at her. On a lesser but more gradual scale than his wake-up call from Satch, his interactions with Greta Martin had also made him feel alive again. The officer was an attractive woman in a natural kind of way. A brunette with short hair and brown eyes. She was fit and looked sleek in her uniform. Had a nice smile when she used it. Jason figured that being attracted to Sergeant Martin was another step in the right direction. A tiny step, but still a move forward.

She nudged him, and he walked with three deputies in front and three behind. Greta was on one side of him, and another male officer stood to his left. Out in front of them, Jason saw the back of Hatty's head. He squared his shoulders as they exited the courtroom into a hallway. Then down the staircase to the second floor. And seconds later, to the ground level. As the doors swung open, Jason wondered what the rest of the day held for him.

He'd bond out. Satch would take him home. And then . . .

I'm going to get hammered.

He didn't even feel guilty for the thought. He was an alcoholic. He'd been arrested for a crime he hadn't committed. He'd just agreed to represent himself pro se. A ridiculously foolish decision. He needed a drink. While incarcerated and detoxing, he had been able to avoid thoughts of alcohol. But now . . . with his release looming . . . they consumed him. He'd have Satch stop at the filling station off 431 at Gunter's Landing. He'd get a six-pack of good beer. An IPA of some kind. Once he had a nice buzz, he'd take a dip in the lake.

And switch to vodka.

By the time his nostrils breathed in his first gust of fresh air coming out of the exit, Jason could almost feel the burn of the liquor going down his throat and the hollowness that his mind would become as thoughts of Jana, Trey Cowan, Tyson Cade, Nola, Niecy, Chase, Harry, Matty Dean, and all the other people who tortured him dissipated to nothingness. Like when the cable would go out as a kid and the television screen would show only snow, the sound of white static ringing in his ear. Comforting. He longed for it.

He hated the channels of his life.

Jason smelled a fruity fragrance that had to belong to Sergeant Martin. He glanced at her and thought of saying something flirty as he saw a sheen of sweat on her neck. As he opened his mouth, the words were drowned out by a sonic boom.

Jason felt his arms being jerked down, and Sergeant Martin covered him with her body. Now, the only thing he could smell was smoke. His face rubbed against the hard asphalt. Out of his peripheral vision, he saw fire.

An explosion.

"That was the district attorney's car!" one of the officers screamed.

"Back in the courthouse!" Another yell. "Back! Everyone back!"

As Jason felt himself being pulled up from the ground, another explosion rang out.

"Shit!" Martin screamed. "Shit!" She again pulled Jason down, and they were now both crouched in a half squat. Several of the other officers had splintered off. Jason heard screams above them but couldn't make them out. He saw the door being opened, and then Martin was on her feet and pulling Jason back inside.

"What in the hell is going on?" Jason asked. His ears were ringing from the blasts.

"I don't know," Martin said. She reached inside her pockets and pulled out a key. "Hold out your hands."

Jason did as he was told, and she uncuffed him. "Stay with me," she ordered.

All of a sudden, Wish French came inside the doors. His face was ashen. His hands shaking. "My car . . . I was about to get in."

"Are you OK, Mr. French?" Martin asked.

He managed a nod.

"There's a bomb threat for the courthouse!" a deputy cried from up the stairs. "Got to evacuate. Everyone out!"

Jason felt dizzy. He looked at Martin, who studied the district attorney. "Mr. French, we need to get out of here."

"Can't go out there," Wish said, his voice regaining some of his confidence. He glanced at the stairs.

"Front's our only option," Martin said, pulling Jason toward the first step.

"This is your fault," Wish said, his voice oddly monotone as they began to ascend the stairs. "You're a clown, Rich. Everything you participate in becomes a circus. Any blood that's shed today is on your hands." He coughed. "Just like Tyson Cade's, you murdering sonofabitch."

"Come on," Martin implored. "He's in shock."

"Your fault!" Wish screamed behind them as they reached the top.

Jason felt his heartbeat pounding, adrenaline fueling his body. Around them, courthouse employees and civilians who'd come to watch the hearing, register a boat, declare their homestead exemption, or any number of other things were running in every direction. The panic in the air was palpable. There had been at least two explosions off Blount Avenue. Satch had warned that the war wasn't over.

Matty Dean is trying to finish it right here, Jason thought.

Sergeant Martin spoke into her cell phone, but Jason could make out only the last two words. "Roger that," she said.

"Squad car is coming up in front of the courthouse. There will be three deputies meeting us at the door."

"Then what?" Jason asked.

"Then we run for it."

———

The sniper was perched in the second-floor window of the Rich Law Firm. Exactly three hundred yards from the front door of the courthouse. He had heard the explosions. He knew it would be a matter of seconds. He didn't need the text reminder, but he received it anyway.

They're coming . . .

He adjusted his scope so that the entrance to the courthouse was between the crosshairs. Then he placed his index finger over the trigger. His breathing was calm. If anything, his pulse had slowed.

He was ready.

———

Jason and Sergeant Martin followed two deputies out the double doors. Their numbers had dwindled in the minutes since the dual explosions, as officers scrambled to respond to the acts of terrorism. In his mind, Jason could still hear Wish French's oddly monotone accusation.

This is your fault.

Jason thought Martin was handling things pretty well, but the whole scene was unsettling. The adrenaline rush he'd experienced had made him hyperalert, and he saw the faces of panic on the other civilians fleeing the courthouse. As they approached the steps leading up to the sidewalk, Jason saw a familiar black Ford Raptor with tinted windows parked next to a cop car. A bald man with a scraggly ZZ Top–style beard hopped out of the passenger side of the vehicle, ran around the front, and started sprinting toward them. "Get down!" he screamed. "Get down!"

Jason heard a noise that sounded like a sharp thud piercing the air. One of the officers in front of him fell to the ground.

"Get down!" Chuck again.

Jason held up his hands reflexively as Sergeant Martin stepped in front of him. Another thud and Jason's face was splattered with a hot, thick liquid. For a second, he couldn't see, and he tasted iron in his mouth. He wiped his eyes and saw bright-red blood on his hands. Below him, Sergeant Greta Martin had fallen. It seemed like half her head was gone. One lifeless eye stared up at him.

Jason tried to yell, but no words came out.

"Get down!" Chuck shouted again, but Jason couldn't move. He gazed out in front of him and saw something that made him question whether he was alive or dead. Colonel Satch Tonidandel had gotten out of the Raptor and was walking down the middle of Gunter Avenue.

He carried some type of assault rifle and was shooting it from his hip toward what used to be Jason's law office. Machine gun patter lit up his eardrums.

Sweet mother of God, Jason thought. Then the air went out of him as Chuck tackled him like he might be a ball carrier in football. Jason fell hard to the ground with the middle Tonidandel brother on top of him. The former captain in the Screaming Eagles knelt over Jason and fired two shots toward the second floor of the old Rich Law Firm building. Then he yelled something into a handheld device. "You got the shooter, Mickey?"

"Negative. I'm in the building and he's already gone. Now I'm just trying to dodge Satch's fire. Goddamnit!"

"Captain Tonidandel, please stand down."

Still covering Jason, Chuck wheeled toward the voice. Over his protector's shoulder, Jason caught sight of Sheriff Hatty Daniels. "Stand down, sir," Hatty repeated. "We got this."

"You got nothing, Sheriff. I only stand down to my brother." Chuck peered toward Gunter Avenue, and Jason did the same.

The colonel stood in the middle of the street, his rifle raised to the air. At least twenty sheriff's deputies had their guns pointed right at him.

"Hold your fire!" the sheriff screamed, running toward the street and holding up her hands. Jason watched the scene unfold as if he were viewing a television show. *Is this really happening?*

"Everyone settle down," Hatty said, turning to the elder Tonidandel.

"Sniper was on the second-floor window of Jason's firm," Satch said, his voice deep and unwavering. No fear. No hesitation. "I had to do something."

"I know," Hatty said. They were both now standing in the middle of the street a few feet from each other. Jason turned and saw that traffic was backed up to the Veteran's Memorial Bridge. "Put the gun on the ground, Colonel. I'll make sure it's returned to you in due time."

Satch squinted at her. "They were going to kill him."

79

"I know. Now, put down the weapon."

Satch laid the rifle on the ground.

"And will you tell your brother to do the same?"

"Put the gun down, Chuck."

"Yes, sir," Chuck said.

Satch moved his gaze to Jason. "You OK?"

Jason managed a nod. He felt numb and nauseous as he rose to his feet. He looked to his right and saw Sergeant Martin's corpse on the ground, blood pouring from her forehead. She had a young son. The boy's father had abandoned them. The kid would be raised by his grandma now. Greta Martin had been kind to Jason. Had treated him like a person.

This is your fault. Wish French back in his thoughts, but Jason felt himself agreeing as his legs gave way beneath him and he sank back down to the concrete, still looking at Sergeant Martin's lifeless eye. She'd made him feel alive.

And now she was dead. Her life ruined. Like all the others.

This is my fault.

15

At 10:30 p.m., Jason posted bond and was released from the Marshall County Jail. What should have been a somewhat momentous occasion that would have drawn a media frenzy was now a mere afterthought, though Hatty had spared no precaution. The pickup occurred in the basement of the sheriff's department. Jason climbed into the front passenger seat of the Raptor. He rolled his window down and gazed at the sheriff.

For a long moment, they just looked at each other. For the past eight hours, Jason had waited in the holding cell. He'd made the necessary arrangements with his bank to post bond. He'd been interviewed by Hatty about what had occurred in the aftermath of the hearing. The trip down the stairs. The explosion outside. The bomb threat. The confrontation with Wish French. The walk back up the stairs. And then, finally, the shooting that had left Greta Martin dead and two other officers wounded. He had spoken while looking down at the table or his feet, unable to make eye contact with the sheriff.

Now, though, he forced himself to keep his head up. "I'm sorry about Sergeant Martin," he managed. "She . . ." He trailed off, unable to continue.

"Me too," she said, her tone short and matter of fact. Then, glancing past him to Satch, she added, "There's a patrol car waiting in the parking lot to escort you home. And another will pull in behind you."

Satch grunted.

"Jason, I wish you would reconsider," Hatty said. "We can't protect you on the outside."

"You almost got him killed today," Satch growled. "He was a sitting duck coming out of that courthouse. I hope to hell you're investigating how that came to be. My bet is that your old pal Matty Dean is behind it."

"We are looking at all angles, Colonel." Hatty spoke through clenched teeth. "And he was almost killed *outside* of the jail. Not in it."

Satch grunted again but said nothing. Jason glanced at him, feeling the edginess. Since the shooting, he knew that Satch, Mickey, and Chuck had been grilled with questions about their reaction to the sniper fire. Satch had shot up a building with an assault rifle. *My building.* Jason half wondered if the colonel had been charged with anything. He returned his focus to Hatty.

"I didn't kill Cade," Jason said.

"And you'll stand trial for it," she fired back. "If you make it to trial."

"What is that supposed to mean?"

"It means I agree with the colonel. I'm not sure we'll be able to prove it, but I do think that Mr. Dean was behind today's attack. And, with you posting bond, there's nothing to stop him . . . or someone else . . . from making another attempt."

"Wrong," Satch said, his voice lower than a bass guitar. "We'll stop him. Just like we did today while your army of deputies sat on their hands."

"The National Guard arrives tomorrow morning," Hatty said. "We'll have reinforcements." She sighed. "At least for a little while."

Satch put the truck in gear. "Are we done, Sheriff?"

Hatty took a step back and nodded. "Be careful," she said, but her voice was washed out by the roar of the Raptor's engine as the truck lurched forward.

Wish French was seated in the war room by himself when Hatty entered. The lights were out. No other officers were present. Hatty sat across the table from the district attorney. Neither spoke for at least a minute.

Finally, Wish coughed and tapped his fingers on the table. He gave his head a jerk. "I grew up in Scottsboro, did you know that?"

Hatty said nothing. She was exhausted, but she doubted she'd ever sleep again. Greta Martin's ruined face was an image that would be permanently emblazoned on her mind. *My employee. My responsibility.*

"Went to Scottsboro High. Then Alabama for undergrad and law school. I was clerking in the DA's office in December 1972." He tapped his fingers again on the table. "I'd been a lawyer for less than three months and was getting ready for my first felony trial. Bob Collins was the sheriff, and I worshipped him. It was First Monday. You ever hear of that?"

Hatty shook her head.

"It was a big gathering on the downtown square the first Monday of every month. In the beginning, farmers would come to town and sell and trade cattle, but by the early seventies, it was really more like a huge outside flea market. People everywhere. Gossiping. Ladies would get dressed up." He smiled, but his eyes were sad. He ran a hand through his thick hair. "On the first Monday of December 1972, a lawyer named Loy Campbell had just walked his little girl to school. He could have driven her, but decided to walk. When he got in his car, he turned the key and . . ." He licked his lips and clapped his hands. "Boom! I was on the square a mile away. Had just eaten breakfast at the Variety Bake Shop, and I could hear it. Word spread like wildfire. Campbell hadn't been killed, but he was hurt bad." Wish placed his hands in his lap and slumped in his chair. "He'd been a lawyer for over twenty years. Good reputation. But he'd gotten on the bad side of a landowner named Hugh Otis Bynum. Ever hear of him?"

Hatty crossed her arms. She figured this trip down memory lane was Wish's way of dealing with the trauma of the day, but, at least right this moment, the distraction was welcome. "Vaguely. He was tried for attempted murder, right?"

Wish grunted. "By the by God attorney general of Alabama. Bill Baxley. I remember the trial. Bynum owned most of the land in Jackson County. I wasn't sure he'd be convicted . . . but he was. That trial cemented my desire to be a prosecutor. I wanted to put folks like Hugh Otis Bynum where they belong."

"Wish, are you OK?"

He ignored the question, pointing at her with a shaky index finger. "I'm not aware of another car bombing in these parts since Loy Campbell's 1971 Pontiac sedan blew up. Not until today."

"Have you been to the hospital, Wish?" Hatty asked. "Don't you think you ought to get checked out. I mean, you're kinda . . ." She trailed off.

"Kinda old." He snickered. "I'm fine."

She fixated on his dark suit. The glow from the hallway's fluorescent fixture gave off just enough light for Hatty to see the streaks of white along the front of the coat. *Smoke,* she thought. "How close were you?"

He folded his hands. "Twenty feet. Maybe closer."

"What happened after?"

"It's all a blur. A bunch of officers came running toward me, but I couldn't hear anything. I still feel a ringing in my ears."

"Did you go back inside the courthouse?"

"For a few minutes."

"Did you see Jason Rich and Greta?"

He leaned his elbows on the table and rubbed his face. "Yes."

"What did you say?"

"I don't really remember, Hatty. I think I called Rich a clown. I mean, this circus today—"

"Would have happened regardless of who we arrested. Tyson Cade was a folk hero on Sand Mountain. His murder prompted a retaliation."

Wish rested his chin on his hands. "That your theory?"

"You have anything better?"

He shook his head sharply. "No. But Rich and Cade had a history. I'm sure it was worse because of his involvement."

"The National Guard arrives in the morning. So do the feds. Two car bombings on the square are above our pay grade."

"And the circus goes full Barnum & Bailey." Wish leaned back in his chair and scowled.

"When was the last time you were in your car?"

"Right before court. I parked it on the square around eight fifteen and came inside."

"Unlike the story you were telling, the detonation device wasn't the ignition switch."

He chuckled. "I guess I can be thankful for that."

"Which means someone planted the bomb with a timer."

He studied her. "You some kind of bomb technician, too, Sheriff?"

"Just using basic deduction. If that was the case, then whoever planted it could have done it before you even got to the courthouse. Where were you last night?"

He scratched his neck and closed his eyes. "I worked at the office until around six and then had dinner at Wintzell's with my church men's group. We normally get together on Tuesday evenings at a different restaurant."

Hatty processed the information. She wanted to ask more questions, but she figured the feds would cover every conceivable angle. She stood and paced to the end of the long table. "I've scheduled a press conference for tomorrow morning at eight thirty a.m. It'll be at town hall. I'd like you to be there."

Wish was brushing the dust off his jacket. He seemed to have checked out.

"Wish, we have to show the county that we are on top of things. That we've recruited reinforcements and that we are going to keep the people here safe."

The district attorney snorted. "Safe." He slammed his hands on the table and stood. "I became a career prosecutor because of that car bombing in 1972. Because of H. O. Bynum and Loy Campbell. Because of Bob Collins and Bill Baxley." He sneered at her. "This has to stop, Hatty. We are going to take down Jason Rich, because that is our job. We're gonna try that SOB right over there in that courthouse even if we have to enlist the whole National Guard. And either before or after we send that prick to prison, we are going to take down whoever blew up my fucking car."

"Matty Dean." Hatty spoke just above a whisper, feeling hate pulse through her veins.

16

The fire crackled as the man dropped another piece of wood into the chimney. He sat in the hickory rocker and stared at the blaze. Waiting.

Just as he had in his bass boat earlier in the day.

He heard a key being inserted into the front door of the cabin and the door squeak open. Then footsteps treading light.

Lu sat on the couch across from him. Matty didn't look at her. "What happened?" he asked.

"Your sniper hit three officers and killed one of them."

"But not Rich."

"One of the deputies stepped in front of him. Took the bullet that would have gotten him. After that . . ." She trailed off. "I'm sure you've already heard the rest."

Matty grinned. "Must have been quite a sight. That crazy bastard firing a machine gun at Rich's law office while striding down Gunter Avenue like Rambo."

"We were gone by then," Lu said. "The diversions worked. The district attorney's car went up first, and the random vehicle at the driver's license office exploded ten seconds later. Butch called in the bomb threat right afterward, and then it was complete chaos. They took Rich out the front exactly like we thought." She paused. "The plan worked. Our sniper just missed."

Matty gritted his teeth. "There's a first time for everything, I guess."

For a moment, silence filled the cabin, the only sound being the crackling of wood on the fire. "So . . . what now?" Lu asked. She had risen from the couch and was standing by the flames. "I hear the sheriff has called in the National Guard. And you know Rich will have those crazy Tonidandels guarding his every move."

Matty stared at her. She wore jeans and a gray sweatshirt. Her brown hair was covered by a mesh trucker cap pulled low over her eyes.

Matty took a deep breath and slowly exhaled. He'd always been a deliberate man. Not prone to big risks.

Today had been a calculated gamble. He knew his plan would work, and it had.

The sniper just missed.

Matty gritted his teeth again. *And Satch Tonidandel happened.*

Matty again inhaled a deep breath through his nose, letting the air out even slower. He rather enjoyed meditation. It was something he practiced when he fished. Usually before starting and then again several times during a day on the lake. The breathing exercises kept him calm. His head cool and focused. He knew that sometimes the best of plans weren't executed.

It wasn't the miss that bothered him. It was a miscalculation. "The Tonidandels . . . ," he started, reaching into his pocket and pulling out a box of toothpicks. ". . . especially the colonel . . . have gotten completely out of hand." He put the tiny stick in his mouth and worked his jaw. "They don't act like normal citizens. They're literally treating this thing like a war." He chuckled. "I mean, who brings a machine gun to the courthouse square?"

"They're all ex-military, right?"

"One Hundred and First Airborne. Screaming Eagles. All decorated . . . especially the colonel. All crazier than shithouse rats."

"War make them that way?" Lu turned and knelt in front of him.

Matty snorted. "Actually . . . no. The brothers had a reputation before going to Afghanistan. They've lived over there on Mill Creek forever. Their father had also been in the army. A Vietnam vet. Probably the craziest of the bunch. When he got out, he was a bricklayer. Died in the early eighties. Massive heart attack. The mom was a fry cook at the Huddle House at night. I've heard she was even meaner than he was. She also died young, but I'm not sure of what. The boys practically raised themselves."

"How do you know so much about them?"

Matty continued to peer past her at the fire, which was now really roaring. "Like I told you before, Tyson gave me the task of taking them out too. So I've been asking around. Studying them. They've been a thorn in our side ever since Jason Rich came home. I wasn't exactly sure how far they would go for him, but I found out today."

"The colonel could have been killed. Probably should have been killed. Either by our sniper or by the sheriff's department."

Matty nodded. "He's willing to go all the way. He'll die for the sonofabitch." He worked the toothpick end over end in his mouth. "And his brothers will too."

"So what do you want to do?" Her mouth formed a tiny grin.

"You already know," Matty said, touching her nose with his index finger.

"I'm sorry about today," she said.

"Not your fault. I'm the one who picked the sniper. I chose to target Rich first."

She rested her elbows on his knees. "I know you wanted to end it."

Matty continued to work the toothpick. "But it wouldn't have ended. That's where Tyson and I had it wrong. We thought killing the lawyer would send the brothers into a spiral, and we could have picked them off then." He scratched his nose and scoffed. "But that's not how they're wired, and I should have known it. Even if we'd gotten Rich, the Tonidandels would still be out there . . ." He stared at her. ". . . and they would have come after us."

"But that's suicide."

"You heard what the colonel did today. That basically was suicide. He just didn't die." He shook his head. "Those bastards don't care."

"So we make them the focus. Instead of going after Rich, we take out the brothers."

Matty Dean bit down on the toothpick and snapped it in half. He spat the remains out on the sawdust floor. Then he peered down at Lu and nodded. "One by one."

17

When Jason walked through the door, he felt like a stranger in his own house. He'd been gone for—how long? A week? He wasn't sure, but it felt much longer than that. Up until his arrest, he'd spent two weeks in a drunken haze.

Now, as he walked into the living area with its couch and fireplace, there was no sense of being home. As if on autopilot, he trudged into the kitchen with its long island and gazed out at the lake through the bay window.

He was still alive. The bullets that were fired from his old law office building had been meant for him. But they'd wounded two officers instead.

And the third shot had killed Sergeant Greta Martin. The image of Martin's head bleeding onto the sidewalk, her lifeless eye staring up at him, would haunt his dreams for the rest of his life.

Jason turned and opened the refrigerator, then stared at its barren contents. A gallon of spoiled milk. A carton of eggs. A half-eaten pack of bacon that had probably expired. A package of Greek yogurt.

And finally, four beers, all IPAs from the Singin' River brewery in Florence. They were Mickey Tonidandel's favorite, though Jason had bought this batch for himself. He didn't remember when or where he'd purchased the six-pack. He'd probably been drunk when he'd gotten it. He grabbed one of the beers and set it on the counter. Then he popped the top on the can and brought the beer to his nose. He smelled the citrusy hops and breathed it in, closing his eyes and again seeing the ruined face of Greta Martin. The smell of the IPA was replaced by Martin's perfume. He'd caught wind of it just before she took a bullet for him.

Jason felt tears welling in his eyes, and he leaned against the island. Martin was yet another casualty.

My fault, he thought, slapping his palms down on the marble top.

"Jason?" The voice came from the front door, and Jason recognized it as belonging to Mickey, the youngest of the Tonidandel brothers. Jason straightened his posture and brought his hands to his face, then rubbed hard. He glared at the full can of beer and left it sitting on the counter as he walked out of the kitchen. When he saw Mickey, he knew something was wrong.

"Satch wants a word."

"About what?"

"He didn't say. Just told me to bring you. Said it was important."

Jason rubbed the back of his neck, disoriented. All he wanted to do was drink the beer that he'd left on his counter in about three gulps. But instead he followed Mickey out the door.

"Chuck is covering us," Mickey said as they walked up Jason's driveway and crossed Mill Creek Road.

"Do you really think Dean would come after me here?"

"We don't make assumptions, Jason. And we take nothing for granted."

Mickey walked around the back of the plywood house, and Jason saw the huge plume of smoke wafting into the air.

Satch Tonidandel was throwing a black bag on top of the blaze. In the county, garbage pickup was spotty at best, and many folks took matters into their own hands. *Taking out the trash,* Jason thought, remembering how Satch had admonished him the first time he'd walked over here to request their help. That had been over a year ago during Jana's trial. At that time, Jason had been scared of Satch and his brothers.

Now they were the only friends he had left.

Jason sat in one of the lawn chairs that had been placed in front of the fire, and Satch took a seat beside him. Jason could see that Mickey was standing guard in the front yard. He didn't know where Chuck was, only that the middle brother was out there somewhere covering them.

Satch cleared his throat and spoke in his customary gravelly baritone. "In military conflicts, you have to understand your enemy. His motives. Desires. Strengths. Weaknesses."

Jason said nothing, staring at the fire. The garbage bags and other debris made crackling sounds, and he was close enough that his face felt hot. Part of him wanted to lean forward and let himself be consumed by the flames. Going out with the trash sounded about right to him.

"Matty Dean is a different animal than Cade," Satch said, taking a stick and leaning forward, stoking the fire as he spoke. Frustration had crept into his tone. "Older. More experienced. Word on the street is that he killed two of Sand Mountain's top dealers within twenty-four hours of Cade's death."

Jason blinked and turned to him. "A power play?"

The colonel continued to dig at the fire. "Probably. These two guys were younger. Maybe they thought they could get the jump on Dean." Satch hesitated with the stick over the flames. "To be honest, I didn't figure Dean as a leader. I saw him as a finisher, but not a point guard. James Worthy as opposed to Magic Johnson. You understand?"

Jason gave a knowing smile. "What is it about the eighties and you, Colonel?"

Satch glared at him, still holding the stick over the fire. "What do you mean?"

"I mean, you watch *Dallas* and *Magnum, P. I.* and *Falcon Crest* and *The Fall Guy* at the exact times they came on during the eighties. You have a photographic memory when it comes to eighties sports." Jason paused. "Who won the 1983 NBA title?"

"Moses and the Sixers. Dr. J's first title."

93

Jason held out his palms. "Who shot J. R.?"

"Kristin. His sister-in-law. Everyone knows that."

"1985 Super Bowl?"

"Bears."

Jason chuckled. "What is your fixation with the eighties, Colonel?"

Satch watched the fire, his eyes distant. Wistful. "I'll tell you some other time." Then he sighed and ran a hand through his beard. "Look, Jason. I was wrong about Matty Dean. He may not be as brilliant or charismatic as Cade, but he's more than a henchman." Satch set the stick on the ground and leaned back in the lawn chair.

"What are you saying, Satch?"

He gave his head a jerk. "Hell, I don't know. It took Lincoln forever to make Grant his number one general in the Civil War. Same with the South. Robert E. Lee didn't start out as the general of the Army of Northern Virginia. Even though he was the most qualified and the smartest, he was passed over." Satch grabbed the stick again and dug in the dirt. "I'm wondering if that's what's happened with Dean." He glared at Jason with his snake eyes. "And that he might just be the smartest and meanest of the bunch."

Jason waited, knowing that the colonel would have a punch line. Satch Tonidandel didn't waste words.

"You should be dead, Jason. Dean's plan today was sound. A sniper had three good shots at you. Normally, it only takes one. I think the chaos of everyone abandoning the courthouse probably cost him some accuracy. Still, he should have gotten you." He paused and wrapped his hands around the back of his neck. "Most good long-distance rifles have five shots, but he didn't get any more than three."

Jason managed a tiny smile. "That's because of you."

Satch gaped up at the sky and nodded. "I'm sure Dean didn't account for a crazy colonel showing up with an assault rifle."

"Probably not. How'd you know where the sniper was?"

"Mickey was scouting the buildings around the square. He saw a window down at your office and some movement about thirty seconds before the shooting started. I was on the Blount Drive side of the courthouse, so I floored the Raptor. Told Chuck to cover you, and I acted on instinct."

"You could have been killed by the police."

"It was a split-second decision."

"Thank you," Jason said. "You saved my life . . . again."

"*Thank you* are two words you never have to say to me. I have never felt more alive in my life outside of my time in the army than I have in the last year." He coughed, started to say something, and then coughed again. He spat on the fire, and Jason noticed a red tinge to Satch's saliva.

"Are you OK, Colonel?" Jason asked, his heart fluttering.

He grinned, staring at the fire. "I shot up a law office today with a machine gun. I had at least twenty pistols pointed in my direction. What do you think?"

"You just spat blood. The question stands. Are you—"

"Lung cancer," he interrupted. "Diagnosed two weeks ago."

Jason felt his stomach clench. *"What?"*

"I go to the VA hospital once a year for a checkup. This year, they did a chest x-ray. I've got a mass as big as a damn grapefruit in my right lung. PET scan showed it's spread." He spat again at the fire. "Fuck it."

Jason stood from his chair, feeling dizzy. "What kind of . . . treatment are they putting you on? Chemo? Radiation?" He paused, catching his breath. His heart was now racing. "Can they take the tumor out?"

Satch snorted. "None of that shit matters."

"Colonel, don't be so flippant. This is your life you're talking about. Aren't you going to fight?"

Satch pierced Jason with a stare that would melt rock. "You're one to talk. Sitting over there boozing it up every day. Doing everything you can do to kill yourself the last month. Fuck off, Jason. You do you, and I'll do me."

Jason sat down in the lawn chair. His shoulders sagged. "It's not the same," he said, his voice weak.

"The hell it ain't. You are self-destructing and you damn well know it. It is the worst cop-out in the world. You're an alcoholic, you weak-kneed sonofabitch, and you were handling it for a while. But now you've fucking quit. You might as well be shooting yourself every day with a tiny pistol that'll eventually kill you."

"There are treatments for cancer," Jason said.

"And every damn one of them just about kills you with no guarantee that it'll help. I'll lose my hair. My weight. My strength." He gave his head another jerk. "I'm not going to wither away and make it easy for Matty Dean to kill us all. *No fucking way.* I'm going out in a blaze of glory."

Jason thought he understood. "That's what today was then. You *wanted* to be shot. Sure, you hoped to save me, but if you could go down in battle, you'd have a noble death. A soldier's end."

Satch said nothing.

"I'm right, aren't I?"

"You're wrong. My goal is never to *go down*. My only objective is to defeat the enemy. Now stop cross-examining me." Satch's tone was lower. Menacing. "I want to talk about something else."

"OK, shoot."

"What were you doing the morning of Cade's death?"

Jason sighed. "Satch—"

"I have to know. What were you doing?"

"Same thing I've done since my license was suspended. Drank myself to sleep. Woke up. Started drinking again."

"Wrong. You did something different on that day, and you didn't tell me, Chuck, or Mickey you were going anywhere. Now . . . why in the hell were you on Hustleville Road just after Cade was shot?"

Jason glared at the fire. He knew if he were ever to win the looming trial against him for murder, a jury would have to believe his answer to that very question. "I was drunk. I . . . I was angry. I drove into town, intending to buy more alcohol, and ended up on Hustleville Road. Based on Harry's reconnaissance last year and reports that you and your brothers had given me, I knew Cade liked to go to the Alder Springs Grocery at midmorning. I drove past the store, and I saw him. He was walking inside. I turned around. I'm not sure what I was doing. I drove a couple more miles and made a U-turn. I thought about pulling into the store, but I guess I either thought better of it or chickened out."

"You're lucky you didn't kill somebody driving drunk like that," Satch said, shaking his head. "Unbelievable. Did you have your Glock 17 with you?"

Jason nodded.

The colonel cackled. "And why exactly did you buy that gun?"

"I wanted a handgun with more power. That would be accurate from longer distances."

"Why?"

Jason kept his eyes glued on the fire until the colonel finally broke the silence.

"You realize how all this looks to the police? Jason, you bought that gun from our range. That means we have a record of the purchase." He sighed. "Chuck will probably be a witness against you since he handles all the paperwork."

Jason felt his cheeks getting hot.

"I hate to even ask . . . ," Satch began, gazing up at the sky. ". . . but where is the Glock 17 now?"

"I threw it in the lake."

"You did what?"

Jason cringed. "When I heard the cops pulling up the road right before I was arrested, I panicked . . . and I threw it in the lake."

Satch chuckled and scratched his beard. He looked at Jason, squinting, and then coughed again. When he finally stopped, he was laughing. "Are you shitting me?"

"No."

Satch leaned over and grabbed his stick. Then he stood and pressed the twig into the fire. "You realize how guilty that makes you look."

Jason leaned forward, placing his face in his hands. He groaned. "Yes."

"I was wondering how in the world Sheriff Daniels could pin this on you, but it looks like you have made it impossible for her not to arrest you."

"I didn't do it, Satch. Cade had a lot of enemies. I'm the patsy here. I think this was another power move by Matty Dean. Or revenge by the former sheriff."

"Richard Griffith?"

Jason nodded. "He's gone AWOL, and his linkage to Cade brought him down. He had motive."

Satch cocked his head in a "maybe" gesture.

"A full investigation will reveal that there were a lot of people who had motive to kill Tyson Cade. I mean, we know Griffith killed Sergeant Kelly Flowers last year. And you know as well as I do all of the murders that Matty Dean is responsible for. And he currently has a warrant out for him. He's a fugitive, for God's sake, and yet they've charged me with killing Cade."

"Prosecutors and detectives love physical evidence, and there's a mountain of it against you and none against the folks you've just mentioned."

"That's because they are taking the lazy way out. Shining the spotlight on the easy target."

Satch gazed at him for a long time. "Sounds like you *might* be up for this fight, Counselor. That is, if you can stop being a raging, stinking drunk."

Jason flinched. He knew he deserved the rebuke, but it stung worse coming from the colonel.

"You told the judge you were going to defend yourself today." Satch guffawed. "You can't even take care of yourself."

"Colonel—"

"I'm not finished." He continued to stoke the fire. Then he finally tossed his stick on top of it and rubbed his hands together. When he looked at Jason, his face shone in the glow of the burning trash. His eyes radiated intensity. "Why don't you call Bo Haynes over in Pulaski. He helped you last year, and he's a badass attorney."

"Bo is Hatty's lawyer, Satch. He has a conflict of interest."

"Then what about Izzy?"

At the mention of his former partner's name, Jason closed his eyes, and visions stormed his brain. Izzy cradling her knees and shaking in a hotel room in Pulaski as Tyson Cade told them both that Harry wasn't coming back. Then his investigator's lifeless eyes. Jana scowling at him with her perpetually disapproving look. His nieces, Niecy and Nola . . . Nola diving into the lake and him pulling her out. Nola telling him that he was a trigger for her alcohol and drug abuse before she left for good. Ashley Sullivan's green eyes. Chase's broken expression the last time he'd seen her. Finally, his father, Lucas Rich, who'd died of a heart attack in the house across the street. Who'd never approved of Jason's tacky billboards or really anything that Jason had done in his life. Of the moment after the civil trial he'd won last year in Florence. Walking in front of the empty jury box and thinking of his father. And of Jana.

He'd never be rid of the ghosts.

"You can't do this by yourself, Jason." Satch again. He was standing over him now.

Old Lucas didn't like to lose, Jason. Wish French in his head.

And that's all he ever did when he faced me. Jason ground his teeth together and closed his eyes tight.

And soon, you'll be following in your daddy's footsteps . . .

99

Jason grabbed hold of his knees and pressed himself off the chair. He looked at the colonel and wiped his eyes. "I have to make things right."

"You can't do that by being convicted of murder."

Jason stuck out his jaw. "Who says I'm going to be convicted? I'm two for two in that courthouse."

Satch's eyes narrowed into tiny slits. "You really want to represent yourself on a murder charge? Isn't that crazy?"

"No crazier than walking down Gunter Avenue firing a machine gun from your hip. In fact, some would say it isn't in the same universe of crazy as that."

Satch kicked at the ground. "I'm a soldier, Jason. I was doing what I do."

Jason felt a surge of adrenaline rush over him. He thought about his closing argument in front of the jury in Lauderdale County last year. The relief and immense satisfaction of hearing the jury's verdict after working so hard to get to that point. He remembered flexing in the men's room stall after his electric opening statement in Jana's case and the nerves he'd felt before the beginning of each of his jury trials. The anxiety. The excitement. The feeling that there was no place he'd rather be. Then his mind drifted to the disapproving stares of the members of the disciplinary commission of the Alabama State Bar when they'd handed down their suspension. And of the emptiness he'd felt every day since that had led him back to the bottle.

"I'm an attorney, Colonel," he finally said, feeling emotion welling within him. His greatest defuser . . . more than lifting or watching old wrestling videos or even hanging out with Ashley Sullivan . . . was *working*. "I need to do what I do." He thought of the untouched can of Singin' River IPA still sitting on the kitchen counter at his house. "It is the only way I can get my career . . ." He bit his lip. ". . . and my life back."

Satch stared at the flames. "You're sure?"

"I need this, Colonel," Jason said. He had begun to walk around the fire. "I'm not exactly sure why I came back home. I mean, Jana was obviously a big reason. My dad. My alcoholism." He snorted. "It's been a shitstorm every step of the way."

Satch grunted his agreement.

"But now I've got to finish it. I have to try this case. I have to do my job." He paused. "And I have to win."

For a long moment, the only sound was the crackling of the embers. Finally, Jason approached Satch. His voice shook as he spoke. "But you're right about one thing. I can't do it by myself." He extended his hand. "Will you help me, Colonel?"

Satch finally moved his gaze from the fire to Jason. His eyes burned as bright as the blaze. He gripped Jason's hand. "Let's finish it."

PART THREE

18

The truck stop was hopping at 9:35 p.m. Matty Dean flicked cigarette ashes on the asphalt and admired the neon lights that blazed from every window of the convenience store. Then he regarded Interstate 65. How many miles had he logged on the primary connector of Birmingham and Nashville?

No telling, he thought, inhaling another blast of nicotine. He wasn't much of a smoker, but he had gravitated toward the cancer sticks in the days since the bombing on the square and the failed assassination attempt on Jason Rich.

Matty had never been in charge before. His role was always as enforcer. He was normally the one carrying out the tasks, not sitting in a fishing boat waiting to hear whether the plan was successful.

Maybe I'm not cut out for this shit, he thought, watching the line of trucks that had parked for the night. He saw an interior light in one of them switched on and then off.

That was the signal. Matty dropped his cigarette and smashed it with his foot. He reached into his jacket pocket and grabbed the pint of Jack Daniel's. He sipped from it and squinted. Then he screwed the top back on and took out his phone. He clicked on her number while continuing to stare at the rig where the signal had come from.

"Hey," Lu said. "Where are you?"

"Doesn't matter. What's the word?"

"My source says there won't be another hearing until the arraignment, and Rich was given an extra few days to obtain a lawyer given all the extenuating circumstances."

"And what about the brothers?"

"Butch has been tailing Mickey, and Chief has been watching the middle one, Chuck. They both go to their shooting range quite a bit. They're always armed, and it's going to be difficult to get a clean shot."

"Tell me something I don't know. What about the colonel?"

"As far as we can tell, he hasn't left his house since the bombing."

"That's almost two weeks."

"I know. It's odd. But, hell, you said yourself they are all crazy as shithouse rats."

Matty smiled, wrapping his jacket tight around him. It was now early December, and cold weather had begun to set in. He glanced at the rig, and the light again switched on and off.

Patience, he thought, feeling a tingle in his loins. His heart rate sped up. He was beginning to crave this fix more and more. It was as if the pressure of his job, the expectations, the responsibility, all of it . . . was too much. He didn't have Tyson anymore to dote on. To protect.

Matty bit his lip.

"You still there?" Lu asked.

"Yeah. Just thinking."

"We'll get them. There's more of us than there are of them. Eventually, they'll let their guard down . . . and we'll knock them off."

"I know," Matty said, licking his lips, watching the rig, thinking of what was about to happen.

"I miss you," Lu said.

"See you soon," Matty said, then clicked the call dead. He breathed in the cold air and exhaled.

Then he walked toward the rig. Halfway there, the interior light clicked on and off a third time.

Matty picked up his pace.

———

Inside the diner, a man watched through the window. He wore a camouflage jacket and a John Deere trucker cap. A plate of meat loaf and mashed potatoes had been placed in front of him. The man had lost around fifteen pounds since Matty Dean . . . or anyone else . . . had last seen him. His face, once clean shaven, was now covered with a thick brown beard.

Inside the diner, he knew he looked like any other trucker who'd stopped for a bite and a brief respite.

But he was not a trucker. He was here because of Matty Dean.

He sipped from a mug of coffee and glanced behind him and around the vast space. He knew he hadn't been tailed, but he still liked to check. Force of habit from his days in the department. He'd worked for twenty years like a dog. Went from a traffic beat deputy to sergeant, then detective, then chief deputy sheriff, and finally . . .

He winced as he sipped the bitter liquid. All Richard Griffith had ever wanted was to be the sheriff of Marshall County. "Griff," as most folks called him, had won his first election for the job in 2010. For almost nine years, he'd been the most powerful law enforcement officer in the county. But with power came temptation . . .

He'd overspent on his house. Lost interest in his wife. Started having an affair with the sister of one of his subordinates. When the underling officer began to blackmail him, he'd gotten into bed with someone even worse than another woman.

Tyson Cade . . .

Griff asked his waitress for the check and continued to watch Matty Dean head toward the line of rigs that had stopped over for the night. *What is this?* he wondered. *A drug deal?*

Some other kind of arrangement? He figured the man he was watching was behind the attack on Jason Rich two weeks ago. There could be any number of nefarious reasons for Matty to be climbing up into the sleeper berth of that truck.

Griff squinted through the window as the waitress left him his ticket. He laid a ten and a five on the table and walked toward the door.

Once out in the cold, he exhaled, his breath forming a cloud of smoke in the air. He walked to his pickup truck, a used Ford F-150 that had once been his "off-duty" vehicle but which was now his only car and, at least for the past few weeks, his home. He got into the vehicle and reclined his seat.

He'd positioned his truck where he could watch the line of rigs. *What is this?* he wondered again.

Griff knew he was playing with fire. He could be outed at any moment. He'd been foolish enough to deal with Tyson Cade, and he'd lost everything.

His wife.

His family.

His job.

Even his mistress.

And while all these losses stung, the one that hit him the most was the loss of his identity. He'd been a lawman. The sheriff. He'd had power and status.

Now he was a nobody. *And I'll never get it back,* he knew. He hadn't even defended the divorce petition. He'd just agreed to all of Cheryl's terms. He had weekend visitation for his kids, but he hadn't seen them yet. He was too ashamed.

Griff had spent his life upholding the law. But over the past eight months, he'd killed Sergeant Kelly Flowers in cold blood, and his actions had led to the murder of Officer George Mitchell.

He was shocked that Tyson Cade hadn't put a hit out on him.

Maybe he did, Griff thought, still staring at the rig. *Maybe he did, and somebody got to him first.*

A tiny smile formed on the former sheriff's lips. *Should've killed me when you had the chance, you sonofabitch.*

With George Mitchell dead, there wasn't enough evidence to charge Griff with Flowers's murder, but everyone who mattered knew he'd done it.

Initially, once he surmised that George was going to roll on him, he'd run and gone off the grid, living like a nomad. He'd heard about George's murder while driving I-65. He knew then he was unlikely to face prosecution because George was the only person who could have testified against him.

But still he had lain low, figuring he was next. A week went by. Then another. By week three, Griff found himself back in Marshall County. He'd passed Branner's Place and the Alder's Spring Grocery on Hustleville Road.

And he'd paid Tyson Cade a visit, too, though the drug dealer never saw him.

His grin widened. He glanced at himself in the rearview mirror, seeing the tiny gap in his front teeth that he'd had since a bad hop in Little League skipped over his glove and hit him in the mouth.

There wasn't much that could make Richard Griffith happy these days. But thinking of Tyson Cade lying on his back on the cold asphalt adjacent to Hustleville Road gave him a great sense of peace.

Griff tensed as he saw movement from the rig. Matty Dean was walking down the steps. He looked back and said something to a person who was still inside. Then he walked up a step and leaned forward.

A goodbye kiss, Griff thought. He knew there were a lot of female truckers, so the gesture didn't surprise him all that much. But knowing that Matty Dean had a girlfriend might provide some leverage. For six months, Tyson Cade had used blackmail to terrorize him.

But now Griff had nothing to lose. And Cade was dead . . .

Griff stared at Matty Dean as he walked toward his vehicle.

You're next . . .

19

The mornings were Jason's favorite time on the lake. As a kid, he and Chase had taken kayak rides in the summer into the main channel in the early mornings before the boats and Jet Skis took over. They'd chew gum and pretend it was chewing tobacco and spit into the water. They'd talk about pro wrestling storylines or the latest movie they'd watched. This was before puberty had changed their relationship, when they were just two lonely kids who'd found solace in their easy friendship.

In the winter, they wouldn't venture as far. On weekends, they would go toward the back of the cove, where the natural spring created a nice current of cold water that allowed for greater depth near their boathouses. Jason had always enjoyed maneuvering his craft around the logs and clumps of brush and grass in the shallower area near the spring. And the colder air meant fewer bugs and less chances of seeing a snake.

Jason shuddered, both from the chilly wind and the thought of a slithery moccasin. He reached for his phone, but then smiled, as he'd left it at the house. He closed his eyes and listened to the sounds of Mill Creek. The spring's water breaking on limestone rocks. The faint hum of cars on the Highway 79 bridge. The rustling of the bare tree limbs as the breeze whipped through them.

When Chuck Tonidandel's deep and haunting voice sang the first line of "Amazing Grace," Jason felt a warmth come over him. He opened one eye and saw Chuck singing the hymn while reeling in his fishing line. The big man's eyes were also closed, his neck cocked upward. As if he were singing directly to God.

Which he is, Jason thought, folding his arms across his chest and humming along.

On the morning after being released on bond, Jason had woken with the sun and drifted down to the boathouse. Chuck was perched in a lawn chair, holding the King James Bible open with both hands. An AR15 was draped across his lap. On a whim, Jason heard himself asking the middle brother if he wanted to take a kayak ride.

Expecting some version of "You're crazy as hell to want to get on the water in this cold," he received, instead, a hard slap on the back and a "Let me get my ride."

Turned out Chuck enjoyed at least one weekly trek on the water come wind, cold, or rain. He owned a paddleboard and a kayak and alternated which craft he'd use based on how he felt that particular day. The fact that Jason had never known, or perhaps hadn't taken the time to know, this information about Chuck was a tad unsettling.

What else don't I know about the brothers? He'd thought about Satch's nostalgic devotion to eighties sports and entertainment, and Mickey's new love interest that he'd met while fishing. Jason had been so wrapped up in himself and his own problems that he'd been blind to what was right in front of him.

Over the course of the past twelve days, Jason and Chuck had started each morning with a trip to the back of the cove. By now, the excursions had become a bit of a ritual. They'd paddle their respective kayak to the cove, Jason normally leading the way so that Chuck could cover him. Then, once there, Chuck would read aloud his daily devotional, after which they'd fish with cheap reels Chuck had gotten from the Waterfront store a mile down 79. Occasionally, when one of them caught something, usually a bream, they'd admire it and let it go.

Of the three Tonidandels, Chuck was the quietest. He rarely talked on their rides other than to help Jason bring in a fish or untie a knot in his line, which happened several times in the beginning, as Jason had never been much of a fisherman. But, almost two weeks in, Jason was pleased that he was beginning to get the hang of the task, which had a monotonous pleasure to it. It reminded Jason in a weird way of sitting in his dad's law firm library as a kid, pretending to do his homework but watching his father work instead. Lucas would talk to himself sometimes, trying out an argument, and Jason would strain to hear his words. So different, yet both activities got Jason out of himself, focusing completely on something else.

Then, it was his dad. Now, it was the lake and the fish that swam below the surface and his quiet friend, who read from his *Jesus Calling* book in a gentle voice, as if he were reading to himself, and then put one of his big paws on Jason and prayed, usually for their safety but also for guidance and strength and "to do God's will."

Jason would say "Amen," and he liked to think that Chuck was right. A week ago, Chuck had surprised Jason again by breaking into "Jesus Loves Me" while he fished. The captain's vocals were pitchy and his voice cracked at times, but he sang without embarrassment or self-consciousness.

Jason thought there was an odd and simple beauty to it. A big, quiet bald guy just . . . singing. Jason had seen so many awful things in the last year and a half . . . *and done so many awful things in my life* . . . he wondered if it was possible that a holy being could be watching over him. As he stretched his back muscles in the small craft and felt the sun on his face, he had to admit that he felt a sense of peace.

Sadly, that peace never lasted.

"Ready to roll?" Chuck sang the question in tune with the chorus of "Amazing Grace." Without waiting for an answer, the middle brother moved out of the narrow spring and back out into the cove, continuing to hum the classic hymn until he broke full out into the last verse at the top of his lungs: *"When we've been there ten thousand years . . ."*

Jason stifled a laugh and moved his kayak past Chuck, finding that he was humming along. He worked the paddle to the left and then the right, balancing the craft as it moved swiftly above the surface. His arms and back ached with the movements, but it was a good pain. Not unlike working out, but oddly better. His mind began to think about the ground he'd covered since the shooting on the square . . . and what still remained to be done.

In the past twelve days, he'd reached out to each of his former clients, making sure they'd found new representation, and he'd started having telephone sessions with his old psychologist, Celia Little. He'd never thought the appointments helped much in the past, but truth be known, he hadn't committed himself. He wasn't sure if he was any more disciplined now, but he was making an effort. He'd also begun to do some preliminary research on the charges against him, making lists of people to contact, potential witnesses, and alternative theories. He was working again, and it felt good.

And he'd reached out to his remaining family, but the reception had been lukewarm. He hadn't been able to get Niecy on the phone. She'd wished him well in her texts, but like always, she seemed guarded and acted as if she didn't want to be involved. *Smart girl,* Jason thought. Jason had managed a phone call with Nola as well, but their exchange had been uncomfortable. He told her that he missed seeing her, which was the truth, but she hadn't offered anything but a "Yeah" in return. They'd compared notes on detox, as she'd had to go through that herself last year. She said she was doing well in Birmingham and looking forward to starting Alabama in the fall, but she offered no details on her life. Nothing about friends. Boyfriends. Her job.

She's afraid that being a part of my world will trigger her again. If he had to guess, he figured that Niecy was in her sister's ear, advising Nola that she was better off moving on. If that were true, it was good advice, and he couldn't begrudge them their decision to stay away. *It's what I should want . . .*

And yet, he still missed them and longed for a connection.

He sighed. He was making progress. But there was still a big box that he hadn't checked.

Jason slowed his movements as Chuck came to a stop a hundred yards from Jason's boathouse. The big man was about to bring it home.

"I once was lost, but now I'm found. Was blind but now I seeeeeeeeeeeeee." He held on to the last note for all he was worth, and Jason was glad they weren't in a room with any glass.

"Bravo," Jason said, giving an eighties end-of-movie slow clap that the colonel would have appreciated.

"Thank you," Chuck said, peering up at the sky, and Jason wasn't sure if he was talking to him or to God. Then the captain addressed him. "You all right, Jason? Awful quiet today."

Jason guffawed. "Says the man who barely talks at all, and when he does it's normally in Bible verses." Jason looked at Chuck, but the middle Tonidandel was still watching him. Waiting.

"Got a huge decision to make," Jason admitted. "The deadline for me to pick advisory counsel is coming up in a few days. I've put in a call to someone . . . and I'm waiting to hear back. If she says no . . ." He trailed off and felt his arm being grabbed.

"Matthew chapter seven, verse seven," Chuck said, his tone low and soft. "Ask, and it shall be given you; seek, and ye shall find; knock, and it shall be opened unto you."

Jason squirmed, awkward. "Um, yeah, Chuck. OK." He looked at his arm. "You can let go now."

"You have to believe, Jason." His tone was intense. Chuck wasn't as large a man as Satch, but at six feet one and a stocky 225 pounds, he was strong as a bull and, with his bald head, he reminded Jason at times of the wrestler Bam Bam Bigelow. With his fierce glare, he was definitely giving off Bam Bam vibes right now. "Mark chapter eleven, verse twenty-four," Chuck continued. "Therefore I say unto you, What things soever you desire, when ye pray, believe that you receive them, and ye shall find them."

Jason nodded and then looked away. "OK, man."

"*Believe*," Chuck repeated, his voice a whisper, finally letting go and forging his kayak ahead.

Jason took another deep breath, watching the smoke drift out and above him as he exhaled. There had been several of these tense encounters with Chuck, where he would quote scripture and implore Jason to pray and believe. And while Jason appreciated what the middle brother was doing, he found himself building internal walls up whenever the subject of faith was broached. He wanted to ask Chuck how he'd come to be such a man of devotion, but he was afraid that the answer might be worse than not knowing.

He sighed and began to paddle again. Up ahead, Chuck was docking at the boathouse and pulling his kayak up the steps. Meanwhile, the colonel was waiting, hands on hips, gun stuck through the waistband of his jeans. As Jason got within earshot, Satch squatted down closer to him. "You have a visitor," he said.

Jason raised his eyebrows. While he'd engaged in many phone calls, he hadn't seen a living soul in person other than the Tonidandel brothers in twelve days.

"Who?" Jason asked.

The colonel smiled. "You'll see."

———

Jason's heart leaped when he saw her. She was standing in front of the couch in the den with her hands clasped behind her.

Isabel "Izzy" Montaigne was a small woman not much over five feet tall. She had dark hair and a petite build, but what she lacked in physical stature she made up for with an energy, spirit, and work ethic that had made her the best law partner Jason could have ever asked for. And a wonderful friend.

"Hey, Jason Rich." Her voice caught in her throat as she said both of his names, which was an Izzy thing that she sometimes did when she was trying to make a point.

Jason's stomach tightened. He hadn't seen her since Harry's death five months ago. So much had happened since . . . "Hey, Iz," he managed.

She walked over to him and stood for a second, shaking her head. Then, tears filled her eyes and she embraced him, squeezing his neck so hard that Jason almost lost his breath. "I'm so glad you're all right," she said. Then she turned to Satch and gave him a hug too. For a moment, the colonel was stunned, but he eventually put his arms around her. "It is good to see you, Izzy."

"You, too, Colonel. I heard about what happened on the square. You saved his life."

Satch nodded. "Just . . . doing what we do."

"Well, thank you."

"Iz, you shouldn't have come," Jason finally said. "It's too dangerous for you to be here."

She crossed her arms. "Well, that's not very nice. Besides, you said in your message that you wanted to talk with me."

"I meant over the phone."

"You didn't want to see me?"

"I don't want you to get hurt." He sighed and rubbed the back of his neck. "But I do need your help."

"Figures," she said, forcing some sassiness into her tone. "Well . . . spit it out."

Jason glanced at Satch. "Colonel, would you mind waiting outside?"

Satch grunted and turned for the door. "I'll be out front, and Chuck is still in the back."

"Where's Mickey?" Izzy asked.

"Little brother's on a date," Satch said, slamming the door behind him. She glanced at Jason. "A date?"

Jason chuckled. "Mickey met a girl bass fishing last summer, and it's blossomed into a romance."

"I didn't think the Tonidandels did anything normal."

"Mickey . . . is probably the closest one to normal." Jason snorted. "But that's not saying much." He rocked on his heels. "But I damn sure appreciate them. They're . . . all I have left."

She frowned. "Not true. You have two nieces that love you, and . . . you still have me."

"Do I?" Jason studied his old friend, taking in the hurt. Then an image of Harry came to him. Black T-shirt, dark jeans. Piercing blue eyes. Crooked smile. He could almost hear his old friend's voice. *"Be easy, J. R. She's been through a lot on account of us."*

Jason sat down on the couch and gazed at the hardwood floor. His face felt hot. He was ashamed. Harry Davenport had been a good man. The best investigator he could have ever asked for and an even better friend. Harry and Izzy had both tried to steer Jason away from coming home to Guntersville to help Jana, but Jason hadn't listened. He'd felt like he had to do it.

Now Harry's dead . . . My fault. All of it. Izzy should tell me to go straight to hell.

He remembered the phone call from Tyson Cade and the terrible hours after learning that Harry was never coming back. Harry had been tracking Matty Dean during the Cowan trial—Jason's stubborn attempt to play Cade's game. Despite Harry's admonitions that they needed to stay in their lane, Jason had put his friend in harm's way.

Izzy and Harry had been so happy. They might have been married by now. Perhaps a kid would have come a long in a little while. But all those hopes and dreams died somewhere behind the Sundowners Club in Pulaski, Tennessee, almost six months ago.

If Jason had to guess, Harry's corpse was now somewhere in the deep waters of the Tennessee River.

He felt movement, and then Izzy was sitting next to him. She grabbed his hand, and Jason couldn't look at her. He wasn't a crier, but his eyes were stinging now. In the days since his return home, he'd felt better, but he'd avoided giving in to his feelings. Now, the dam felt ready to break.

"Izzy, I'm so sorry about Harry," he said, still staring at the floor. "I think about him every day. I know it was my fault that he died. I overreached, and the people I love all got hurt." He wiped his nose. "You. Harry. Nola."

"I forgive you, Jason Rich." Izzy's voice was soft, and she spoke right in his ear. She had put her arm around him, and he leaned into her. "I forgive you for all of it."

"No," Jason whispered.

"Yes." She nudged him with her elbow, and he finally looked at her.

Tears had streaked her cheeks, but her voice was strong. "You did what you thought was right, and Harry was a grown man. He loved you. I . . . love you. We all did the best we could do. It was just . . . an impossible situation."

"I should have backed off."

"You couldn't do that. With Jana's case, you were trying to help your sister. And with Trey Cowan, Cade blackmailed you. He was going to hurt Nola. And Chase. And you know he would have done it." She rubbed the back of his neck. "It was impossible."

"I shouldn't have had Harry tail Matty Dean. I should have stuck to practicing law."

She snorted. "Jason, Harry was an Army Ranger. He was as equipped as the colonel and his brothers at taking care of himself." She glanced down at the floor and then back up at him. "And he'd be furious that we were sitting in here feeling sorry for ourselves because of him. That's what finally helped me move on. I know Harry would want that."

"I can't," Jason said. "Too much has happened."

"Yes, you can." She slapped him on the knee. "And you will." She rose from the couch and walked out in front of the fireplace.

"So does that mean you'll help me?" He smiled at her as he leaned back against the cushions and wiped his eyes.

She grinned back. "You are so slick, aren't you? Even when you're pouring your heart out, you always have an angle. If I didn't know how much you loved Harry, I'd almost think you faked those tears to get what you wanted."

"I love you, too, Iz, and I miss you. I miss working together." He sighed. "I miss working period. I trust that you've been getting a lot of calls from our old clients."

Her grin spread. "Yes, I have."

"I'm glad," Jason said, meaning it. In the days after his suspension, in the few semisober moments he'd managed, he'd referred all his existing clients to Izzy. During his follow-up calls since the shooting, it appeared that most of his clients had taken his advice and retained her.

"Once again, you've saved my career," Izzy said. "Just like when you hired me out of law school when no one else was interested."

"Best decision I ever made." He paused, feeling hopeful. "Iz, on this murder charge I'm facing, I need to retain advisory counsel, and—"

"Nope." She gave her head a quick jerk. "Not only no, but hell no. You don't need me. I can't help you win this case. I'm not a criminal defense attorney, I'm not from Marshall County, and I have never even tried a case to a jury in my life." She winked at him. "I'm you two years ago, Jason, but with much less experience."

"I won, Iz. *We* won. And we can win this one too. I'm innocent. I did not kill Tyson Cade. You know I couldn't have done that. Look, I'm going to try the case myself. I'm not asking you to represent me. I'm really just asking you to do what you've always done in every case I've ever handled. Except this time, sit next to me during the trial."

She crossed her arms and gazed down at him. "I can't, Jason. I'm too busy trying to get my new firm going. Helping your old clients. Being your advisory counsel will take me away from them. Is that what you want?"

"This is my life, Iz. If I lose . . ." He trailed off.

"Jason, if I thought I could add something that might help you win, then I would do it in a heartbeat, but we both know that all I would be is a crutch. A warm blanket. Someone for you to vent to."

"You're a hell of a lawyer, Iz. You know how to work up a case as good as anyone I know. You're a fantastic researcher and investigator. And, last but most definitely not least, I trust you, and I can't imagine trusting another lawyer with this assignment."

She approached him and put a hand on his shoulder. "I appreciate that, Jason Rich. I really do. It means a lot. If I was on trial for my life in Guntersville, I would want you. But here's the deal. You're from Marshall County. And you're now three for three in jury trials and undefeated in murder cases in the jurisdiction where this case is being held. I get why you want to handle this yourself. You've become a great trial lawyer." She squeezed his shoulder. "I'm not there yet, and, even if I was, you need a local attorney. Not a Birmingham lawyer with a funny name."

"Isabel Shasteen Montaigne is a beautiful name," Jason said, and he put his arms up to block a fake punch that Izzy was threatening to throw.

"Look," she said, running her hands through her hair, "I'm happy to help with administrative tasks. You need some help with research, tracking down a person . . . you want to discuss strategy, any behind-the-scenes investigation, I'm in." She paused and squinted at him. "But seriously, for the person that will be there with you in the courtroom, we both know you need someone local," she said. "And I know exactly who that someone should be."

He put his arms down, and she punched his shoulder.

"Ow!"

"See. You're sitting there thinking that talking to me was a waste, and I'm about to save the day for you."

"Izzy, what are you talking about? *I'm* the local connection. What I need is someone I can trust, and who I work well with. *You're* that person."

"No. I think you can trust who I'm thinking of. This lawyer . . . owes you one."

Jason inspected the floor, but then his eyes shot up. "Shay?"

Izzy shot finger guns at him. "Don't you think the former district attorney is itching to get back in the courtroom?"

"But I'm the reason she lost the election. The Cowan case pretty much sunk her boat."

"You also saved her life, remember?"

Jason rubbed the back of his neck. "You want me to team up with Shay Lankford, a career prosecutor?"

"Can you think of anyone more qualified to try a murder case in Marshall County?"

Jason opened his mouth, but then closed it.

"Didn't think so," Izzy added.

Jason stood and walked toward the front door. Then he turned around and gazed at his former partner. "You're crazy, you know that?"

She nodded. "Damn right. I learned from Jason motherfuckin' Rich. But we both know it's not crazy. It's—"

"Genius," Jason said, smiling at her.

20

Shay Lankford lived in Grant, Alabama, about two miles from DAR High School. Satch parked the Raptor out in front of a one-story frame house that was painted light blue and had a red door.

"This is the address Izzy gave us," the colonel said, grunting.

"You think it's a bad idea," Jason said.

"No. It's a great thought. I just think she'd be crazy to say yes."

"And why's that?"

"Because she's a career prosecutor, and she didn't lose the election by much. Why in the world would she want to get involved in this mess? Seems like the better political strategy would be to lay low and wait for the new district attorney to make a mistake." He paused. "Like Wish did."

Jason chuckled. "You don't think I can win, do you?"

"Didn't say that."

"You're thinking it, though."

"Will you get the hell out of this truck and pull the Band-Aid off? I'm losing seconds of my life, and I might not have many of those left."

Jason saluted him and climbed out of the passenger side of the truck. He strode toward the red door, which seemed an odd choice for a blue house, and glanced at his phone. He had a text from Izzy.

Asked her yet?

Jason inspected the screen, feeling grateful. It felt good to be texting with his old partner again. Like old times, almost.

At her house right now, he responded and slipped the phone in his pocket.

He trotted up the steps to the small landing and stood on a brown mat that said "Welcome." He felt foolish. Like he might be some kind of door-to-door salesman from years gone by. Jason sighed and knocked three times. *Satch is right. Smart idea but no way it works.*

A few seconds later, the door swung open, but it wasn't Shay Lankford who stood behind it.

The woman had curly silver hair and round spectacles and wore a white sweatshirt with "Seaside" written in light-green letters across the front, a pair of black joggers, and tennis shoes.

"Hello . . . ma'am. I was looking for Shay Lankford."

The woman crossed her arms and squinted at him.

"Do I have the right house?" Jason added with a sheepish smile.

"Yeah, you do. I'm just surprised to see you." She rubbed her hands down her pants and then extended her hand. "Beth Lankford. I'm Shay's mother."

Jason shook her hand and grinned wider, his mind racing. *She lives with her mom.* He wasn't sure what he was expecting, but this was a bit of a surprise. "It's nice to meet you, Ms. Lankford. Is, uh, your daughter home?"

"No, she's not. But . . . she has a lunch break around noon."

"Could I come back then?"

"You could." Beth smiled. "Or you could take a walk with an old woman. I was just going to take Lucy out for her daily."

"Lucy?" Jason asked, raising an eyebrow.

"Yeah. Let me get her, and I'll be right out." She turned and left Jason standing on the stoop. He looked over his shoulder at Satch, who was leaning against the truck. The colonel held out his palms.

Jason returned the gesture. Seconds later, Beth Lankford was back and holding a leash. Attached to it was a chocolate Labrador retriever.

"This is my Lucy," Beth said, ruffling the dog behind the ears, which the animal greeted with a snort.

"She's not overly social, but she won't nip you." Beth walked down the stairs with the dog behind her. Without turning around, she said, "You coming?"

Jason glanced at Satch and chuckled. Then he jogged a few steps to catch up.

———

After walking down the street past several houses, Beth veered off the road onto a path between the trees. Jason had kept quiet so far, not exactly sure what to say and figuring Beth would start talking when she felt like it. However, once they were off the asphalt and walking along the dirt, he couldn't help himself.

"Where are we going?"

"You'll see," she said. As smoke lifted above her, Jason rubbed his arms together. He had dressed in jeans and a button-down but should have brought a jacket. The air was cold and crisp and now, as they walked along the trees, it was even chillier. He looked over his shoulder and saw Satch, who was walking ten yards behind them. The colonel had pulled his handgun out of his pocket and was holding it at his side. He glared at Jason, clearly not enjoying this detour. *Anybody could take a shot at me in here . . .*

He almost laughed. That was true wherever they went, and Satch had confirmed with Mickey, who was at the bottom of the mountain, that no one had followed them. *Relax . . .*

"What's his story?" Beth asked, jerking her head toward Satch. "Your driver."

"He's a bit more than that."

"Security, I'm sure. Heard about the shooting at the courthouse." She sucked in a breath. "You sure seem to attract the drama. I guess I'm glad Shay wasn't there for that."

"You should be. The district attorney's car blew up. He was . . . lucky."

She snorted. "Wish French is a jerk, but there's no place for terrorism. I'm glad he's OK." She looked at Jason. "And I'm glad you are too. The officer wasn't so lucky, though."

Jason flinched. The funeral for Sergeant Greta Martin was held last week. The National Guard, which was still in town, had maintained a peaceful presence at it. Jason had wanted to pay his respects, but Hatty and Satch had warned him against it.

Instead, he'd written letters to Greta's mother and young son and also made a sizable donation to the GoFundMe account that a sheriff's department's deputy had started for her family. It was the least that he could do, and it felt woefully insufficient.

"No," he finally said. "She wasn't." He paused, thinking about what Wish French had yelled his way just before the shooting. "My fault."

Beth scoffed. "A bit full of yourself, aren't you?" She shook her head. "You sound like my Shay. Always thinking the world revolves around you." She stopped for a moment, leaning down and handing Lucy a treat. Then she took a small bottle of water out of the pocket of her pullover, unscrewed the top, and poured some of it in the Lab's mouth.

Rough life, Jason thought, smiling at the dog.

"You know what I believe, Mr. Rich?" she asked, straightening up and yawning.

"No, but I suspect you are about to tell me."

She put her hands on her hips. "Sometimes . . . shit, excuse my French, happens."

He stared at her. "Greta Martin was killed protecting me. The bombing was likely a diversion to set up the shooting. The whole thing . . . was my fault."

She glared back at him. "Well . . . did you kill Tyson Cade?"

"No ma'am, I did not."

"Well, if that's true, then it wasn't your fault that you were at the courthouse."

Jason held her gaze and finally looked away.

"Got you there, didn't I, Counselor?" She started walking again before he could respond. He caught up to her, and felt now as good a time as any to dive in.

"How's Shay been doing?"

Beth worked her jaw a bit before responding. "She's a fighter, my Shay. No quit in her. But . . . with what happened at your office and almost being killed . . . and then losing the election on the heels of that . . ." She shook her head. "I think she's not sure what to do anymore."

Jason grimaced. "That could also be said was my fault."

"No, it wasn't. Being a political figure comes with risk. When you lose a case, it hurts your chances. Those are just the breaks."

"Shay's a very good lawyer."

"So are you," Beth fired back.

"So . . . she's been doing some teaching?" Jason asked.

"Yeah, just up at the school. Shay graduated from DAR." Beth smiled. "Was a cheerleader and ran track." She gave her head a jerk. "What does Forrest Gump say? My girl Shay could run like the wind blows." She cackled. "Anyway, she wanted to keep busy, but I don't think she was ready to go back to practicing law."

"Why not?" Jason asked.

"The only job she's ever known has been in the Marshall County DA's office. First as an assistant for many years under Wish and then as the DA." She shrugged. "She's . . . just not sure what's the next step."

Beth stopped for a moment and gave Lucy another treat and sip of water. The dog enjoyed both and then relieved herself. Beth pointed toward the horizon. "This is pretty much the highest point on Gunter Mountain. It's always been my favorite place. It's where I go when I'm sad." She bit her lip and gazed wistfully over the mountain. From this vantage point, Jason could see Lake Guntersville, Highway 431, and the farmland beyond it. He took a deep breath of cold air and looked behind him. Satch was now five yards away, his arms folded in front of him. The gun was now in his pocket.

"I also come here when I'm happy. To celebrate a victory, like when Shay won her election a few years ago." She sighed. "Shay likes to run this path, and Lucy loves the walk."

"I can see that," Jason said, smiling down at the Lab.

"But the thing I like to do most when I come here, Mr. Rich, is to pray." She watched Jason with wistful eyes. It was easy to see where Shay had gotten her beauty. Beth Lankford, even with her blonde hair turned silver, was an attractive woman with violet eyes that had a searching quality about them. Jason felt like she was examining his soul, and finally turned away. She looked back when he felt his hand being grasped.

"I pray for good health. I thank God for my life. For Randy, God rest his soul, and all the years we had together. All those wonderful days living right on this mountain. The fun trips to the beach. Shay's ballgames and track meets in high school. The graduations from high school and law school. You see, Mr. Rich, it's important to be thankful. Grateful for the good things." She gritted her teeth. "There's plenty enough bad things to think about. Why not be grateful? For good dogs. For my wonderful daughter." She squeezed his hand. "And for the man who saved her life."

Jason kept his eyes on the ground.

"I don't know why you came here today, Mr. Rich, but I have wanted to thank you for a long time."

"Ma'am, I probably cost your daughter her job."

His hands were now being gripped so tight that he almost yelped. "But you saved her life. You covered her body with your own. She's all I've got, Mr. Rich. You understand that, don't you?"

127

He finally looked at her, and she had tears in her eyes. "Yes, ma'am."

"Now, close your eyes."

"Why?"

She chuckled and wiped her eyes. "Because, you silly man, I'm going to pray for you."

"For *me*?"

"For *you*, Jason Rich."

Jason closed his eyes and felt the cold breeze on his face. He was reminded of his morning trips to the cove with Chuck these last two weeks. The prayers and the songs. The warmth he felt then was on him now. He wasn't sure if he believed in all the things that Beth Lankford and Chuck Tonidandel did. But if there was a Jesus. If he did still exist and walk with us and talk with us, as the song went . . . Jason figured that he did it here. On top of Gunter Mountain with this beautiful soul. And in the cove at Mill Creek with his quiet but intense friend.

"Dear God, thank you for Jason Rich, who saved my precious daughter, Shay. Please be with him. Guide him and watch over him. Please bless him and whatever business he has with my girl. Thank you, Lord, for this man. For this day. For your son, Jesus." She paused. "Amen."

"A . . . men," Jason managed.

"Amen." Satch's gravelly voice startled Beth, and she looked past Jason to the colonel. Then she turned back to Jason and leaned closer to him. "You know, that man kinda looks like my Randy. If he'd shave that god-awful beard."

Jason smiled and felt her nudge his elbow.

She cocked her head. "He also kinda favors Walt Longmire." She let out a breath she'd been holding. "Mercy, I love that show." She rubbed her hands together and retrieved the leash from the ground. Jason hadn't even realized that she'd dropped it. Lucy had been walking along the mountain's edge, sniffing and snorting. Now, Beth hooked the leash back to the dog's collar and began to walk in the opposite direction.

"You two like chicken salad?" she asked, as she strode past the colonel.

Satch was shaking his head at Jason. "Uh, yes," Jason said. "Love it." He followed her. "Why?"

"Because that's what's for lunch."

———

The house was like a shrine to Shay. Photographs of her from birth all the way to the district attorney's office covered most of the three-bedroom home. Jason and Satch sat at a circular wooden table, drinking sweet tea and watching Beth make the sandwiches. She hummed an old country song, "More Than I Can Say," as she worked, swaying back and forth and occasionally having to elbow Lucy away. The dog had both paws on the counter, sniffing and barking and trying like hell to snatch a bite of food. The only part of the song that Beth would sing was "Whoa, whoa, yeah, yeah," and Lucy would howl along with her. Jason wondered how many times this ritual played out between dog and master, and couldn't help but grin. He winked at Satch, but the big man didn't return the gesture. The colonel looked like a wild animal that had been caged and hadn't said a word since entering the house.

When the front door squeaked open, Jason felt his stomach tighten, and then it twisted further when he heard her voice. "Mom!"

"In the kitchen, hon."

Lucy ran toward the voice, and Shay entered the kitchen with the dog standing on her hind legs and trying to lick Shay's face. She wore dark jeans and a khaki blouse, and her dark hair was tied up in a micro bun. Even as a substitute teacher with a dog hanging on her, she looked like the impeccably dressed and hard-nosed prosecutor that Jason remembered.

"Stop it, girl," Shay said, setting Lucy's pads on the floor. When she saw Satch and Jason, she stopped in her tracks. "What . . . *in the world?*" She locked her gaze on Jason. "What . . . are you doing here?"

"Shay, mind your manners, hon," Beth interjected. "I invited Mr. Rich and Colonel Tonidandel in for lunch." She turned from the counter and winked at Jason. "Chicken salad on wheat?"

"Yes, ma'am," Jason said, returning the gesture.

Shay looked from Jason to her mom and then finally stepped forward. Her face had turned red from either anger, embarrassment, or both. "Whatever, then, I guess."

"Sit down and hold your tongue, daughter," Beth said, placing paper plates on the four placemats on the table. Each one contained a sandwich, sea salt chips, and a pickle. Jason smiled and felt a genuine warmth come over him as everyone sat at the table.

"Colonel, would you mind saying the blessing?" Beth said.

Jason glanced at Satch, who continued to look as uncomfortable as Jason had ever seen the big man. For a moment, he thought Satch was going to decline the offer, but then Satch surprised him.

"Uh . . . God is great. God is good. Let us thank him for our food . . . amen."

"Amen!" Beth said, her voice infectious with its energy. She leaned across the table and squeezed Satch's hand. "Thank you, Colonel. Now . . ." She looked at all of them for a second. "Let's eat."

The chitchat during the meal focused, surprisingly, on Satch Tonidandel's military career. Beth Lankford peppered Satch with questions about the One Hundred and First Airborne, the Screaming Eagles, his brothers, the skirmishes he'd been in, the type of vehicles they rode in, what it was like to fly in a helicopter, the landscape of Afghanistan, and on and on. Satch's answers were mostly cryptic and uninformative, but that didn't seem to quell Beth's enthusiasm.

Finally, Shay stood from the table and put her half-eaten sandwich in the trash.

"Not hungry, baby?" Beth asked.

"Not really," she answered, turning to Jason. "I have twenty minutes before I have to go back to the school. Can we cut the bull and get to it? Why are you here?"

"Shay—"

"I've minded my manners long enough, Momma. Would you please excuse me and Mr. Rich?"

"Of course," Beth said, glancing at Satch. "Care to see my back porch, Colonel?"

Satch grunted and looked at Jason, who nodded. Then he followed Beth out of the opening to the den. "How tall are you, Colonel?" Jason heard Beth ask, and then their voices were out of earshot. He smiled up at Shay and pointed to the chair she had just vacated.

"Please. Would you mind sitting?"

Shay crossed her arms. "I'd rather stand."

"OK," Jason said. "Why . . . the hostility? I thought we had turned a corner after the shooting."

"That was before the election." She glared at him. "I lost."

"I'm sorry. I did still save your life. Your mom seems to think that was more important."

Shay snorted. "Mom is at the smelling-the-roses part of her life. I'm not." She paused. "Look, I thanked you for what you did, and I meant it, Jason. That was very brave. But . . . everything since then . . ." She stopped, and her look softened. ". . . for both of us has been a complete—"

"Disaster," Jason finished the thought. "I know. I was hoping we could do something about that."

Shay ran her hands through her hair and recrossed her arms, saying nothing.

"Please sit down," Jason said.

"No. Spit it out. Why are you here? Shouldn't you be working up your defense to the murder charges the new district attorney has brought against you?" She shook her head. "Representing yourself. I

131

mean, are you really that stupid?" She sucked in a breath. "Or maybe conceited is the word. Narcissistic."

"They all probably apply," Jason said. He snickered, but Shay didn't join him. He took a deep breath himself and cleared his throat. "I need advisory counsel . . . and I was hoping—"

"Are you out of your ever-loving mind?" Shay cut him off and walked toward the door.

"Shay, wait." Jason got up and jumped in front of her.

"Get out of my way or I'm going to scream."

"I need your help. No one has more experience with murder trials in this county than you. No other criminal defense lawyer has even half the trial experience. Please, Shay. It would be a way for you to get back in the game."

"Who says I want back in the game? I'm a prosecutor, Jason, and regardless of your record against me, I'm a damn good one."

"Do you honestly think I'd be here if I didn't already know that?"

"Get out of my way, Jason. I'm going to be late."

"Shay, please."

"Now, Jason. Or I really am going to scream."

He stepped aside, and she brushed past him. "You're really gonna let that prick get the best of you?" Jason asked behind her. "Wouldn't you like to get back at Wish?"

He followed her to the front door, where she had stopped with her hand on the knob.

Jason spoke in a firm voice from behind her. "I realize that I was gone from Guntersville for a long time, but I know the history and I've heard the rumors. You were Wish's top assistant for years. You waited for him to announce his retirement before you ran, and didn't Wish say he was going to support you? But then he changes his mind and runs against you. You won the first election. Then, the next term comes around, and the sore loser runs against you again. *You.* His right hand for all those years. Doesn't that make you a bit mad?"

"Go to hell, Jason."

He ground his teeth. "I'm already there, Shay. And I need some help getting out. I need *you*."

She peered down at the floor. "I can't," she said. "Not after . . . all that's happened."

"You never struck me as a coward."

She finally turned, her eyes intense. "I'm not scared, Jason. Not of Wish French. Of you. Or of getting shot at again."

"I'm innocent," Jason pled.

"Until proven guilty," Shay said. "I know the drill pretty well. But I've been paying attention to the evidence. You look guilty as hell."

"That's why I need you. Shay, you know me. You know I couldn't have done this."

"I don't know you, Jason. Just because we had two trials against each other and shared a near-death experience . . . you think that makes us friends? From what I hear, the state will have no problem proving its case."

"I was framed." He gave a sheepish smile. "Or I'm just incredibly unlucky."

"Like O. J., right?" Her voice dripped with sarcasm.

"I didn't kill him, Shay. You owe me, damnit. Please. Your mom says you haven't been sure what to do since the election, and this teaching gig is just a bridge to the next life. What I'm offering is a tremendous opportunity. Help me win. Defeat Wish French in his own backyard. Show all the people who voted against you that they got it wrong. You know that you're the better lawyer. Show them."

Shay's lip started to tremble, and she bit down on it. "I'm sorry, Jason. I . . . I just can't."

"Yes, you can," he said, taking a step back. "But you're wrong about one thing. You are scared. Scared that maybe you'll lose again. And this time to Wish."

She shook her head and smirked at him. "You're really something, you know it? Think you can just knock on my door, charm my momma, and get me to say yes because you're Jason Rich. And then when I bring up some reasonable questions and concerns, you act like a five-year-old. Do you think insulting me is the way to change my mind?"

Jason forced a grin. "Complimenting you wasn't working."

"Nothing's going to work, Jason. Like I said . . ." Her voice cracked. "I can't do it. I can't go in that courtroom again."

"Shay—"

"Shut up. I'm saying no, Jason. Now tell my momma that I've gone back to work." She turned around and grabbed the knob again.

Jason opened his mouth but stopped himself as the door slammed shut. He walked forward and watched from the window as she climbed into her car and peeled out of the driveway.

He leaned his head against the glass as the reality of the situation hit him. He'd be trying this case by himself. His advisory counsel would be a goon appointed by a judge who hated him.

"Damnit," he whispered.

21

Hatty Daniels drove through the streets of Guntersville, trying to keep her mind off all the horror she'd witnessed over the past few weeks. The remnants of the National Guard's occupancy of the town remained present, with guardsmen still flanking the courthouse and the sheriff's department, though their numbers had shrunk considerably since the days immediately after the bombing and shooting.

The federal presence was all but gone too. Agents had interviewed Wish French, Hatty, and pretty much everyone in the district attorney's and sheriff's offices along with dozens of bystanders present near the courthouse at the time of the incidents. But despite the best efforts of the FBI, there'd been no leads. No suspects had risen to the surface except the shadow of a man who'd been on the run from the law for months.

Matty Dean . . .

Hatty gritted her teeth as she drove over the Veterans Memorial Bridge and gazed to her left and right at Lake Guntersville. At 4:30 p.m., the sun was setting to the west over the trees that guarded Camp Cha-La-Kee. Hatty's phone began to ring, and she glanced at it. The screen read "Wish."

Hatty sighed, not wanting to answer but doing so anyway. "Hey."

"Where are you?"

"Agent Tidmore is flying out from Huntsville International at seven, heading back to DC. She wanted to have a last briefing."

"Why wasn't I notified?"

Because you're not in the sheriff's office, Hatty wanted to say, but instead she maintained diplomacy. "There wasn't time. I'm sure it will be the same old, same old we've heard since the beginning."

"What a complete cluster," Wish said.

Hatty stayed quiet but nodded as she drove.

"How can they have no leads?"

"How can we have no leads?" Hatty echoed the question. "You know how the Sand Mountain meth business works. How many years did we try to nail Tyson Cade with no success? And now that Dean's running it, things seem even more stealthy. No one's seen him in months. No one in Alder Springs or Albertville or anywhere else on Sand Mountain will talk. It's like they are more scared of him than they were Cade." Hatty almost said *Maybe because they think Dean killed Cade* but held her tongue. "We both know, and I think the feds do, too, that Dean was behind everything that happened on the day of the hearing."

"We just can't prove it," Wish said. "All right, call me when the meeting's over."

"Ten-four," Hatty said, and clicked End.

As she drove Highway 431 toward Huntsville, questions abounded. *If Dean is behind the bombing and shooting, what's his endgame? Why would he want Jason Rich dead? Why would he want Wish French dead? Or was Wish just the diversion to get Jason in the open, as Colonel Tonidandel said?*

Hatty tended to agree with Satch, so the question came down to Dean's motive to want Jason dead.

Which is easy, she thought. *Don't overthink it.* If Dean believed that Jason killed Tyson Cade, then Dean would want to kill Jason for revenge. He wouldn't want to wait for a jury to decide. That's not Sand Mountain justice. He'd want to finish it, once and for all.

Hatty was nodding along with those thoughts, but another one crept into her subconscious. *What if Dean killed Tyson Cade?* If so, then wouldn't Dean want to close the loop and kill Jason Rich too?

That way . . . *case closed.* Dean wouldn't want pesky Jason Rich, who had been a thorn in the drug trade's side since his return to Guntersville almost two years ago, to have a chance to launch a defense and shine the spotlight on Matty.

And Dean will be Jason's defense, Hatty thought, as she passed Keller's Tackle Shop and into Madison County. *So much speculation,* she thought. *And no physical evidence to back it up. Still . . .*

Hatty knew firsthand how resourceful Jason Rich could be. He would sling as much dung on the wall as he could and see if any of it stuck.

Where are the holes? she wondered. Something about Jason's arrest, despite all the evidence, had always felt wrong. She knew she was biased. Hatty liked Jason. Even admired him. She hated that her first big act in office was to prosecute him for murder. Hated it.

But it's the job . . .

As the last hints of light evaporated, Hatty passed through New Hope and then Hampton Cove. Ten minutes later, she pulled into a parking space in downtown Huntsville and walked to a tiny restaurant called Jack Brown's Beer and Burger Joint.

Agent Tidmore was seated at a high table with two stools, drinking what looked like a craft beer. She toasted Hatty as she sat down. "Hatty."

"Sheila," Hatty said, taking her seat. "You wanted to see me."

"Come on, have a beer."

"I don't drink beer."

"Well then, try the Elvis burger. It's delicious."

"Not all that hungry either. You said this was important."

Sheila Tidmore had short blonde hair and wore a white blouse and black pants. She'd been all-business during her three weeks on the job, but apparently she wanted to relax before she got on an airplane home. Hatty tried not to begrudge her. *I might do the same thing.*

"It is," Sheila said, taking a sip of beer.

A waiter came over, and Hatty ordered a Diet Coke. Then she looked at Sheila and raised her eyebrows. "Well?" Hatty asked.

"We received an anonymous tip early this morning. Came from a burner phone. We couldn't trace it. The caller disguised his voice, so he kinda sounded like Supreme Leader Snoke in the new Star Wars movies. Seen them?"

Hatty shook her head. "What did the caller say?"

"That he'd seen Matty Dean outside of the Love's Travel Stop in Columbia, Tennessee."

Hatty's heart rate sped up.

"Identified a rig that Dean had apparently been sleeping in. Gave us the plates."

"Have you run them?"

Sheila grinned. "We've done more than that. We've found the guy."

Hatty's heart was pounding now. "And?"

"The trucker's name is Ben Raggendorf. He's from Ardmore, Alabama. Drives for McLemore Foods. Has a wife and two kids."

"Has anyone spoken to him?"

"Not yet. We are going to follow him for a while to see if we can get a read on Dean. If he knows Dean, and Dean's been sleeping in his rig . . ."

Hatty squinted at her. "You think they might be having an affair?"

Sheila took a sip of beer. "We don't know anything yet, but . . . that seems like a possibility." The agent's eyes were dancing with excitement. She licked her lips. "Ever hear any rumors of Dean being a homosexual?"

Hatty shook her head. She felt dizzy. "None. What about Raggendorf?"

"We're doing some digging. Nothing so far."

"What if he doesn't lead you to Dean?"

"He may not, but we are going to give it a few weeks. Then we'll interview him."

"So the FBI is staying on the case?"

"Absolutely," Sheila said. "We believe the only explanation for the bombing is the Sand Mountain drug trade, but we have been unable to gain leverage on any suspect. But since there's already a warrant out from your office for Dean's arrest, we may be able to bargain with him."

"He'll never talk. Even if you get him, he'll stay silent."

"What if we catch him in an illicit homosexual love affair?"

Hatty shrugged. "Not sure that's going to matter to any of the drug dealers he works with. If Dean is in charge, and we think that he is, then the shooting and the bombing in November shows that he has the full support of the Sand Mountain drug trade behind him."

Sheila sighed and stared at her beer. "Look, it's a lead. It's something. I wanted you to know about it before I went back to Washington. We aren't abandoning this investigation, Hatty." She leaned closer. "We have your back."

Hatty stood from the table. "Thank you, Sheila. Please have your agents contact me if they're able to take Matty Dean into custody."

"Of course." The two women shook hands, and Sheila held on to Hatty's, giving it a squeeze. "Sure you don't want to join me?"

Hatty frowned. "I can't." Then she turned and headed for the door.

———

As if on autopilot, Hatty drove from downtown Huntsville to Bridge Street off Research Park Boulevard. She parked near her favorite bar. When was the last time she'd been here? Six months?

Hatty gripped the wheel, staring at the front door as two women entered holding hands. She didn't want to have anything in common with Matty Dean. She didn't want to feel any empathy for the man who'd tried to kill her last year.

But she knew what it was like to live a lie. Or, at least to present an on-the-surface image that was a far cry from reality.

She thought of the trucker Ben Raggendorf, who was married to a woman and had children. What could this stakeout do to him if it produced dividends? If it turned up Matty Dean in Raggendorf's rig?

Hatty watched another couple—two men this time—enter the bar. She grabbed the door handle. She could go in for a drink and then leave.

No. She put her vehicle in reverse and then pulled out of the lot. A few minutes later, she was on Highway 431 East to Guntersville.

Hatty forced herself to concentrate on her breathing. She was cracking under the pressure. If she was seen at a Huntsville gay bar, it would be a death warrant to her political career in Marshall County.

Sighing, she took out her cell phone. She had to stay focused and busy.

She checked her recent calls and dialed the number for Wish French.

"Well?" the prosecutor answered on the first ring.

"The feds have a lead on Matty Dean."

22

Highway 79 was the primary throughfare between Guntersville and Scottsboro.

Hence the nickname "Scottsboro Highway." On the bridge that separated the main channel of Lake Guntersville and the tiny cove of Mill Creek, there was a rocky area where fisherman enjoyed practicing their craft in the dark.

On this early December night, with temperatures hovering in the midforties, few had braved the cold. But at least a handful had.

Two heavily clothed figures held rods and reels and sat on a rock about midway down the bridge.

"Hard to believe we aren't the only ones out here," Lu said, casting her instrument and slowly beginning to bring it in. She hadn't even bothered to bait her hook.

Matty was reeling his line back in. "Not for me. Been watching this house for a while now. There's always somebody fishing this spot. That's why it's such a good cover."

"You and Tyson used to do this?"

Matty grunted but said nothing. He peered across the cove to Jason Rich's house. He could see a figure on the dock holding a long gun of some kind. He took the binoculars out of his pocket for a quick look. "Bald head, so that's Chuck."

"The preacher," Lu said.

"I don't think that's an official title or anything, but he is the religious nut of the group." Matty chewed on the toothpick that had been dangling out the side of his mouth. "Any updates on their whereabouts?"

"Satch and Jason went to Grant today. We couldn't follow them up the mountain without being seen."

Matty cast his line again. "Huh. Any thoughts as to what they were up to?"

"No, but they were gone awhile. Came down about three hours after they went up."

"Well, that's interesting."

"Want me to dig further?"

"Not yet. Don't want to waste time on that. How about the other two brothers?"

"Chuck mostly guards the water side of the house. He attends the Guntersville Baptist Church every Sunday. We haven't seen him go anywhere other than worship service and the range." She paused and, even though it was dark, Matty could tell the next words were said with a smile. "But the youngest one has a girlfriend."

Matty stopped gnawing at his toothpick. "Really now?"

"She lives off of Highway 69. Small house a mile or so from Brindlee Mountain High School. We tailed him to her home last night. They went to Crawmama's, split a couple of pounds of crawfish, and had a few beers. Came back to her house, and Mickey didn't leave until this morning." She paused. "Butch said he had a spring in his step on the way to the truck."

Matty took the toothpick out of his mouth and flung it in the water. Then he stood and eyed Jason Rich's house again. "That's a damn fine report, Lu."

"You want us to take out the girl too?" Lu asked.

"Only if we have to."

"When?" She stood and leaned into him, brushing her hand across his groin.

Matty Dean continued to gaze at the house. The downstairs lights were on and, if his ears weren't deceiving him from this far away, he heard music.

"Matty?" Lu leaned forward and kissed his ear.

"Soon," he finally said.

———

There were three other fishermen on the rocks below Highway 69. On the Scottsboro end of the bridge, a man smoked a cigarette and watched Matty Dean and Lu Stephens climb into an SUV that pulled to a stop next to them. This man wore faded jeans and a lined blue jean jacket. When he was sheriff, Richard Griffith's hair was cut short, but now his locks were longer and unkempt, covered by a mesh John Deere cap. He reeled in his line and watched them leave.

He didn't follow. By now, he knew where they were going. He'd followed Matty Dean for a good two weeks. Like his predecessor, Tyson Cade, Matty had his habits.

Being predictable had eventually caught up to Cade.

It'll get this sonofabitch too . . .

Griff moved his eyes to Jason Rich's house on the water. He squinted at the man on the dock, who was holding some type of semiautomatic rifle.

Griff couldn't believe he'd let any of these bastards get the best of him. He'd once been the most powerful man in Marshall County, and now he was an outcast. Cain after murdering Abel.

This was his land of Nod.

Griff took another drag from the cigarette, smiling inwardly at the thought of the anonymous call he'd made earlier today. Griff might be a pariah now, but he still had contacts within law enforcement that owed him. He'd made a few calls after taking down the plates on the rig that he'd seen Matty Dean entering and exiting at the truck stop.

Sure enough, he'd struck gold. The drug dealer was carrying on with a family man from Ardmore, Alabama, named Ben Raggendorf. So . . . the next time Matty Dean had the itch to have his cornhole penetrated, the FBI would be waiting.

Cade was gone. Dean would be soon. Griff glared across the cove at the lawyer's home, knowing that revenge was a dish best served cold. He had time. Plenty of it. *The rest of my miserable life.*

The people that brought him down would pay.

Every damn one of them . . .

23

Jason's eardrums pounded with the beat of James Brown's "Get Up Offa That Thing." He danced around the garage, sweat pouring off him. He'd been working out for the past three hours with the Godfather of Soul blaring the whole time. There were few playlists that made it virtually impossible to feel bad, but this was one of them. Between sets, he pretended he was Apollo Creed doing the "Living in America" dance before the Ivan Drago fight in *Rocky IV*. The irony of this ridiculous line of thinking didn't escape him: Creed was killed in the ring immediately after this scene in the movie.

Was death next on the horizon for Jason Rich?

He'd escaped it almost two weeks ago, but, as Satch said, the war had only begun. Would he survive it?

He didn't know, but he was not going to go down as a drunk. Matty Dean might kill him, but alcohol would not.

Jason got on his treadmill and began to run. When he and Satch had gotten home from Shay's house, he'd wanted so badly to have a beer. A shot. A pull from a bottle of whiskey. Hell, a swig from a can of Busch Light would have tasted like the golden nectar of the gods.

He hadn't expected Shay to say yes, but nevertheless the whole interaction had left him weak and strung out. From the beauty of being prayed for by Beth Lankford to the harsh rejection by Shay. Even the awkwardness of seeing Satch Tonidandel blessing the food. It was all too much. The best and worst thing about being in an alcoholic haze was that you couldn't feel anything.

He'd felt everything at Shay and Beth's, and it was overwhelming. There was no liquor or beer in his house, and he wasn't going to make a run. He wouldn't let it break him again no matter how bad he wanted it.

Jason picked up his pace, feeling his heart beg for oxygen. When he'd gotten home, he'd done a polar plunge into the lake. The shock of the cold water had been good for him, but his brain was still scrambled. He'd forced himself to eat a turkey sandwich and drink milk and then went down in the basement. He watched WrestleMania III in its entirety with Mickey. Everyone remembered that one for Hulk Hogan slamming Andre the Giant, but Jason preferred the match between the "Macho Man" Randy Savage and Ricky "the Dragon" Steamboat for the Intercontinental title. For his money, that was the best high-stakes wrestling match of all time. Steamboat won in the end, but the match solidified Savage's greatness as a technical performer.

He and Mickey had spent most of the match mimicking the Macho Man's catchphrase, "*Ohhhh yeahhh!*" When it was over, Jason was amped up and feeling a tad better. Old-school pro wrestling had been a good defuser for him, but he needed more.

So he'd blared the James Brown playlist and hit the weights, going through all his full-body moves. Bench. Deadlift. Pull-ups. Shoulder press. Farmer's carry. Then he'd moved on to a few isolation moves. Dumbbell and hammer curls. Sideways and bent-over flies for his shoulders. When he was sufficiently pumped, he'd hopped on the treadmill. He'd done an hour of running, jogging, and walking and, after a short break, was at it again. The urge for a drink was almost gone.

I can win this case by myself. I don't need Shay. I don't need anyone. I'm Jason motherfucking Rich. I'll let Barber appoint a local, and I'll tell whoever it is to sit at the table and keep their mouth shut.

"Dude, are you still at it?" Mickey came into the garage wearing a tank top and pulling on the back of his mullet. The younger Tonidandel had worn a perma-smile all afternoon and night, and Jason figured he knew why.

"Just a few more minutes."

"This isn't enough," Mickey said, ambling over to the dumbbell rack and picking up the twenty-fives. "Temporary relief ain't what you need." He curled the dumbbells up toward his shoulders, and his biceps bulged.

Jason slowed his pace to a walk. "So, now that you are getting laid on a regular basis, you're a great philosopher, huh?"

Mickey continued to curl the weight. "Ohhhh yeaaaaaahhh!" he screamed, keeping a crooked grin on his face. "In all honesty, J. Rich, it helps. The release of the poison, am I right?" He cackled.

"If you say so."

"You know, I haven't had a girl since Afghanistan. Didn't really want one. I guess I was afraid, you know." He continued to work the weights like they might be two twelve-ounce longnecks instead of twenty-five-pound dumbbells. Jason had lost count of the reps. He was also a bit dumbfounded. He'd never had a conversation like this with any of the Tonidandels except Satch, and even the colonel was tight lipped. He remembered that Satch had applauded Harry Davenport for trying to make a life after the war. He and his brothers were still fighting . . .

But maybe Mickey isn't anymore, Jason thought. If that was truly the case, he was happy for his friend.

"What were you afraid of?" Jason asked, finally stopping and stepping off the treadmill. He felt a bit dizzy and reached for a bottle of water.

"Everything," Mickey said. "Well, I guess that's not true. I think the main thing I was scared of was feeling . . . anything . . . again. You know what I mean?"

Jason remembered his walk with Beth Lankford. The emotion in her voice as she prayed for him. The love that he'd felt. And then the anxiety, excitement, and, ultimately, the disappointment of his talk with

Shay. He looked away from Mickey to the lake. "I know exactly what you mean."

A few seconds later, he felt a strong hand on his shoulder. "You gotta have people in your life, Jason. For a long time, I thought I could live with just Satch and Chuck. I thought that's all I needed. That I was no good for anyone else. That all I'd do is hurt them. You know?"

Jason felt a lump in his throat but managed a nod.

"But being with Tiffany has changed that for me. I feel . . . different." He pulled on his mullet again. "I want to do more things. Not just be here and the gun range."

"Mickey, any time you want to leave, you have my permission, man. You and your brothers have done enough for me."

"I'll never leave you, J. Rich. Satch won't allow it, and I won't ever go nowhere unless the colonel gives his approval." He paused and took a step toward the lake. He waved at Chuck, who stood guard by the boathouse, and the middle Tonidandel gave a salute back. "But, when this is over . . . I think I'll be ready to move on from here." He turned back to Jason. "Maybe you should do the same."

Jason averted his eyes, thinking of his parents and his sister. Of being raised in this home and of finally coming back to Mill Creek almost two years ago. He took a deep breath and exhaled into the cold air. "I'm not sure I could do that."

"I wasn't sure I could ever enjoy a woman's company again," Mickey said, throwing up his hands. "But one day, God or a breeze or both led my bass boat in her direction."

"So romantic," Jason teased.

"Ain't it?" Mickey fired back. "Whatever . . . I guess all I was trying to say is that you need people in your life. People you care about."

Jason shook his head. "Everyone who gets close to me gets hurt."

Mickey pointed at Chuck and then beat on his chest with a fist. "Not everyone." He winked and walked past Jason. "You know I'm right."

Jason watched him go and then turned back to the water, looking past the fishermen on the bridge to the half moon above. Could he ever leave this place?

He sighed, thinking of Jana and Harry and Chase and Nola. Finally, he closed his eyes and leaned his sweat-streaked head against one of the brick columns.

Will I ever be able to move on?

24

Shay Lankford rose early and did her habitual morning run to the edge of the mountain. The cold, almost freezing air felt good on her face, and she found that her pace was faster than normal today.

She'd done a meditation that morning from one of the many self-help apps on her phone, and her mind was clear. She went cliffside, as she'd done so many times with her momma. To think. To cry. To pray. Her momma had taken Jason Rich and Colonel Tonidandel here yesterday, and Beth Lankford had prayed for Jason.

Momma had told her all about it over dinner last night. She'd been so chatty that Shay had finally left the table, saying she was tired and not feeling well.

Momma had asked her to rethink Jason's proposition, but what was there to think about? She was a prosecutor. That's all she'd ever known. *And I'd still be the district attorney if Jason Rich had never come to Guntersville . . .*

. . . and I might also be dead.

She'd slept fine and got up, like always, at 5:00 a.m. Now, as the sun rose over the mountain, and sweat beaded on her forehead despite the cold, Shay figured it was time to go back into town. She hadn't been into Guntersville since the election. Instead, she'd hidden in Grant with her momma.

Hiding. The thought gave Shay an awful taste in her mouth.

"You never struck me as a coward." She heard Jason Rich in her mind, and she ground her teeth together as she arrived back in the house. She entered the kitchen and smelled bacon and coffee.

"Breakfast, hon?"

"Not today, Momma."

Beth frowned at Shay, waiting.

There was a long silence between them. Then Shay bit her lip and stared down at the floor. "I'm going into town." After a few seconds, she glanced up at her mom, who was staring at her with her hands on her hips.

"'Bout damn time."

———

Shay decided to have coffee at JaMoka's a block from the courthouse. When she walked in the door, she saw Barry Martino sitting by the window. His eyes widened when he saw her. "Hello, Shay." He stood, and they shook hands. "It's great to see you." He sounded genuine, though Shay had never cared much for Barry, who just happened to be the dean of the local criminal defense bar. She couldn't count how many cases they'd had against each other over the years.

"You, too, Barry. Still denying and defending?" She forced a smile.

"All day long," Barry said, winking at her. "What have you been up to since the . . ." He trailed off, clearly not wanting to say *election*.

"Just taking a break. Doing some teaching up at DAR."

"Well, we miss you around here. I hated going up against you, but at least I knew I was getting all the documents I requested. With Wish, it's always a box of chocolates." He leaned close to her. "I voted for you. I hate having to deal with that cocky SOB again."

Shay wasn't sure that was a compliment, but she nodded. "Thank you. Gonna get some coffee now."

"Take care."

Shay ordered an espresso and a bagel and sat at a circular table by the front. Coming to the coffee shop a block from the courthouse before work had become a habit of hers during her tenure as a prosecutor for two reasons. One, it was a great place to interact with criminal defense attorneys like Barry, who sometimes were more forthcoming in an informal setting. She'd ironed out many a plea deal over coffee.

Two, it was important to see and be seen by the local townsfolk. The barbers. The retail salesman. The other restaurateurs. And the patrons of those establishments.

She'd learned that lesson from her mentor, who she'd accompanied here many times during their years of working together. And if she knew Aloysius French, she figured he'd be swinging through the front door any minute.

Why? she thought, as she smiled at the clerk at the cash register and took a sip of her drink. *Why in the hell did I come here? Am I a glutton for punishment?*

The door jingled, and in came county commissioner Rex Patterson, and behind him a tall man with thick silver hair.

Shay bristled at the sight of Wish and, without conscious thought, ran her hands down her skirt. She'd dressed in her finest burgundy suit. The one she liked to wear when it was time to make closing arguments. She felt good. Strong. But also a bit weird.

It had been over a month since she'd had coffee at JaMoka's, but it felt like a lifetime ago.

Because it was . . .

Patterson walked to the cash register, looking at the day's special, and didn't see Shay.

Wish, however, made eye contact almost immediately. Though he hesitated for a moment, he managed to recover and shake hands with Barry Martino, who acted as if the king of England had just entered.

Good old kiss-ass Barry, Shay thought. *Always tells people what they want to hear.*

She wondered if the criminal defense guru had even voted for her as he'd said he had. The truth was a malleable subject for Barry Martino. Twistable. Manufacturable. Clear as mud.

Shay felt dirty watching the two men back slap each other. *How can I cross over to the dark side?* she thought, nauseous as she watched Barry. But then, turning her attention to Wish, she wondered who was bullshitting who in their conversation.

It was like watching two rival boxers try to be nice to each other. *Maybe both sides are dark . . .*

When Wish had finally had his ass thoroughly vacuumed with Barry's lips, figuratively speaking, he began to stride toward Shay, then stopped and sat down without invitation. "So . . . how are you?" He asked the question in a low tone as if he were a close friend attending a reception after a funeral and trying to have a real moment with the aggrieved spouse.

"Just peachy," Shay said. "How about yourself? Stab any old friends in the back today?"

He frowned and crossed his arms. "Shay, come on. That's not what happened between us, and you know it."

"That is what happened . . . and everyone knows it. Go ask your pal Barry over there. You know what he just told me?" She gestured for him to come close, and she spoke in the same tone that he had. "That he voted for me, because he couldn't stand you."

Wish gave a toothless grin. "If he did vote for you . . ." He glanced at Barry and back at Shay. ". . . it's because he thought he had a better chance of beating you than me. Like Jason Rich did. Twice."

Shay felt her face grow as hot as the burner on a stove. She crossed her legs and then her arms. She knew it was a defensive gesture, but she had to control herself. It would not be good to lose her cool in this situation.

"You want something, Wish?" Patterson asked from behind them, and the district attorney glanced that way.

"Regular coffee, Rex. Thanks." Then he leaned across the table and spoke while looking Shay directly in the eye. "I didn't betray you, Shay. On the contrary, I did you a favor. You weren't up to the task of succeeding me." He chuckled. "It was like putting a dog out of its misery."

"You won by two percent. Fifty-one to forty-nine." She kept her voice measured. "That's not much of a victory."

"Counts the same as a landslide." He stood and winked at her. "And let's be glad that I did win. The last thing this county needs is Jason Rich defeating the district attorney . . . *again*. Bye, Shay."

———

Shay busied herself by surfing the net and her social media apps while Wish and Patterson drank their coffee at a table right next to her. She picked at her bagel, sipped her espresso, and tried to ignore them. Several times, she caught the commissioner looking at her. When the two men finally got up, the politician leaned toward her. "Nice to see you, Shay. What are you doing these days?"

"Oh, nothing much." She forced a grin. "Still licking my wounds, I guess."

"Well, we hope to see more of you," Wish said, walking toward the door.

"Oh, you will," she said. "I can promise you that." The commissioner turned to Wish and blinked before looking back at her. "Well, have a nice day."

"You too."

She watched the two men leave, feeling irritated and embarrassed. After waiting a safe amount of time, she threw the rest of the bagel in the trash and headed for the door, still holding her coffee but not sure she could drink any more of it. *Why did I come here? What did I expect?*

The county commissioner had looked at her like a stranger. An outsider, which of course she was now. And Wish treated her the same as he always had. Like an underling. Never a peer. Not even when she was handling all the tough cases for the office right before their first election six years ago.

And not now.

As she reached the door, she noticed that Barry Martino was still at his window seat. He was watching her with a curious look.

"Gonna work from here today, Barry?" It was a somewhat serious question. With laptops and electronic filing, remote work was not only possible but sometimes preferable. During big cases, she liked to come here or to the library to get a little space away from the telephones.

"Yeah, a little. Slow day. All of my cases this week pled out on Monday." He paused, then sighed. "Actually expecting a rather big appointment soon."

She raised her brows. "You don't sound all that excited about it."

"That's because I'm not. Your buddy the billboard lawyer needs advisory counsel. A little birdie told me that Barber is going to appoint me." He chuckled. "Will probably be the easiest gig ever. He's going to represent himself, so I'll just be eye candy."

Shay couldn't help but giggle. Barry wasn't an unattractive man—he had brown curly hair, a long forehead, and glasses and always wore suspenders over a button-down shirt with his suit pants—but he wasn't exactly Brad Pitt.

"I was speaking figuratively, although I clean up OK." Now Barry laughed. "I guess I'm a bit wary of getting involved after the shooting last month." He paused again and fidgeted in his seat. "Whoever tried and missed may try again."

Shay nodded. She had thought the same thing when Jason asked her to get involved yesterday. It wasn't just a request to take a case. Criminal work had a dangerous side to it, but representing Jason Rich, or prosecuting him for that matter, had become like swimming in shark-infested waters.

"Well, who knows, maybe Jason has someone else lined up," she said, winking at him. "See you around, Barry."

————

Around 10:30 a.m., after driving to the Sunset Drive Trail and drinking the rest of her coffee with a view of the lake, Shay headed back into town and parked by the courthouse. At this time of day, she knew that most of the hearings would be over. If there was no trial, then the circuit courtroom would be open.

She walked briskly up the steps, thinking of what she would say if anyone saw her. The best she could come up with was getting a passport, which was done on the basement floor. It wouldn't explain what she was doing in the courtroom, but she guessed she could fall back on a half truth: while she was here, she wanted to check out her old stomping grounds.

She trotted up the steps and went through the maze of hallways that led to the courtroom. She opened the double doors, and sure enough, the space was empty. Just spectator benches, the long divider, and then two counsel tables, the jury box to the left, and at the very front, the judge's pulpit. If there was any place in the world that she felt comfortable, this was it. For twelve years, six as an assistant and six more as the head prosecutor, she had tried cases in this courtroom. This was her sanctuary. This . . .

. . . *is home.*

She walked down the aisle that separated the spectator benches and through the gate to the area where the magic happened. She'd tried over a hundred cases in here. Felonies and misdemeanors. Traffic court and domestic violence. And, of course, the big ones. Three rape trials, all victories for the state. And five murder trials. Three wins, two losses.

Unfortunately, the two losses were her last memories of this place.

The last thing this county needs is Jason Rich defeating the district attorney . . . again.

Wish French's voice rang in her head, and she sat down at the prosecution table. She sighed and gazed at the jury box. The losses weren't her fault. The last one wasn't even technically a defeat, since she dismissed the charges before the jury came back with a verdict.

She rose and pushed her chair in. Then she walked a few paces over to the defense table. In twelve years, she had never defended a case. She'd only prosecuted them.

It's all I know, she thought.

But, as she looked to the right of the judge's platform and saw the framed photographs of judges long since gone and then turned in a circle, breathing in the scent of the room and feeling the energy that even an empty courtroom gave off—that sense of an impending battle or one that had just taken place—she had to admit one more thing.

I miss it.

25

"You sure about this?"

Satch's voice was as gravelly as ever as the Raptor turned off Hustleville Road into the Alder Springs Grocery.

"Got to start somewhere," Jason said. "Might as well be here."

"It doesn't come without risk. This was Cade's territory. Now it's Dean's." They parked by the pump, and Satch got out of the truck and stuck a credit card in the terminal. Then he unscrewed the gas lid and picked up the handle for unleaded. Once the gas began pumping, he hooked the latch so it would run until full. Jason walked around the front of the truck. "I'd prefer you wait in the cab," Satch said.

"Nope," Jason said, walking toward the entrance. "Chuck and Mickey are behind us, right?"

They looked over their shoulders and saw the other two brothers pulling into the lot. Mickey got out and stood by the hood, while Chuck jogged around the back of the station.

Good grief, Jason thought, wondering how he could be in a universe where these types of maneuvers were necessary and then seeing an image of Greta Martin's ruined face.

"Let's get on with it," Jason said, thinking he was beginning to sound like one of them. Satch grunted, as if maybe he agreed with the thought.

The door jingled as they walked inside. Jason turned to the desk clerk, and his spirits immediately sank. The man behind the counter eyed him with a weary gaze.

"How you doing?" Jason asked.

"I'd be better if you'd get on with your business and get out of here."

"It's a free country, and we're buying gas."

"You can do that at the pump," the clerk snapped.

"I'm a tad thirsty too," Jason said.

The man smirked. "Heard that about you. Don't sell none of that here."

Jason blinked at him.

"We came in for a Coke, dipshit," Satch said, walking past Jason to the clerk. "We also wanted to speak with Marcia Darnell. Goes by Dooby."

"Well, she ain't here." The clerk's voice rose a bit, and he brought his hand under the counter.

Satch reached across and grabbed the clerk's hand before it could go any lower.

"I'm going to call the police," the clerk said, his tone now a wail.

"And tell them what? That you almost went heel on us when we asked for a Coke?"

"You're assaulting me."

"No, sir," Satch said. "I'm defending myself." He let go of the man's hand and unbuttoned his jacket, showing the handgun tucked in his waistline. "Now we're going to get a Coke and a snack. We're gonna fill two tanks of gas up." He paused. "And you're gonna tell us how best to reach Dooby Darnell."

"We'll get the information eventually," Jason added. "Her contact information is discoverable, and we'll issue a subpoena."

"Dooby's been through a lot."

"We aren't planning to hurt her, just talk with her," Jason said. He stepped forward and was now standing beside Satch. "I didn't kill him, sir. I'm innocent."

He smirked again. "I got no love for Tyson Cade. But some folks around here do. I'd watch my step if I were you."

"That's why we're here, numb nuts," Satch said. "Now give us her digits before I lose my patience. And also an address."

The clerk took out a sticky notepad and scribbled on it, snatched off the paper, and flung it at them.

Satch caught it in the air. "Thanks," he said. "Is there anything else you can tell us about the murder of Cade?"

"Only that your boy there looks guilty as hell, and a lot of folks around here aren't too happy about it."

Satch grunted. "Get me a Dr Pepper, would you, Jason? And a damn PayDay too."

"Yes, sir." Jason walked to the back of the place, scanning as much of it as he could. There were two bathrooms and a storage closet in the back and then coolers of drinks lining the walls. In the middle were three aisles of conveniences. No alcohol. But there were cigarettes behind the counter.

He grabbed a Diet Coke for himself and Satch's items and walked back to the counter. He flung two hundred-dollar bills on the counter. "Keep the change. If you have any more information about Cade, his murder, or anything you think I might like to know, there's more where that came from."

"I don't want your money, sir."

"Take it," Satch said. "That's an order."

"I'd like you gentlemen to leave. My next call is to the sheriff's office."

"Be sure and tell the sheriff that I don't plan to press charges on you attempting to shoot me," Satch said. "At least not yet. But if you so much as move from this counter on our way back to the truck, I will press charges. And if you draw on me, my two brothers will send you to where Cade is." He paused. "Got me?"

"You're crazy."

Satch grunted and then walked past Jason to the door.

"Remember what I said." Jason patted his back pocket. "I'm innocent, and I'd really like to catch the man who killed Cade."

"Fuck you," the clerk said, spitting the words.

"No thanks."

———

The clerk's name was Frank Crutcher. Once Satch and Jason had walked a few feet outside, he snatched his cell phone and clicked on the number. "You told me to call if I saw him. Well, he and that big-ass Tonidandel were in here a few seconds ago. They threatened me until I gave them Dooby's number. I think I'm going to call the police."

"No," Lu said. "You did right by calling, Crutch. We have to be patient. We knew they'd eventually come."

"I don't want them back out here."

"Patience," she said. "I doubt you'll see them again."

———

As Satch took the gas nozzle out of the Raptor, Jason patted his shoulder. "Colonel, what was that in there?"

"He had a gun under the counter. I was protecting you."

"You pretty much destroyed any chance of us coming back here. I suspect the first call he's going to make in there is to Matty Dean."

"So you're thinking what I'm thinking." There was a glint in Satch's eye.

"I can't even begin to understand you, Colonel."

"If Matty Dean was behind Cade's murder, it stands to reason he has an in with someone at the Alder Springs Grocery. What was the Darnell woman doing watching the murder anyway? She wasn't behind her counter. You can't see the area where Cade was killed from back there."

Jason turned and inspected the yellow crime scene tape that still draped the area behind the pump. He looked from it to the front door. Satch was right.

"So you think Darnell might have been in on it?"

"If Dean is the reason Cade is dead, then I think that's a strong bet."

Jason scratched his neck and thought it through. He gazed at Mickey, who continued to watch the store and also Hustleville Road. He couldn't see Chuck, but knew the middle brother was still around back. "So we need to find Darnell."

Satch took the sticky note the clerk had given him and handed it to Jason. "No time like the present."

26

They drove to the house first, which was only a mile from the station. It was a one-story plywood shack with rotting wood. Jason guessed there were, at best, two bedrooms. The lights were off, and there was no car in the driveway.

"Doesn't look promising," he said, and Satch grunted as he pulled to a stop on the curb.

"Wait here," Satch said, then hopped out of the truck and strode toward the door. Chuck and Mickey had driven past them and were scoping the neighborhood. If they had seen anything, they would have called.

Jason watched as Satch knocked on the door. After a few seconds, the colonel knocked again. Then he walked around to the back of the house. Finally, he trudged back to the truck. "Nothing."

Jason glanced at his phone and then the sticky note. "All right, let's call, but—"

"She ain't gonna answer."

Jason tried the number. After seven rings, he ended the call. "Damnit."

"I'm betting our buddy at the Alder Springs Grocery knew a little more than he told us."

"And I'm surprised he wasn't more forthcoming," Jason said, rolling his eyes. "With you being so nice and all."

"I would have gotten nothing playing nice. Folks on Sand Mountain are tough, smart, and mean. They only respond to one thing."

"And what's that?"

"Fear." The colonel turned the Raptor around and headed back toward Hustleville Road. "That's how Cade was able to obtain information, and you can bet for damn sure it's how Matty Dean will keep getting it." He turned left. "What do the young folks say these days? Don't hate the player. Hate the game."

Jason felt a chill inside the cab of the truck despite the heat being on.

He had a feeling Satch had been playing that game his whole life.

———

They made one stop on the way home. Satch pulled into Guntersville High School with Mickey and Chuck right on his heels. "Just drop me off at the front," Jason said.

"Can't do that, Jason. Where you go, I go."

"I have to do this by myself, Colonel."

Satch parked the truck and cut the ignition. "I'm going to walk you in and wait outside the door."

"OK."

"All right then."

They got out and started to walk to the entrance. Mickey and Chuck had gotten out of their truck and were both leaning their backs against the front bumper. Mickey took a step forward.

"I'm taking your advice," Jason said, peering at the youngest brother, who slapped him on the shoulder. Then Jason glanced at Chuck, who had leaned toward his ear.

"Believe," the middle brother whispered, putting his big palm on Jason's heart. *"Believe."*

"All . . . right," Jason said, raising his eyebrows. He never quite knew how to take Chuck's intense admonitions.

Jason moved his eyes from Chuck to Mickey and finally to Satch. Then he walked inside the school, which had let out for the day and was mostly empty except for one room. He strode with purpose down the hallway, grabbed the knob, and then looked back at the colonel.

"I'll be right here," Satch said.

Jason nodded. Then he opened the door and saw a lot of familiar faces. How long had it been since he'd been here? When had he quit? He took a seat and felt their eyes on him. "Hey, everyone," he finally said. "My name is Jason . . . and I'm an alcoholic."

27

Ben Raggendorf pulled his rig into a spot along the line of tractors to the side of the truck stop. He called home and spoke to both his son and daughter for a few minutes each and then his wife. He went inside the diner and ate the meat-and-three special and had a piece of pecan pie. Then, after he was sufficiently full, he walked back to his rig and lit a cigarette. He hadn't seen his "friend" yet, but that didn't mean the man wasn't here. He climbed up into the sleeper berth and took out his toys. There were times when he felt guilty about what they were doing, but he had his rationalizations ready.

He hadn't left his wife. He was a good provider. He worked like a dog. And he loved his family very much.

Nothing about what he did here changed any of that. It's just . . . like his friend called it . . . he had an itch, and if he didn't scratch it every couple of weeks, he couldn't seem to function. Kind of like smoking, really. When the urge came, it was almost impossible to control it.

He took another long drag on the cigarette and blew a puff of smoke in the air. He glanced at his watch and then the diner. *Where is he?*

———

Matty Dean pulled into the truck stop at just after nine. He was feeling pretty good and in the mood to celebrate. They'd sold more meth in the last week than they had in the prior month. It was like everyone was getting their Christmas stash. Cocaine purchases were also up. His team was killing it, and everyone seemed to be bullish on their prospects for the new year.

Tyson was gone, but Matty was settling in. He wished he could enjoy the fruits of his labor a bit more. But the warrant for his arrest was still out there, and after the bombings and shooting last month, the heat on him had intensified. He knew the feds were focused on finding him.

He also knew that habits could kill.

As he pulled into a parking place in front of the diner, he peered into the huge glass window and felt a tingle of fear. There appeared to be around fifteen people inside, most of them men. Did they all look like truckers?

Things were going his way. It was only a matter of time before one of the Tonidandel brothers went down. By the time Jason Rich was tried for murder, his security detail would be gone.

No mistakes, Matty thought, knowing that every time he came here, he was rolling the dice. Habits could kill . . .

He continued to focus on the people in the diner. Most were eating. Some were drinking coffee. All wore typical trucker garb. Jeans. Flannel. Caps.

But there were two in a booth that were clean shaven. One wore green-and-black-plaid flannel and the other red and black. They looked right off a Target rack. Matty gripped the wheel. Was he being ridiculous?

He closed his eyes and thought of what he was about to do. Of what he'd been doing at this very truck stop with the same man for almost seven years.

He again studied the two men. No beards. Both with short hair. New clothes.

Feds.

Matty backed out of his parking spot and pulled into one of the pumps. He didn't need gas, but he didn't want to make any sudden movements. He put his vehicle in park, took his pistol out of the glove compartment, and stuck it in his pocket. Then he got out of his car and pumped the gas, still watching the inside of the diner. He glanced to the line of rigs and saw his friend. Smoking a cigarette. Eyeing him.

Matty took a deep breath and exhaled. Could he be overreacting?

No. Matty Dean had good instincts, and he always trusted them. The feds were here.

And they were here for him.

Inside the diner, Griff ground his teeth together. He'd watched Matty park, and he wanted to scream at the dumbass federal agents sitting across the diner from him. They had to have a picture of Dean, but old Matty was a bit of a chameleon. No distinctive look. He had a beard, but so did 90 percent of the men at this truck stop.

He's right fucking there, Griff screamed in his mind. He glanced at the agents. He knew it was them. Knew it had to be them because of their new flannel shirts, clean-shaven appearance, and military haircuts. Even with caps on, the high and tights and new flannel were a dead giveaway.

Matty will make them too.

Griff stood from his table and put a five-dollar bill down for his coffee. He walked out of the diner and saw Matty at one of the pumps. Then he observed the line of rigs, where Ben Raggendorf was smoking a cigarette.

He hadn't told the feds his name, just given them the plates. He didn't want to broadcast too much about himself.

Griff was about thirty feet from Matty. The former sheriff felt for the gun in his coat. It was too lit up here to shoot him. He turned and looked at the agents inside the diner.

Clueless. Blowing their one opportunity.

Matty Dean wasn't stupid. He'd never come here again. He'd never see Ben again.

Fuck, Griff thought. He thought of Tyson Cade lying on his back outside the Alder Springs Grocery on Hustleville Road. He'd wanted to bring Tyson in when he was sheriff. Then he'd become the drug dealer's bitch. Then . . .

He touched the handle of his gun and again peered from Matty to the federal agents that were squandering their one opportunity. He sighed and turned toward his car. *Patience,* he told himself, as he tried to control his breathing. Dean would go down just like Cade had. He just had to have . . . *patience.*

Once inside his vehicle, he let out the breath he'd been holding. The reality of his situation began to dawn on him.

I'm going to have to do it myself.

28

Jason decided to eat dinner with the Tonidandels. It was Wednesday night, which meant Satch liked to watch *The Fall Guy* right at 7:00 p.m., just as he'd done as a kid back in the mideighties. Mickey had picked up a pizza, and Chuck started the weekly bonfire out to the side of the house to "take out the trash."

Jason rather enjoyed these interludes. It was a break from reality, which was much needed right now. The day had been a . . . *step in the right direction? Maybe?*

Jason watched the theme song—still awesome after all these years— and then grabbed a couple of slices of pizza and a bottle of water and went outside. He sat in a lawn chair next to Mickey, who was chowing down on a piece of pepperoni.

"Date tonight?" Jason asked.

"Nah. She's visiting her folks in Gadsden."

Jason nodded. "Thank you for the talk last night. It helped me today."

Mickey nodded and took another bite of pizza. It looked like he wanted to say something, but he didn't. Jason heard footsteps approaching, and both men shot off their chairs, with Mickey drawing his pistol.

"Relax, it's me," Chuck said, his bald head now visible in the light of the fire.

"What's up?" Mickey asked, but Chuck was peering at Jason.

"You have a visitor."

———

Shay Lankford sat at the kitchen table. She hadn't turned any of the lights on.

When Jason entered the room, he put his hand on the switch but then let his arm fall to his side. He took a seat next to her and then gazed past her to the large bay window that framed the lake. The half moon cast a glow over the middle of the cove. When was the last time he'd sat here? Jason wondered. Had to be before Nola left. On the few occasions when they ate dinner together. Before that, he and Chase had eaten here quite a bit. For a couple of months after Jana's death, Jason had known a blissful peace with his childhood sweetheart. But then, like everything in his life, that relationship had blown up.

He turned and peered out the other window, seeing Chase's barren house. She hadn't put it up for sale, and he didn't think she ever would.

He also doubted she'd ever come back as long as he was here.

"Aren't you going to say something?" Shay asked.

"I was figuring I'd wait you out."

He finally looked at her. She wore a dark suit, likely red, though it was hard to tell in the near dark of the kitchen. A little dressy for substitute teaching.

"You have a beautiful home," Shay said.

"It was Mom and Dad's. The family homestead."

"Funny," she said. "I didn't think we had a single thing in common. But I'm living in the home I grew up in too."

"Your mother prayed for me yesterday. She's an amazing lady."

Shay placed her hands on the table and leaned back straight in her chair. "I think she's going to be praying for you quite a bit now."

Jason grinned. "Why's that?"

"Because, if the offer still stands, I'd like to be your advisory counsel."

Jason looked at her. His eyes had adjusted, and he could tell that her top was dark red. He'd seen her wear it in court. Her brown eyes radiated intensity and perhaps a bit of anxiety too. Jason extended his hand. "Deal."

She shook his hand.

Jason's grin widened. "Like the meeting of the Mania and the Madness."

Shay frowned.

"You know, when Hulk Hogan and the Macho Man finally teamed up after being enemies for years."

Shay's frown turned to a grimace.

"Never mind. Like Rocky and Apollo?"

Now, she finally smiled. "I get that one. You can let go of my hand now."

Jason glanced down and then unlocked his grasp. "I'm sorry."

"Jason, we have a lot of work to do."

"I know."

"And, based on everything I've heard and seen so far, the case looks bad."

Jason gazed past her to the window again. Like always, there were fishermen on the rocks below the bridge. Didn't matter how cold, hot, or wet. They were always there. He turned his face to Shay. "What changed your mind?"

"Honest?"

"I'd like to know."

"You were right. I miss it. I miss the courtroom. I miss the work . . ."

"And?"

"And this may be the only chance I ever have to go up against Wish French in a case that matters." She glared at him. "And I have to win."

Jason felt a surge of relief and adrenaline run through him. "Me too."

Shay pushed herself out of her chair and walked out of the kitchen.

"Where are you going?" Jason asked.

She looked at him over her shoulder. "To get to work."

29

Hatty was catching up on some paperwork Thursday morning when Wish French walked into her office without knocking.

"Jason Rich has retained advisory counsel." He flung a piece of paper on Hatty's desk.

She looked down at it and read the notice of appearance. Then she read it again, trying hard not to smile.

"Well, that's a bold move," Hatty said, gazing up at Wish. The prosecutor's face was flushed.

"He's a one-man circus, and this is just another attempt to distract from what's really going on so that he can get away with murder."

Hatty crossed her arms. "Wish, you aren't afraid of going up against your old apprentice, are you?"

He snatched the notice out of Hatty's hand. "I'm not afraid of anything, Sheriff. I just wanted you to see the latest lunacy from our friend Mr. Rich."

"Lunacy?" Hatty asked, shrugging. "You know anyone besides yourself that has tried more murder cases in that courtroom than Shay?"

Wish said nothing.

"Seems pretty smart to me."

———

Once her door was shut and Wish gone, Hatty walked to her window and scanned Blount Avenue. She smiled and then snorted. *Good for you, Shay.*

She had always liked the former district attorney. Even last year when her own world was turned upside down and she had to force the sheriff's department to do right by her. Shay Lankford had never been her enemy.

And, when Hatty was appointed sheriff and then won the election in a landslide, she had hoped to work side by side with her friend.

But now, in the first big case of her term, she'd be working against Shay.

Hatty's smile faded. And, if she knew her old friend, they were in for one hell of a fight.

30

LAW OFFICE OF SHAY LANKFORD, ESQ.

The sign was up by noon on Thursday, replacing **THE RICH LAW FIRM**. Jason had agreed to lease his old law firm's space to Shay and give her an advance on the first six months' rent. It was the least he could do for her agreement to assist him, though he knew he needed to make it clear this morning that an assist was all he wanted.

"I'm representing myself, Shay. You're my copilot, but I'm flying the plane. I hope you can live with that." It was the first thing he said to her once they were seated across from each other in the old law library that Lucas Rich had spent most of his time in.

"I hope you can live with it," Shay fired back, leaning across the table. "Why exactly would you want to do this yourself? It seems so . . . foolish. And risky."

"You want the company line or the truth?"

She folded her arms and squinted at him. "Both."

"The elevator answer is that I don't trust anyone else to do it. No one has more experience in this county defending high-stakes murder trials than me. So I'm going with the fastest horse, and Secretariat around these parts . . ." He thrust his thumbs into his chest. ". . . is me."

She bristled and then smirked. "Well, that sounds like something Jason Rich would say, and . . . there is definitely some truth to it."

"Right? But here's the thing. It's bullshit."

"OK then, so what's the real reason."

"The truth . . ." Jason's hands had started to shake as emotion and intensity began to get the better of him. ". . . is that I *need to work*. I need to throw myself into the investigation and the strategy of a case. When my license was taken away, I couldn't function, and I started drinking again. I guess I've realized that *the work* . . . more than anything else . . . is what got me through the pain."

"What pain?"

He shook his head and spoke in a low tone. "Life's pain. My dad not being proud of me. My sister being a gaslighter and dying in my arms. My nieces shunning me because I'm an alcoholic and have brought nothing but problems on them. Chase . . ." He trailed off and shook his head. ". . . leaving me. Harry getting killed because of me. Everything."

For a long few seconds, Jason stared at the table. He'd said the same to Satch, but it felt different sharing such raw feelings with Shay. Though he didn't know her as well, the moment felt oddly intimate. "If I don't have my work . . . ," Jason continued, looking up at the ceiling to avoid eye contact, ". . . and I may never have it again if we lose . . . then I'm afraid my desire for alcohol will consume me."

Silence filled the library, and Jason's gaze moved to the framed portrait of his father. Had he ever shared his feelings with his father like this? *No.*

Then why had he chosen to tell Shay such deep secrets? *Because she has to trust me. And . . . because I wanted her to know.* It felt good to get it off his chest. He sighed and looked at her, and saw that she was staring at him, her expression neutral. As if she were sizing up a hand of cards. "I'm sorry," Jason said. "You asked . . . and I thought if you were going to go down this road with me, you needed to know."

"Thank you," she finally said.

There was a stare-off for a couple of seconds, and Jason finally rubbed his hands together. "All right, so what's our first move?" he asked.

"Shouldn't I be asking you that, Captain? I mean . . . you are flying the plane and all." She smirked but then winked, and Jason felt a ripple of relief wash through him.

"I wasn't telling you I'd agree with it. Just asking for my partner's input."

"Ahh. Well . . ." Shay got up from her chair and paced around the large library with its shelves of outdated court reporters, hornbooks, and yes, even a fiction shelf with the best of Greg Iles, Michael Connelly, Sandra Brown, and Jason's new favorite author, S. A. Cosby. "Remember the last time we were in this room?" she asked.

"George Mitchell's confession," Jason said. "How could I ever forget?"

"I was so tired that day. The trial was almost over. I could tell it was going off the rails. And then . . . George told us what really happened. And then he had his head blown off on the steps out there."

Jason fixated on the portrait of his father that hung on the wall adjacent to the fiction shelf. "That won't happen today. Chuck is outside. Mickey is parked across the street, and Satch is in the lobby."

"He's a hell of a receptionist."

They both laughed.

"I admire how those brothers adore you. It's like you're one of them."

Jason continued to inspect the portrait. "They feel like my family now."

"You're lucky to have them."

"I know."

She followed his eyes. "What was he like, your father?"

Jason guffawed. "He was everything that I'm not. Smart. Reliable. Disciplined. Revered in the community. Respected by the bar."

"And yet you've probably made ten times more money and have won the two biggest criminal trials in the county's history. Your legacy dwarfs his."

Jason shook his head, feeling heat behind his eyes. "Nah. I'm a clown."

"No, you're—"

"You said it yourself, Shay. When I took Jana's case. And I know you've thought it a thousand times. I bring the circus with my billboards, my outrageous behavior, my unpredictability."

"But that's what makes you hard to beat," Shay said. She was standing by his side now. "All of those things."

"I've just been lucky. And my good fortune ran out when the bar suspended me."

For a long moment, there was silence. "You aren't going to do this the whole case, are you?" she asked.

"What?"

"Feel sorry for yourself. It's really unbecoming. You're so much more attractive when you're being an arrogant asshole."

Jason managed a chuckle. "Uh . . . thank you . . . I guess."

"And I know what our first move should be." A wide grin came to Shay's face.

Jason cocked his head. "What?"

"You know what I hated most about dealing with you, Jason?" She didn't wait for him to respond. "Exactly what you said. You bring a certain chaos to every case you handle. It's distracting. Aggravating. It takes the spotlight off the case and puts it on you . . . or wherever you want it."

Jason watched her, waiting.

"But, as much as I hate how you are, you know who hates it even worse?"

Jason smiled wide, figuring he looked just like one of his old billboards. "Wish."

Shay cackled. "It's time for us to bring the circus back to town."

31

Wish French arrived home at a little before 6:00 p.m. He walked straight to the bar in the den and made himself a bourbon and branch. He stared at his reflection until he couldn't bear the sight anymore. Then he took a long sip.

For at least a minute, he walked around the empty house. There were pictures of his wife, Stella, and daughter, Julie, over the mantel. At Julie's birth. Her graduation from high school and college. Her marriage to Steve, a banker in Birmingham. And of Julie's two girls, Amy and Christine, both now fully grown.

When was the last time he'd seen his daughter or grandchildren? Last Christmas for two blinks. Before then . . . he couldn't remember.

Wish sighed and retreated to his home office. He flipped on the television, hoping to catch the evening news, and plopped down in his chair. He had nowhere to be tonight. Since Stella's passing two years ago, he tried to stay busy with church and his friends, but such a mundane existence didn't satisfy him.

That's one of the reasons he had run for another term. The sheer boredom of growing old alone.

Alas, that wasn't the only one.

Wish gazed at the photograph of his son, Patrick, on the bookshelves to the left of his desk. Wearing his Guntersville High football uniform and striking the Heisman pose with his left arm extended out to stiff-arm a would-be tackler. He'd been an All-County defensive back. A straight-A student. A good kid by anyone's estimation. He'd gone to the University of Alabama in 1997, and Wish had high hopes that he would come back and practice law in Guntersville. Perhaps they could have had a family practice together.

Instead, Patrick was killed while driving back to his apartment drunk after a fraternity party. His blood alcohol content was three times the legal limit. Wish hadn't even known his son drank. He hadn't known about the peer pressure to binge drink in college. He'd been too busy working and making a living.

Patrick's death had changed everything.

Ruined, more like it, Wish thought. It had been over twenty years. Wish had been in his early fifties at the time. Well into his second term as district attorney. What would have happened if Patrick had lived? Would he and Stella have been happy their last two decades together? Would he have strayed with other women? Would she have still become an alcoholic? Would his relationship with Julie have been healthy? Would he actually have a relationship with his daughter instead of being simply her financier?

Wish sighed. Who the hell knew? But there was one thing he was certain about. He wouldn't still be prosecuting cases at seventy-one years of age if Patrick French was still around.

He placed his face in his hands and rubbed hard, trying not to think about the job or the big development of the day. *I probably brought that on myself . . .*

The news came on, and the anchor had excitement in her voice. "We're going to start tonight's broadcast with an impromptu press conference called by Jason Rich, the man accused of the murder of Tyson Cade and known all over the state of Alabama for his Get Rich billboard campaign. Let's go live to Tracy Gwaltney, who is at the Rich Law Firm with the defendant and his attorney."

"Well, hello, Guntersville, yes, we are live here at the new office of former prosecutor Shay Lankford, which just so happens to have once been the office of the Rich Law Firm. Mr. Rich has asked to make a statement, and his attorney, Ms. Lankford, will then also say a few words."

"Jesus H. Christ," Wish whispered, taking his hands off his face and glaring at the television.

"Thank you, Tracy," Jason said, looking directly into the camera and pausing for a full two seconds. "I did not kill Tyson Cade," he finally said, his voice firm and defiant. "I am not a murderer. I was a lawyer, and I plan to be one again. I will defend myself against the charges brought by the state, but will not do so alone." He paused. "The former district attorney of this county, Ms. Shay Lankford, will be by my side."

The camera shifted its focus to Shay, who wore a black suit, her dark hair falling down to her shoulders, her eyes intense. "It is my privilege to be here with Mr. Jason Rich. As everyone in this city and county knows, I was the district attorney of Marshall County for six years. I loved my job. I went up against the man sitting next to me twice in court." She glanced at Jason. "He is an excellent attorney, and he also saved my life last year on the steps of this very office. He is innocent of the charges brought against him, and I am proud to be part of his defense team." She licked her lips and leaned forward, glaring now at the camera. "As a political figure in this county for quite some time, I know *exactly* what is going on here. The meth trade in Marshall County is a volatile industry. Tyson Cade had many enemies. Jason Rich was one of a long list of potential suspects. One name you haven't heard from the sheriff's office is Matthew Dean. There is a warrant for Dean's arrest. He is the new methamphetamine czar of Sand Mountain, and he stood to gain the most from Tyson Cade's death."

"You crazy bitch," Wish said, taking out his phone and sending a text to Hatty. You watching this?

Two seconds later, a reply came. Yep.

"A little over two weeks ago, Mr. Rich was brought to court for his initial hearing. After the hearing was over, he was almost shot coming out of the courthouse. A sheriff's deputy . . . Greta Martin . . . was killed. Two other officers were injured. Ask yourself something: Who wants Jason Rich dead?" She paused. "The same person who killed Tyson Cade."

Wish called Terry Barber without even thinking about it.

"Hello."

"Are you watching this, Terry?"

"Wish, it's not proper for you to call me—"

"Proper! Are you watching the news? The former district attorney is pissing all through my jury pool."

"I'm calling an emergency hearing in the morning."

"You better."

"Don't make threats to me, Wish."

"Not a threat, Terry. We both know I own you. I expect there to be consequences." He hung up the phone and continued to stare at the television set. Shay was still the focus. She had paused for effect and was clearly waiting to bring it home.

"Like I said, I was in politics. I know how things work. Tyson Cade's murder is a big deal. The sheriff's office needed to make an arrest. They needed a patsy. They needed a scapegoat."

"I can't believe this," Wish whispered.

Shay glanced at her partner as the camera angle widened to show both of them. "Need a scapegoat?" Shay asked the screen, pointing at Jason. "Get Rich."

32

The hearing was set for 11:00 a.m. That gave enough time for another group of National Guardsmen to arrive and surround the courthouse. They were needed not just to protect those inside and out from another possible bombing or ambush, but also because protesters holding "Need a Scapegoat? Get Rich" signs were everywhere. Jason had asked Izzy to get some folks down here to make a commotion, and his old partner had come through. He might not have his license anymore, but he still had some of his war chest left, and it was amazing what people would do on the spur of the moment for a few hundred dollars. Jason liked to think that some of the people outside were there because they genuinely believed in his innocence, but he wasn't that naive. Money talked, just as it always did.

Shay wanted the circus, and Jason had brought it.

To say that Judge Terry Barber looked angry was an understatement. He was already sitting at the bench when Jason and Shay arrived, thinning hair in disarray, glasses off, face puffy and red with bloodshot eyes to match.

Press and spectators had been banned from the courtroom, but the air still felt thick and stuffy.

Wish French was standing beside the bench with an exasperated grimace on his face. He didn't wait for Barber to begin. "I hope you two are proud of yourselves. You've now poisoned the entire jury pool with your little stunt. I would expect such shenanigans out of you, Mr. Rich, but Shay . . ." He trailed off. "What in the world is wrong with you?"

Judge Barber beat the bench with his gavel twice. "I'm holding you both in contempt. Calling a press conference in this case given what has already happened was unethical and untenable. I won't stand for it in my courtroom. You can look out the window and see what your actions have led to. Do you have anything to say for yourself, Ms. Lankford?"

Shay didn't hesitate. "I said it all last night. This case has been a witch hunt from the start, and Mr. Rich deserves a fair shake. There was no gag order. What we did was completely within the bounds of law. There are no grounds for contempt."

Barber leaned back in his chair and took a sip of water that didn't go down right. He began to cough. When the fit ended, he scowled at them. "You're most certainly in contempt. You'll both spend the night in the Marshall County Jail. I'm tempted to report you both to the bar, but what good would it do? You're already suspended, Rich. This is your mulligan, Shay. I always thought you were a capable prosecutor, and I'm going to assume this idea was Mr. Rich's as he technically is representing himself and you are merely present in an *advisory* position." He coughed some more. "Do I make myself clear?"

"Yes, Your Honor," Shay said.

"Yes, sir," Jason added.

"From this point forward, there is a gag order in place for this case. Any press release or comment to the media of any kind will result in a much more serious contempt charge." Again, the judge coughed. He picked up his glass of water, seemed to remember that it had caused his fit, and set it down. Jason thought the Honorable Terry Barber looked more agitated than perhaps he should, but who the hell knew?

His Honor sighed and glanced at his bailiff. "Get them out of my sight."

As they were being led out of the courtroom in handcuffs, Jason whispered to Shay.

"Hell of a first day."

"We needed to get their attention. And don't act like you haven't spent a night in this jail before. You're a damn honors member."

Jason squashed a chuckle and looked over his shoulder at Barber, who remained seated on the bench, and Wish French with his perfect suit and hair. He figured that if his father was here, he'd probably be standing with those two bastards and shaking his head. Or maybe he'd be trailing behind Jason and Shay.

As Jason was pushed out the double doors and a squadron of National Guardsmen joined the deputies, he sighed. It was odd the times he thought about his father. Almost always during times of shame. And sometimes in moments of pride. He thought of the trial victory in Florence last year. Waiting around until everyone was gone and facing the empty jury box. Giving the Macho Man yell and thinking of Lucas Rich.

The memories were painful.

———

With the courtroom empty, Wish stared up at Barber. "Good job, Terry."

The district attorney began to walk toward the exit.

"They'll probably file a motion to transfer venue now," Barber said. "I would if I were them." He coughed. "A lot of judges would grant it."

Wish turned and leered at his old friend. "But you won't."

33

Matty Dean had a temper. He just didn't let it control him. That had been one of Tyson's faults. Youth or an excess of testosterone had made the boy king hotheaded at times. If not for Matty's influence, Tyson's fury might have ignited more than it had.

Matty preferred to use the energy brought on by anger. To let it smolder and cover him from head to toe. He knew there were times that an action called for a reaction.

And there were times to wait in the grass like a copperhead. Right up until your enemies were in striking distance.

The press conference hadn't changed anything. He'd been wanted by the sheriff's office before Jason Rich and Shay Lankford made a spectacle of themselves. Now, though, the case, which had already gained a good bit of attention, was back in the public eye, and his name was being thrown around as a suspect.

That's what angered him the most. He'd already had to face the hidden accusations behind the stares of his own people. He'd killed Reg Strassburg and Tanner Sparks because of those stares. It showed a lack of respect that Matty Dean wouldn't tolerate.

Now business was booming, and no one seemed to care that much. *But I care.*

Matty gawked at the lake from the kitchen window. At this time of the morning, the sun was full in the sky and, it being Friday, there were already a few fishermen on the water braving the cold.

Matty looked around at the rustic but comfortable accommodations. One thing he'd learned from Tyson was the importance of inside sources.

But unlike his old boss, Matty preferred subtlety. He had spent a lifetime developing relationships in and out of the meth world. He'd helped powerful people, and he'd kept a list.

And now that he was a fugitive, he was checking off names.

He took his coffee and walked to the den with the large deer head on the wall. The bar with several bottles of Maker's and Jack Black. The stairway that led to a couple of small bedrooms with bunk beds. And then the hallway that took him to the master.

He'd been smart to call this favor in, but he wasn't taking any chances. He only traveled at night and was driving a car registered to the owner.

A perfect cover, he thought, walking again to the window. He missed his old boat. The runabout that they'd arrested him in.

But, as he spied the boathouse, he saw a fishing skiff that he figured he'd have to test out in the near future.

It pays to know the right people.

His phone rang, and he looked at the screen. Lu.

"Yeah," he answered.

"Rich and Lankford have been held in contempt and are spending the night in jail."

He nodded to himself but said nothing.

"Tonight might be a good time to take a shot at the youngest Tonidandel," Lu said, her voice playful.

"Might be. You think you'll get a shot?"

"They don't have to watch his ass tonight."

188

Matty rubbed his chin and watched a fisherman edge close to the boathouse and throw his line toward it. He knew that a lot of the biggest catfish could be found under and around docks and boathouses.

"When are you going to invite me over to your new digs?" Lu asked, a tease in her tone.

"Soon, Lu. Soon."

"Good."

He licked his lips. Sometimes an action required a reaction. "And Lu."

"Yeah."

"If you have the shot tonight . . . take it."

34

At noon, the doors of Jimmy's Lounge in Madison, Alabama, opened. Griff walked inside feeling defeated and needing a drink.

He'd lost his tail on Matty Dean this morning. He knew he shouldn't be surprised or disappointed. Dean was a veteran who was also a fugitive. The man knew how to change his shape, his look, and his scenery.

I gave them the SOB on a silver platter.

Griff tasted acid in his throat and ordered a beer from the barmaid. He'd been so close to obtaining his revenge on the old meth dealer. Apprehension by the feds would have almost been better than killing him.

Almost . . .

Griff sighed and sipped from the bottle. He needed some rest. When was the last time he'd had a decent night's sleep? Since moving out of the home he'd shared with his wife and kids in Guntersville, he'd lived mostly out of his car. Sleeping at truck stops and RV parks. He'd gotten a lot of texts from his ex-wife, but almost all of them said that the sheriff or Wish or someone with the media wanted to talk with him.

About George Mitchell's unsolved murder. A crime that some thought he had committed. *Not true.*

Griff had killed one of his officers, but it hadn't been George.

He sighed and took a long pull off the bottle. Kelly Flowers had started off as a good cop. Griff had hired him. Trained him. But then Kelly had fallen in with Cade.

And then I did too. And then . . .

He often woke up in the middle of the night with those last few seconds playing in his mind. Of pulling his truck up to Branner's Place. Of seeing Kelly walking toward him with that cocksure grin. Of watching the smile replaced with curiosity and then fear.

Of pulling the trigger.

"What in the hell are you doing here?"

Griff's eyes shot up, and he saw a woman standing in front of him. She was dressed in joggers and a hoodie and held a duffel bag. In a few short minutes, she'd be dancing one of the poles in here.

"I wanted to see you."

"Well, I don't want to see you. Not now. Not ever. And you have a hell of a lot of nerve showing up here." She leaned forward and grabbed the table with both hands. *"You killed my brother, you sonofabitch."* She spat the words at him and waved at someone behind Griff.

"Bella, you can't believe that," Griff said. *Why shouldn't she believe it?* he thought. *It's true . . .*

"Oh, I believe it. Just because you weren't charged doesn't mean you didn't do it. If George hadn't been killed, he would have put you under the jail. Wonder who made that happen?"

"It wasn't me," Griff said, grateful to not have to continue lying. "I promise. I didn't kill George."

"But you did kill Kelly. I know it. You told me that Trey killed him, but it was you. You have my family's blood all over your hands."

A large man wearing a black T-shirt and jeans walked over to the table. "Everything all right, Bella?"

"No, Victor. This man was putting his hands on me the last time he was in here. I'd like you to escort him out."

"Bella, please."

191

"All right, mister, you heard the lady. Let's not have a scene, OK? It's too early for me to have to open up a can of whup ass."

Griff gaped at the bouncer and then up at Bella. "I need to talk with you."

"No, you don't." Her voice cracked on the last word. "You need to talk with God. You won't be getting any forgiveness from me."

"All right, buddy, let's go," Victor said, putting a hand on Griff's shoulder.

"I'm going," Griff said, standing up and wriggling out of the big man's grasp. He held up his hands and saw that Bella was still watching him. Her arms were crossed and her cheeks were streaked with tears. "I'm going," he repeated, staring at her.

"Don't ever come back," she said through clenched teeth.

———

Out in the parking lot, Griff sat inside a five-year-old Toyota Corolla. He'd traded in his truck for the small sedan, figuring it would be better for travel on the interstate and less visible.

But now, he'd lost Dean's trail, and he felt strung out and restless. All he'd wanted was to see Bella. Talk to her. Smell her scent.

Addiction came in many forms. He'd basically pissed his whole life away because he'd gotten a taste of Bella Flowers a year ago and couldn't get enough of her. Cheryl was a good woman, but she'd been a prude between the sheets. Griff hadn't been with many women. Bella had showed him things.

The affair had been wrong. And it had cost him his life.

And yet . . . he still wanted it. Needed it. He took a deep breath and exhaled, smelling his stale breath. He winced as he remembered how Bella had looked at him.

She hates me.

Just like Cheryl. And my kids.

Everyone.

He pulled onto University Drive and stopped at a convenience store. He wanted to get drunk but decided against it. He needed to rest but knew he couldn't.

Why did I come here? he thought. *For forgiveness? For a piece of ass? Both?*

No. While either of those would have been fine and he would have gladly accepted them, he had come to lick his wounds. He'd hoped Bella would help in that regard.

Griff sighed and stepped out of the car. He bought a cup of coffee and a Little Debbie oatmeal creme pie. It was time to go home. Back to Marshall County. Tyson Cade was dead, but there were others who needed to join him. He may have lost Dean's scent, but he'd find it again. As he trudged back to his vehicle, his focus returned. As did one undeniable truth.

These wounds won't heal.

35

The door to the holding area slid open with a whoosh, and Sheriff Hatty Daniels stepped through. She walked toward the cell with two guards. One in front of her leading the way and one in back. The lead guard took out a set of keys and opened the first cell, and Hatty walked through the opening without breaking stride. "Leave us," she said, not looking at the officers.

"We'll be right down the hall, Sheriff."

"Good," Hatty said, placing her hands on her hips and staring at a woman she'd once worked with for the better part of a decade.

"Hatty," Shay said, her voice a tad hoarse as she rose from the cot in the corner.

"Shay."

For a full beat neither of them said anything. Finally, Hatty took a step closer. "It's good to see you." She managed a smile but felt sad.

"You too," Shay said.

"That press conference was quite the spectacle. Jason's idea?"

Shay shook her head. "Mine."

"Really?" Hatty crossed her arms. "How does it feel to join the dark side?"

"Different," Shay said. "I didn't think I could do it. I was substitute teaching at DAR."

"Still living with your sweet momma."

Shay's face finally broke, and she smiled. "She asked about you. Told me to tell you hi." The former prosecutor waved.

Hatty brought up her hand. "Hi to Beth. I miss her. And you." During their time working together, Shay had asked Hatty to join her and Beth for dinner a few times, and Beth had peppered Hatty with questions. And when Hatty was appointed sheriff, Beth had prayed for her.

"We miss you too."

Hatty surveyed the tiny cell. "What made you get involved?"

"I don't know. Several things. One, criminal law is all I know. If I can't be a prosecutor, then that only left criminal defense."

"You could have easily gotten an assistant DA job in Jackson County. Or Etowah. DeKalb."

"Didn't want to work that far away from home. And, frankly, didn't want to work for anyone. Once you've been the top dog . . ." She trailed off.

"Did Wish have something to do with it?"

Shay gave her the side-eye. "I'd be lying if I said no. Going up against Wish in court is something I've always dreamed of. And he's such a prick."

"No argument on that from me."

"Taking him to the woodshed would give me great satisfaction."

Hatty approached Shay until she was just a foot away. "You know that's not going to happen, don't you? I hated to arrest Jason, but he's guilty, Shay. He killed Tyson Cade, and I don't even blame him all that much. But I have to do my job."

"And I know you will," Shay said, extending her hand.

The two women shook.

"You really think you can win?" Hatty asked, taking a step back.

Shay walked back to her cot and plopped down. "I still haven't told you the main reason I took this case. My experience and Wish are part of it, but not the big thing."

"What is?"

Shay stared at her. "Jason Rich has tried two cases in that courtroom over there, and he's won them both. He's not a clown like I thought and like Wish still thinks. He's smart . . . and he saved my life." She hesitated. "I couldn't say no."

Hatty maintained eye contact for a moment and then turned for the door. "Guard."

As the officer's footsteps approached, Shay spoke from behind her. "And Hatty?"

"Yeah," the sheriff said, looking over her shoulder.

"We're going to win."

36

Crawmama's was Mickey Tonidandel's favorite restaurant. He and his brothers typically went once a month, but this particular Friday, he'd taken someone else with him.

Tiffany Shrout cut hair at a beauty salon in Arab. She had naturally curly locks herself and applied a pound of makeup to her round friendly face. The first time Mickey had met her was when they started fighting over a fishing hole near the Paul Stockton Causeway. The argument ended in laughter, and they had shared the spot. Tiffany had cooked the fish they'd caught later that night at her place, and the day ended with Mickey's first sexual experience with a woman since he'd returned from Afghanistan.

Tiffany might dress a tad fake, but she was fun to be around and seemed to enjoy Mickey's sense of humor. He figured he'd introduce her at some point to his brothers, but, for now, he was trying not to over-think things. He'd meant what he said to Jason. You did need people in your life. Tiffany had proved that to him. He was thinking of maybe moving from Mill Creek. Or at least getting his own place. But he knew what Satch would say if he asked now.

Not until the war is over.

Mickey knew not to argue with the colonel. He also knew that, on that point, Satch would be right.

"What you thinking about, boyfriend?"

Mickey grinned and tossed a fry in his mouth. He'd already devoured two pounds of crawfish by himself and three cold Miller Lites. "How I'm fat and happy."

"Well, I'm glad you're happy, but you ain't fat. Besides, I've got a way you can work off these calories when we get home."

"Uh-huh," Mickey said, kissing the air in front of him, and Tiffany did the same from her seat.

"When are you going to introduce me to your brothers?"

The grin left Mickey's face. "Oh, I don't know. They're pretty busy at the range."

"Well, take me there. You know I love to shoot."

I love this woman, Mickey thought. *She fishes like Bill Dance, fucks like a porn star, and shoots like Sharon Stone in* The Quick and the Dead . . .

"Makes you horny, doesn't it?" Tiffany asked, then ran her tongue across her teeth.

"All right, we need to get the check."

He stood while Tiffany let out a cackle. Yes indeed. He thought he might love this woman.

———

Crawmama's didn't have much of a parking lot. There were a few places in back, and then you just did the best you could. Sometimes, if the crowd was big enough, a person had to park at the Foodland Plus shopping center across the street.

Mickey Tonidandel had done that tonight. As the department store was now closed, the area was dark with only a few light poles.

Lu Stephens sat on the driver's side of her truck. She'd parked a few spaces away from Mickey, and there were cars in between them. She'd had some time to think about how she was going to do it, and she knew her plan would work. Butch had wanted to be the triggerman, but she wasn't willing to take a chance. She didn't want to lose her son. Nor did she want the mission to fail.

She had the window rolled down and was smoking a cigarette. Her trusty sawed-off shotgun was lying across the cab. Her phone dinged, indicating a text.

They're getting the check. Almost go time.

Lu had never been a soldier, but she knew how to handle a gun. Her father had been a hunter, and she'd spent many a morning in a duck blind with him, or a deer stand. She was an only child, and her mom had died in childbirth. Her father had raised her until he'd dropped dead of a heart attack when Lu was seventeen years old.

Since then, she'd been on her own. She didn't have the money for college, so she'd made ends meet mowing grass, fixing cars, and repairing toilets. Doing the things that Jeremiah Stephens had taught her. But while she was a good mechanic and handyman, the pay wasn't that great.

Methamphetamine had been her way out. Growing up off the grid in Albertville with a single parent had taught her a lot about life. She'd lost her virginity when she was fifteen years old to a friend of her father's who'd come over to borrow a wrench and ended up forcing himself on her. She hadn't told anyone about it, but she learned her lesson. The next time the man came over when her dad wasn't there, Lu had hit him in the shin with a Louisville Slugger—Lu was a pretty good high school softball player—and then had put the barrel end of a twelve gauge in his mouth. She hadn't pulled the trigger, and the man limped away and never bothered her again. Unlike Lu, he talked, and she got a reputation for being a hard-ass woman.

Lu sometimes still cried at night when she thought of how well earned her reputation was. She'd never known innocence. Even as a child, she'd felt guilty for killing her mother. Her dad never made her feel so; Lu just did. But for Lu, Jeremiah and Susan Stephens might have had other kids whose delivery might not have been so volatile.

I was born in death, and bringing it to others has been a talent of mine since my first breath.

The thought calmed her as she sat in the parking lot. She was a killer. She hadn't killed the man who'd raped her, but she had become an enforcer in King Hanson's and later Tyson Cade's meth operation. She made sure deals went through and that the folks in the operation did what they were supposed to do. She'd paid her dues and built her rep with King, but she'd really come into her own with Tyson, and there was one big reason for that.

Matty . . .

She'd take a bullet for her new boss, who'd been her supervisor since she'd joined the meth trade. Matty was smart, cunning, and fun. She loved him more like a brother than a man. Her advances toward him were to make him feel good. She knew the truth about Matty. Could tell it in the uneasy way he looked at her. In the lack of any activity below the belt when she touched him.

If he ever wanted sex, she'd gladly oblige. But it would be out of loyalty and respect more than attraction. Those two traits meant more to her than anything else. And regardless of his sexual orientation, Matty Dean garnered both.

She watched through her window as Mickey Tonidandel and Tiffany Shrout walked hand in hand across the street toward the shopping center. Lu clicked the latch on the door and got out of her vehicle. She dropped her cigarette and stomped on it with a flip-flop. Then she smoothed out the dress she was wearing. She opened the back of her truck and pulled out a black overcoat and slipped it on. Then she walked around the truck to the passenger side, reached through the open window for the sawed-off shotgun, and began to walk toward the couple.

Too easy, she thought. "Excuse me, the battery on my car is dead. Do you think I could get a jump?"

Mickey blinked and then nodded, releasing Tiffany's hand. "Sure, ma'am. I got some cables in the back of my truck." He turned his back on her, and Lu undid the button on her coat and pulled her weapon.

"Mickey!" Tiffany screamed.

"I wouldn't." The voice was harsh gravel, and it was right in Lu's ear. A long-barreled pistol pressed into her neck, and a strong hand gripped her waist. "Now, I want you to drop that gun and walk backward to your truck."

"You're a dead man," Lu whispered, still pointing her weapon at Mickey, who had now turned around and was standing stock still. Tiffany was trembling a few feet away from him. "And you better not move, Mickey Mouse, or you and your cunt are both going to hell."

"The only people dying tonight and meeting the devil will be you and your son. If you don't drop the gun and walk backward to your truck."

"My son is—"

"Standing in back of Crawmama's waiting for you to pick him up. He's in the crosshairs of my brother Chuck's thirty-ought-six rifle, and Chuck is a *very* good shot. Your boy Butch's brains are about to join all the possums' and squirrels' and other rodents' corpses who haven't successfully crossed Highway 431."

"You're a fucking liar."

"No, ma'am. I'm fucking crazy. And my trigger finger is getting itchy." He pressed the gun harder into her neck and then moved the muzzle up until it dug into the side of her forehead. "I don't want to kill you, Lu. Don't give me a reason."

"How do you know who I am?"

"Because I'm Satch Tonidandel. I've lived in Marshall County all my life, and I've hung out with more ne'er-do-well no-count pieces of shit than I care to tell. Everyone in Alder Springs, Albertville, Boaz, and

Sand Mountain knows about badass Luann Stephens. You working for Matty Dean now?"

Lu grunted. The barrel of the gun was beginning to hurt.

"Give him a message for me, would you? Tell him that he's going to need more than his enforcer and her shitleg son to get the jump on three Screaming Eagles."

"You're hurting me," Lu said, forcing weakness into her tone.

Satch let up on the pressure, and Lu wheeled toward him, swinging her gun at him. Satch ducked and grabbed her by the throat. He squeezed and lifted her off the ground. When she dropped the gun, he let go, and she dropped to her knees, scratching at the asphalt for her shotgun. When she looked up, Satch was pointing his pistol and her gun at her face. "Get in the truck right now," he said.

Lu got up and coughed. Her throat ached. "Next time, I'll have every man and woman in our operation with me."

Satch snorted. "Well, you're goin' to need them all."

Mickey joined him, having pulled his own gun. Satch took the shells out of the sawed-off shotgun and flung the weapon in the back of Lu's truck.

"Are you going to hurt my son?"

"No, I'm not. Get in the fucking truck, Lu."

She stood her ground. "Why are you showing us mercy? We wouldn't have done that for you, and we won't going forward. I'd cut your throat in your sleep."

Satch took a step toward her. Then another. He gazed at her. The colonel's eyes were ice cold. Lu felt a chill that had nothing to do with the temperature.

"Because this war, regardless of how much I'm relishing it, has to end at some point. When that happens, you could be in charge." He paused. "And you'll know that my brothers and I spared your life."

"Well, that don't mean shit to me," Lu said. She spat on him.

Satch made no move to wipe the saliva that ran down his cheek. He pulled out his phone. "Chuck, do you still have Butch in view."

"Yes, sir."

"Good. Fire on my order."

"Say when."

"No!" Lu screamed.

"Perhaps if mercy to you isn't good enough, then the fact that we spared your only son his life will mean something to you."

Lu glared at Satch. Her hands were shaking. She wasn't sure what to say. "I can't make Matty back off. He blames Jason Rich for Tyson's murder. I mean, so does the damn sheriff's office, but it's different for Matty. He'll never stop."

"And neither will we. Not until Dean is buried in a hole next to Cade."

"You'll never get Matty. He's too smart. Too unpredictable. And he has friends in places you'll never suspect."

"He sent you and Butch to pick Mickey off tonight, and you both ought to be going back in pine boxes."

Again, Lu said nothing. "Please don't hurt my son," she finally said, hating her weakness. She dropped her eyes.

"Holding for the order," Chuck's voice blared from the phone.

"Stand down," Satch said.

"Ten-four."

Satch ended the call and lowered his gun. He stepped closer to her. She could smell his rustic scent. Feel the intensity radiating from his eyes.

For a long moment, Lu glowered at him. "Did you really show us mercy because you want the war to end?"

Satch shook his head. "War is all I have to live for."

"Why then?"

Satch gave his head a jerk but said nothing. Finally, he grunted. "Your boy's waiting on you."

Lu walked around the front and climbed inside. She felt his eyes still on her, and she rolled down the passenger-side window. "What?" she asked.

"Bye, Lu."

She blinked and then gazed over the wheel through the windshield at the cars passing on Highway 431. Cars carrying people in both directions who had no idea that Lu's entire world had almost been shattered. "Bye . . . Colonel."

37

Matty Dean needed a fix. He seemed to crave it more and more now. He'd always been a disciplined man. Sex had no power over him. That control had made him dependable. Steady. Dangerous.

But since he took over for Tyson, the urges were greater. What the hell was wrong with him? He was sixty-one years old. He'd sowed his wild oats a long time ago. He'd had sex with women. With men. He'd played pitcher and catcher. He'd gone to Vegas and cross-dressed for a week. He'd experimented with every kind of drug known to man. He should be past all that, right?

Tyson . . . He thought of his boss. The man's self-assured violence. How Matty would sometimes leak in his shorts when Tyson would break down a plan.

With him gone, Matty felt strung out and hollow. He'd never made so much as an advance toward Tyson Cade, but he figured the other man had known.

Tyson was too smart not to know. Why else had they spent so many nights together on the boat? Tyson had known how Matty felt and had exploited those feelings for his own benefit. He knew Matty would do anything for him.

He betrayed me . . .

Matty felt heat behind his eyes and shook his head. He remembered being arrested on his boat last October. Of spending the night in jail.

Of being released on bond and Tyson's patronizing words. Of being told to kill George Mitchell and then having another warrant taken out for his arrest. He'd been used by Tyson. His loyalty taken for granted. Tyson had chewed him up like one of the Twinkies the young man had so enjoyed.

"You all right, Matty?"

He blinked his eyes and gazed at the other man. Frank Crutcher was an old friend who'd been in the business almost as long as Matty. Retired military whose primary role these days was the assimilation of information.

"So, Rich and the brothers were all there?" They'd met in the parking lot of Top O' the River. Matty was in the passenger seat of Frank's Silverado. He wore a cap, and his mostly salt with a few specks of pepper beard was thicker than the photographs they had of him. Matty almost guffawed at the ridiculousness of being worried about being captured. With his wrinkles, hair color, and stooped build, he looked like any advancing-middle-aged man in America. The ultimate cover.

"I told Lu, I only saw Rich and the colonel." His voice was slow. Methodical. "The colonel made threats, and I gave them Dooby's contact information."

"Not anything current, I hope."

"Her home address, but she hasn't been there in a couple months."

"And the phone number?"

"Current, but Dooby's too smart to answer it."

"Where is she then?"

Frank held up his hands. "I don't know. She quit a day after Tyson's murder, and no one's seen her since."

"Not even Trudy?" Matty glanced toward the restaurant.

"I just spoke with her, and she said she hasn't heard a thing."

Matty rubbed his chin. "You believe her?"

"Trudy Cowan is no liar."

Matty thought it through. "Trudy went through a lot this past year with Trey. She might not be all that friendly toward us anymore."

"You want me to talk with her again?"

"Not right now. Just keep your ears open, Crutch."

"Will do. How you holding up?"

"What do you mean?"

"You know. Warrant out for your arrest. The former lady prosecutor talking all that nonsense with Rich on the television the other night."

Matty chuckled. "Oh, I've got a pretty thick skin. That's all bullshit." He took a breath, and the scent of the car had a trace of body odor. He exhaled and grabbed the handle.

"What are you doing now?" Frank asked.

"Got other appointments. Day isn't done."

"Good seeing you, man. Let me know if you ever want to go fishing or drink some whiskey." He patted Matty's shoulder, and for a second, Matty wondered if the invitation was for something else entirely.

"Thanks, Crutch." He took three hundred-dollar bills out of his wallet and gave the cash to him. "Let me know if those crazy Tonidandels are back in the store. I'm going to teach those fuckers a lesson." He thought about Lu's assignment for the night. *Hopefully, I already have . . .*

"Will do."

Matty stepped out of the truck, his heart racing. Perhaps Crutch's overtures had simply been innocent. Maybe he really just wanted to go fishing and have a drink. Or maybe he wanted exactly what Matty wanted.

Or maybe it was a trap.

His instincts weren't sending up any smoke signals, so he'd pressed the eject button. He had too much on his mind, and he needed to keep moving. He walked down Val Monte Drive toward Legends on the Lake, and his phone buzzed.

"Yeah?"

"Hey," Lu said.

"Well?"

"We never got a good shot. Mickey's brothers were with him."

"No worries. They'll let their guard down eventually." He ended the call as an SUV slid to a stop behind him. He opened the door and glanced at the driver. Chief Parrish's massive arms draped over the wheel.

"Where to?" Chief asked.

"I left the loaner car at the Scottsboro Walmart."

"That's a haul. Where you staying these days?"

"Safe," Matty said. He trusted no one except maybe Lu with his whereabouts. "Anything happening?"

"Actually . . . yeah. Mind if we stop at Branner's Place? We got a deal cooking with a Huntsville teenager. Son to a multimillionaire oral surgeon whose wife is also a doctor. They got no time for the kid, so he's into everything."

Matty smiled, thinking of Tyson. *You'd love this one, T. C.* "Ducks on the pond," Matty said as the vehicle surged forward.

38

Lu stared at the phone. She and Butch had gone to Giovanni's off 431 for a pizza. Butch was eating and watching the NBA game on television.

Lu had barely touched her food. She wasn't much of a drinker, but she thought she might get a six-pack of something on the way home. Giovanni's didn't serve beer, but they had the best pizza around, and that's what Butch said he wanted.

She watched him, envious of his utter obliviousness to what had just happened. Butch was a big man like his father. Six feet two and well over two hundred pounds. He had a bit of a belly, but he was a strong kid and good with a gun. Lu had taught him everything her father had taught her. How to fish. How to shoot. How to hunt.

Everything except how to be a man.

Butch was now in his midtwenties. He was tough and strong, but he wasn't smart. On that particular quality, he'd taken after his father, who'd left them both when Butch was a baby. Lu hadn't blamed him. They'd had a one-night stand after a night of drinking and hadn't used protection. It was stupid and careless.

But Lu was forever grateful for the son they'd created and was glad that the sperm donor hadn't been around to interfere with his raising.

I almost lost him tonight.

Lu clasped her hands together to keep them from shaking. She'd never lied to Matty Dean before. Not in over twenty years of working together.

Why had she lied tonight? Shame at being shown up? Guilt for failing the mission assigned her? Fear at both of those things? She watched Butch put a piece of pizza in his mouth and wash it down with a Dr Pepper. The small restaurant was full, as was typical on a Friday night. The air smelled of pepperoni and garlic and cheese. There was laughter coming from the table adjacent to them. A teenager celebrating a birthday. Next to the family and against the window was an elderly couple sharing a small supreme.

Life was being lived in here.

Hers had almost been taken tonight, but that would have been OK. Losing her son would not have been. She was a tough woman, but she wasn't sure she could handle that.

Why did I lie?

She saw an image of Colonel Tonidandel in her mind. *Why did he show mercy?*

Lu took a sip of water. She thought she knew.

She also thought she knew why she'd lied to Matty.

And both realizations scared her to death. She sighed and focused on her son.

This is a dangerous game . . .

39

When Jason and Shay were released from the Marshall County Jail on Saturday morning, they were escorted to the basement parking area of the sheriff's office. Jason hoped this would be the last time he was ever in this spot again. The dark, tight space with only police vehicles gave him the creeps.

But not as much as the man waiting on them did.

"Judge Barber issued a gag order right after he held you two in contempt." Wish handed a piece of paper to Jason, who glanced at it and then gave it to Shay.

"Well, I guess we won't be holding any more press conferences," she said.

"You're a joke now, Shay. Just like him. Happy?"

She puckered her lips and cocked her head. "Actually? It's been a while since I had this much fun. Seeing you and Hatty with your panties in such a wad kinda makes me giddy."

"I know you, Shay. I trained you. I made you." Wish paused. "This isn't you."

"Wish, I made you look good for a lot of years. Let me ask you something about that trial record you're so proud of. How many of those murder trials that you won did you handle by yourself?" She looked up at the parking garage's concrete ceiling. "Hmmm. Seems like I might have been the one doing the heavy lifting in pretty much *all* of them." She leaned toward him. "You don't have me to do the work for you this time."

A Ford Raptor pulled to a stop, and Satch got out of the driver's side. He looked at Jason and gave a wry smile. Jason had made his one phone call last night and given Satch specific instructions for pickup. There had been some arguing, but the colonel finally relented.

"I'll be in the lead," Satch said. "Mickey is behind me, and Chuck's behind him. We've recruited help for the house today."

Jason raised his eyebrows.

"Virgil Onkey and his son Wyatt," Satch said. "They've had a little trouble with the law over the years, but I trust them. Both served with us overseas." Satch nodded. "Good folks to have on our team."

"Sounds good."

"I'll be waiting out front."

Satch hopped back in the Raptor and drove out of the garage. Seconds later, another car skidded to a stop in front of them. Jason grinned wide as he heard the district attorney hiss behind him.

"Jesus H. Christ," Wish said.

The car was a midnight-black Porsche. Mickey had pulled it forward just enough to see the license tag.

GETRICH

"Enjoy the circus," Wish said, stepping away from Shay.

"What I'm going to enjoy . . . ," Shay said, ". . . is beating your ass." She got in the passenger side, and Mickey slammed the door shut behind her. The youngest Tonidandel winked at Jason. "Right behind you, J. Rich."

Jason saluted him.

He climbed into the car and felt an odd combination of calm and excitement. The way you felt when you were in a cozy theater about to watch a movie you'd been waiting on for a while. When was the last time he'd been this excited to be alive?

None of it made sense, but Jason knew better than to fight the tide. *Roll with it, baby.*

"Siri, play my theme song!" he yelled, winking at Shay. Then, rolling down his partner's window as AC/DC broke into the opening riff of "Highway to Hell," Jason screamed at Wish French.

"Hey, Wish!"

The district attorney turned as he was about to walk inside.

Jason extended his middle finger and then peeled out of the parking garage. Once they were in the light, Jason saw them.

Beyond the National Guardsmen that surrounded both sides of the road was a crowd of people. Some were holding signs that said, **NEED A SCAPEGOAT? GET RICH**. Jason rolled down his window and cranked the music.

"Are you crazy?" Shay asked.

"I like to leave a wake," Jason said. "Learned it from my sister."

Cheers and jeers rang out on both sides. Jason saw another sign that said **NEED A MURDERER? GET RICH**.

As he turned onto Blount Avenue and vocalist Brian Johnson began to shriek the opening lyrics to Jason's favorite song, Shay looked at him. "This is kinda fun," she said.

"What?" he asked, pushing the accelerator to the floor and rolling up the windows.

"Being bad."

He guffawed as the Porsche followed Satch's Raptor up the Veterans Memorial Bridge.

Shay sighed and her face became tense. "Now comes the hard part."

"What's that?"

"Winning," Shay said. "None of this matters—"

"Unless we win," Jason interrupted. As the Porsche ascended to the top of the bridge and Jason gazed to the right at the mansions on Buck Island, he pushed a button, and the top lowered on the Porsche.

"Oh my God! Are you nuts? It's freezing?" Shay screamed, rubbing her arms and laughing.

Jason arched his head back as the frigid air caught him flush in the face. He squeezed the wheel and gave a Ric Flair "Wooooooooooo!"

We're going to win, he told himself, seeing a vision of Jana and then his father. And then the inside of the cell he'd just spent another night in. The same type of cell he could spend the rest of his life in if he was found guilty of murdering Tyson Cade.

I have to win.

PART FOUR

40

On January 7, 2020, at 10:30 a.m., a Marshall County grand jury indicted Jason James Rich for the murder of Tyson Kennesaw Cade. The indictment was a mere formality, but it was still big news in Marshall County and throughout the state of Alabama.

Almost exactly twenty-four hours later, Jason and Shay sat across from each other in the office library, both going over their copies of the indictment and the order for an arraignment.

Jason had decided to forgo a preliminary hearing, and Shay had reluctantly agreed. While giving up a right of the defendant was almost never advisable, Shay knew that Wish French was unlikely to give them anything they didn't already know, so the whole song and dance would be a waste of time. That meant the case was immediately bound over to the grand jury, and the indictment had come swiftly.

"Arraignment is set for January 10," Shay said, peering down at the order. "We'll serve our discovery that afternoon." In the days since Shay joined him, they had hired two paralegals to handle electronic filing and all administrative tasks, and Jason was glad to finance these new additions. He knew he could spare no expense.

"I've drafted it," Shay said. "And it's pretty detailed."

"Using your inside knowledge, I'm sure."

"Absolutely," she said. "I've put a draft in your office. Let me know what you think."

"I'm sure it's fine."

"I've got something else cooking too."

"Mmm. Sounds yummy."

"I'm not sure how helpful it will be, but no other defense attorney in town could pull it off."

"That's why you're on the team."

"We also need a profiler," Shay continued. "Someone who can do a deep dive on the victim and all of our alternative suspects. The more we know, the better chance we'll have of sprinkling reasonable doubt. I have a few thoughts on this, but not sure how willing my folks will be to get involved. Most of their work has been for the state."

"I've got a guy," Jason said. "I'll call him today. I may need permission first from an old friend, but he's good. He's who shone the light on George Mitchell in the Cowan trial."

"Get him," Shay said. "Whatever it takes."

"Yes, ma'am. So who are our alternative suspects? Matty Dean has to be at the top."

Shay nodded. "Then Richard Griffith. No one's seen Griff since the Cowan trial, but he's got to be looked at pretty hard. A lifelong cop who lost everything because of his association with Cade. His family. Job. Everything. Him going AWOL and his name recognition should make for an explosive part of the trial."

"We know he was having an affair with Bella Flowers. Maybe she knows something."

"If she does, I doubt she'll tell us."

"Maybe, maybe not. She has to know by now that you wanted to prosecute Griff for her brother's murder after the dismissal of Cowan."

"She does know. I told her."

"Then maybe you should talk with her again. Last I spoke with her, she was a dancer at Jimmy's Lounge in Madison."

Shay rolled her eyes. "I bet you hated that interview."

"It was a tad awkward, but you gotta do what you gotta do. I can't go that far out of county, so you'll have to handle it, or we can sick Hooper on her."

"Hooper?"

"My profiler. You're gonna love him."

"All right, Dean and Griff are natural alternatives, but what about the checkout clerk?"

"Dooby Darnell," Jason said. "We've struck out with her so far. Phone number goes straight to voicemail, and address is abandoned."

"This is the info you got from the new clerk at the grocery."

Jason nodded. "Who was none too pleased to see us. I've got the Tonidandels trying to find her. They know the Sand Mountain landscape better than anyone, but so far they haven't found anything." Jason snapped his fingers. "I'm going to reach out to Trudy Cowan and maybe Trey too. They live in Alder Springs."

"And they owe you. Trey looked guilty as hell for Kelly Flowers's murder. Your work in that trial was extraordinary."

Jason gazed at his partner, who was now hammering away at the keys on her laptop, not paying him any attention, completely focused on the task at hand. "Thank you."

"The state's file will probably have a statement from Darnell. That ought to help some. That store was right in the heart of Tyson Cade country. I'm sure she knew him well."

"I'll get with the Cowans."

Shay stopped typing and looked at him. "Could either of them be alternative suspects?"

Jason looked down at the table. He knew there was no love lost between Trey Cowan and Tyson Cade. Could Trey have gone after him? Jason didn't think so. Trey didn't come off as a violent sort, and the trial last year had established his lack of expertise with guns. Still . . . *This is my life. We have to exhaust everything.* "It's possible," he finally said.

Jason was now staring at the wall, as the memories of last summer and fall came back to him. "There's also someone else."

"Who?"

"Colleen Maples. I called her as a witness during the Cowan trial. She was pretty much destroyed by Kelly Flowers, and she knew Flowers was working for Cade."

"Seems a long shot that she'd be involved in shooting Cade."

"Maybe not as the triggerman, but . . ."

Shay crossed her arms. "OK. Worth looking at. Do you want to take her?"

Jason sighed. "Not really." He had almost fallen off the wagon with Colleen. "But I will."

"OK. Sounds like a good division of assignments." Shay stood and folded up her laptop.

"Where are you going?"

"JaMoka's. Need a caffeine pickup and also wanted to see if there was any gossip about the case. It's a favorite spot of the criminal defense bar." She paused. "And of Wish French. I'd ask you to join me, but—"

"But I'm not one of the cool kids," Jason said, winking at her. "I get it. Go forth and learn something that helps us."

"I'll try." She crossed her arms. "What are you going to do?"

Jason cleared his throat. "Gonna see an old friend."

"About the case?"

Jason shook his head. "About something else."

41

They met at Charburger. The iconic grease joint off Highway 69 was a favorite of Jason's all the way back to childhood, when his parents would pick Jana and him up from a week at nearby Camp Cha-La-Kee and take them for a burger, fries, and a shake. When he walked inside and saw the old booths and the smell of onions frying on the grill hit him, the sensation brought on other memories. Lake summers. Suntan lotion. Chase in a bikini top and jean shorts, smacking Hubba Bubba original flavor and fishing off the dock. Old Lucas Rich, who always wore a short-sleeve button-down and slacks on the weekend as opposed to the long sleeves he'd don during the workweek, folding up his napkin and placing it down the front of his shirt, sipping Coca-Cola, and peppering Jana with questions about camp, occasionally asking Jason how his week had been. Their father letting them order shakes that were a bit too big so he could finish them off under the weight of their mother's disapproving eye. His doting mom, making sure they had napkins and silverware and that their mouths stayed clean. Did she ever even eat?

Jason paused for a moment at the entrance and allowed himself to . . . what? Smell the roses? That didn't seem appropriate given the setting, but perhaps figuratively it was. Amazing the nostalgia that an old booth and a blast of onions and grease could bring back. As he strode to the booth in the rear, where Ashley Sullivan sat examining the menu, he knew he had a long way to go to get his life back. But feeling gratitude for his childhood had to be a positive development.

When she got closer, he felt his heart rate pick up and butterflies in his stomach.

Ashley Sullivan wore jeans and a light-green blouse that matched her eyes. Her red hair had a few curls, and she was sporting bangs today, which was new. It had been almost eleven weeks since they'd seen each other, but it felt like eleven years.

"Hey," he said.

"Hey, back," she said, sliding into the seat across from him.

"Thank you for agreeing to meet," Jason said. Ashley was the president of the Alabama Lawyer Assistance Program and had been his mentor after Jason's first emergency suspension from the practice of law. That discipline had spawned from Jason taking a deposition while intoxicated. He'd been suspended for ninety days and required to go to rehab at the Perdido Addiction Center. One of the state bar's requirements after he was discharged was that he have a mentor from the Lawyer Assistance Program. When Jason hedged on picking a lawyer role model from a pool of candidates who he thought hated him, Ashley volunteered for the job. As she worked in Cullman, which was only an hour away, it was an easy commute for Jason that he had come to enjoy.

Over the course of a year and a half, they had become friends. Last summer and fall, Jason began to have other feelings for her. After his activities in the Cowan trial had led to a two-year suspension by the bar, Ashley comforted him, and he told her he wanted more than a friendship. Her response still stung. It related to the instruction a flight attendant gave parents when a plane was going down . . .

"You're still wrestling with your own oxygen mask . . . Until you get yours on, you aren't going to be good for anyone else."

Jason knew what she meant. He wasn't ready for a serious relationship. He was still on the edge of a relapse, which, of course, occurred right after his suspension.

"I almost didn't come," Ashley said, smiling and pushing a stray hair out of her eyes.

"But?"

She sighed. "But I missed you. And I've been very worried about you. I wanted . . . to call sooner. I just . . ."

Jason stared at a bottle of ketchup. "I don't blame you. I've been a trigger for other addicts my whole life. Chase. Nola. They were both worse off, because of being around me. You would have been no different." He continued to focus on the condiment but felt his hand being touched. "Besides, it's been a tad dangerous to be near me lately." At this, he turned around and saw Satch Tonidandel sitting at a table near the front door, drinking a milkshake. The colonel had arrived before Ashley and scoped the place, and Chuck was watching the parking lot. Jason wasn't going to take any chances with Ashley. It was selfish to have this meeting. He was putting her in danger.

They already know about Ashley, he told himself. *She doesn't live here, and her connection to me, at least on the surface, appears purely professional. She was my mentor. A colleague. Nothing more . . . nothing less . . .*

If only that were really true, Jason thought, nodding at Satch, who sipped from his milkshake, before turning back to Ashley.

"I heard about the bombing and the officer being killed. I'm sorry."

"Yeah, it was a bad scene." He paused. "Ashley, I don't want anyone I care about to get hurt. I've told Nola and Niecy to stay far away. I don't want you to get hurt either. I just . . . had to see you."

"It's OK." She frowned. "What about Chase?"

"Haven't heard from her since the Cowan trial . . . and I doubt I will."

"I'm sorry."

"I'm not. I was bad news for her. I hope she's happy wherever she is." Ashley squeezed his hand. "You're a good man, Jason."

"No, I'm not," he snapped back. "I'm a narcissist. An alcoholic. I'm selfish. I'm impatient." He sighed. "I could go on and on. Begging you to meet me is another example of all of the above."

"No, it's not. We're friends, and you reached out to me. I'm glad you did. When you are trying, you have a certain charm. That's what was so worrisome about your fall after the suspension. You quit."

Jason looked away.

"Why did you stop trying?"

"I guess I just figured it didn't matter anymore. That I'd done the very best I could. I won the Cowan case, which was impossible. I was proud of how I handled myself. I stayed sober despite the craziness of Chase and Nola leaving. And then the board slams me with two years, and you tell me you aren't ready for anything . . ." He trailed off.

"That's a cop-out," she snapped, removing her hand from his. She looked away from him. "Your life always matters. There are never any guarantees. Uncertainty is part of it. It goes hand in hand with the first rule of AA. You have to surrender control. *Completely.*"

"I know," Jason said. "You're right. About everything. Then and now. I wasn't ready then. I'm still not. I've been walking a tightrope between sobriety and full-out alcoholism for almost two years, and I'm still on it. I don't trust myself, so why should you? And my behavior after the suspension was shameful. I was using those failures as an excuse for drinking."

"A poor excuse," she added.

For a moment, there was silence, and a waitress came by for their orders. Jason wasn't hungry. He felt ashamed and embarrassed. He ordered a cheeseburger, fries, and a Coke as if on autopilot. Ashley did the same. They waited for their drinks. When the sodas were placed on the mat, Ashley put both hands on her glass and finally spoke. "I don't want to ever be a trigger for you, Jason."

"You aren't," he said. "You never were. To use your terminology, being with you has always been a defuser for me. Like lifting, watching old wrestling videos, music. It takes my mind off drinking."

"I'm glad," she said. "But I think you might be lying."

"No," he said. "I'm not. I feel uncomfortable right now, but I don't want a drink." It was the truth, and it felt weird saying it out loud.

"What do you want?"

Jason took a sip of Coca-Cola and held back a burp. He thought about the question. "To be a better man?" He didn't mean for it to come out as a question, but it had anyway.

Ashley laughed. "You are such a bullshitter."

"The truth would be a bit crude." He grinned at her, feeling a tingle in his loins. When was the last time he'd had that sensation?

Since I was with Ashley the last time, his brain answered.

She blushed and drank from her glass. "So . . . I hear you have a new partner?" She cocked her head at him.

"I didn't think you would want the job."

She rolled her eyes. "How many layers of bullshit do I have to get through to have a real conversation with you?"

"Several . . . probably."

"I think you made a wise choice, by the way. Hiring the former prosecutor. Bold." She paused for a moment. "I don't know Shay, but I've heard really good things. Smart. Hardworking. Fair."

"I'm lucky to have her," Jason said. He started to say more, but, before he could, a plate was pressed in front of him. He leaned down and breathed in the wondrous goodness of the burger and the salty fries, and his tummy rumbled. His stomach had settled down, and he was now hungry. Ashley Sullivan, his best defuser, had worked her magic again. He took a huge bite and made sure to chew slow. He wanted to savor the food and the company for as long as possible. He thought of Satch enjoying his milkshake and imagined his father downing the last of the chocolate shake that Jason always used to order but never could quite finish.

"Miss." He waved his hand at their server. "Could I order a chocolate shake?"

"Of course, hon. How about you?" She turned to Ashley.

"No thanks." She was squinting at Jason. "But I might have some of yours."

The tingle was back with a vengeance. "Sure."

She crossed her arms. "There's one other thing I noticed about Shay. I'm sure you've noticed it too."

"Oh, what's that?" He popped a fry in his mouth, and it burned his tongue.

"She's pretty."

Jason chewed fast as his mouth cursed him for not going in slow. "I hadn't noticed."

Ashley brushed a bang out of her face and shook her head. "Bullshit."

42

The crowd at JaMoka's was thin. Shay sipped her espresso and ate a bagel. The only lawyer in the place was Barry Martino, who was back in the window seat and typing furiously on his laptop.

As Shay turned to leave, Barry made the whole experience worthwhile. "You need to watch Wish and Barber."

"Oh." Shay turned to him. "Working 'from home,' Barry?" She made quote symbols with her hands. "Again."

"I work from everywhere. But, now that you're on my side of the bar, fair warning. You aren't Michael Jordan anymore. You won't get the calls."

"I see. Are you insinuating that the poor old criminal defense bar doesn't get a fair shake when going up against the district attorney?"

"Not insinuating," Barry said. He flipped his long hair, which he'd done up in a ponytail today. "I'm saying it. Especially now that Wish is back in the driver's seat. He's got a way of saying something that's completely incorrect in a way that sounds like it's straight from McMurtrie's Evidence hornbook."

"Seldom right but never in doubt," Shay added, nodding.

"Amen," Barry said.

"You sure were kissing Wish's ass the other day," Shay said. "I thought they were going to need pliers to get your lips unlocked from his hindside."

Barry grinned. "I rarely represent defendants who aren't guilty of something, Shay. It's the nature of the game. That means favorable plea deals are the best way to help my clients." He sighed. "And to get those, I have to grease the district attorney. I'm sure if you counted the pecks on your cheeks, I'd be in the lead like Secretariat at the Belmont."

The comment bordered on inappropriate, but Shay couldn't help but laugh. He was right.

"One more thing," Barry said. "With Wish, I much prefer cases in front of Virgil Carlton as opposed to Barber. Carlton is an asshole, but he calls balls and strikes and keeps things objective."

"You think Barber's dirty?"

Barry's grin widened, but his eyes were cold and clear. "As a pig in mud."

———

Shay walked out of JaMoka's and fell in step with Mickey Tonidandel, who had been watching the place from the outside. "Where're you headed?" Mickey asked.

"I'm going for a run, Captain."

"Right after coffee?"

"It's for work," she said, walking fast, not wanting to lose momentum.

"I have to follow you. The colonel's orders. But . . . I don't run."

When they had crossed Gunter Avenue, Shay asked, "Where's your truck?"

"Behind Jason's office."

She cleared her throat. "Behind whose office?"

"Uh, sorry. Behind your office."

"Can you drive me to the Sunset Trail?"

"Ma'am, I can't provide cover from the water. I think it's too dangerous."

"Too bad. It's the only way I could secure this meeting." She began to walk again. "And it's worth it."

———

Mickey dropped Shay off where the Sunset Drive Trail began, which was just off Lurleen B. Wallace Drive. Shay had changed at the office into joggers and a fleecy hoodie. Aviators covered her face.

She walked the first hundred yards and then began to pick up her pace. She saw a figure a couple hundred yards ahead of her that was wearing a similar outfit. Shay increased her pace and concentrated on her breathing. She ran three miles five days a week, but normally in silence. To her left, she saw Mickey's Ford F-150 truck easing along the road. She knew the captain was frustrated with her, but there was no way around it.

When she was a few feet from the person in front of her, she cleared her throat. "Mind if I join you?"

"Shay?" Emily Carton's face broke into a smile. "Of course."

"How do you like being the county coroner so far?"

"It's great," Emily said. She wore a gray headband, and her hair was already matted down with sweat. Shay knew the woman had already run a couple miles and was on her way back, as opposed to just starting like Shay. "The people have been awesome."

"The job's beneath you, and we both know it," Shay said.

Emily said nothing for a second. Then she sighed. "Dad asked me to do it, and I couldn't say no. It'll only be one term."

"I'm sure that's what Clem said when he started six terms ago."

Emily frowned. "He actually served seven."

"Exactly."

"What do you want, Shay? I'm sure this isn't a coincidence. Especially since we used to run together all the time and you know my routine."

"Wish hasn't shown me a damn thing yet."

"Well, as I understand it, the defendant isn't technically allowed any discovery until after the arraignment." She paused for a breath. "Which hasn't happened yet."

"True, but my office always produced our file before the arraignment. It was a courtesy that I learned from Wish."

"Maybe he's become a bit harsher in his advanced age."

"Or maybe he's just an asshole," Shay fired back.

"Maybe that too."

"I'm going to learn everything eventually, Emily, but I'd really appreciate the head start. Jason wants this trial fast tracked."

Emily shot her a glance. "How does it feel working for the enemy?"

"Honestly? I'm struggling with it. But with Wish French on the other side, it's hard to feel like we are doing wrong."

"What about Hatty? How does it feel going against her?"

Shay let out a breath. "Hard. I love Hatty. I had hoped to work with her."

"Would have been pretty awesome to have a woman district attorney, sheriff, and county coroner." Emily's face finally relaxed a little bit. "Let's walk for a while if you don't mind. This talking and running is putting a stitch in my side."

Shay slowed her pace to match Emily's.

"I went to the scene that morning. It was a beautiful day. I mean, gorgeous. Not a cloud in the sky."

Inside her pocket, Shay had her phone turned to the camera function. She hit the record button, hoping it would catch the sound. There was nothing unethical about tape recording a conversation without the other person's notice in Alabama, but it still felt wrong to Shay. Especially with a friend like Emily. But, alas, taking notes might draw suspicion. Talking to her at all at this juncture was a risk for Emily that could put her future in danger.

It's just the job, Shay said. *I want Jason to hear this, and I don't want to forget anything.*

"How long after the murder did you arrive on scene?" Shay asked.

"Not long. Dispatch got the call a few minutes after Cade was shot. Came in from an eyewitness who had been pumping gas."

"Name?"

"First name was Candy." Emily sighed. "Wish you would have called beforehand. I can't remember the last name off the top of my head."

"If I had called, you wouldn't have agreed to meet me."

Emily shrugged her agreement. "What did Candy say?"

"She responded after the shooting. Saw Cade on the ground."

"Did she know who he was?"

"No. She's not from the area. Visiting her mother in Albertville, who lives off Highway 75. I think Candy was from New Hope."

"What else?"

"Cade said something before he died."

"Go on."

"He said, 'I can't believe the bastard got me.' Then he said your client's name."

Shay scoffed. "You've got to be kidding?"

"I'm not. She also remembers seeing a dark SUV leaving the store, and a stoplight video puts Rich's maroon Explorer on Hustleville Road a few miles from the scene approximately ten minutes after Candy called 911."

Shay said nothing, feeling a sinking sickness come over her. She tried to hide it. "Any other witnesses?"

"The clerk. I think her first name is Dooby. Sorry."

"Marcia 'Dooby' Darnell," Shay added.

"Right. She saw the shooting. She had come out of the store to give Cade his change. Cade turned toward her, and he was shot."

"So the perp was firing from the direction of the store?"

"Yes. Probably a larger handgun. Based on my analysis, I'd say it is a larger-barrel nine millimeter." She paused. "We haven't found the murder weapon, but . . . it is consistent with a Glock 17."

"Why do you say that?"

"I really shouldn't say any more. You'll get all of this in discovery."

"Then there's no harm in telling me now." Shay snapped the words, letting her irritation show. She had been a hard-nosed prosecutor, but she hadn't played games. It was frustrating to know that Wish was holding out on her, but not surprising. "Emily, come on. You're better than this."

The coroner stopped walking and studied the lake. She leaned over and touched her toes, stretching her hamstrings, and then sipped from a water bottle. She spoke without looking at Shay. "The sheriff's office issued a warrant to search the Tonidandels' gun range. They found a purchase order for a Glock 17 made in early November by Jason Rich."

Shay felt a flutter in her stomach.

Emily cleared her throat and wiped sweat from her brow before continuing. "Rich also had a Glock 43X. That gun was found at his house. I tested the 43X with the bullet fragments uncovered from the victim's body and determined that it was not the murder weapon." She turned her head and stared at Shay. "But I wasn't able to test the Glock 17, because it wasn't discovered at Mr. Rich's home or either of his two vehicles during our search. It's missing . . . and is presumably wherever your client disposed of it after he shot and killed Tyson Cade."

Shay held Emily's gaze, but her heart was pounding. She struggled to blow off the coroner's well-reasoned conclusion as Emily began to walk again. "Oh good grief," Shay managed, following after her. "Don't be so glib, Emily. Cade had a lot of enemies, namely the wanted fugitive who now runs his outfit. This is a frame-up job and you know it."

"You sound convincing, Shay, but do you really think a jury is going to believe that? If Dean did it, then why did Cade identify Rich with his—what do you lawyers call it—dying declaration?"

"I can't answer that."

"Maybe because he saw his shooter?"

"Or maybe because he made the same presumptions that the sheriff's office and the new district attorney are making."

As they reached a bench, Emily sat down and began retying her shoes. "That's all I know. Because of when the call came in, we can identify time of death almost to the minute. I don't have my report in front of me, but it was approximately ten thirty a.m. We know Jason Rich was close by. We know he had a gun consistent with the murder weapon. We know he trained with it at the gun range owned by the Tonidandels. We know he was seen close to the scene right after the murder, and we know the victim identified Rich as the killer just seconds before he breathed his last." She finished her last knot and stood up, placing her hands on her hips. "Shay, you're good. But come on. Jason Rich is guilty. Have you ever seen evidence more damning?"

Shay wasn't sure if she had. It was as ironclad a prosecution case as she could ever recall.

"Is there anything . . . good you can tell me?" Shay finally asked, giving her old friend a tired smile.

Emily returned the gesture. "Only that no one . . . except maybe Cade . . . saw Jason Rich pull the trigger." She held out her palms. "That's it." She leaned over and touched her toes again and then stood back up. "Shay, I have to go. Please don't mention this conversation to anyone else."

"I won't. I need Candy's last name."

"And you'll get it from the district attorney when you request it." She started walking and spoke without looking over her shoulder. "Like everyone else."

Shay watched her leave and realized her legs felt weak. She sat down on the bench and gazed out at the water. Had she read the situation wrong? Could Jason really have done it?

She took in a deep breath of damp lake air and exhaled. She wasn't sure. But she understood now why Hatty was so adamant that Jason was guilty.

With all that evidence against him, how could he not be?

43

"Where's the gun?" Shay spoke through clenched teeth after she played the recording for Jason. They were back in the library. Jason was actually on a high after his lunch with Ashley Sullivan, but any good vibes quickly dissipated as he listened to the new county coroner break down the evidence against him.

The only thing new was the dying declaration of Tyson Kennesaw Cade.

Which is kind of a big deal . . .

"Damnit," Jason said, running his hands through his hair.

"Answer the question."

"I don't know," Jason said. It wasn't technically a lie. At this point, it was possible that wind and storms and a changing tide could have taken the gun far from his boat dock.

"I don't believe you."

"Shay, I spent the two weeks before my arrest in a drunken haze. I wasn't in my right mind."

"You were lucid enough to buy a Glock 17 that the sheriff's department hasn't been able to find. Do you have any idea where it might be? If you are innocent and we can locate the gun, it might completely absolve you of the murder. You understand that, don't you?" She paused. "Or maybe you got rid of the gun. Drove by a bridge like Waylon Pike did when your sister hired him to murder Braxton Waters and dropped it in the lake. Like sister, like brother, huh, Jason? Didn't want a ballistics expert like Emily Carton to match your gun to the bullets found in the victim's corpse, so you disposed of it."

"You're wrong," he said, feeling shame from his head to his toes. *Like sister, like brother . . .*

Jason knew dropping the gun in the lake made him look guilty as hell. He couldn't tell Shay. Especially not after what she'd just said. He'd defended Jana, who had, in fact, hired a handyman to kill her husband just as Shay claimed. Jason had helped a guilty client get away with murder.

She'll think I'm trying to do the same . . .

If I tell the truth, then I might as well pick out my prison cell. He sighed. *But how can I win this case if I don't testify? And if I take the stand, am I going to perjure myself?*

Jason didn't think he could do that. He gazed past Shay to the framed portrait of his father. *No,* he thought. *I won't lie under oath.* He moved his eyes back to Shay. *But if I tell her the truth now, she may walk away. It looks like she already wants to.*

"Jason . . ."

"Shay, I know as a prosecutor, you are trained to look only for the truth. But when you're a criminal defense lawyer, the focus is different."

"How so?" She was gritting her teeth again.

"Our focus has to be on what the state can prove beyond a reasonable doubt and on doing everything we can do to cloud that picture."

"Spoken from a man who has spent a career settling PI wheels cases."

"And who has successfully handled two capital murder cases in this county," Jason fired back.

Shay stood and walked toward the door. "I have to get out of here."

"You can quit whenever you want to," Jason said. "I'm sure the last thing you want to do is start your second career with a loss to Wish French."

"Fuck you, Jason. You're welcome, by the way. There's not a criminal defense attorney in this county or state who could have had an informal discussion with the county coroner prearraignment."

"I know that, Shay, I appreciate it. And we have some leads. Candy isn't that common a name, and New Hope is a small town. I'll have our investigator find her. And the info on Dooby Darnell sounds very fishy. Giving Cade his change?"

Shay nodded. "That does sound odd. Almost as if—"

"She might be in on it," Jason completed the thought. "It takes a village to frame someone."

"We have to find her."

"And we will. I'm gonna work on that tonight."

For a moment, the two stared each other down. Finally, Jason took a tentative step toward her. "Stay with me."

Shay waited in the doorway for a long three seconds. Then she gave a swift nod and left Jason alone with his thoughts.

He stayed in the library for a long time. He stared at his father's portrait and tried, for the umpteenth time, to put the pieces together for the morning of November 13, 2019. He'd woken up drunk. He'd started drinking again. He'd gotten his gun. The Glock 17. He'd driven to Alder Springs. Turned onto Hustleville Road.

Had he wanted to kill Tyson Cade?

Like sister, like brother.

A desire had been building for almost two weeks. He'd bought a new gun. Had done nothing but think about Harry and Jana and Braxton and Niecy and Nola and Izzy and Chase. And everyone in his hometown who'd had their life ruined or taken by Tyson Cade.

Why did I throw the gun away when I heard the police sirens? He squeezed his eyes shut, trying to think. Had he blocked it out? Had he done something so awful that he simply couldn't remember?

Have I lost my mind?

Jason felt tears forming in his eyes, and he wiped at them. He gazed at his father's gray eyes in the painting.

Like sister, like brother.

44

Some folks said that Memory Hill Cemetery in Albertville was haunted.

Weird cold spots. Odd noises. There was even a tale about hearing a young girl's voice singing "Amazing Grace."

Matty Dean was aware of the rumors. He'd lived in Marshall County his whole life and had half a dozen relatives buried in this vast space, including his parents.

Matty wasn't sure if he believed in ghosts, but there were times when he hoped the stories were true. He'd never experienced anything supernatural here or anywhere else. He'd like to believe there was something else out there, but he knew the harsh truth.

Life wasn't about spirits or angels. There were no cosmic forces. No religion.

Only choices.

He stared down at the headstone. He leaned a Twinkie and a Sun Drop up against it and squatted down, running a thumb over the name.

Tyson Kennesaw Cade.

The grave had been placed next to Tyson's mother, Ruthie Cade. Tyson had given Matty specific instructions on how he wanted to be buried. Next to his mom. No church funeral. Not even a graveside service.

He hadn't wanted any fuss. Just to be returned to his mom. That was it.

Matty wiped tears from his eyes. "I'm sorry, T. C. I really am. I wish you were still here. I wish . . . things had been different."

He rose to his feet and surveyed the vast lawn. Some of the markers were huge with a full paragraph written on them. But most, like the one for Tyson Cade, were a mere two feet by two feet with a name and two dates with a dash between them.

"We're gonna finish this," Matty said, staring at the grave. "Rich, the Tonidandels, the new sheriff . . ." Matty peered up at the sun, which was beginning its descent. "I won't rest until it's finished. I promise you that."

Matty stood by the headstone for several more minutes. Then he kissed his hand and placed it on top of the concrete. "Miss you, man. And . . . I'm sorry."

———

Matty took his time walking back to the car. He had some decisions to make. The Rich murder trial was beginning to pick up speed. An arraignment in two days. Then trial. Rich and his new partner would not sit still. They would stay mobile. Investigating. Meeting with witnesses. Doing all the things that lawyers did.

There will be opportunities, he thought, getting closer to the vehicle and making eye contact with the driver. *There already have been . . .*

He sat in the back, and the black SUV lurched forward. Butch Stephens was driving, and Lu was sitting next to Matty. There was no one in the passenger-side front seat. "You OK?" Lu asked, rubbing his leg.

"Fine. Look, Lu, what are your thoughts on taking another crack at Rich after the arraignment?" He knew the answer but wanted to hear her say it.

"Too risky. National Guard everywhere. Tonidandels too. I don't think we'll get a shot, and even if we do, the chances of getting caught are much greater now than at his hearing."

"I agree," he said.

Silence as the vehicle pulled onto Highway 431. "Matty, have you thought about just letting the district attorney and the sheriff do their jobs. If Rich goes to prison for the rest of his life, isn't that the best revenge? A lawyer losing his future in a trial. Seems perfect."

She had a point. "It does," Matty said. "But he's not enough. I want to take down the Tonidandels. I owe the sheriff one too. If we had killed her last year when we had the chance, Tyson might still be alive. Griff might not have been made. The whole thing might have turned out different." He paused. "We can't have Hatty Daniels in that spot. She's been a thorn in our side, and she has to go."

Lu said nothing.

Matty turned to look at her. "What? You disagree?"

"Haven't you been saying that Tyson took on too much? Tried to control everything. That's why they got him." She looked away from him. "I don't want that to happen to us."

Matty put his hand on the back of her neck and squeezed. Then he turned her head to face him. "*Us?* What do you mean . . . us?"

"I meant you."

Matty pinched her cheek. "I have to avenge Tyson. He was a god to our people. They expect that, and . . . I want that."

"I think you overestimate what our people want. It's been two months. *Our people* just want affordable meth and protection from prosecution."

Matty leaned away from her. "What's going on with you? I thought you understood how important it was to me to finish things. Tyson told me to take out Rich and the Tonidandels, but Rich got to him first. I have to finish it, Lu. For Tyson . . . and for me."

"I do understand," Lu said, scooting closer to him. "But, I'm worried that our people may see your actions more as a personal vendetta than a business decision."

"Is that how you feel?"

She touched his hand. "I just don't know that it's worth it, Matty. You're the boss now. Business is good. Why take any unnecessary risks?"

Matty ignored her and rolled down the window. The blast of cool air hit him, and it felt good. He left it open for a full minute, trying to clear his head of the doubts Lu had planted. Finally, he couldn't bear the chill anymore and clicked the up button.

Had he heard any noises in the cemetery? Little girls singing hymns? Strange spots that were even colder than the January chill?

No, he thought. But he had heard the voices in his head . . . and perhaps those coming from under the grave, and they were singing a different tune than Lu Stephens.

Finish it . . .

As the SUV pulled into a used-car dealership off Highway 75, Matty was opening the door before Butch brought the vehicle to a stop.

"Matty?" Lu's voice was higher than normal. Desperate?

He put one foot on the asphalt and gazed at her. "I'm taking you and Butch off the Tonidandels' detail, Lu. Chief's gonna take over."

She recoiled as if he'd struck her in the face. "Matty, I'll get them. I always do."

He shook his head. "I know you would, but we need to make a change. Chief is ex-military and has some friends from his time in the army who are even more ornery than him."

"At least let us help," Lu said. "I've been tracking them for weeks."

"And you haven't found an opening," Matty snapped. "I want to make a change. Besides, I need you for something else."

"What's that?"

He scrutinized her, seeing the hurt in her eyes. "This isn't a demotion, Lu. I'm just rearranging the deck to utilize my talent better."

"What do you want, Matty?"

"How well do you know Dooby Darnell?"

She blinked. "I mean, we aren't best friends or anything, but I'm from the Sprangs. Everyone knows everyone. She's brought her and her momma's car into the shop a few times. I heard the rumors about her and Tyson . . ." She hesitated. ". . . hooking up. And I've also heard she hasn't worked at the Alder Springs Grocery since Tyson was killed. Why?"

Matty patted her knee. "I need you to find her."

45

Jason sat at the booth, picking at his catfish. He'd barely eaten since his tense encounter with Shay at the office, but he knew he needed to keep moving. The day had been an emotional roller coaster, and he was fighting an all-too-familiar urge.

Satch had driven him here, and the colonel was sitting alone, two tables down. Chuck was watching the parking lot, and Mickey had stayed to guard the house.

One of the only bright spots of his defense of Trey Cowan last year were his visits here, at Top O' the River restaurant, with Trey's mother, Trudy. She had smiled when he sat down in her section, though Jason could tell that many of the other patrons were uncomfortable.

It wasn't often that a man charged with murder ordered catfish in the same restaurant as you. The fact that an assassination attempt had been made on Jason a couple months ago probably wasn't doing anything to ease concerns. After a few minutes, Jason noticed that only he and Satch were sitting upstairs. The place had cleared out.

He hated that his presence was hurting a local institution. He'd been a bit more incognito at lunch at Charburger, sitting in a back booth, but it was a smaller spot, and he'd met Ashley early in the lunch hour.

Top O' the River was a huge, open place. He'd begun to hear the murmurs the minute he walked in the door, and they hadn't stopped once he sat down. Trudy had brought a menu over, and Jason had ordered his usual. When he told her he needed to talk with her, even her good vibes evaporated. By the time she ambled over a few minutes after setting his plate down, she looked exhausted. "I suspect I know why you're here."

"How've you been?"

"Better," she said. Then she reached across the booth and put her hand on top of his. "But I've also been worse. Jason, I'll never forget what you did for Trey. If there was any way I could help you, I would."

"But . . ."

"But I don't know where Dooby is. We're friends. We have been forever. And I haven't seen her since Tyson's murder."

"Has she called? Texted? Written a letter? Anything?"

Trudy pulled at her ear. "She called a week after she left. Said she couldn't stand everyone's stares and needed some space. I think she may have gone to Florida to live with her sister, Anna."

"Where in Florida?"

"Fort Walton. Anna's a waitress at Hightide. Ever been there?"

Jason shook his head.

A vacant smile came to Trudy's face. "We went to Fort Walton once as a family. When Trey was a boy. Stayed with Anna. She has a place a couple miles from the ocean, but there are a lot of great public beaches in that area. For three days, Walt and I drank cheap beer and ate seafood while Trey swam until his arms and legs were burnt crisp. We ate at Hightide twice. They got clam strips there. You ever had 'em?" She shook her head. "Better 'n shrimp or crab claws, if you ask me."

Jason took a sip of tea, enjoying the warmth of Trudy's memory. He remembered a few similar trips with Jana and his folks to the beach as a kid, but they'd never been to Hightide. "Isn't Fort Walton pretty close to the 30A area where Walt works?" Jason knew it was, but he was trying to keep her talking.

"Yeah."

"Have you spoken with Anna since the shooting?"

"I called her and asked if Dooby was there. She said no."

"Do you believe her?"

She sighed. "Who the hell knows, Jason. Dooby is an eyewitness to Tyson Cade's murder. That makes her a rather important person to the sheriff's office, the district attorney . . . and to Tyson's successor."

"Matty Dean," Jason said.

Trudy frowned, and her face paled. "I never liked that man."

Jason leaned closer. "What can you tell me about him, Trudy?"

"Not much. Matty's always played things close to the vest. But he was Tyson's right-hand man for a reason. When Tyson needed dirty work done . . . and I think you know what I mean by that . . ." She trailed off, and her face got even whiter.

Jason winced, seeing an image of Harry Davenport's dead eyes. "I know exactly what you mean."

"I know." Trudy squeezed his arm. "But I've heard rumors of a rift between them before the shooting."

Jason felt a flicker of life run through him. "What kind of a rift?"

"Matty wasn't too happy about being arrested right before Trey's trial. He blamed Tyson."

"Where did you hear that?"

She looked behind her shoulder and then back down at the table.

"We're the only ones here, Trudy."

She snorted. "And whose fault is that? You've cleared the place out."

"Please . . . who told you about Matty being unhappy with Tyson? That's a potential motive for murder. I'm grasping at straws here. I believe that Matty Dean framed me for Tyson's murder."

"I can't, Jason."

"Trudy, I represented Trey, and we won. He could have gone to jail for a crime he didn't commit. Please . . . I need your help."

Trudy sighed. "I heard it from Dooby. A couple of days before Tyson was killed."

"Good grief," Jason said, sitting bolt upright in his seat. "Trudy, it's even more critical now for me to find her. Is there anything you're not telling me about Dooby?"

Trudy shook her head, but her eyes were hollow, and she looked like she might be sick. "I'm sorry, Jason."

———

Jason followed Satch to the Raptor with his mind racing. "We have to find her, Colonel. She may be the key to this whole thing."

Satch stopped when they reached the truck. He put his boot up on the trailer hitch and leaned his elbow against the top of the tailgate. "You think Trudy's shooting straight with you?"

"Yes," Jason said. "I mean. I guess. Why would she lie?"

"There's a code of honor on Sand Mountain, Jason. They watch after their own. Didn't you say Trudy spoke pretty highly of Tyson Cade? That he looked after her after her husband left."

"Yeah."

"Well, maybe Trudy's looking after Dooby Darnell. The woman is obviously smack-dab in the middle of this thing. And if Matty Dean did get her involved . . . then he might be wanting to be rid of her."

The lifeline that Trudy Cowan had just provided him was precarious, and Jason felt a sinking sensation in the pit of his stomach. "All the more reason to find her."

46

No one would confuse the Hampton Inn off I-59 in Gadsden for the Ritz Carlton Atlanta.

But, as hotels went, it wasn't awful. Breakfast was free every morning, there was a fitness center with some dumbbells and a treadmill. Best of all, there was a Mexican restaurant located literally in the parking lot that had two-dollar margaritas from four to six every evening.

Marcia "Dooby" Darnell sat at the bar of the Old Mexico Cantina & Grill and sucked salt off the rim of her glass. She'd already drained one margarita and was thinking of having another. It was 5:45 p.m., and the crowd was beginning to thicken. She needed to order some food, but she wasn't hungry. She missed her home.

She even kinda missed her job.

But she didn't miss Tyson Cade.

I'm glad he's dead.

Barely a day went by when she didn't relive the seconds right before the shooting.

"Another one, hon?" The bartender was a twentysomething woman named Mandy. Dooby had introduced herself several times, but Mandy's eyes never seemed to register recognition. As always, she looked at Dooby like she was a complete stranger.

Which, of course, I am. Drinking at the same watering hole every night doesn't make me an old friend, and Mandy only works twice a week.

The other bartender, a short man with a mustache named Earl, did sometimes address her by name. *But he works three nights a week . . .* She gritted her teeth. *. . . and he wants to get in my pants.*

Dooby had told Earl that her name was Marcia, as she didn't want to draw attention to herself, so it took her a few seconds sometimes to even realize he'd called after her. It was her daddy who'd called her Dooby; she'd never escaped it and had grown to embrace the nickname.

"Ma'am," Mandy repeated. "Can I get you another margarita? It's last call for happy hour." Dooby was about to say no, but then she saw a familiar face walking toward her in the mirror.

"Sure. Why not."

"Coming right up."

The man sat in the vacant seat next to her and ordered a Tecate beer. Once the full drinks were in front of them, he turned and held his bottle out for a toast.

She clinked it with her glass.

"To Tyson Cade," he said.

Dooby frowned. "I'll drink to that bastard's death," she added, before licking the salt on the rim and taking a long sip. The second drink was a little stronger than the first, and Dooby winced as the tequila burned her throat. "What's new?" she asked.

"Nothing yet. The arraignment is tomorrow. Then we'll know the trial date."

"Crutch, I can't hide out here forever. Matty—"

"Won't find you. I promise." Frank Crutcher's voice was firm, and he tugged on the bill of his cap. "But we have to be careful. Have you seen anything fishy or unusual?"

"No. But I'm so restless. I work out. I watch Netflix. I come here and drink. I miss my friends. My life."

"Do you miss worrying about Matty Dean slitting your neck?"

She held her glass with both hands to keep them from shaking. "I do that anyway. Staying here doesn't take the worry away. And I'm going to have to come back eventually."

"Not unless you are subpoenaed. And they can't subpoena you unless they can find you."

"Are you sure?"

Frank nodded. "Once we know the trial date, we'll regroup. But if it's only going to be a few more months, you better get used to your current surroundings."

Dooby gazed up at the ceiling. "Do you really think he'll kill me?"

"Dooby, look at me."

She rolled her eyes, sighed, and then finally peered at Frank Crutcher.

"If Matty Dean finds you . . . he will kill you."

She reached for her drink and took a long sip, spilling a bit down her chin. *"Why?"*

"You know damn well why."

Tears filled Dooby's eyes, and she tried to gather herself. She noticed that Mandy was watching her.

"Just hold tight," Frank said. He had lowered his voice to a whisper. "You had to do something. You said it yourself."

Dooby nodded and drank the rest of her glass in one gulp. Some of the ice got on her face, and she wiped it off.

"Dooby, you've got to keep it together."

"What am I going to do?"

He grabbed both of her hands. "You're going to be patient and not bring any attention to yourself. Just like you been doing."

"And what if Matty finds out that you've been helping me?"

"He won't," Frank said.

She felt a tickle in her throat and coughed, and then she looked at her reflection in the mirror. "I'm scared."

"I know," Frank said.

She turned to him. "I'm so scared."

47

As expected, the gallery was empty when Jason and Shay were escorted inside the double doors of the courtroom. Four National Guardsmen were in front of them and four in back. Taking no chances, despite the military presence, Jason had Satch stationed right outside the door. Mickey was in the lobby. And Chuck was running reconnaissance outside.

Judge Terry Barber was already seated at the bench with a court reporter at her desk below the pulpit. Wish French was standing in front of the prosecution table, and Sheriff Hatty Daniels was right beside him.

"Let's get this over with," Barber said, holding up his hand to the court reporter. Then he gave the thumbs-up and cleared his throat. "State of Alabama versus Jason James Rich." He gazed over the bench with his spectacles pushed low over his nose. Gone was the usual nasally southern arrogance of his tone. Barber had been almost giddy during the Trey Cowan trial last year and also the petty trespass charge the state had brought against Jason during the Cowan matter. He seemed to enjoy the theater of trial and loved being at the center of it. Now, though, the weight of what had already happened in this case appeared to be wearing him down. An officer was dead. The National Guard surrounded the courthouse. There were no spectators. Terry Barber looked like he'd rather be almost anywhere else. "This is the arraignment of the defendant," Barber said. "Are there any matters to take up before Mr. Rich enters his plea?"

"None, Your Honor," Wish French said, buttoning his coat and then frowning at Jason.

"No," Jason said.

"All right then. Mr. Rich, you have been charged with first-degree murder by intentionally taking the life of Tyson Kennesaw Cade. How do you plead?"

"Not guilty."

"OK, Counsel, please approach. Wish, what are you thinking with respect to a trial date?"

"We could be ready tomorrow, Judge. It's really up to the defendant."

Barber scowled. "Well, tomorrow's out, and I've got trials set for every week in February. The earliest I have is March 9." He glanced up at Jason.

"Your Honor," Shay started, "we probably need a bit more—"

"That's fine," Jason interrupted. "March 9 . . ." He stared at Wish. ". . . works for us."

"Very well then. Sheriff Daniels, I trust that you have provided a safe way for Mr. Rich and Ms. Lankford to exit the courthouse."

"Yes, sir," Hatty said.

"Good." Barber stood and pressed his glasses back. "I'll see you all on March 9."

———

"Are you crazy?" Shay asked Jason as soon as His Honor was out of earshot. "That is less than two months away. How in the hell are we going to be ready in seven weeks?"

"We will be," Jason said.

"Should've listened to your partner, Rich," Wish said, pausing as he walked by them. "If you're up for serving twenty years in prison, we can probably work out a plea bargain. What are you? Thirty-five? Thirty-six? That puts you out in your midfifties. A lot of life left."

"No thanks," Jason said.

Wish took a step toward him, staring at Jason with a cocksure grin. "You know, I really thought you and old Lucas Rich were like night and day, but I'm starting to see similarities. Lucas could be a hothead too. Especially when he was losing." Wish leaned closer. "I saw that side of him a lot." The district attorney turned and headed for the double doors.

Jason wanted to yell "Fuck you" but stopped himself. He looked at Shay, but she, too, was scowling at Wish.

"Are you two ready to go?" Hatty asked.

Jason moved his gaze from Shay to Hatty and then back to Shay. "Hey, lookee here. The three amigos back together again."

Hatty and Shay both rolled their eyes. "The Guardsmen are waiting," the sheriff said.

Shay grabbed her briefcase and purse while Jason snatched his file jacket from the table. "We can do it," he said to Shay. "We'll be ready."

"You better hope we are."

———

Satch dropped Shay off at the office. "Have my men been watching your place?"

"Yes, they have. I think my mom is worrying them to death, though. They'll all probably be shot while she serves them lemonade."

"She's a fine lady."

"I know, Colonel. Thank you." She touched his shoulder. "And thank you for the protection."

"Virgil and Wyatt Onkey are two of the best. I'd have them watch my own mom . . . if she were still alive."

She gave him a tired smile. "Thanks again."

———

Satch was halfway back to Mill Creek before Jason said a word. He hadn't said anything to Shay on the short drive from the courthouse to the office. He knew he was in the doghouse with her, but he had decided to trust his instincts.

The universe likes speed. It was something he believed. If it was worth doing, it was worth doing fast.

It was Friday morning. January 10. Almost exactly two months from trial. Eight and a half weeks, not seven. He would have reminded Shay of her miscalculation if she was still in the car, but she wasn't.

By the time the Raptor was turning onto Mill Creek Drive, he'd received a text from his new partner.

I hope to hell you aren't taking the day off. We have a lot of work today. Are you OK with the discovery I've drafted?

Jason chuckled. He was again reminded of how fortunate he was to have Shay on his team.

Discovery is fine. Please serve ASAP. I have a meeting.

The three dots appeared immediately on his phone, followed by:

With who?! We're a team, Jason. We make decisions together. We talk with each other before we interview witnesses.

Jason sighed but then smiled as he saw the familiar figure chatting with Chuck and Mickey in front of his house. He typed out a quick return text.

I'm meeting with the profiler I told you about. The one that's going to dig up all the dirt and scoop on Tyson Cade, Matty Dean, Richard Griffith, Dooby Darnell and whoever else we think might be involved in Cade's murder.

Hooper? Shay responded.

"The man, the myth," Jason said out loud before texting back the thumbs-up emoji.

48

Albert Hooper didn't need much convincing. "You had me at twenty-five thousand flat fee." He held out his hand, which Jason shook.

"Hooper, this is going to be dangerous. Much worse than the help you gave on the Cowan trial."

"Are you kidding? Jason, I've been keeping up with this case. The most famous lawyer in the state is on trial for the murder of a meth lord and he's defending himself pro se and there's already been an assassination attempt on his life. I'm in, man." Hooper wore a button-down collared shirt with the script *A* of the Alabama Crimson Tide, khaki pants, and penny loafers. He resembled a fraternity pledge at the University of Alabama. He had a pudgy belly, a round face, and dark hair that he rarely combed. To say that he didn't look the part of a hard-boiled investigator was an understatement.

Hooper had been recommended by a lawyer out of Pulaski named Bocephus Haynes. Bo had done some work for Hatty Daniels last year, and his path had crossed with Jason's. They'd become friends, and Bo's advice had been helpful to Jason. He'd called Bo yesterday and obtained his blessing to use Hooper.

"Glad to hear it." Jason clapped him on the back. "And I hope you're ready to start. Trial is set for March 9."

"I can't wait," Hooper said, walking to his car, which was a tan Nissan Maxima with a "Tide Pride" bumper sticker. He pulled out his laptop and a duffel bag and pointed at the house. "In fact, I've already started. Let's go inside and I'll show you."

"OK," Jason said. "What's with the overnight pack?"

Hooper raised his eyebrows up and down and glanced at Mickey Tonidandel. "Always bring one just in case."

"In case what?"

"I get a tempting offer . . . like buckets of beer and crawfish at a place called Crawmama's."

Jason gazed past him to Mickey and held out his palms. "You really think that's a good idea after what happened last time?"

Hooper frowned. "What happened last time, Captain?"

"No big deal. We stopped a woman and her son from trying to kill us. Just another night in Marshall County. You're still in, aren't you?"

Hooper looked at Jason and then back at Mickey. Then he grinned wide, showing a set of bleached white teeth. "RMFT."

Mickey guffawed. "Roll motherfucking Tide." He looked at Jason. "I think I'm gonna like this guy."

49

Jason sat at the kitchen table alone. He drank unsweet tea and gazed out at the lake. After Hooper had filled him in on his work so far, Jason had declined dinner at Crawmama's. Though the food sounded great, his psyche was fragile, and seeing the other men drink might act as a trigger for him.

Satch had also stayed behind, and he was outside guarding the house. He'd be there until his brothers returned. If the colonel was truly sick, he was doing a hell of a job disguising his condition.

Of course, a man like Satch Tonidandel probably had a much higher threshold for pain than most normal humans.

Jason took out his phone. He had a couple of texts from Izzy, checking in on his spirits after the arraignment. Without conscious thought, he thumbed a response. **All good.**

But all wasn't good. He was tired. Lonely. And a bit overwhelmed by the task in front of him.

Hooper's work was helpful. He'd tracked down the listings of property owned by Richard Griffith. It was a good way to find the former sheriff, and Jason would probably start on that this weekend. What exactly would he say if he was able to find the onetime lawman? The man who had murdered Kelly Flowers in cold blood but had gotten away with it because Matty Dean, or perhaps Griffith himself, had killed George Mitchell.

What were you doing on November 13? Were you close to the Alder Springs Grocery? Did you kill Tyson Cade?

Jason sighed. Griff, as Hatty called him, had proved himself slippery and quite the survivor. Why would Jason's case be any different?

Still, the property he owned was something. Griff's criminal record was, as you'd expect, completely clean. No lawsuits either. Only a divorce from his wife. And while divorce files had been very helpful in his last two murder trials, Griff's was a dead end except for the timing.

Cheryl Griffith had filed her petition to dissolve the marriage two weeks after the close of the Cowan trial . . . and exactly one week before Tyson Cade was shot to death.

Cheryl still lived in the home she and Griff had once shared on Neely Avenue. According to Shay, Griff had disappeared during the investigation of him in connection with George Mitchell's murder. Alas, no charges were filed after George's death.

Jason started a list. They'd need to meet with Griff's ex and go from there. A meeting with the former sheriff might go nowhere, but they could at least serve him with a subpoena. That would get Wish's attention. Given Griff's motive and prior stature in the community, crossing him would still be a big moment in the trial. Even if he denied any involvement, Jason could hopefully plant the seeds of doubt.

Richard Griffith had been investigated for murder.

Matty Dean was a fugitive.

Weren't both better alternatives for the killing of Tyson Cade than Jason?

And what about Marcia "Dooby" Darnell? Jason's drunken haze of a memory and the PTSD he'd suffered since the shooting at his office had blocked a lot out. He was still struggling with his own actions on the morning of November 13. But . . .

. . . *I never spoke with Dooby Darnell.*

If Dooby was involved in some way with the murder of Tyson Cade, then Jason could definitely say that he never spoke with her about it.

That's something, he thought. He wrote "no connection to Dooby Darnell" on his pad in a box to the right.

He sipped the tasteless tea and smiled. He enjoyed brainstorming a case. Got a thrill from seeing pieces come into place.

Hooper had also gotten the last-known address of Dooby Darnell, which matched what the new clerk, Frank Crutcher, had provided. There was, in fact, a sister in Fort Walton, Florida. Anna Darnell. Hooper had volunteered to fly down and see if Dooby was there, but they both doubted she would be.

Too easy. If she was, in fact, hiding out because she was afraid of Matty Dean, then the last place she would go is Fort Walton. She'd be found, and she'd put her family in danger. Where could she be then? And had Trudy Cowan been telling the truth?

Jason finally stood and walked out into the sunroom. From here, he could see the back of Chase Wittschen's house, which had been unoccupied since the Cowan trial. *Where are you, Savannah Chase Wittschen?* he wondered. He hoped, wherever she was, that she had found some peace.

She would have never found it with me.

He'd now been to three AA meetings, and one thing he'd heard several of the members say was that they didn't start healing until they learned how to be alone. To deal with the pain and know that it wasn't going to kill them. And to eventually . . . let it go.

Jason walked out onto the deck and viewed the bridge over Highway 79. Then below him to where Satch Tonidandel held an AR15 and leaned against a brick column on the patio downstairs. Jason almost said something but thought better of it. He went inside the house and passed the kitchen and then looked at a closed door that he hadn't opened since he'd been home. His parents had built Jana a suite during high school. Up there was her room, and Jason hadn't been able to look.

It was sacred ground.

But, on this Friday, January 10, approximately sixty days from the trial of his life, he figured what the hell. He opened the wood door and began to climb the steps.

50

On the rocks below the Highway 79 bridge, Matty Dean glared across the water at the soldier standing guard over Jason Rich's house. "What do you know about him?" he asked.

Chief spat in the water and cast his line. "Same as you. None of it good."

"I'm surprised Lu never was able to get a shot."

Chief grunted. "Maybe she had one and didn't take it. Or missed."

Matty regarded the big man, thinking about the doubts Lu had raised about their mission after he'd visited Tyson's grave. *I just don't know that it's worth it . . . why take any unnecessary risks?*

"You think Lu would lie?" Matty asked.

"If she was embarrassed about coming up short . . . yes, I do."

Matty threw out his own line. "Doesn't matter. Is there anything new?"

"The other two brothers went into town. Rich has got some kind of computer nerd working the case for him, and they are going to dinner with him. Guy named Albert Hooper."

"Guys like that can be very valuable."

"Want me to take him out?"

"Not yet. Going after this Hooper . . . or even Mickey Tonidandel's girlfriend is going to be gratuitous and just make them more determined. It won't *hurt* them."

"And you can bet they'll have security too. The Tonidandels aren't completely alone. They've got Virgil and Wyatt Onkey watching his lady partner's house."

"Goddamn. When did those two get out of Pell City Correctional?"

"Not that long ago. They're crazy as hell . . . but also very loyal to Satch. He was their colonel too."

"What about your crew?" Matty asked. "How loyal are they?"

"They'll do whatever I tell them."

"How many?"

"Counting me? Ten. All skilled in the use of assault rifles. And any other weapon used to kill. I also have two cousins that were marines. Big time meth heads now, but they're on board." He paused. "Twelve total."

Matty nodded. "I like those odds." He reeled in his line and then pointed at the house. "Before trial, I want to wound that sonofabitch. I want him to bleed. I want him to understand that he doesn't have the high ground. Once we hurt one of the Tonidandel brothers—and I don't care which one—we can start picking off the others, including the IT nerd and the youngest brother's girlfriend. I want the colonel to understand that he's dealing with Matty *fucking* Dean. And I want Jason Rich to realize that going to prison for the rest of his life might not be the worst thing." Matty licked his lips and threw out his line.

"Do I make myself clear?"

"Yes, sir," Chief said.

51

The king guest room on the top floor of the Hampton Inn Gadsden could hardly be described as a penthouse suite. But it wasn't uncomfortable. Dooby lay on the bed, her phone in hand. She had so many text messages from friends that she had not returned. Crutch had managed to get word to her sister, Anna, that she was OK. He'd also verified with the nursing home that her mother was stable.

And with one exception, Dooby had managed to avoid contact with anyone from Alder Springs.

It was hard hiding out. But when she even thought about answering the phone, all she could see in her head was Matty Dean. Tyson had done things to her that still haunted her dreams. It was why she had agreed with the plan.

She'd heard the rumors about Matty. Knew what a dangerous man he could be. Knew that Lu Stephens worked with Matty and that the woman was meaner than a pit viper.

As Dooby's phone began to vibrate and the screen read "Trudy Cowan," she closed her eyes. She needed human contact.

If she didn't talk to someone besides Crutch soon, she might bust. She'd thought of inviting Earl, the bartender from Old Mexico, to come over. But she hadn't been with a man since Tyson, and she knew she wasn't ready. Besides, what if he was like Tyson? What if he wouldn't stop if Dooby said no.

Tears streaked her face, and she pulled the covers over her head.

Her phone continued to buzz.

52

When Trudy Cowan arrived home, she was exhausted. All she wanted to do was open a cold PBR, eat a can of StarKist tuna, and watch old MASH reruns until she fell asleep in her recliner. But when she opened the door, she saw a woman waiting for her in the kitchen.

"Hey, Miss Trudy."

Lu Stephens was sitting with her feet on the table. A sawed-off shotgun lay on the place mat in front of her.

"How'd you get in my house?" Trudy asked.

"Door was open. Like always."

Trudy knew that it wasn't open. She had become religious about locking her door since Trey's arrest for murder last year and having a brick thrown through her window during the trial. She faked a smile. "Well now, Luann, how are you?" She trudged to the fridge and pulled a can of Pabst Blue Ribbon out. "Beer?"

"No thanks."

Trudy opened hers and took a long sip, knowing that this surprise visit couldn't be a good thing.

"Actually, Miss Trudy, I'm not too good." She tapped her fingers on the shotgun. "You see, I need to speak with Dooby Darnell, and she's done run off and disappeared."

"I know," Trudy said, taking a seat across from Lu at the table. "I think she was really spooked by what happened." Trudy paused. "I mean, she was right there when Tyson . . ."

"I need to talk with Dooby, Trudy. And something tells me that you know where she is."

Trudy gazed at the can of beer. She'd lied to Jason Rich last night, and she'd felt guilty about it. The billboard lawyer had helped her son. She owed him. But . . .

. . . *I knew this day would come.*

Everyone in Alder Springs knew how close Trudy and Dooby were. She figured a visit like this was inevitable, but it still caught her off guard. "Why do you need to see her?" Trudy asked.

"Oh, my friend Matty has some questions he wants to ask her."

Trudy felt her stomach roll. She didn't think she could drink any more of the beer and doubted she'd be able to eat anything either. "What's he want with her?" Trudy snapped the question, meeting Lu's eye. The two women scrutinized each other. Trudy had no weapon, but she'd been good to Lu when the other woman was younger.

"Same reason the sheriff's department wanted to talk with her. He has some questions about Tyson's death."

"Or maybe he wants to make sure she never tells what she knows."

Lu put her hand on the sawed-off shotgun and scooted the handle closer to her. Almost half the weapon was hanging off the table. "Trudy, I think you know where she is. And I think it's in your best interests to tell me."

"My best interests? You gonna come into my house and shoot me, Luann? If I don't give you what you want, you're gonna just kill me? That my repayment for watching after you when you was in high school and your daddy died?"

"I'm not going to hurt you, Trudy. I couldn't do that. Now Trey's a different story. He's already caused our operation quite a bit of trouble, and my son, Butch, is actually watching him tonight. Said he's doing a little fishing. I'd hate for him to have a boating accident."

"You little cunt bitch."

Lu grabbed the gun and pointed it at Trudy. "Now that's no way to talk to someone who's holding your son's life in her hands. And if you keep calling me such ugly names, I may just end you too."

Trudy felt nauseous. She wasn't sure if Lu was bluffing, but she'd be damned if she wanted to fuck around and find out.

Lu cocked her gun and stood. "I got shit to do, Trudy. Where's Dooby?"

Trudy swallowed, feeling her heartbeat thudding. *God forgive me.* "Gadsden." She whispered the words. "She said she's in Gadsden in walking distance to a Mexican restaurant."

"Very good, Trudy."

"You're not going to hurt my boy, are you?"

Lu walked past her to the door. She held the sawed-off shotgun out, and the biceps on her arm bulged. Trudy had never realized how strong Lu was. Physically and in every other way. "Only if you're lying, Trudy."

"I'm not," Trudy managed.

"I hope not," Lu said right before she slammed the door shut.

———

Trudy drank her dinner. After confirming that Trey was still alive, she killed four PBRs at the kitchen table. By the time she crushed the last can, her hands had finally stopped shaking. She took out her phone. She wanted to call Dooby but knew she couldn't. If Lu got wind that she'd helped Dooby escape, then she'd be back. If Tyson Cade were still running the Sand Mountain meth operation, Trudy knew that tonight's episode would never have happened. She had practically raised Tyson. *He took care of us . . .*

As she finally sat in her recliner, she didn't bother turning on the television. Trudy closed her eyes and prayed.

God forgive me.

53

Matty Dean was in the car with Chief when the call came in. He listened to her talk and then made up his mind in a half a second. "Go. Now."

"On my way," Lu said. "And when I find her?"

"Hold her until I get there."

A long pause. "You're coming too?"

Matty chewed on a toothpick and nodded. "Call when she's with you."

"Yes, sir."

"Where we going?" Chief asked.

"Hampton Inn off 459 in Gadsden."

Chief entered the address into his GPS. "Thirty-five miles. Fifty-two minutes."

Less than an hour, Matty thought, as Chief pressed the accelerator down.

54

Lu had Butch pull into a parking space once they arrived at the hotel. "Wait here," she said, then hopped out of the truck and speed-walked toward the entrance to the hotel. After the automatic sliding door opened, she ran toward the front desk. "I need to find my sister, Marcia Darnell. I know she's been staying at this hotel for a while on a work assignment, but I can't remember the room number, and she's not answering my calls. Her momma's had a heart attack, and she needs to come home right now. It may be too late as it is. Can you please help me?"

The receptionist was a thin balding man probably in his late twenties, early thirties. He talked with a lisp. "Let me see here. Oh dear. OK. I know that name." He glanced above his computer at Lu. "I can't tell you her room number. It's company policy."

"Her momma's about to die, and you want to talk about company policy. Tell me the damn room number or I'm going to knock on every damn door here."

"Why don't I just ring the room, and then—"

"Didn't you hear me? She isn't answering the phone."

"Ma'am, I can't."

"Give me the goddamn room number!" Lu screamed, walking toward the elevator. "I'm going to start at the top and work my way down. Every room. You're gonna have a lot of complaints."

"I'll call the police."

"Call them. I don't care. I have to find my sister."

She pressed the up button to the elevator and saw the receptionist coming around the desk. "I'm going to take you to the room."

Lu started to object but then forced herself to smile. "Oh, thank you so much."

———

Dooby was still lying in bed with the covers pulled over her head when she heard the knocks.

"Dooby, open up! Open up right now!"

She ran to the door and cracked it. "Crutch? I thought you had gone back—"

"Let's go."

"But my things."

"Forget them. There's no time."

"What's going—"

"Matty's on his way. He'll kill you if he finds you."

"Let me get my—"

But Frank Crutcher pulled her through the door and pushed her toward the stairs. "There's no time."

———

After three knocks with no answer, Lu began to fake whine. "Can you please open this door? My sister is a deep sleeper, and I have to bring her home."

"Ma'am, I don't—"

Lu screamed in a high-pitched yell and didn't stop. The man took out a card and opened the door.

When Lu stepped inside, her heart sank.

"No one's here, ma'am," the receptionist said. "Gosh, I hate to invade people's privacy like this. Maybe she's out for a late dinn—"

But Lu was already gone. Running toward the stairs with her phone out. "Butch, she's gone, and she left all her shit in the room. Eyes and ears open, son. Watch the entrance." Lu ran down the steps as fast as she could.

——

Crutch walked Dooby to the employee exit in the back. "Trust me, Dooby. This is the only way."

"What is? What are you talking about?"

"Just keep telling them the same thing, OK?" He didn't wait for an answer and pushed her through the door.

Dooby stopped when she saw the car waiting on her. She wheeled back toward the door. "Crutch?"

But he was gone.

A person got out of the driver's side of the car and opened the back door, motioning for Dooby to come. *No,* she thought. *This is wrong.*

She stepped backward toward the hotel and looked down the hallway. Lu Stephens was walking toward her. "Dooby, wait. I just want to talk."

But Dooby's feet were already moving for the car. She hopped in, and the sedan sped away. A minute later, it was on Highway 431.

Dooby was breathing hard, trying to put together the pieces of what had just happened. Finally, she looked at the woman driving.

"Sheriff? What are you doing here?"

Hatty Daniels, dressed in jeans and a black sweater, rolled down the window, put a portable siren on top of the car, and turned it on. Then she gazed at Dooby through the reflection in the rearview mirror. "Shouldn't I be asking you the same question?"

55

Matty Dean rarely lost his cool. It almost never paid to do so. But he was getting tired of failure.

"Somebody must have tipped her," Lu said. "Or she has a guardian angel."

"Somebody my ass," Matty hissed. "Trudy Cowan called her the second you left. Didn't you warn that bitch what would happen to her and her son if she interfered?"

"Matty, I really don't think Trudy—"

"Enough. Too much talking and not enough action. Are you sure it was the sheriff that picked her up?"

"Not a hundred percent. But it was a Black woman driving with Marshall County plates, and she put a siren on top of her car. That's when I stopped tailing her."

"Damnit," Matty hissed. They were standing in the parking lot between the hotel and the Old Mexico restaurant. Matty and Chief. Lu and Butch. Several others had joined them. Matty had wanted to create a wall around the hotel, so he had called in reinforcements. Alas, Lu was right. Someone had warned Dooby of the ambush.

"If not Trudy, then who?" Matty asked. "Who's the rat?"

"The Cowans have been fuck-ups ever since Trey's injury," Frank Crutcher said, pulling down on the bill of his Braves cap. "Might be time to put them out of their misery."

Matty nodded. "I agree."

"But Matty, given what just went down, I think the best strategy right now is to sit tight," Frank added. "I'll take care of Trudy and Trey after Rich's trial." He grinned, showing two capped front teeth. "I'll do it real quiet like. It'll look like an accident."

"He's right," Lu said.

Matty put his hands on his hips. "Anyone else have any ideas?"

Silence. They either didn't have any thoughts, or they were afraid to speak their mind. Matty wasn't sure what he preferred. He had to be respected, but he also had relied upon these men and women his whole life. "Speak up."

"Like Crutch said, I think we should wait until the trial is over to do anything else," Lu finally said. "Rich is guilty. The district attorney will send him to prison, and then we can knock out the Tonidandel brothers." Lu spoke with confidence, and Matty saw several of the team nod.

"No," Matty said. "I've seen Rich wiggle his way out of two no-win situations. I'm not going to watch him do it again."

More silence.

"What do you want to do, Matty?" Lu asked. "His house is a fortress. You've said so yourself."

"We have to spread them out. Create another diversion. Hit them at a weak link and draw their fire."

Chief was nodding. "That'll put them out in the open."

Matty glared at Lu, who held his gaze. "Won't it look kinda fishy to the sheriff and the district attorney if another attempt is made on Jason Rich's life?" she asked. "They might start to think he's innocent."

"I don't trust them to give Tyson justice." Matty paused and moved his eyes to each of them. "So if we have a chance to deliver it . . . we will."

56

Jason woke up Saturday morning on his sister's old bed. He'd spent most of the night looking at old photo albums and yearbooks from high school. It was remarkable how similar the room looked to the way Jason remembered it. It was like Jana moved off and neither his father nor mother wanted to change anything. Even the posters of NSYNC and Britney Spears were still on the wall.

And while the rest of the house had taken on a new feel since Jason had been living here, up in this room, the sights and even the smells were straight out of 1997. He didn't look back on his childhood with a lot of fondness, but he missed his parents. And as Jana had predicted, he missed her too. He had fallen asleep looking at pictures from the family's one and only trip to Disney World in 1995.

Jason had turned his phone to silent mode. Upon waking, he saw that he'd missed three calls from Shay last night and another this morning. He trotted down the stairs, started a cup of coffee in the Keurig machine, and called her.

She answered on the first ring. "Where the hell have you been?"

"Sleeping," he said, his voice scratchy from lack of water.

"Sheriff Daniels took Dooby Darnell into protective custody last night. Apparently she'd been hiding out at a hotel in Gadsden, and Hatty got a tip that her life might be in danger."

"Are you serious? How'd you hear about this?"

"Actually, Wish called. He was furious. He thought you might have sent the Tonidandels after her."

"What? He needs to have his head examined. Satch was here all night, and Mickey and Chuck took Hooper to Crawmama's. We're clean." He walked to the coffee maker and grabbed his mug, breathing in the aroma. "Besides, Wish knows damn well who would want to hurt Dooby Darnell."

"Matty Dean," Shay said. "But the tip Hatty received didn't say who the threat was coming from. Just that Dooby was in danger."

"Good grief," Jason said. "I was thinking about the case a lot last night, and Darnell is the key. There is no link between me and her. I didn't speak with her. I didn't have her phone number. There is no way that she can say that I asked her to do anything."

"And yet she walks out of the store with Tyson Cade's change."

"And he turns around just long enough to be shot."

"Coincidence?" Shay spoke in singsong voice.

"I think not," Jason finished the cliché, before adding, "But that's what Wish will say. Cade forgot his change. Darnell was being a good citizen. She's an eyewitness and nothing more."

"We have to make the jury believe different," Shay said.

"Where are they keeping her?"

"I don't know, and I doubt we will. But at least we know she's safe and that she'll be available for trial."

Jason sighed. "Beggars can't be choosers. Hey, Hooper got some information on Griff. Properties he owns, et cetera. We need to go over it."

"Good deal. I've also found the other eyewitness. Emily Carton had said her name was Candy, and I tracked down a Candy Atkinson in New Hope. Left several messages for her, and she called me back yesterday evening. She's actually coming to Guntersville this afternoon for some shopping and will meet us at the office at four thirty. That work for you?"

Jason chuckled. *It's not like I have anything else to do.*

"Something funny?"

"No. I'm going to get dressed and come into the office. Meet you there?"

"I'm already here. See you in a bit."

———

Cassandra "Candy" Jean Atkinson was the prosecution's dream witness in every sense of the word. She taught AP English at New Hope High School. Her husband, Daniel, was an assistant district attorney in Madison County. She had several cousins in Marshall County but had grown up in New Hope. She was attractive with brown hair, brown eyes, and a petite figure, but she wasn't striking or over the top. She dressed conservatively in jeans and an orange sweater. She remembered the murder of Tyson Cade like it was yesterday.

And she recalled his dying words like he'd just said them to her again.

"'I can't believe the bastard got me,'" Candy said. "I asked who, and he said 'Jason Rich.'"

Jason took notes while Shay asked most of the questions. "Ms. Atkinson, did you see this man at the scene?" She pointed across the table at Jason.

"No, ma'am. Everything is kind of a blur after the shooting, but I didn't see him." She managed a sad smile. "And I would probably have recognized him, because I've passed so many of his billboards over the years." She looked at Jason. "No offense."

"None taken," Jason said.

"You said you remembered seeing a dark-colored SUV?" Shay asked.

Candy nodded.

Then they'd walked out of the office to the road. Satch Tonidandel was standing up Gunter a few hundred feet, and Chuck was stationed at the other end. "Ms. Atkinson . . ." Shay brought her up to the maroon Explorer, which Jason had driven to the office so they could have this moment with Candy. "Is this the dark SUV you saw?"

Candy squinted at the vehicle and put her hands on her hips. "It could be. I mean . . . it very well could be, but I can't say for sure."

"Fair to say you have doubts that this might not be it."

She cocked her head. "Yeah, I guess. I mean, all I remember is that it was dark and that it sped away. This . . . is dark, but I was kinda thinking it was darker. Like black."

"You just can't say one way or another, can you?" Shay asked.

"No, I can't."

"And if I ask if you have doubts as to whether this vehicle is the one you saw, you'll say that you do, in fact, have doubts?"

Candy waited several seconds and walked all the way around the Explorer. "Yes, ma'am," she finally said. "I think I'd have to agree that I'm not sure this is it."

"Thank you," Shay said.

Once Candy had left the office and it was just Shay and Jason in the library, Jason couldn't contain himself. "Wooooooooo!" he yelled. "That's what I'm talking about. That was a master class in cross-examination, partner."

"Won't count until we pull it off in court."

"I don't see her lying."

"Me neither. But the concession on the dark SUV doesn't do that much to counter Cade's dying declaration."

"She didn't see me there and can't identify my Explorer as the 'dark SUV' that she saw. It's something."

Shay finally conceded with a weary smile. "It's something." Then she began packing up her briefcase. "Listen, I've been here since seven, and I need to get home to Mom."

"Grab a bite to eat first?" Jason asked. "Celebrate the first good news we've had in the case?"

She gazed at him and then down at the table. "I can't, Jason. Sorry."

"Hey, no worries. I . . . never mind. Great work today."

Shay headed for the door.

"Are you working tomorrow?" Jason called after her.

She stopped at the open door and then peered back at him. "We've got two months to trial, Jason. I'll be working every day. You?"

"Every day," Jason repeated, trying to sound confident.

Any good vibes he'd begun to feel were gone in an instant.

57

Matty Dean finally couldn't take it anymore. Twenty-four hours after the failed bust of Dooby Darnell in Gadsden, Matty was on Highway 79 headed to Birmingham.

He'd felt the stares and the whispers of his crew. He could sense the increasing doubt in Lu Stephens's eyes. Something he wouldn't have thought was possible. *What's going on with her?* He cranked the radio, and David Lee Murphy sang "Dust on the Bottle."

Matty had heard of the Peter principle. That some people were not cut out for leadership roles beyond a certain level. He'd always been a fixer. An enforcer. He killed people. He cleaned up messes. That's what he did for Tyson, and he was the best. He wasn't the Godfather folding his hands into a tent while others did the killing.

He was Luca Brasi.

He'd known what he needed to do to seize command. He'd also know that Reg Strassburg and Tanner Sparks had come to kill him in Mentone. He couldn't have just said, *No worries, fellas, I just want to keep doing what I was doing.* They'd have killed him anyway. He had too much sway in the network and must be put down like the old dog he was.

Matty didn't regret killing those bastards. He'd do it again in a heartbeat.

That's what I'm good at.

He blinked and glanced at his reflection in the mirror of the car before returning his eyes to the blacktop. He'd been a good enforcer. What did the great running backs in football say? *I could see the field.*

He knew how to set a trap, as he'd done to kill the billboard lawyer's investigator. But Harry Davenport had been out of the war for many years before Matty brought death to him. Satch Tonidandel seemed to still be over there.

And his brothers would die for him. And all three of them would take a bullet for Jason Rich, of all damn people.

Matty didn't get it. But as he eased onto the I-65 ramp, he began to realize that he was playing this all wrong. Delegating the Tonidandels to Lu and now Chief was wrong.

His plan to kill Jason Rich at the first hearing may have failed, but it wasn't due to poor planning. It was due to execution.

Matty had always come up with the plan and executed it himself. That's what had made him so valuable to Tyson.

He rolled the windows down and felt the cool air fill up the Lincoln. The song playing now was Conway Twitty's version of "Slow Hand," and Matty sang along. The distance was helping, just as he knew it would.

But he knew something else would help too.

He'd met Ben Raggendorf at a bar on Ninth Avenue in downtown Birmingham about seven years ago. Ben had been attending a commercial driver's class during the day and staying at a hotel near the bar. They'd had a few bourbon drinks and talked about outlaw country music and fishing. They'd left at the same time, and Ben had invited Matty to have a drink at the hotel bar with him. They'd brought their glasses to Ben's room, and . . .

Matty felt his heart racing at the memory. He'd been with a few men over the years, and the night with Ben followed the same pattern. Strange city. Gay-friendly bar. Meeting someone in town for business who had a hotel room. Boom.

He'd known something was different about him since he'd started getting erections in the boy's locker room after football practice his first year of high school. Then, his junior year, there had been a school trainer that was helping him deal with a nagging hamstring injury. He felt the man's hard penis rubbing against his leg through his shorts, and it made him hard too. Eventually, he started seeing the trainer even when he wasn't hurt anymore. And their sessions involved more than the hamstring . . .

The man eventually left for another job before Matty's senior year, and Matty never saw him again.

Since then, Matty Dean had been firmly in the closet.

Perhaps if Matty were younger and had the skills of someone else, he'd come out. Maybe enjoy a more overt gay lifestyle.

But he'd been a drug dealer and a killer all his life. It was all he knew.

Matty parked a block from the bar where he'd met Ben. He hopped out and checked his phone. A text from Chief said that Mickey Tonidandel was out with his girlfriend, Tiffany, with Chuck watching his back. The colonel was apparently taking the night off and was at the family homestead, watching Jason Rich's house.

The lawyer was also home while his new partner, the former prosecutor, was with her momma up on Gunter Mountain, walking the mom's Lab in the woods behind their house.

As Matty strode down the sidewalk, he thought, *That mountain has several ways up and down . . .*

He opened the door to the bar and saw a couple of men sitting alone. He ordered a bourbon and branch. He knew it was risky coming here. Ben might have the same idea. But he was tired and edgy and needed the thrill of what was about to come. He saw a man wearing suit pants, a white button-down, and a tie and sat down next to him. The man had a goatee, but the sides of his face were clean shaven. Matty leaned toward him.

"Evening," Matty said.

"Hey," the man said, his eyes darting around the place. Nervous. He drank a sip from his martini glass, which was almost empty.

First time? Matty wondered, smiling to himself.

"What kind is that?" Matty asked.

"Dirty vodka."

Matty waved at the bartender. "Another one for my friend here." He smiled at the man, who nodded.

"Thank you."

"So what brings you to Birmingham?"

"I'm a banker from Little Rock. Met with some clients earlier and . . ." He hesitated. ". . . spending the night at the Tutwiler."

Matty smiled. "That's a nice place," he said, thinking that the formula was about to play out again.

Same old, same old.

58

On Sunday morning, after his morning kayak ride with Chuck, Jason did something he hadn't done since he was a teenager.

He went to church. Mickey Tonidandel had been invited by his girlfriend, Tiffany, to attend services at a nondenominational chapel in Arab. Right before he was leaving, he asked if Jason wanted to go.

Jason had planned to head to the office but decided calling in some divine intervention might not be a bad idea. Dress was casual, according to Mickey, but Jason still wore slacks, a button-down, and a sport coat.

Chuck, who attended every Sunday at the Guntersville Baptist Church, decided to tag along both for security and to worship.

As they left the house, the colonel declined an invitation.

"It's a nice morning," he said, peering out at the water. He'd set up a lawn chair between Jason's house and Chase's so he could watch the road and the water. He leaned forward and rubbed his hands over the portable propane firepit. His brothers had offered to alternate taking the night shift, but Satch wouldn't have it. "Think I'll just have some coffee and stay right here." He coughed, and it looked like he was holding in a fit. "Ask the Lord to forgive my sins."

"Yes, sir," Jason said. As he and Mickey crossed the street to Chuck's pickup, Jason looked over his shoulder at Satch, who seemed to have lost a little weight. Or maybe it was just how he was sitting in the chair. "You noticed any changes with him?"

Mickey stopped and put his hands on his hips. "He's been coughing a lot, which I guess has to be from the cancer." He scratched his neck. "Still kinda hard to believe that he's sick. The colonel . . . has always seemed invincible." His voice shook, and he cleared his throat and spoke in a quieter tone. "Sleeping a tad more too. The courthouse shooting took a lot out of him, as did our run-in with Lu Stephens at Crawmama's."

The boys had briefed Jason on that encounter. "You still think it was the right decision not to tell the sheriff about that?"

There was a long moment of silence. "Jason, that was the colonel's call. And, over the years, I've learned not to question him. He's the reason I'm alive. Chuck too. We're good soldiers, don't get me wrong, but I woulda been killed overseas if it wasn't for Satch. He, uh, he's just . . ." Mickey looked away as his eyes misted over, and Jason swallowed hard. The Tonidandels weren't an emotional crew, but the love between the brothers was obvious. ". . . he's a special man," Mickey continued. "I just don't see how anything could kill him. Not even cancer."

Jason wiped at his own eyes and studied the colonel, who was standing and staring at the lake. A powerful wave of gratitude came over him. He'd reread *The Secret*, by Rhonda Byrne, again over the past few weeks since rededicating himself to his recovery. He knew gratitude was a powerful process, and he'd tried to be more thankful for what he had instead of fretting about what was gone.

He'd lost a lot, but he'd gained three brothers.

At least, that's how he thought of the Tonidandels now.

"You boys coming?" Chuck asked from the driver's side of the truck. "The Lord waits for no one."

Jason smiled, still looking at Satch. *Thank you,* he thought.

Then he hopped into the back seat of the truck.

Up on Gunter Mountain, Shay Lankford ran laps on the track of DAR High School. She and her mother had already attended the early service at Grant United Methodist, and now it was time to work.

Though she loved the run through the woods, sometimes she just liked to pound out laps, where she didn't have to think about where she was going or even the next step. While she ran at a steady pace, she could lose herself in the case.

Its facts, legal conundrums, and witnesses. As the miles piled up, many times her mind would clear and a strategy would unfold. An idea. Something.

Today, nothing came to her except a belief. One that had been building since he'd come to see her for the first time. Since her momma had told her that she'd prayed for him. Solidified by Candy Atkinson not being able to identify his SUV.

He's innocent. Regardless of whether this case was a frame-up or just a case of being very unlucky, Jason Rich did not murder Tyson Cade. She felt it in her bones.

Which upped the stakes even more.

There was another reality that was also beginning to rise to the surface. And Shay hated to even acknowledge it, but damnit, the feeling was there. It had probably been there for a while, like a rock in the lake or a fossil underground. Shay was thirty-five years old. She hadn't had a serious relationship in almost a decade. Her life was the job.

That was her kinship to Hatty Daniels. Why she'd so looked forward to them working together. A shared singular focus.

But her near-death experience on the steps of her new office and the former site of the Rich Law Firm, together with her loss in the election, had changed her. She had tried to fight her new feelings, but that was as pointless as swimming against the current.

As she slowed her pace to a walk and wiped sweat from her brow, she thought about Jason's harmless invite to dinner yesterday. She'd said she couldn't go, not because she didn't want to go. She'd said no because she was scared.

Shay couldn't afford to feel anything for her client, but those feelings were there. She grabbed a water bottle she'd left on the bleachers and took a long sip. She gazed out over the football stadium. She felt energized, as she knew she would.

She also sensed butterflies in her stomach.

Shay giggled and then stifled it. She shook her head and began to trot home.

I like him, she finally admitted to herself. She inhaled a breath of cold mountain air and then exhaled, watching the smoke cloud made by her breath rise above her. Her heart was racing, and her brain was wired. She'd tried hundreds of cases, but she knew that being Jason Rich's advisory counsel might very well define the rest of her career . . .

. . . *and my life.*

The stakes couldn't be higher.

59

Matty Dean fished on the dock of the lake home he was squatting in. The place was in Langston, Alabama, which was a hard place to get to by car but fairly easy by boat. Matty felt completely refreshed after his evening in Birmingham. He'd left the hotel at three this morning, having accomplished his objective with the trip. He'd gotten the banker's number but given fake digits for himself. Just like a high school girl.

Matty grinned and felt a tug on his line. He'd slept for a few hours when he arrived back here, but he was too wired to snooze long. He'd gotten his fix . . .

. . . and I have a plan.

As he began to reel the catch in, which appeared to be a modest-size catfish, his phone vibrated. He clicked on the speakerphone button and continued to bring in the fish. "Yeah."

"Rich and the younger two brothers went to church in Arab," Chief said, his voice a tad amped up. "The lady lawyer is running at the DAR track with Wyatt Onkey watching her. Virgil is back at the house."

"Did you scout out my ideas yet?"

"Oh, yeah, and you were spot on. There's a half dozen good exits down Gunter Mountain. You want to attack tonight?"

Matty unhooked the catfish and threw it in a pail. He might have to do a fry this evening. "Not yet, Chief. I want them to get lazy. A little too confident." He hesitated. "I also want to see the terrain myself."

There was a pause. "Um, Matty, you trust me, don't you?"

Matty Dean didn't trust a living soul. He almost laughed at the question. "Of course, Chief, you're a good man. But I'm not delegating this assignment. I want your help, but this hit is my detail. Understand?"

"Yes, sir." The tone was amped back up, and it sent a shiver of adrenaline through Matty.

"Bye, Chief." He clicked the phone dead and closed his eyes, thinking of how much he loved control. Both having it . . . and giving it up.

It was a dance Matty had always liked.

He'd relished being dominated by Tyson. Taking his orders. And he would have done anything for him. He'd savored relinquishing control last night. Knowing full well that it was all an illusion. Sexual dominance was nothing more than a fad. A breeze that changed from day to day for Matty Dean.

Real dominance was knowing you were smarter than your opponent.

And knowing you would go further than they would to win.

And executing your own plan and not being afraid to pull the trigger.

Matty saw a vision of the fight that was coming. The Tonidandels were good. And Jason Rich was scrappy.

But this is what I do.

Matty began whistling a sad David Allan Coe song . . . and recast his line.

60

Jason enjoyed the church service. Though he got plenty of stares, and Tiffany gave Mickey the stink-eye for bringing him, the people were kind, and several introduced themselves.

On the way home, Jason asked Chuck to make a detour. He wanted to check the properties owned by Richard Griffith that Hooper had found.

The first was a rental house on Loveless Street within walking distance of the Rock House restaurant. Jason knocked on the door, and a woman answered. Other than sending checks to a PO box number to Richard Griffith's attention, she and her family had no contact with the former sheriff. Jason asked for the box number as well as Griffith's phone number, and the woman hesitated for a few moments before saying she didn't feel right about giving that information to him.

"Please, ma'am, I really need to speak with him." Jason figured it was the same cell number that Shay already had—she'd tried dozens of times to contact him already with no answer—but maybe he had a different line for personal business.

"I'm sorry, sir. Ever since . . . you know . . . the stuff that's happened in the last few months, we really don't want to have much contact with sheriff . . . uh . . . I mean, Mr. Griffith. We're looking for another place to rent."

"OK," Jason said before turning away and calling Hooper as he walked back to the truck.

"Jason, this better be good. Sundays are sacred."

"I'm sorry. Did I catch you at church?"

A snort. "NASCAR, man."

"Ah, when does the race start?"

"Not till seven, but I'm pregaming by watching the second half of the 2018 National Championship Game. 'And the Crimson Tide . . . will not be denied!'" He mimicked a broadcaster's voice and sounded half-drunk. "By the way, Crawmama's was outstanding."

"Good deal, man. Listen. Richard Griffith has a PO box number. Just spoke with the woman leasing his rental house downtown, and she sends him a check once a month to a PO box, but she wouldn't give it to me. Need you to track that down."

"Will do."

"Thanks. Any leads on Matty Dean?"

"Not yet, but I'm working on it."

Jason fought the urge to say something sarcastic. Albert Hooper was a bit eccentric—*like every damn body in my life*—but he'd saved Jason's and Trey Cowan's collective asses during Trey's trial last year. Sometimes you just had to let people be themselves to get the most out of them.

Jason smiled as he climbed back into the truck. Where had he heard that before?

He wasn't sure, but it sounded good. Maybe he was learning something on this journey called life.

Or maybe I'm completely and utterly full of shit.

That sounds about right. Jana's voice. Jason grinned wider. It had been a while since his deceased sister had slid into his subconscious.

"Where to now, hoss?" Chuck asked. Next to him, Mickey was playing with his cell phone. "Tiffany sure is lighting me up about bringing you to church. Says it wasn't proper to bring someone so controversial with me without clearing with her first."

"Well, that *was* pretty insensitive, little brother," Chuck said, his tone serious. "Be sure to ask where she keeps the jar."

"What jar?" Mickey asked.

"The one with your dick in it."

For a moment, there was silence. Then Chuck howled with laughter, and it sounded a bit like a donkey. Then he glanced up. "Lord, forgive my ornery words and behavior."

"Yeah," Mickey added, and Jason could tell he was trying not to laugh too. "Lord, forgive him."

"Griffith owns thirty acres near Marshall Medical South in Boaz," Jason broke in. "Can we head that way?"

"Let's do it," Chuck said. Then, giggling, he added, "Need to find that penis, Mick. Next thing you know, you'll be mowing her yard and painting her house. Paying her light bill too."

"Big brother, when was the last time you saw a vagina up close? The late nineties?"

"Lord, forgive us," Chuck said, still giggling as the truck bolted forward.

———

The land in Boaz wasn't quite big enough to be considered a farm, but it was still a nice spread. Huge lawn in front and then a field in the back that might be large enough for a small crop but was currently eaten up with weeds and in desperate need of a good bush hogging. Jason knocked on the door, but there was no answer. No cars in the driveway. He peeked inside the detached garage. No vehicles there either.

Dead end, Jason thought, knowing they had to check these boxes. Jason had brought his briefcase with him, as the next stop was the office.

He took out a piece of paper, thought for a few seconds, and scribbled a note on it. Then he placed the page in the mailbox.

"Done all we can do," he said.

"Next stop?" Chuck asked.

"DQ?" Mickey asked. Both brothers looked at Jason with hopeful glances, like dogs begging for a treat.

"Christ, why not."

———

Twenty minutes later, Jason walked into the office library holding his briefcase in one hand and a chocolate dipped cone from Dairy Queen in the other. "Damn, you have to eat these fast or they'll melt all over you."

Shay didn't even glance his way. "We have a meeting with Dooby Darnell at the sheriff's office tomorrow." She paused and looked at him. "Wish and Hatty will be there too."

"Good freakin' grief," Jason said, flinging the rest of the ice cream treat in the trash and taking a seat. "A lot of good that'll do us."

"She's under police protection, and this was the only way she would talk to us."

Jason forced the frustration out of his tone. "All right. Better than nothing. I drove by the properties owned by Richard Griffith. They were dead ends." He quickly relayed what happened at both places, leaving out the part about the note he'd left in the mailbox.

"So we have Matty Dean on one hand and Richard Griffith on the other," Shay said, standing up and pacing around the conference room table. "Both could be the ringmaster of Cade's death and would have had the motive and the means to do it. We're a bit shaky on opportunity. Neither was identified near the crime scene as you were, nor do they live close by."

"I can see where that would be a problem."

"It's a hole. A pretty big one. But . . . we've also got Dooby Darnell as an accessory. If Griff had a relationship with Dooby, that's news to me. I plan to ask her tomorrow, but I suspect the answer will be no."

"She could also lie tomorrow. Griff could have approached her not as an old friend but as someone with a common interest."

"True, Jason, but that's a stretch. She probably does know Dean, and there is a good chance that Dean was who was planning to kill her Friday night."

"I agree. And why would he want to do that other than to get rid of the evidence? If Dooby confesses the truth on the stand, then Matty goes down."

"If . . . he's the one who killed Cade."

"What if he's not?" Jason asked.

"But if not Griffith or Dean, who? Dooby didn't pull the trigger. She had to have help." She stopped pacing. "Didn't you say Trudy Cowan buttoned up pretty tight when you tried to talk with her about Dooby?"

Jason frowned. "Yeah."

"And aren't Trudy and Dooby the best of friends?"

Jason looked at the backs of his hands. "So what, Shay. Do you really see Trudy for this? I mean, she's a tough woman who could definitely fire a long-barrel pistol, but—"

"Not Trudy." She paused. "Trey."

Jason opened his mouth, aghast at the suggestion. *"What?"*

"Think about it, Jason. Cade played Trey for a fool. Cade had to have known that it was his inside source, Griff, who killed Kelly Flowers. He blackmailed you to represent Trey and basically did everything he could do to ensure that you lost. To make himself look like he was taking care of his Sand Mountain folks. All the while he was actually protecting his own ass."

"But the case was dismissed. Trey is a free man."

"A free man with a grudge against Tyson Cade."

Jason shook his head. "I don't see it, Shay. Trey went through a lot, and I know he hated Cade. But I don't see him as a killer."

"You're saying that because you represented him." She paused. "How's he been since the trial?"

"I don't know."

Shay squinted. "I do." She slid a printout over to him. "Two public intoxication charges in the past sixty days." She paused. "Both *after* the murder of Tyson Cade."

A gust of depression rolled across Jason. "Good grief."

"Sometimes people don't live happily ever after, Jason." She walked around the table and stood over him. "Especially on Sand Mountain."

61

Trudy Cowan hated to lie.

But that's all it seemed she'd been doing lately. To Jason Rich. To Lu Stephens. But especially . . . *to myself.*

She'd tried to go about her business this weekend without panicking, but she'd heard what happened.

Dooby was in the protective custody of the Marshall County Sheriff's Office. She'd thought she would have heard from Lu by now. She had slept with her twelve gauge the last two nights and would again tonight.

She walked out of her house, carrying the gun, and got in her car. Then she turned left onto Hustleville Road. She was glad that Dooby was OK. They'd been friends forever, and Trudy didn't want anything bad to happen to her.

But she'd be lying if she said that was the sole reason she hadn't shared much with Jason Rich or only shared with Lu when the mercenary bitch threatened violence.

Trudy Cowan was no fool.

In the weeks after the murder charges were dismissed against her son, she'd noticed a change in Trey. And not for the better. Instead of relief at having his life set free, he seemed to spiral back into his old ways. Drinking too much. No direction. And, worst of all, seeing his ex-girlfriend.

When Trudy arrived at the home where she knew Trey was staying, she sighed. *When does this end?* she thought. Trey was twenty-four years old. When would protecting him cease to be her responsibility?

She walked toward the front door, knocked twice, waited, knocked three more times, and when there was no answer, tried the knob. It was open.

When she walked in, the powerful skunk-like smell of marijuana hit her like a left jab from Muhammad Ali. She coughed and stepped into the foyer, seeing a woman sitting at the kitchen table. She wore a pink robe open down the middle.

"Where's my boy?"

"Hey, Trudy," the woman said, standing. "Want a drink?" She grabbed a handle of vodka.

"Colleen, where's my son?"

"In the back sleeping. He's real tired."

"I bet. Why don't you cover up your cooch, hon? What you're selling, I ain't buying." She walked away and heard Colleen laugh behind her.

Trudy found Trey lying face down on the bed. He was naked, and there was a half-drunk pint of Jim Beam on the nightstand next to an ashtray. The pot scent was even worse in here.

"Come on, son. We're going home." Trudy snapped the words off, looking on the floor for his clothes. She threw his jeans and underwear at him. "Now."

When Trey didn't move, Trudy went back into the kitchen. Colleen had now tied her robe and was drinking straight from the handle.

Trudy filled a glass with water, took it back to the bedroom, and flung it on Trey. "Get up, goddamnit. Right now. My next move is blowing a hole through the ceiling with a twelve gauge."

Trey rolled off the bed and onto the floor. "What the . . . Momma?"

"Get dressed. I'll be waiting in the truck."

"I live here now."

"Not anymore you don't. This is a house of sin, and I won't stand for it anymore. You're better than this, Trey. After all Mr. Rich did to keep you out of prison and after everything I've done my whole life to make sure you followed the straight and narrow, look at you. Smoking pot and getting drunk every day and screwing a dime-store hooker."

"Don't talk about her that way."

"I'll call a spade a spade. Fucking Kelly Flowers for drugs. Now she's messing around with you because no one else will touch that stank twat." She ground her teeth together. "Only a loser."

Trey had put his underwear and jeans on. He stared at his mother while holding his T-shirt. "Momma, Colleen is my girlfriend. If you don't like it, that's too bad. I love her."

"Bullshit."

"I do. And she loves me."

"All that woman loves is vodka and THC. She threw her life away, and now she's drowning and taking you with her."

"That's not true." He put on the shirt and placed his hands on his hips. "I'll talk with you, Momma, but I'm not going anywhere."

Trudy just stared at him. What had she hoped to accomplish coming over here? "Did you talk with Dooby Darnell before Tyson was killed?"

Trey blinked. "What?"

"I didn't stutter."

"I mean, I'm sure I did. The Alder Springs Grocery is my go-to place for gas."

"You know what I mean."

"Momma, what's this about?"

"I'm sure you know who's running the Sand Mountain drug trade now."

"I mean, not exactly, Mom. I knew Tyson was in charge because he never missed a chance to tell me. But . . ."

"You suck at lying, son. You worked several deliveries for Tyson. I'm not an idiot."

Trey looked down at the floor. "Matty Dean, I assume."

"You assume right." She paused. "Are you working for that SOB? Is that why they haven't killed me?"

"*What?*"

Trudy wanted to slap him and pulled her arm back to do so. She stared into his eyes and saw nothing but the dull gaze of a pothead. She lowered her hand. "Oh, fuck it. Why do I even bother?"

"Mom, I'm not working for Matty Dean."

But Trudy was walking toward the door.

"Wait, Mom."

But Trudy continued to walk. How could Trey afford all this booze and pot?

"Mom, stop!"

She wheeled on him when she reached the opening to the kitchen. Colleen was now drinking vodka from a glass at least, but her robe was back open. Trudy gritted her teeth again. "For the last time, Colleen, will you cover yourself?"

Colleen didn't. "Why don't you get the hell out of my house?"

"I'll leave when I damn well want to. Why aren't you working? Lose your nursing job too?"

"It's my off day, bitch."

"Don't call my momma that," Trey said.

Colleen placed a joint in her mouth and lit it. She said nothing, instead blowing a puff of smoke in the air.

"Mom, I'm sorry. Why'd you come here?"

Trudy blinked her eyes and glanced at Colleen, who continued to smoke at the kitchen table. The woman's eyes didn't look as dead as Trey's, though.

"Are you part of it?" Trudy spat the question at Colleen before looking at Trey. "Do you both work for him now?"

"Mom—"

"Did you . . ." But she couldn't ask him in front of Colleen. Not this way. "I need you to come see me. Sober and not stoned either. We need to talk."

"I have to work tomorrow," Trey said. "I'm refereeing a game in Scottsboro."

"Soon, son." She grabbed the knob and spoke without looking at him. "You better not be lying to me."

———

Trey Cowan watched his mother leave and then glanced at Colleen. She stood from the table, and the robe slid off her body.

"Follow me," she said.

He did as he was told, his eyes glued on her beautiful naked backside. When they reached the bedroom, she leaned over and grabbed the handle of the bottom drawer of her dresser. "I hope you didn't show your momma what's in here." She opened it and took out a stack of ten one-hundred-dollar bills. There were ten other stacks like it in the drawer. "Just one, OK, baby."

"One what?"

She undid the paper band on the bundle and then lay on the bed with the cash on her stomach. "Come here," she said.

Trey followed her instructions. Just as he'd done when Matty Dean's messenger had come to him in early November. He was a free man, but he had no prospects in life. No college degree. No talent for anything anymore but throwing a football flatfooted and hitting a baseball. Not good enough to play in the Majors. Not smart enough to do anything but work for the city . . .

. . . and maybe do a few side ventures for the local meth operation.

Trey took off his clothes again. He took the joint out of Colleen's mouth and took a drag before placing it in the ashtray.

He felt guilty that his momma was so upset, but he was tired of being everyone's bitch. He'd been Tyson Cade's for too long, and it wouldn't have been long before Cade would have had his claws dug in again.

So he'd done what he did. *No regrets,* he thought, putting a hundred-dollar bill in his mouth and then his face between Colleen's breasts.

None at all.

62

To say the mood in the conference room was tense would be an understatement.

Marcia "Dooby" Darnell sat at the end of the long table. Sheriff Hatty Daniels and Wish French were on one side, and Jason and Shay were across from them.

"Ms. Darnell, thank you for agreeing to this meeting," Hatty began. "And we appreciate your cooperation with the sheriff's department."

Dooby stared at the table, saying nothing.

"Well, I think these lawyers have some questions," Hatty said, glancing at Jason.

Wish French was quicker on the trigger. "Ms. Darnell, I know this has been a stressful time for you, and I don't want to make it any worse. We took a statement from you right after the murder of Tyson Cade. Do you remember talking to Sergeant Greta Martin?"

"Yes." She looked up at the district attorney. "She's dead now, isn't she?"

"Yes, she . . . is." Wish glanced down at several sheets of paper in front of him. He slid one across the table to Dooby and another to Shay. "We received your discovery package, and this statement, as well as others taken by the sheriff's department, will be produced to you later this week. Here is a courtesy copy since I'm going to be referring to it with Ms. Darnell." Then he returned his focus to Dooby and glanced down at what must be his copy of the same page. "Ma'am, what I've given you is Sergeant Martin's summary of her interview with you. As you may or may not recall, you were very upset . . . as anyone would be . . . after the shooting and were not able to write a statement yourself. Can you please look over Sergeant Martin's report and tell us if you think it accurately summarizes your memory of the events of the morning of November 13, 2019?"

While Dooby Darnell began to read the report, Jason scooted closer to Shay so that he could read the same. The description was short, sweet, and only a paragraph.

> *According to Ms. Darnell, Tyson Cade had bought a couple of items, a Twinkie and a soft drink, and had paid with a twenty-dollar bill. He had left before Ms. Darnell could give him the change, which was a little over fifteen dollars. She walked outside and yelled for him, telling him he'd forgotten the change. He turned around, and she heard at least five gunshots. Mr. Cade fell down to his knees and then over on his back. Ms. Darnell could remember nothing else, apparently going into shock. When the first responders arrived, they found her sitting up against the front of the building staring out at Hustleville Road.*

Dooby nodded and peered up from the page. "That's all I remember."

"Thank you," Wish said. "That's all I have."

Shay and Jason shared a glance. There was a lot they wanted to ask Dooby Darnell, and this would probably be their only opportunity to do so before trial. Some of the questions they would really like to know the answer to without the district attorney present, but that wasn't possible. Shay cleared her throat. "Ms. Darnell, do you know why you are in the protective custody of the sheriff's department?"

"I got a tip from an anonymous caller that Ms. Darnell was in danger," Hatty said.

"Thank you, Sheriff, but I'd prefer to hear from the witness." Shay glared at Hatty and then looked back at Dooby. Jason was reminded that Shay was once a powerful figure in this building, and old feelings died hard. There was a shared history between Shay and Hatty, and he suspected that Shay's orders had normally been followed.

"Just like the sheriff said." Dooby's voice was timid. Scared. "I was in danger."

"Did you also get a tip?"

Dooby nodded.

"Shay, I fail to see how any of this has any bearing on the trial of Jason Rich," Wish said, exasperation in his tone.

Shay ignored him, staring at Dooby. "I think when an eyewitness gets her life threatened, that it actually does have some bearing on the trial. Who notified you of the danger, Ms. Darnell?"

She blinked and looked at Hatty. "I don't know. Got a call from a number I didn't recognize. Told me to leave the hotel, so I did."

"Why were you in Gadsden to begin with?"

She swallowed. "Just needed to get away. Was afraid after what happened to Tyson."

"Afraid of what?" Shay snapped.

Dooby placed her hands over her face. "I don't know. I just haven't been right since the shooting. I've lived in Alder Springs my whole life. I needed to get away."

"I'm sorry, I don't understand. You needed to get away from what?"

"I think you're badgering the witness, Shay," Wish said.

"You needed to get away from what?" Shay repeated the question, speaking through clenched teeth.

"Everything," Dooby finally said. "I was getting all these looks from people. Friends. Neighbors. Like it might have been my fault since I was there. I don't know. You just don't understand how people in the

Sprangs . . . folks on Sand Mountain . . . felt about Tyson. There was a lot of fear, but folks also loved him."

"Why?" Jason asked. It was the first word he'd said, and his voice seemed to startle Dooby.

"Because he took care of us. If anyone was in trouble or needed a hand, he'd lend money or get some of his people to help out. I know he helped Trey Cowan last year when he was arrested. Trudy's my friend, and I know Tyson helped Trey get you as his attorney."

Jason leaned back in his seat. He almost said something, but Shay jumped in. "Did he ever help you, Dooby?"

She nodded. "My momma's in the nursing home. She ain't doing all that good, and those bills ain't cheap. Tyson paid the monthly charge." She wiped her eyes again.

"What nursing home?"

Dooby sniffled. "Marshall Manor."

"Is she still a resident there?"

"Yes."

"Ms. Darnell, who's been paying those bills since Mr. Cade's death in November?" Shay pressed.

Dooby opened her mouth, then bit down on her lower lip. "I . . . I don't know."

Shay glanced at Jason and then back at the witness. *Could be something,* Jason thought. *Or it could be nothing. Cade's successor might know about this arrangement and be continuing to honor it.*

"Did you like Tyson Cade?" Shay asked.

She nodded. "I did."

"Were you friends with Tyson Cade?"

"I guess you could say that?"

"More than friends?" Shay asked.

"What?" Dooby wrinkled up her face.

"Did you have a sexual relationship with Mr. Cade?" Shay pressed.

Jason had confided to Shay that Cade told him last year that his alibi for the Kelly Flowers's murder was being in bed with Dooby Darnell. Jason figured that if Tyson was willing to tell him, it was probably pretty common knowledge on Sand Mountain.

Dooby's eyes watered, and she glanced at the sheriff. "Do I have to answer that?" Her voice was timid.

"You'll have to answer it at trial," Shay said.

"I'm not sure her personal relationship with the victim is relevant," Wish jumped in. "So I respectfully disagree. And she doesn't have to answer anything today. This is a voluntary interview, and she can end it at any time." He gave Dooby a reassuring pat on the back, and Shay squelched the urge to gag.

Dooby gazed down at the table.

"Ms. Darnell, I will ask this question at trial, and a judge will force you to answer. I can promise you that."

"Shay, you're harassing—"

"No, I'm not," Shay snapped. "She is the last person to have seen the victim alive. Her relationship with him is pivotal to the—"

"Yes," Dooby interrupted, looking up from the table and crossing her arms. Her voice was breathy.

Shay glanced at Jason and then back at the witness. "And was that something you wanted?" Shay asked. "Or was it something Tyson demanded in exchange for helping your mother?"

Dooby held Shay's gaze. "I wanted it." Her tone was defiant.

"Was he ever abusive to you?"

She shook her head. "No."

"Did he ever come to you for information?" The Tonidandel brothers, during their investigation of Cade during the Cowan trial, had heard from numerous sources that Dooby Darnell was a source for Tyson Cade.

"Sometimes."

"And did he often tip you large amounts if he was happy with the tidbits you gave him?"

"Sometimes."

"Prior to November 13, 2019, had you ever given him change for a purchase before?"

"Yes."

"Had you ever gone out of the store and stopped him to remind him that he'd forgotten his change?"

"I can't remember."

"When you called after him, did he turn to face you?"

"He was already facing me."

"So he walked backward to his car?"

"I don't know. I just know he was looking at me when I asked him."

Wish French coughed and cleared his throat, and Jason pointed at the summary that Wish had provided when the interview started. "The statement here says that he did turn around when you called after him," Jason said. "You told Mr. French that everything on this page was accurate. Is that not true?"

"It is true."

"So Tyson Cade did turn around when you called after him?"

"Yes," she said, clasping her hands together.

"And then he was shot."

"Yes."

"Who do you think was trying to kill you Friday night, Ms. Darnell?" Jason asked.

She glanced at him. "I have no idea."

"Are you familiar with a man named Matty Dean?" Jason looked at Hatty as he spoke.

"Yes."

"Isn't it true that Matty Dean is now the meth king of Sand Mountain?"

"I wouldn't know."

"Right," Jason said. "Well, if Matty Dean was in the meth operation and he thought you might have had something to do with Tyson's murder, he probably wouldn't like it, would he?"

"This is ridiculous," Wish intervened. "You don't have to answer that, Ms. Darnell. Can we keep this professional, Shay? Can you tell the clown to either keep his mouth shut or wait outside?"

"I'd like an answer to my question," Jason said.

"I don't know," Dooby said.

"So you watched—" Jason started, but Shay held up a hand and peered hard at him.

"Ms. Darnell, have you ever spoken to or had any contact with former Marshall County sheriff Richard Griffith?" Shay asked.

"No," Dooby said, wrinkling her face in confusion. "Never."

Shay crossed her arms. "Have you told us the truth today?"

"Yes, ma'am," Dooby said.

"Thank you."

———

Hatty Daniels had a sergeant escort Dooby out of the conference room. "You guys really think Dooby Darnell went out of the store to give Tyson his change?" Jason asked.

"That's what she said," Wish fired back. "And if she hadn't done that, you would have just shot him in the back. Which I'm sure was your intention anyway."

Jason felt a lightning bolt of anger seize through him, but he knew he couldn't act on it. He remembered something Knox Rogers had told him while he was prepping for Jana's trial. A lesson the old medical malpractice attorney had learned from Professor Tom McMurtrie at the university. *Never let them see you sweat.* Always act like whatever happened was exactly what you expected in front of your opponent. And most especially before the jury. "Nice try, Wish," Jason said, turning his back on the prosecutor. "Oh, Sheriff, have there been any developments in your department's investigation of the assassination attempt on me after the first hearing in this case?"

"No, Jason. There haven't been."

He glared at her and then at Wish. "Well, I certainly hope you haven't given up. I'm sure Sergeant Martin's family feels the same way."

"We haven't," Hatty said.

"This meeting is over, Rich," Wish said. "Get the hell out of here."

"Glad to," Jason said. "Shay."

Shay stood and extended her hand to Hatty. "Thank you for arranging this meeting, Sheriff."

"You're welcome."

"We may want to talk to Ms. Darnell again closer to trial."

"That will be up to her."

"Of course," Shay said, then walked out of the door held open for her by Jason without acknowledging Wish.

"You got nothing from this," Wish said, his tone condescending. "Your plan was to shoot him in the back."

Jason looked past him to Hatty. "Where are things with the search for Matty Dean, Sheriff?"

He left the question on the table as he closed the door shut.

———

"That change anything for you?" Wish asked, looking up at the ceiling as he ambled around the conference room table.

"It is odd that she waited so long to tell him about the change," Hatty said. "And awful convenient for the killer. A much easier shot to hit someone standing still that's facing you than a moving target walking away from you." She hesitated. "But no. Nothing's changed. I'll say this though. I hate this case. And while Jason may be guilty, there's not a doubt in my mind that Matty Dean tried to kill him on the square two months ago. And I'd bet my life savings that it was Dean who put Darnell in danger Friday night."

"You think?" Wish asked as Hatty moved for the door.

"I know," she said, pausing with her hand on the knob. "And you know what else?"

"What?"

"I think Ms. Darnell knows more than she's saying."

63

Neely Avenue was a curvy street that offered lake views and privacy. According to Hooper's report, Richard and Cheryl Griffith had bought their home in 2005, and Cheryl was still the owner, taking the property in the divorce settlement.

Jason and Shay pulled to a stop at the curb. Jason was sitting shotgun in Shay's Honda Accord. Behind them a hundred or so yards was Satch Tonidandel in the Raptor. As Jason and Shay got out of the car, Satch did the same and stood against the front of the truck.

"He's dutiful, isn't he?" Shay asked, picking up her pace.

"He is," Jason agreed. "But, given what's happened to me in the last eighteen months, I'm glad he's on my side."

"Me too," Shay said. They paused at the steps leading up to the door. "Based on my recollection of Griff and Cheryl's relationship, she's a stay-at-home mom. The kids are now in school, and that's her green Yukon in the driveway."

"So she should be home."

"Yep."

"How did you think it went with Darnell?" Jason asked. They'd barely said a word on the ten-minute drive from the sheriff's department to here.

"I think the cross of her will be all about the questions, not so much the answers. She probably isn't going to admit anything, but her actions look fishy as hell."

"I agree."

"And her body language screams that she knows more. At least it does to me."

"I think the same."

"So, like Candy Atkinson not being able to identify your SUV, it's something. Nothing more. Nothing less. But if we get enough some-things, then we might be able to raise reasonable doubt. Speaking of which, we need to subpoena Marshall Manor's billing records and see who's paying those invoices now. That could be another something."

Jason punched her lightly on the shoulder. "You're starting to sound like a criminal defense attorney, Counselor."

Shay ignored the compliment and stared at the door. "All right, I know her, so let me lead." Shay trotted up the steps and knocked several times. Jason stood behind her.

Seconds later, a woman cracked the door but left the chain latch attached. "Yes?"

"Hey, Cheryl."

"Shay?"

"Can we come inside?"

The woman blinked. "What's wrong?"

"Please, Cheryl. It's about Griff."

"Why didn't you call?"

"Because I didn't have your number, and I didn't want to ask any-one in the sheriff's office for it." That was technically a lie, as Hatty had given Shay the number for Cheryl Griffith right after the former sheriff disappeared. Shay had even tried to call it a few times with no answer. Shay told Jason that, even if she were to answer now, which was unlikely, they would get more out of an in-person visit.

That is, if she let them in.

For a long moment, Cheryl stared above them to some unknown spot out on the road. Her eyes were vacant. Weary. "What's this about?" Cheryl finally asked.

"Please, it won't take but a few minutes. We just have a couple questions."

Cheryl Griffith looked at Jason and then Shay. "It's about your case, isn't it?" She directed the question to Jason. "Think Griff might be involved in it too. That it? Want to blame him for something else?"

"Please, Cheryl, I know this has been a tough time for you."

"You don't know shit, Shay."

"I know I lost my job too. Just like Griff."

"Not like Griff. All you did was lose an election. Griff lost *everything*." Her voice cracked, and she looked away, clearly trying not to cry. It was obvious that, divorce or not, she still carried feelings for her ex-husband.

"I'm innocent, ma'am," Jason said. "I don't want to go to prison for a crime I didn't commit. We think your husband might be able to help us. All we're asking for is a few minutes of your time."

"Please," Shay said. "I think we might be able to help each other."

Cheryl rolled her eyes and made a motorboat sound with her lips. Then she undid the latch and let the door swing open. "Well, come on then."

———

Five minutes later, they were seated in the living room, each holding a cup of coffee that Cheryl had made with her Keurig machine. Though they hadn't been given a tour of the place, Jason saw no pictures of Richard Griffith anymore. There were shots of the kids and a few of older people that Jason guessed were grandparents on Cheryl's side. But none of the former sheriff.

"I don't have a clue where he is," Cheryl said. "If that's why you came, then you're out of luck. I haven't seen him since he was terminated as sheriff, and neither have the kids."

Jason glanced at Shay. Not exactly a bombshell, but the information was still surprising. "How long have y'all been divorced?" he asked, already knowing the answer but trying to get her talking.

"Since early December. I filed a couple weeks after the Cowan murder trial . . . after he was fired. Griff didn't contest it."

"So Griff hasn't been exercising his visitation rights?" Jason asked.

"No . . . not yet." Her lip started to tremble. "I think losing his job and the scandal was too much for him. Being sheriff was everything to Griff. But then he got messed up with *that woman*, and she was like a cancer on his whole life."

"What woman?" Jason asked, again knowing full well what she was about to say.

"Oh, come on. That was the reason he was fired. He was having an affair with Bella Flowers, Kelly's sister. Kelly found out about it and threatened to go public. And . . ." She trailed off. "Look, I divorced my husband, but I still care about him. I can see how it happened. I was home with the kids all the time. Never interested in . . . you know, and then he meets *that woman*. And she's nothing but boobs and ass and is all over him." She shook her head and looked away from them. "It doesn't excuse what he did. To Kelly or to anyone else."

"He was never convicted . . . or even charged with Kelly's murder," Jason added.

"That's because someone killed George Mitchell, right?" Cheryl asked.

"Pretty much," Shay agreed.

"When was the last time you heard from him?" Jason wanted to steer back to the reason they had come.

"Like I said. The day before he was terminated."

"Where do you think he might be?"

Cheryl sipped from her mug. "I don't know. He loved his farm out in Boaz. That's where I would check." Jason thought of the note he'd left in the former lawman's mailbox. "After that, I don't know."

"Has anyone else tried to reach out to you?" Shay asked. "The new sheriff, Hatty Daniels. The DA, Wish French?"

"Both of them have. Multiple times. So has the *Advertiser-Gleam.* I've told them the same things I've told you."

"Have you thought of filing a missing-person's report?" Jason asked.

She glared at him. "He's not my husband anymore. And, whether he was charged or not, he's a murderer. If he never comes back, I'm not sure that wouldn't be the best for everyone. Including Lida and Richard."

"What grades?" Shay asked.

"Lida is in fifth and Richard third."

"Do they miss their dad?" Jason asked.

"Well, of course they do. But they've heard the rumors. Kids are mean. I think they're embarrassed by him. And I think Griff knows that. He was a very prideful man . . ." Her voice broke again. ". . . he would never want his children to be ashamed of him."

"Cheryl, did Griff ever mention Tyson Cade or Matty Dean or anything about the Sand Mountain drug operation to you?" Shay asked.

A bitter smile came to her face. "He never talked work with me at all. I was nothing more than an ornament on his arm. I helped him fulfill the image of the hardworking family-man sheriff." She wiped her nose. "And the sad thing is that I don't so much miss him. But I miss what we were. I miss going to church and seeing people smile and nod at us like we were somebody. Now we get side glances and head shakes. Whether Griff is around or not, his stench is all over us." She paused. "Once this school year is over, I'm going to sell this house and move to Huntsville."

A sad silence came over the room. Jason finally stood. "Thank you, Ms. Griffith."

"You know, you two are the first houseguests I've had in three months." She continued to sit in her chair, staring at the wall.

"Thank you, Cheryl," Shay said, squeezing the other woman's shoulder before walking toward the door.

———

"Sad," Jason said, once they were back in the car.

"Awful."

"Do you think she's telling the truth?"

"Yes, I do. I don't think you could fake that kind of despondency." Shay put the car in gear. Jason glanced behind them, and Satch was following in the Raptor.

"We need to check out the Boaz property again," Shay said. "And we may want to stake it out."

"I'm working on that angle," Jason said.

"Good."

"I think our goal is just getting Griff to trial," Jason said as she turned right onto Blount Avenue. "I doubt he's going to be all that responsive to us, but we need him there."

"Agreed," Shay said. "It's another cross where the questions are more important than the answers. Planting those 'somethings.'" She turned left past the courthouse to do the loop that would put them back on Gunter heading to the office.

Jason began to think out loud. "The problem is that while Matty Dean is a known fugitive, and Dooby Darnell is subject to a firm cross on the odd timing of her giving Tyson his change, everything with Griff is based on hearsay. My, your, and Hatty's recollection of George Mitchell's confession just before George was killed is inadmissible. It would be great if we had some witness who could place a motive for killing Tyson Cade on Griff's shoulders." As Shay parked the Accord at the office, Jason continued, "That's also kinda the case with Dean. I mean, what is his motive other than speculation about wanting to be the head guy or perhaps frustration at being arrested, as Trudy Cowan suggested to me? That's not much. I think our theory has to be that Dooby was in on the murder, and so Griff or Dean or someone working for Dean had to be the shooter."

"Correct," Shay said. "We're just weak on motive. And we have to consider something else."

"What?"

"That maybe Dooby was working for someone else."

64

Trey Cowan waited until around 3:45 p.m. to swing by his mother's house. Trudy worked from 7:00 a.m. to 3:30 p.m. at Sand Mountain Used Auto and then three nights a week as a server at Top O' the River. She was off tonight, and he knew she was probably looking forward to an evening of putting her feet up and maybe some *Longmire* reruns.

Trey sighed as he walked toward the front door of the house he was born and raised in. He knew he should give his momma some of the money he'd gotten, but he couldn't risk it. Colleen had made him promise to wait.

Trey felt guilty. About misleading his momma. About everything. He knew he should have been grateful to have a new lease on life after the trial.

But he wasn't. He was still the shooting-star ex–high school football star that everyone whispered about behind his back. How great he could have been if he hadn't broken his leg. And what a loser he'd turned out to be.

He was tired of torturing himself, so he'd listened to Colleen. Falling back into a relationship with her in the aftermath of the trial was probably not the soundest decision he'd ever made. But what the hell? She asked him to come over a week after the dismissal, and he'd agreed. He was lonely and cash poor, and she took care of one of those problems.

And Matty Dean had taken care of the other.

When he entered her house, Trudy was sitting at the kitchen table with her feet resting on one of the other chairs. She had a cold can of PBR pressed to her forehead. "You got some explaining to do," she said.

"Momma, I'm fine. Really. I like Colleen. I know you don't, but it's my life."

"I brought you in this world, Trey, and by God I'll take you out. Colleen is using you."

"And I'm using her."

"Well . . . good. I guess." She took a long sip of beer. "Where were you on the day Tyson was killed, Trey?"

"I was with Colleen," he said.

"Where?"

"At her house. Still asleep when the shooting happened."

Trudy closed her eyes. "All right then." She hesitated. "Are you telling me you had nothing to do with it?"

"Yes ma'am," Trey said.

Her eyes opened, and she drank the rest of the beer in one gulp. Then she belched. "I don't get it, then."

"Get what?"

"Everything." She grunted. "Come here. Give your momma a hug."

Trey did as he was told. As he breathed in the first scent he could ever remember in his life, a laser of guilt burst through the marijuana haze. He'd lied a lot to himself over the past few years, but he'd never lied to his momma.

He squeezed his eyes shut and hugged her tight.

———

Trudy sat at the table until well past dark. She drank five more PBRs and was almost shitfaced. She knew Trey wasn't being truthful. Could read it on his face as easy as if it was printed on his forehead. She loved her boy, and he'd been an incredible athlete.

But a scholar he wasn't. Nor was he good at manipulating the truth. And a mother knows her son.

Had he killed Tyson Cade? Been in on it in some way?

Yes. She felt it in her bones, and it made her so damn angry. How could he be so stupid? So ungrateful to her and to his own damn lawyer who had saved his ass.

Trudy belched and walked to the fridge. She pulled out another PBR from the case and popped the top. She heard knocking on her door and hoped it was her neighbor Paul from across the street. He was about her age and widowed, and they enjoyed a good romp every once in a while, which somehow didn't get in the way of their friendship. They liked each other's company and enjoyed getting each other off. That was enough.

Trudy burped again, ran a hand through her hair, laughed at the absurdity of trying to clean up for him given her drunken condition, and opened the door. If it was Lu Stephens, Trudy hoped the death would be quick and painless. *Just take my fucking head off with that sawed-off shotgun, you bitch.*

But it wasn't Lu.

"Trudy, how are you?"

"Mr. Rich, I'm surprised to see you here."

"Please, Trudy. It's Jason. We've been through too much to be so formal."

"All right then. Well, come on in, Jason. There's beer in the fridge."

"I'm an alcoholic, Trudy."

"Well . . ." She scratched her head. "There's bourbon in the pantry."

Jason blinked and then laughed. "No thanks."

Trudy sat back down at the table, where she'd made a pyramid with the other six cans she'd drunk.

"Did you have a party earlier?" Jason asked.

"No. Trey came by."

"Ah, good. That's actually why I'm here. Was hoping to get in touch with Trey. You know, during the trial last year, he was always in the custody of the state. I never had to call him on the phone or go see him. I was hoping you could give me his number and tell me where to find him."

"Why do you want to see him?"

"Well, if I told you, I'd have to disclose some of the information he gave me during the case. It'd be a breach of the attorney-client privilege."

She took a sip of beer, her mind scrambled. "You think he can help you in your trial."

Jason nodded. "I think he might."

"I think you're wrong," Trudy said.

"Why don't you let me be the judge of that?"

"He's living with Colleen Maples. She lives over by Cha-La-Kee. I think you know the address."

"Really? They got back together?"

Trudy took a long pull from the can. "Much to my chagrin." She walked over to the kitchen counter where she'd laid her purse, took out her phone, and texted Jason the contact information for Trey.

"I just sent you his number, but he'll never answer it. Best just go see him."

Jason crossed his legs, watching her. "How's he been doing?"

"Not worth a damn," Trudy said. "Staying high most of the time. Still working for the city, but I don't see how he's holding down that job."

"I'm sorry to hear that. Had hoped the dismissal of the charges against him would give Trey a new lease on life.'"

"Me, too, but he takes to drink, smoke, and easy pussy just like his daddy did." Trudy killed the rest of the PBR in one gulp. "I hear Dooby is being protected by the sheriff's office."

"That's right," Jason said. "I actually spoke with her today."

"How's she holding up?"

"She looks very scared to me. Apparently, she was almost killed on Friday night in Gadsden."

Trudy crushed her beer can. She tried to add it to the pyramid, and they all crashed. "Screw it."

"Do you know why she was in Gadsden?"

"No, I don't, Jason. I don't know shit from Shinola." She stood and walked into her den. She plopped down on her old La-Z-Boy recliner. "But I do know this. If Matty Dean killed Tyson Cade, then he's going to make damn sure any link to him is dead before the trial." She thought of Trey. His lies. And she shivered. She reclined the chair and sighed.

"You OK?"

"Jason, I know Tyson was a scary young man. Capable of the worst kind of evil. He did awful things, but he could also be kind. He helped me after Walt left. I know what he did for Dooby . . . and I know what he did to her."

"What did he do to her?"

Damnit. Trudy blinked at him. *You're drunk, woman. Just shut the hell up.* "I don't know. I think he may have expected certain physical pleasures from Dooby in exchange for paying for her momma to go to the nursing home."

"I see. Doesn't sound so kind."

"No, it don't." She shook her head. "I guess that was one of Tyson's talents. He could use people and still get old fools like me to say he wasn't all bad." She put her hands behind her neck. "I think he must have been using Matty Dean."

"Why do you say that?"

She rubbed her temples with her thumbs. "Because I've heard that Matty was really devoted to Tyson. Even let himself get passed over so that he could work for him."

"Why?"

Trudy gazed at him, blinking, trying to keep her words from slurring. She was running her mouth, and she couldn't stop it. "The rumors I've heard are that maybe Matty had kind of a . . . what would you call it . . . man crush? Something like that." She whistled through her teeth. "Maybe more than that," she mumbled.

"An obsession?" Jason offered.

Trudy snickered. "Fancy words. Whatever it was, Tyson was the kind of person who would take advantage of the situation."

"Interesting," Jason said. "Might give Matty a motive for murder if his feelings weren't being reciprocated. Or if he figured out he was being used."

"Might," Trudy said, her voice thick with fatigue. "I don't know. None of this makes sense to me. I don't think you're guilty, but I just don't see Matty Dean for it either. Even though . . ." She trailed off, again thinking of Trey and his lies. Was he working for Dean?

"Even though what?"

"Jason, I'm a tired old woman. I'm drunk too. Don't listen to me. Just go on now. Leave me be. I need to rest."

"Yes, ma'am," Jason said, getting up and heading for the door.

"Jason."

He turned and waited.

"If Matty did have something to do with it, he'll try to kill anyone that was involved and cover up the truth."

"I understand. That's what you just—"

"But if he didn't have anything to do with it . . . and he thinks you did . . . he's going to try to kill you."

"He's already tried once."

Trudy leaned the recliner back even farther. "He'll try again."

65

At 8:55 p.m., the Raptor stopped at Richard Griffith's spread in Boaz. "I can't believe I let you do this," Satch said. "I mean, of all the dumbass, stupid things—"

"It's done," Jason said, hopping out of the passenger seat holding an envelope. Satch cut the lights on the truck, and the house in front of the football-field-size lawn was barely visible.

"Jason, you realize that if the former sheriff is as unstable as his wife seems to think he is, then you've just given him a great chance to take a shot at you." Satch had climbed out of the driver's side, and now both men leaned against the front bumper of the vehicle.

"Sometimes, the risks are worth the rewards."

"Rewards? What do you possibly hope to gain from this?"

"I trust my instincts, Satch. It's a teaching I learned from *The Secret*. When the universe gives you an impulse, you act on it or you lose the opportunity."

The colonel grunted. "Secret my ass. How long are we going to wait for him?"

"The note said nine, and it's . . ." He took out his phone and glanced at the screen. ". . . Eight fifty-seven. At least fifteen or twenty minutes."

Satch coughed and stepped away from the truck.

"You OK?"

"Fine."

Jason considered asking again about treatment options but didn't figure now was the time. The colonel was on edge. Jason had sprung tonight's assignment on him without much warning, and he couldn't send Chuck or Mickey out ahead for any reconnaissance on the back end of the property. *Flying blind.*

The younger Tonidandels were behind Jason and Satch, but not in view of the house. Chuck was supposed to establish a position in the rear of the home.

"Something he should have done hours ago given how dangerous an animal we may be trying to corner," Satch had said on the way over.

Jason was still feeling a little weird after his meeting with Trudy. *Trey and Colleen?* He was surprised and disappointed. While he had grown to respect Colleen Maples during last year's trial and appreciated her willingness to testify in Trey's case, she was in a downward spiral, drinking vodka every night to kill the pain. She'd burned Trey before, and he hoped she wouldn't do so again. Given Trey's arrest record since the trial, Jason didn't figure Colleen was doing his old client any favors.

"Look at that," Satch said. "The house."

Jason leaned forward and saw porch lights flash on and off. Five seconds passed, and they flashed again.

"I think that's an invitation," Satch said, his tone grave.

"Then let's take it," Jason said.

Satch grunted. "All right, get in. We ain't walking across this lawn."

They drove up the driveway and parked behind the detached garage. Jason saw no cars anywhere, and the lights were now off.

"Easy now. Me first," Satch said. He got out of the truck and walked around the back of it. When Jason saw him again, the colonel held a pistol and was standing in front of the passenger-side door.

"Show yourself," the colonel said.

Silence.

"I'm on the porch," a voice finally spoke from the darkness. "Tell Rich to come on up."

"You show yourself first," Satch said.

"I don't take orders from you, Colonel. Rich asked for this meeting. He can put his big-boy britches on and meet me on the porch."

Jason opened the door into Satch's body, and the colonel moved out of the way.

"I'm coming with him," Satch said.

When the former sheriff didn't answer, Satch led Jason toward the steps. It was still too dark to see anything but the shadow of a swing and a ceiling fan. The wooden stairs creaked as the colonel took them with Jason behind.

"Put the gun down, Colonel."

"I don't take orders from you either," Satch said.

Jason could now see a figure sitting in a rocking chair. He could also see a long-barrel pistol lying on his lap. *A Glock 17?* Jason wondered. *Or something similar . . .*

"How about telling your muscle to wait by the truck, Jason. I didn't agree to this meeting for a gunfight."

"I'm not going anywhere," Satch said. "But I'll put my gun on the railing if you'll do the same."

"All right," Griff said, then stood and placed his weapon on the wooden barrier.

Satch followed suit and continued to stand next to Jason.

"What do you want, Jason?" Griff asked, his tone sharp. No bullshit.

Now that his eyes had adjusted to the darkness, Jason could see the man. He wore jeans, a flannel shirt, and a blue jean jacket with some kind of thick lining. "Nice place you have here," Jason said, gesturing with his left hand toward the expansive lawn and then glancing at the window to the right of Griff. There were no lights on inside the house. "Do you use this place for hunting?"

"I don't use it for much of anything anymore," Griff said. "But . . . for a time, we had corn in the pasture behind the house, and we'd have a dove shoot. Always a good campaign event." He grimaced. "Won't be having any more of them."

"Do you live here?" Jason asked. He hadn't seen a car or a truck in the driveway, and there were no lights on in the garage. Jason guessed there could be a vehicle in there, but he doubted it. The whole place felt . . . barren.

"What do you want, Jason? It's cold out here, and I don't have all night."

Jason rubbed his hands up his arms. The temperature was probably in the low fifties, but the wind tonight made it feel chillier. The former sheriff's general disposition certainly wasn't warming anything up. "Your ex-wife says that you haven't seen your kids since you were fired."

Griff worked his jaw. "Are you here to counsel me on the error of my ways?"

"No," Jason said. "Why have you not seen them? And, if not here, where are you living?"

"None of your damn business. You still haven't answered my question."

"I know you killed Kelly Flowers last year. Everyone does . . . whether you were charged with it or not. But I'm curious. Flowers was an inside man for Tyson Cade. So did you take his place?"

Silence as Griff rocked back and forth.

"Were you working for Cade?"

Griff chuckled. "If that were true, why would I tell you?"

"I think it is true," Jason said. "I think you killed Flowers and took his place as Cade's inside man in the department. And then George Mitchell had an attack of conscience, and you got burned."

"I don't give a damn what you think."

"Are you working for Matty Dean now?"

Griff stood from the rocking chair.

"Easy, Sheriff," Satch said.

The use of the prior title seemed to surprise Griff, and he gazed past Jason to Satch for a second. Then back to Jason. "Did you really come out here to ask me questions like that?"

"No," Jason said. He'd stuck the envelope in the back of his pants, and he grabbed it now. "I came here to give you this."

He handed the enclosure to Griff, who tore it open. "Should've known," Griff said, staring at the subpoena.

"Trial starts on March 9. If you give me your telephone number, I'll put you on call so you don't have to sit at the courthouse all week."

"Shay already has my number."

"Will you answer if we call?"

Griff took a step closer. Jason could see the man's blue eyes. "Maybe. Maybe not."

"What's your deal, Sheriff?" Jason decided to use the former title too. A show of respect in the hopes of softening him.

He scoffed. "My *deal* . . . is that I've lost everything. My job. Wife. Kids." He paused and spat over the railing. "And my reputation."

"You did that to yourself." Satch's gravel voice cut through the darkness like a steak knife over soft meat.

"I know," Griff said.

"Did you kill Cade?" Jason finally asked.

Griff shook his head. "I wish I had. And I admire you for doing it." He chortled. "It's too bad that giving someone true justice will put you in prison for the rest of your life."

"I didn't kill him," Jason said.

"Right."

"Are you still seeing Bella Flowers?"

Griff's hands formed fists, then relaxed. "I'd like you to leave now."

"I'm going to ask you again, Sheriff," Jason asked. "Are you working for Matty Dean?"

"Don't you wish it was that simple." The words came out through clenched teeth like a snake's hiss.

"Or are you planning to kill him too."

"Get, Jason," Griff said. "Before the colonel and I see who can grab our gun faster."

"See you in court."

"I'll look forward to it."

———

"What do you think?" Jason asked. They were back in the Raptor headed home. Chuck and Mickey were behind them as they passed into Albertville.

"Hard to know which side of the fence he's on. As a lawman for so many years, he certainly was capable of killing Cade. And if you are right about them dealing with each other, which I think you are, then he'd have a reason to kill the sonofabitch. Like he just said. He lost everything."

"But I've got no one that places him at the scene."

Satch grunted. "And that's the rub. And that's why I like Matty Dean for Cade's murder more than the former sheriff. Dean grew up in Alder Springs. Sand Mountain man all the way."

"We can't place him at the scene either."

"Doesn't matter," Satch said.

Jason looked at the colonel, and the grizzled veteran's face shone in the glow of yet another stoplight on Highway 431. "What do you mean?" Jason asked.

"Remember me showing you my favorite scene from *Dallas*?" Satch had a curious grin on his face.

"Yeah. When Jock gets mad at Ms. Ellie for trying to shut down the Takapa project."

"Remember what he says?"

Jason nodded, as understanding set in.

Satch grunted. "Matty Dean is Alder Springs." He squinted at Jason. "He *is* the scene."

———

Back in Boaz, Griff had to admit that the billboard lawyer was smarter than he looked. *But he can't prove any of it, and neither can Shay . . .*

. . . and I'm still here. A free man.

He made sure all the doors were locked, and he walked across the thirty acres in back of the house. He'd parked on a dirt road he'd cut himself behind a storage barn.

He'd enjoyed the dove hunts that he'd told Jason Rich about. Griff liked shooting guns and, more than that, relished hosting the power players of Marshall County on his land. They'd hunt in the morning and drink beer and eat barbecue with their families in the afternoon. The last event he'd hosted was back in September. He'd brought Lida along for the hunt, and she'd killed her first bird. If he'd remained sheriff, he figured both kids would have joined him next year.

But all those dreams were gone now.

A rustling sound broke his reverie, and he drew his pistol. He slowed his walk and squinted against the darkness. He snatched his phone out of his pocket and flicked on the light.

A coyote was staring at him.

Griff edged closer, looking at the animal's yellow eyes. He pointed his gun at it. The coyote was about fifteen yards away, which would be an easy kill for him.

Griff held up his gun and fired a warning shot into the sky. The animal scampered to the right out of his view.

He reached his car and opened the door, still holding his gun. Feeling the heat on the barrel. He could have killed Rich tonight. Could have shot him and the colonel from the railing of the porch. Had them in his sights. All he had to do was pull the trigger.

Rich was on his list. Why hadn't he done it?

Perhaps it was the brazenness of the note the lawyer had written him. Bravery? Recklessness? Insanity? Who knew what drove the billboard lawyer? But Griff had to admit that he respected the gesture, though he'd known the subpoena was coming.

Griff grabbed the envelope out of his pocket. He took out the court order requiring him to attend the trial of *State of Alabama v. Jason James Rich*. Then he wadded it up and threw it in the back. Would he show up? What had he told the lawyer?

Maybe. Maybe not.

There was a time when court orders to appear at a trial meant something to him. But now he didn't give a damn. All he cared about was inflicting pain on those who had brought him down.

Cade was gone.

Matty Dean was next.

And Jason Rich? Griff spat on the ground before climbing into his car. He turned on his headlights, and the coyote he'd scared off was ten yards away, just off the road, and looking right at him. The animal's yellow eyes shone in the darkness, as did his teeth.

Brave? Reckless? Insane? Griff shook his head and put the car in gear.

The jury was still out.

66

The next morning, Jason and Satch were in the driveway of Colleen Maples's home near Highway 69 at 6:30 a.m.

Satch yawned and sipped from a coffee mug.

"I could've handled this one myself," Jason said.

"No."

"Colonel—"

"Jason, don't think for a minute you're safe. When you think that, you're dead. Matty Dean is going to make another play on us. I can feel it."

Jason thought about what Trudy Cowan had told him last night. *He'll try again . . .*

"This shouldn't take too long."

"I'll stand by the truck and cover you."

Jason walked to the door. He knocked and waited.

A full minute later, a brunette woman wearing green scrubs opened the door. She was still attractive, sexy even, with a curvy figure. She'd made overtures toward Jason last year, but he knew he couldn't get involved with someone who had a drinking and drug problem.

"You should have called," she said, her voice scratchy. Her eyes were puffy from lack of sleep.

"I did. And I texted. No answer, so I thought I'd come over."

"You called and texted last night, and I was going to respond when I got to work."

"I don't have much time, Colleen. I need your help. Can I come in?"

"No," she said, crossing her arms. "I helped you in your last case."

"I know that and appreciate it. I'm sure Trey does as well."

She blinked.

"I know you're seeing him again. Trudy told me."

"I'm sure she mentioned me in the most glowing of terms."

"Please let me in."

"Whatever you have to say, you can say right here. We aren't friends, and I have to eat breakfast and finish getting ready for work."

"Is Trey here?"

"None of your damn business."

"I need to talk with him. And you. I'm sure you know what's going on with me, and I think he might know some things."

"What things?"

Jason felt himself getting angry. He had helped Trey. Colleen, too, in a way. "I think he . . . and you . . . might know who really killed Tyson Cade."

She stared at him. "Jason, I'm sorry you're going through a rough time, but I can assure you that neither one of us has the first clue about the Tyson Cade murder. Do you honestly think Trey would get involved with Cade again after his trial?"

Jason narrowed his eyes. "I think rats and stray cats tend to go back to the same garbage cans when they're hungry. They never get out of their rut because they know they'll get fed."

"You're wrong, Jason."

"Tell your boyfriend to call me. You have my number and so does he." Jason turned his back on her and began to walk to the truck.

"Jason?"

He wheeled around, and she was staring at him, rising up and down on her toes. It looked like she wanted to say something.

"What is it, Colleen?"

"Nothing," she said. Then she slammed the door behind her.

Jason peered at Satch as he walked back to the car.

"That went over like a silent fart in a full elevator, didn't it?" the colonel asked.

"Pretty much."

Jason sat down in the passenger seat. He'd hoped Colleen would help him . . . *and maybe she still will*. There was obviously something else she'd wanted to say. Jason checked his phone. He already had a text from Shay.

We need to discuss a motion to transfer venue. Given Cade's notoriety and yours, I'm not sure we can get a fair trial. I think it's worth a shot.

Jason closed his eyes. He couldn't imagine his trial happening anywhere else. He didn't think the danger posed by Matty Dean would go away if they moved locations.

But what if the jury pool were Sand Mountain heavy.

He opened his eyes and rubbed them. Changing venue was definitely worth considering.

"You hungry?" Satch asked.

"Starved," Jason said. All he'd had so far was coffee.

"Good. I'm going to introduce you to the best breakfast on the lake."

———

The Homecoming Café and Country Store was located at South Sauty Creek in Langston, Alabama. It was a nondescript peach building off South Sauty Road within a solidly struck seven-iron of Lake Guntersville. Chuck and Mickey were already seated at a table when Jason and Satch walked in.

Jason breathed in the aroma of coffee and bacon and couldn't help but smile. He took his seat, and Mickey and Chuck were having a deep conversation. "John Dutton is the by God king of Montana," Mickey said. "He owns everything and ain't afraid to take someone to the train station if he deserves it."

"I hear you," Chuck said. "But Walt Longmire is the by gosh sheriff of Absaroka County, Wyoming, and he ain't afraid to get rough either."

"Good grief," Satch said, sitting down next to Mickey. "Neither of those two youngsters hold a candle to big Jock Ewing."

Mickey giggled. "I swear, Satch. What is it about Jock Ewing and Lady Gaga with you? Jock was only on the first four seasons of *Dallas*, and Lady Gaga's nose—"

Satch thumped Mickey with his index finger on the temple.

"Ouch!"

"You disrespect the sexiest woman alive again, and I'll throw you out of that window."

Mickey was rubbing his head and smiling. "Sorry, Colonel."

Chuck was shaking his head. "Little brother, you know there are three people you can never disrespect around the colonel. Jock Ewing, Lady Gaga, and Francis Poncherello."

"Francis who?" Jason asked, seeing Satch draw back his index finger and aim it at him.

"Ponch," Chuck clarified, his face stoic as Micky tried to keep a straight face next to him. "From *CHiPs*."

"Ponch and John," Jason said, snapping his fingers. "The two motorcycle cops."

"Damn straight," Satch said. "Now, enough of this mess, before I thump all your asses. I'm hungry."

"What's good here?" Jason asked.

"Hell, everything, J. Rich," Mickey said. "Put a blindfold on and point at the menu."

Jason smiled as a waiter brought over a white kettle.

"Coffee?"

"Please," he said, leaning back so she could pour it in his cup.

Jason gazed from Chuck to Mickey and then Satch. Weird how, in the most stressful time in his life, he was finally beginning to feel like he had a family again.

In the dark days ahead, Jason Rich would often think back to this morning. Having pancakes, eggs, bacon, juice, and coffee with Mickey, Chuck, and Satch Tonidandel. He'd remember Mickey's giggles. He'd think of Chuck blessing the food and squeezing Jason's hand when he said amen, just as he did when he prayed on their morning excursions to the cove.

Of the respect the two younger Tonidandels showed their brother.

And the odd, genuine affection that the colonel had for his siblings, and the bizarre reverence that Satch showed eighties television characters.

For a little less than an hour, the four laughed, told stories, and ate the best breakfast on the lake.

Later . . . Jason would be glad that he'd savored this moment. The food. The company. The humanity.

Nothing was ever the same again.

67

With Jason's permission, Shay filed the motion to transfer venue that afternoon. They'd brainstormed it from every angle and felt like it was worth filing. Tyson Cade had been a powerful force in Marshall County, and now Matty Dean was running Meth Mountain. How many potential jurors had been impacted by Tyson or were being affected by Matty? Jason was also infamous in his own right, after handling his sister's murder trial and Trey Cowan's volatile case last year, which involved the death of a police officer. How could the jury be impartial?

Jason briefed Shay on his meetings with Trudy, Griff, and Colleen Maples. She was surprised and a bit angry with how he'd met with Griff. "I worked with him for a decade. I should have been there."

"It was a shot in the dark that paid off. We got him subpoenaed. If he shows, we can cross-examine him. If he doesn't, we have an empty chair and a violated court order. Win-win."

She reluctantly agreed.

The box of discovery responses from the state had arrived that morning, and Jason and Shay spent the rest of the afternoon going over the coroner's report, witness statements, and photographs of the murder scene and the body of Tyson Cade.

The video of the stoplight of the intersection of Martling Road and Hustleville Road was unsettling. Jason saw himself behind the wheel as the SUV passed on the green light. The time was reflected below it. 10:43 a.m.

"The 911 call was made at ten thirty-three a.m. This video is exactly ten minutes later."

Jason felt sick to his stomach.

"This is probably the worst piece of evidence against you," Shay said. "Cade's dying declaration is awful, too, but combined with this video . . ."

"Might be too much to overcome," Jason said.

"We'll need to address it," Shay said. "You could take the stand and tell the jury what you were doing on Hustleville Road just minutes after Tyson Cade was murdered."

Jason closed his eyes. "I was drunk out of my mind, Shay."

"That won't fly, Jason. Unless you want to admit to killing Cade and plead temporary insanity."

He shook his head. "No, I don't want to do that." He sighed. "And I don't think it would work anyway."

"Neither do I."

"So let's start with the truth," Shay said.

"The truth . . . ," Jason began, looking down at the table and then back up at the portrait of his father, ". . . is that I'm not exactly sure what I was doing. I'd spent a lot of time on Hustleville Road during the Cowan trial. I guess I wanted to take a drive—"

"You're lying," Shay said.

Jason turned to her. "I can't tell you."

"Why?"

"Because you'll quit."

"Try me."

"No."

"Jason—"

"I was confused and angry, OK? I bought a Glock 17 because I knew it would be more accurate from a longer distance. I trained with it for almost two weeks. I was half-drunk each time I trained, but I got better every session. By November 13, I hardly missed from a hundred feet."

"The coroner estimates a shooting range of approximately sixty feet," Shay said, her voice distant.

"I could have hit that shot sound asleep and piss drunk."

"Jason—"

"Let me finish. I went out there, and I'm sure I probably thought about killing him. But I didn't go through with it. I chickened out."

"Are you freakin' kidding me?" Shay asked. "So if that's all true, why did you throw away your gun?"

"I panicked. I threw it in the lake. It was stupid."

"Damn right it was. *If* you're telling the truth, the gun might have completely exonerated you."

"I'm telling the truth."

Shay pressed her hands on the table and stood. She paced a couple circles around it. "Well, based on what you just said, it would be malpractice to put you on the stand. You would confirm their entire theory of the case. 'I chickened out' isn't much of an explanation when he was murdered ten whole minutes before you went through that light on Hustleville Road."

"An unlucky coincidence," Jason said, his tone weak. Tired.

"That won't fly with a Marshall County jury. You're smooth, but you won't be able to talk yourself out of that." She hesitated and stared at him with grave eyes. "Wish French would tear you to shreds."

"Don't you think I have to testify?"

"Not if we can show a link from Dooby Darnell to either Matty Dean or Griff . . . or Trey Cowan. Someone other than you. They can't put you and Dooby Darnell together. That's our strongest alternative."

"I'm going to see if I can bump into Trey tonight."

"Do you think he's capable of this?"

"Alone? No. One of our arguments in his trial last year was that he wasn't a good shot and had little experience with guns. But could he be working with Dean in some way? I do think that's possible."

"Let me know what he says." She walked toward the door. "If he's involved, that complicates things because you can't use anything he told you during your representation of him. It would be a violation of the attorney-client privilege."

Jason groaned. *So many complications . . .*

"I'm going home," Shay said. "I want to take a walk and clear my head."

"Shay?"

She stopped and looked at him.

"You can walk away from this," he said. "Withdraw tomorrow. The court will appoint Barry Martino or someone like that. I'll be OK."

"Is that what you want me to do?"

"No," Jason said. "But . . ." He felt his emotions getting the better of him. ". . . I want . . . I need you to believe that I'm telling the truth."

Silence for at least five seconds, and Jason could hear his heart beating.

"I have to go," she finally said.

68

Two hours later, Jason was in the parking lot of Albertville High School. Tonight the Wildcats basketball teams were playing North Jackson. It was 5:22 p.m., and the JV boys game had just ended. The varsity girls would crank up in a minute, but they'd have a different set of referees.

Jason and Satch sat in the Raptor and watched the door. A minute later, Jason saw a tall man wearing a black-and-white referee shirt with a jacket over it walking toward them with his head down.

"Let's do it," Jason said. The two men exited the truck and walked toward Trey Cowan. When Trey clicked the keyless entry to his truck, Jason called after him.

"Hey, Trey."

He stopped and blinked at Jason. "Oh . . . hey, Mr. Rich." The smile was forced. Tight. The gaze distant and a bit bloodshot.

"I need to talk with you."

"Now's not really a good time—" He had opened his door, but Jason stepped between him and the opening.

"Now's all I have, Trey. Your girlfriend wasn't all that cooperative this morning, and you haven't returned a single one of my calls. That seems strange since I saved your ass last year. I would think that you might be a bit more respectful toward me."

"I'm sorry, Mr. Rich. Just trying to make a living—"

"You were asleep this morning and couldn't be bothered. You work for the city part time. According to your momma, your full-time gig is getting stoned and drunk. And according to court records, you've been arrested twice since November."

He blinked and rubbed the back of his neck. "Mr. Rich, I'm sorry about what you are going through, but I can't help you."

"Oh, but I think you can," Jason said. "What were you doing the morning of November 13?"

"I was at Colleen's."

The answer came so quick that it startled Jason. *Rehearsed.*

"Did you have any contact with Dooby Darnell on or before November 13?"

Trey snorted. "Before Tyson died, I used to see Dooby pretty much every day. So what?"

"I think you know."

"I'm tired of this, Mr. Rich. I wish you the best, but I want to go have a beer and see Colleen. Can you get out of my way?"

Jason stared at him, feeling desperate. He stepped away, and Trey climbed inside. When he shut the door, Jason knocked on the window. Trey put the truck in gear, and Jason thought for a moment that he was just going to drive away. But then the window came halfway down, and Jason stared at his former client.

"This is my life, Trey. I helped save yours. To use a sports term, I need an assist. Something. Anything. I think Dooby was an accomplice to the murder. She was working for someone. I just don't know who."

Trey gazed over the steering wheel. He reached into the glove compartment, pulled out a pack of delta-8 gummies, and popped one in his mouth. "Mr. Rich, I know that I owe you one. But Dooby is like an older sister to me. I couldn't do anything to hurt her . . . even if it helped you."

"Please, Trey."

"I'm sorry."

———

Once Trey Cowan was out on 431, he popped another gummy in his mouth and made the call.

"Mr. Rich ambushed me after the Albertville basketball game. I . . . feel really bad about all this."

The voice was sharp and cutting. "Do you feel bad about all that money you made?"

Trey felt an arrow of fear run through him. "No."

"Good. Then keep your mouth shut, and don't worry about Mr. Rich."

"I know him," Trey said. "He won't quit."

Silence on the other end. "Oh, he will. He's going to be very distracted."

"Hey—"

The phone clicked dead.

Trey punched the steering wheel. *This is wrong . . .*

Then he felt the calming effects of the THC kicking in as he turned on his playlist. The first song was "Travelin' Light," by Widespread Panic, and he cranked the volume.

I'm sorry, Mr. Rich . . .

69

Satch and Jason drove down Highway 205 in silence. Once they passed the green sign indicating they were back in Guntersville, the colonel started coughing.

The fit lasted almost four minutes. When it finally subsided, they were passing Lusk Street on 431. Satch punched the wheel. "Damnit."

"I made some calls," Jason said. "There are several oncologists at CCI in Huntsville that will see you."

"No," Satch said. "I'm fine. It's worse at night."

Jason started to say something else, but his phone began to ring. He pulled it out of his pocket and looked at the screen. It was Shay.

"Hey," Jason answered.

"Have you checked your email?"

"No."

"Barber denied the motion to transfer venue."

Jason sucked air through his teeth. "That was fast. Any grounds listed?"

"Nope. Just one word. Denied."

Jason gazed to his right as the Raptor made its ascent over the Veterans Memorial Bridge. The lights on the houses of Buck Island cast a glow over the water.

"Well, I can't say I'm surprised," Jason said. "Barber seemed like a drama queen during the Cowan trial. I'm sure he likes having a big trial in his courtroom. And, hell, if I'm going down, it might as well be here where it all started."

"Don't talk like that. How did it go with Cowan?"

"A dead end. He denies any involvement."

"Do you believe him?"

"I mean, I don't know. He admitted being close with Dooby. They were like siblings. I guess he could be part of a conspiracy to kill Cade." He leaned his head against the cold glass window. "But how are we going to prove that?" He scoffed. "Impossible."

"Jason, what are you doing for dinner tonight?"

He frowned. "Hadn't thought about it."

"Look . . . I've been thinking about the case, and we need to talk."

Great. "Shay, if you want to quit, you can just tell me over the phone. I hate dramatic breakups."

"I don't want to quit. I want to talk, and I'm hungry. Mom's playing bridge with her group of friends tonight, so . . . what do you say?"

Jason glanced at Satch, who stared over the wheel, lost in his own thoughts. There were no plans for dinner. He closed his eyes. There were never plans for dinner. "Sounds good," he said.

70

Henagar, Alabama, was a one-stoplight town in DeKalb County, Alabama. It sat at the very top of Sand Mountain. If Hustleville Road had been the beating heart of Tyson Cade's meth operation, then Henagar would have been the lungs. And if Matty Dean had anything to do with it, both sites would continue to flourish.

Lu Stephens sat alone at the bar at Lemons, which was pronounced *Limoans*. Though the pronunciation sounded French to her, the food was Mexican. And, most importantly, it was quite literally the only place to get a decent margarita in Henagar. Lu was by herself and wished she could stay that way tonight. She was halfway into her drink and beginning to feel the tension being replaced with tequila. She'd been strung out and at loose ends since the unsuccessful takedown of Dooby Darnell last Friday.

And, if she was being honest, she was still reeling from the encounter with Satch Tonidandel outside of Crawmama's a month earlier. She hadn't heard from Matty since Friday, nor had there been any updates on Chief's surveillance of Jason Rich and his team.

All she wanted to do tonight was drink two margaritas and go home, but she was supposed to meet a new client that had a big potential upside. It was the wife of a banker in Chattanooga. Apparently, THC gummies weren't pushing all her buttons, and she wanted something stronger.

Lu got a text and figured it was the woman canceling. Cold feet were part of it in this business. But, instead, the message killed her budding buzz in an instant.

We are making a play.

It was from Matty. He hadn't communicated in any way with her since Friday. Three dots indicated another message was coming.

Need you to stop what you are doing and meet at this address in forty minutes.

Lu gazed at the address and plugged it into her GPS.
Grant . . .
"Oh, Jesus," she thought, leaving the rest of her margarita untouched and throwing a ten-dollar bill on the counter.
She ran for the door, knowing full well what her boss was planning.
He wants to end it tonight.

71

Geno's was the only pizza joint in Scottsboro. Located off John T. Reid Parkway, it was also a sports bar and, according to Satch, always brought in a lively crowd.

The colonel said he'd wait in the truck. Jason offered to get him something to go, but Satch declined.

Jason walked in the door and saw Shay waiting for him in a booth. He strode toward her, his mind lost in negative thoughts. Satch's illness. Trey Cowan's failure to cooperate. Trudy Cowan's haunting eyes. The odd encounter with former sheriff Richard Griffith, which Jason had barely processed.

"You look awful," Shay said as Jason took a seat across from her.

"Thanks."

A waiter took their drink orders. Jason ordered water and Shay a Sprite Zero.

"You can have a beer if you'd like," Jason said.

"I don't drink," Shay said.

Jason surveyed the bar with its various taps of domestic and craft beer. "Looks like they have the Terrapin Hopsecutioner on tap."

"What's that?"

"A great beer," Jason said.

"You miss it," Shay said.

"Miss is probably not the right word. I don't miss hangovers and regrets. Last year, while I was really rolling in my recovery, I thought of not drinking as my superpower. I was so much more productive in my practice. And was able to be present during Nola's crisis. But . . . I do crave alcohol. Especially a good IPA."

"Makes sense. Tell me about your niece."

"Well, I have two. Niecy is a sophomore at Birmingham-Southern. Doing well, making good grades, all that jazz. I think she wants to be a lawyer. I haven't really talked with her much since Jana's death. We were closer when she was little." He shook his head. "And Nola . . ." He trailed off.

"You miss her."

Jason nodded. "I got to know Nola a lot better last year, and, for a while, we were a family. I went to a few meetings with teachers and counselors at the high school. It was like . . . I was her dad."

"Do you think you might want to be a father?"

Jason raised his eyebrows and gazed at her. Shay had dark hair, brown eyes, and olive skin. When they'd worked against each other, he'd only known the immaculately dressed, hard-driving, no-nonsense prosecutor. Not a hair out of place. Makeup perfect. Fit. Strong. Both physically and mentally. But seeing her now, wearing a red sweater and jeans, hair up in a ponytail, light makeup if any, and asking him personal questions, it was like seeing her for the first time. He'd gotten a taste of the more casual Shay during the past months of working together, but she was always so tense. It was hard to really see her.

He saw her now.

"Earth to Jason."

He blinked and started to stammer something but was rescued by the waiter, who put their drinks in front of them. She took their food order, and they decided to split a pepperoni pie. Then Shay's eyes were back on him, waiting for an answer.

"Do I want to be a father?" Jason asked out loud. "Yeah, I guess. I don't know. I doubt I'd be good at it. I was a trainwreck with Nola."

"As I recollect, she was the trainwreck, and you saved her life. Then you sent her to rehab and made sure she got clean. And now?"

"Living in Birmingham with her sister. Accepted to the University of Alabama in the fall."

Shay held out her palms. "I think you're selling yourself short."

"I guess I didn't have a great relationship with my dad. He was always working . . . and he doted on Jana." He took a sip of water. "Tell me about your dad."

"He died five years ago. Pancreatic cancer. I'm an only child."

"Were you and he close?"

Shay nodded. "It's hard to talk about. He was a quiet man. He loved to play golf. He would take me with him to Goose Pond every so often, and I'd drive the cart. He played every Saturday and Sunday with his coworkers."

"What line of business?"

"He was a sales rep for Jenkins Brick for thirty years." She chuckled. "He loved the job because he could entertain clients on the golf course."

"That's awesome. You know, I played at Davidson."

"Really? Davidson? Same place as Steph Curry went for basketball."

"Yep. Three years. Got my game down pretty close to scratch, but couldn't putt well enough to take it any farther. Do you play?"

"A little. Not much. This line of work doesn't allow for many four-hour breaks."

Jason snorted. "Tell me about it. The last time I was on a golf course wasn't even to play golf." He thought of his encounter with Tyson Cade last spring. The blackmail proposal that had led to his taking the Trey Cowan case. Jason shivered at the memory.

"I want to tell you something," Shay said.

Jason felt a nervous tickle in his stomach. *Here it is. Some version of "you'll be better off without me . . ."* "OK," he said.

"If you don't take the stand, and I don't think you should, it is going to be awkward with you trying the case too." She winced. "The whole thing is awkward to begin with. I can't remember the last pro se defendant I went up against as a prosecutor, but it's normally a disaster for the defendant."

"Shay, most defendants aren't trial lawyers with experience defending murder cases."

"True, but I'm sure you've heard the saying."

"A lawyer who represents himself has a fool for a client." Jason rolled his eyes. "Of course, and I hear it in my thoughts three times a day."

"Then why are you doing this?"

Jason stared at his half-empty glass of water, saying nothing. "I told you why. I need to work. If I don't . . ." He focused on the taps over the bar.

Before he could say anything else, the pizza came. Jason dove into a slice, enjoying the greasy thin-crust goodness and again having a pang for a beer. After almost taking down the whole slice in a couple of bites, he saw Shay staring at him. He wiped his mouth with a napkin. "In your phone call, you said you wanted to tell me something."

"Two things actually."

He noticed she hadn't touched the pizza yet.

"First, is that I do believe you. I'm not sure why . . . but I do."

"Thanks. And the second?"

"I want you to let me be your lawyer, not your partner. I think you will have a better chance of winning if you let me do the trial work and you just be the client."

Jason stared at the pizza. This was not what he was expecting.

"What do you say?"

"I can't," he said.

"Why? I want you to continue to work the investigation. All I'm asking is for you to let me handle all the trial parts."

"No," Jason said, his voice firmer than he intended.

Shay flinched. "I don't get it," Shay said.

"That's because you aren't an alcoholic. I want one of those beers on tap right now." Jason glanced at the bar and back at Shay. "I want one *bad*. When I didn't have my practice, I gave in to those cravings. I couldn't . . . stop them." Jason clasped his hands together to keep them from shaking. "Being a lawyer is my identity. Without it, I'm lost, and I can't fight the urge to self-destruct. And . . ." His voice cracked, and he forced himself to swallow back his emotions. ". . . the absolute *best* part of what we do is trying a jury trial. I was a salesman before coming back home. I sold settlements with my billboards and bullshit. My circus, as you and Wish call it. But these last two years have turned me into a trial lawyer . . . and *I love it*. There's nothing like it, and I want . . . I *need* to try this case all the way to verdict." He let out a ragged breath and stared at his plate. "I may never get another chance."

For a few seconds, there was silence. Then he felt her hand on top of his. "Hey," Shay said.

Jason looked up at her.

"I get it." She smiled, and her eyes were warm. "And you will get other chances, because we're gonna win," Shay said. "You and me. What did you call it? The Mega Powers?" She squinched up her face and spoke in a raspy whisper. "Ohhhhh! Yeahhhh!"

Jason laughed at her Macho Man imitation, which wasn't half bad and cute as hell. He put his fist up, and she nudged it with her own. "Thank you," he said. He was physically spent and not hungry anymore. But he was grateful for the company.

"You're wel—" Shay stood from the table without completing the expression. "Something's wrong."

Jason turned and saw Satch Tonidandel walking toward them. "Colonel—"

"We got a problem," Satch said, handing Jason his cell phone.

Jason took it and peered at the colonel, whose eyes were bloodred. Then he spoke into the device. "Hello," Jason said.

"Mr. Rich, I don't think we've ever met." The voice was scratchy, harsh. "But you know me and I know you."

"Who—"

"This is Matty fucking Dean."

72

"I'd like you to listen very carefully, Jason." Matty's voice was deliberate and slow.

Jason, Satch, and Shay had gone outside of Geno's and were listening to the phone on speaker. "Go ahead," Jason said.

"I'm sitting here at the kitchen table of this beautiful home up on Gunter Mountain."

"Oh my God," Shay whispered. Jason looked at Satch, and his eyes were focused on the phone.

"Beth Lankford really is a . . . well-preserved woman," Matty said. "It's hard to believe she's pushing seventy."

"You leave my mom alone, you sonofa—"

Satch put his hand over Shay's mouth before she could say more.

"Ah, good," Matty continued. "I was hoping that you two would be working late. Or maybe you aren't working? Maybe I caught you playing."

"What do you want, Dean?" Jason asked.

"I want you and the two remaining Tonidandel brothers, Chuck and the colonel, to come to Ms. Lankford's address. I want you to park your truck and knock on the door. Someone will let you in. No guns. No funny business. No calling the sheriff's office. If you do any of those three things, Ms. Lankford is dead. Do you hear me?"

Jason's head buzzed with what he'd just been told. "What do you mean *remaining* Tonidandel brothers?"

"Oh, I think the youngest Tonidandel . . . Mickey, right? He'll be unavoidably detained."

Jason turned to Satch, who continued to stare at the phone with dead eyes as he held on to Shay, who was shaking.

"How do I know this isn't a sham?" Jason asked.

Silence and then he heard a gunshot. And a woman's scream. Followed by anguished wails.

"No!" Shay cried.

"Mr. Dean . . . ," Jason stammered.

"Oh, it's Mister now."

"What did you do?"

"Why don't I let Bethie tell you?" He paused and, a moment later, Jason heard panting breaths.

"H-h-h-he sh-sh-sh-shot me."

It was Beth Lankford's voice. Even with the emotion, he recognized it from their walk together and the time in the same kitchen she was being tortured in now. *She prayed for me . . .*

Jason hung his head, while Shay dropped to her knees on the hard asphalt.

"Meet me at the Lankford house in thirty minutes," Matty said. "And remember my parameters. I can't say I get much satisfaction out of hurting Ms. Bethie here." He paused. "But if you're so much as a second late, I'll blow her brains out. Understand?"

Jason peered at his partner kneeling on the ground and then to Satch Tonidandel, who gave him a grave nod.

"I understand," Jason said.

73

They met Chuck Tonidandel at Mill Creek. Satch had tried calling Mickey three times, and so had Jason.

No answer.

After filling in Chuck, the three men and Shay stood in front of the Tonidandels' cabin. The former prosecutor had regained some semblance of control on the way back, and she glared at Satch. "I thought you had someone watching my momma's house."

"I did. Two of the best men I know. Virgil and Wyatt Onkey."

They hadn't tried to communicate with either of the Onkeys, because Satch said they must already be dead.

"What's our plan then, Colonel?" Shay asked. "I assume you aren't just planning to go up there and sacrifice yourselves?"

"He's drawing our fire with your mom," Satch said, his voice weary. "Trying to get us out in the clear, vulnerable, so he can take us down without worry of police involvement. He caught us too spread out. Mickey was on a date with Tiffany tonight. Probably should have had Chuck watching him . . ." He trailed off.

"Mickey's tough, Satch," Chuck said. "There's no way—"

"He's dead." Satch said it with such confidence that it felt like a dagger through Jason's heart. "Look, there's no time for bullshit. Shay, I want you to follow us up the mountain in your car. Do you have a piece?"

Shay nodded.

"Good. Have it on you. We'll make our plan en route by phone. I need to know everything about the location of that house. All angles in and every avenue out."

"I can give you that," Shay said.

"Good."

"Colonel, we both know they aren't going to let my momma go. They'll kill her too."

"If they haven't already," Satch said.

Shay swallowed.

"There's no time for this," Satch said. "Let's roll."

74

Behind the home, along a trail that led to the edge of the mountain, Lu Stephens gripped her sawed-off shotgun and waited. *Jesus H. Christ,* she thought. *He's really going to do it.*

There would be no trial of Jason Rich. No more Tonidandels. She reached inside her jeans and gripped the handgun that she'd brought just in case. She felt adrenaline pulsing through her veins. Matty Dean was back to doing Matty Dean things.

Lu forced a smile and watched the house. *And I'm here for it.*

75

Inside the dark home, four people sat around the kitchen table. It was so quiet that Matty could hear their breathing. They had drugged the dog before going in, and she was taking a nice sedative-induced nap in a closet in the back.

The room smelled of smoke, which lingered from the gunshot, and piss.

And fear . . .

"Won't be long now," he whispered.

The woman, Beth Lankford, was tied to her chair. Blood was running down the back of it. He'd shot her in the ass. He believed the army called that a "million-dollar wound," but he'd have to confirm that with the colonel.

Beth was shaking. Her pants were damp from blood and urine.

Matty felt an electric current of excitement running through him. He'd gotten the jump on them tonight, just as he'd known he would. He'd told no one in his operation about this plan other than Chief, who'd relayed the specifics to his crew.

Patience and brains.

Chief peered through the blinds of the kitchen window. "They just pulled in the driveway. The colonel, his brother Chuck, and Rich just got out of the car."

Matty grabbed a walkie-talkie. "How are we looking from the road?"

"All clear," a deep voice responded.

Three loud knocks rang out from the front door.

Matty looked at Beth Lankford. "Got your popcorn ready?"

76

Shay Lankford parked a mile from the house. She cut a trail through the woods, running as fast as she could with what she was holding. She'd walked with her mother through this very same forest as a child. She'd heard her momma's prayers as they ducked under branches and around trees.

Please hear her tonight, God.

And please hear me. Help us . . . She gritted her teeth as hot tears fell down her cheeks. She couldn't wipe them.

Let me be fast, dear Lord.

And let this plan work.

77

"Open the door," a voice from behind the barrier said.

Jason was holding his breath. He finally exhaled and gasped. He felt like he was about to pass out. The trip up the mountain in the Raptor had been like riding a roller coaster in the dark. Down Highway 79. Up curvy Columbus City Road to its intersection with Old Union. Past the creepy Old Union cemetery, a slew of intermixed trailers, several new homes, and a lot of nothingness until they reached the summit. Jason's ears popped from the elevation change. They'd been on the phone with Shay for most of the ride, first getting the bearings of the house and surrounding area from her. Then the colonel had barked out his game plan, but there hadn't been time to discuss it.

Only to execute.

"On my signal," Satch said. The colonel's voice was razor sharp.

"Open the fucking door!" the man repeated.

Satch grabbed the knob. "You remember what to do, right, Jason?"

"Yes, sir," he managed.

Satch swung the door open and stepped inside. Chuck was behind him and Jason after Chuck. Jason could hear the words of the twenty-third Psalm that the middle Tonidandel was whispering.

"Yea though I walk through the valley of the shadow of death . . ."

All the lights were on. The blinds had been shut. From the foyer, Jason could see Beth Lankford tied up in a seat at the kitchen table.

Blood was oozing down the chair's legs. He saw four men standing around the table. Closer to them, in the hallway that led to the kitchen, were two more men, and, here in the foyer, another three. *At least nine.*

"Now I'm going to pat you down," a huge man said. It was the voice that had been speaking before they came in. He took his time and patted their pants and shirt. "They're clean," he yelled. Then, looking at Jason, he added, "Mr. Dean is waiting in the den just past the kitchen." He pushed Jason toward the hallway. "Go."

Jason walked through the hallway. He smelled smoke and something else pungent and, when he entered the kitchen, he saw what it was. Urine also covered the floor around Beth Lankford's feet. He looked at Shay's mom, and she closed her eyes tight, tears streaming down her cheeks.

The kitchen opened into a nice-size entertainment area with two couches. A man sat on one and gestured for Jason to sit on the other. "Please, sit. All of you."

"Matty Dean?" Jason asked, taking his seat with Satch and Chuck following suit.

"The one and only."

Dean was of average build and looked like the mug shot Jason had seen last fall. Salt-and-pepper hair. Similar beard. Hard to tell his height sitting down, but everything about his appearance was average. Nothing jumped out.

Nothing except the long-barrel handgun that lay across Dean's lap.

"Glad you could make it," Matty said. "I really did hate shooting Ms. Lankford, but I needed to make sure you knew I was serious. I will have to kill Bethie, too, but it'll be quick and painless, I swear."

"Why?" Jason asked. *Got to buy some time. Bullshit is my bread and butter. Come on . . .*

"Because you killed Tyson Cade."

Jason didn't think arguing would do much good. "Why not let Wish French do his job?"

"Because you seem to have a way of wiggling out of unwinnable cases," Matty said. "I don't trust that this prosecutor will have any better luck than Ms. Lankford's daughter."

"Did you kill my brother?" Satch asked, his voice a low croak.

"Yes. He had just dropped his sweet little piece of ass off at her house. We shot up his truck. It's not bulletproof like yours. And when he got out . . . well . . . you remember that scene in *The Godfather* with Sonny?"

"You're lying," Chuck said. "Mickey's too smart to let a pack of mangy dogs get the best of him."

Matty moved his eyes to Chuck and tapped his fingers on the Glock in his lap. "Oh, I wouldn't lie about that."

"Is that it?" Jason asked, nodding at the piece. "Is that the gun that killed Tyson Cade?"

Matty scoffed and picked up the weapon, eyeballing the barrel. Then he pointed it at Chuck Tonidandel. Satch elbowed his brother just as the shot rang out in the den.

Blood flew from Chuck's left shoulder, and he crumpled to the ground.

"Well, shit on a stick, Colonel. You just made a mess." He pointed the gun at Chuck's head, and Satch threw himself on top of his brother. Jason instinctively stood from the couch and saw at least six guns pointed at him. Then the weird sound of static came from a walkie-talkie. "Matty, watch out! The truck is coming straight for the house!"

Jason saw the others turn toward the sound of a rushing engine.

"What?" Matty asked, letting his hand drop a few inches. He opened his mouth to say something else, but then the air went out of his lungs.

The punch delivered from Satch's knees caught Matty square in the chest. The colonel rolled and Jason ducked as a fully loaded 2017 black Ford Raptor crashed into the house going about thirty miles per hour.

As the roof on the side of the house caved in, Beth Lankford's screams mixed with the sound of pistol shots.

Then, from outside the house, came the unmistakable pop of an AR15 assault rifle.

Jason felt hot breath in his ear. "There's another AR in the truck." It was Satch. "I'm going to get it, and I'm dragging Chuck with me. I need you to get up and find Ms. Lankford, OK? Try to crawl out the other end of the house, all right? Stay down and get out as soon as you can."

"Yes, sir," Jason said. "Where's Dean?"

But Satch was gone. Jason crawled toward the kitchen. Everything past it was caved in around the Raptor, whose wheels were still turning and tearing up the hardwood floor. Jason reached Beth and knocked over her chair. He covered her with his body. One of Dean's men that had been run over by the truck was lying dead a few feet away, and a handgun was next to him. Jason grabbed the weapon and squinted against the dusty ruined drywall. There was more gunfire outside. Multiple ARs.

Below him, Beth was whimpering and praying "Please God" over and over again.

"Ma'am, we have to go." He tried to untie her, but it was no use. He didn't have a knife either. Jason squatted and pulled the chair with Ms. Lankford in it toward the den where they'd just been sitting with Matty Dean.

"Back porch is straight ahead," Beth managed. "Lucy is down the hall beyond the den."

"OK." Jason made it to the screen door and pulled Beth and the chair through it. Seconds later, they were outside on the patio and then to the edge of the backyard. "Stay here," he said, feeling dumb as soon as the words left his mouth, as Ms. Lankford was still bound. Jason went back inside the house and down the hallway to the left of the den. He opened one door. *Bathroom.* Then he opened the next one. There were several coats hung on a rack and below them, crumpled on the ground, was a Labrador retriever. "Come on, sweetie," Jason said, reaching down for the dog as gunfire erupted outside the house. The dog must have been tranquilized or drugged because she wasn't moving. Jason reached down and picked her up and stumbled down the hallway. Lucy must have weighed over seventy pounds, and he was struggling with her. He finally made it out to the backyard and knelt next to Beth.

"My sweet girl," Beth whimpered, kissing the unconscious animal.

The air smelled heavy of gunfire. Jason covered Beth and Lucy with his body and tried to keep his eyes open. Inside the house, he heard another crashing sound. And then the roar of the Raptor as it backed up and out of the place. Satch must have gotten in and removed the crowbar that Shay had attached to the accelerator.

Now the colonel was behind the wheel.

Jason saw the Sheetrock-covered truck emerge from the front of the house as the entire roof caved in. *It's gone,* Jason thought, staring at the ruined house. Satch was driving toward a man running along the street. Then the man disappeared under the tires of the Raptor. The truck cut rubber in a circle and drove toward the woods, then stopped at the edge of the clearing, unable to go any farther.

"Jason!" Shay screamed, running toward them, holding the rifle, but dropping it when she reached her mother. "Momma." Shay hugged Beth and tried to untie the knots. "Momma, are you OK? Where are you hit?" Lucy had opened her eyes and was whimpering, licking her master's face.

But Beth wasn't answering or moving.

Jason felt like everything was operating in slow motion. He saw Greta Martin again. And Harry Davenport's dead eyes. Jana on the sidewalk after being shot.

Mickey Tonidandel. *You need people in your life, Jason.*

He let out a sob as he peered down at Beth Lankford.

"I can't tell if she's breathing, Jason. The pulse is faint." Shay had her phone out. "Yes, this is Shay Lankford in Grant, Alabama." She gave the address. "My momma's been shot! Please come fast. This is an active-shooter situation, and there are multiple gunmen. And . . . oh my God."

An explosion came from the house, and the home was now in flames. How many people had died inside?

"Dean!"

Jason turned toward the anguished cry and saw Satch Tonidandel standing in front of the Raptor. Blood streaked his arms and face. His shirt had been torn off his body. He held the rifle in the air and fired off a round, screaming, "I'm still here, motherfucker!"

The big man's voice shook.

"We ain't done!" Satch's yell was like a wild animal's.

"Colonel." Jason walked toward him. When he got within arm's reach, he touched his shoulder, but Satch shook him off and walked toward the woods.

"He's gone, Colonel," Jason said. "It's over. We did it. The plan worked."

Satch spat blood on the ground. He laid his weapon at his feet and sank to one knee. "Nothing's over, Jason," Satch said. "Nothing."

78

It took the whole way down the mountain before Matty Dean caught his breath. Between the adrenaline of the gunfight and the smoke and Sheetrock inhalation after the truck crashed through the house, he was having a hard time getting enough oxygen.

He'd run immediately. The second he no longer had control, he hit the eject button. He was out the back porch in seconds, and he told Lu Stephens to abort mission as he ran toward her. Two minutes later, they were in her car, going down the Gurley side of the mountain. Once on Highway 72 heading toward Scottsboro, he asked her to pull off the side of the road. When she did, he got out of the car and fell to his knees.

Matty puked. Caught his breath. Puked again. He thought of the men inside the house. The Raptor had crushed Chief Parrish. He was dead.

As were most of Chief's men.

He hadn't seen it coming. The colonel had outfoxed him.

But not before I took them down to one. Mickey Tonidandel was dead. Wyatt and Virgil Onkey were too. And if he had to guess, Chuck Tonidandel would be out of commission for months.

All that was left was the colonel . . . *and Jason Rich.*

It was important to be able to calmly assess the situation. He hadn't finished things, but he'd hurt them. The plan had worked.

That would have to be good enough.

"You OK?" Lu asked, as he got back inside.

"I'm . . . great. I told you we'd get them one by one, and . . . we're almost there."

79

Jason sat in the lobby of Marshall Medical Center North. *Déjà vu all over again,* he thought. He'd spent way too much time here in the past couple of years. He tensed when he saw Shay come out of the double doors from the treatment area, her face pale, eyes red. When she got closer to him, she smiled through her tears. "Mom's OK. She's lost a lot of blood, but she'll make it."

A wave of relief rolled over Jason.

"She's more worried about Lucy than herself." Shay wiped at her eyes.

"I'm glad she's gonna be all right," Jason said.

"How's Chuck?"

"Alive, but not good. They had to amputate his arm. He just got out of surgery."

Shay closed her eyes and then opened them. She pointed behind Jason.

He turned and saw Sheriff Hatty Daniels walking their way.

"Shay, how's your momma?" Hatty asked.

"She's OK," Shay said. "Hurt bad, but she'll pull through."

Hatty breathed a sigh of relief and then hugged Shay. "I'm glad." The sheriff turned to Jason. "How's Captain Tonidandel?"

"Chuck lost his arm. Just out of surgery."

"Where's the colonel?"

"He went looking for Mickey."

Hatty winced.

"What?" Jason asked.

"Can you call him?"

"Why?"

"Because we've already found Mickey." Her grave expression said it all, and though Jason knew this news was coming, his legs still shook. "We'll need a family member . . . ," Hatty continued, ". . . to identify the body."

Jason took a step back and collapsed into a plastic chair. He put his face in his hands. In his mind, he could still hear Mickey's laugh from that morning at the Homecoming Café on South Sauty Creek.

Now he was gone.

He felt a hand on his shoulder. "Jason, I'm sorry," Shay said.

———

Twenty minutes later, Satch Tonidandel walked out of the morgue, where Jason was waiting. Hatty followed the colonel out.

Satch looked at Jason, his eyes distant and bloodred. A jacket covered his bare chest.

"Can I see him?" Jason asked.

Satch shook his head, and behind him, Hatty made the same gesture.

Jason's lips trembled. "Colonel, I'm sorry. This is m-m-my fault."

Satch came over and put his big paws on Jason's shoulders. The colonel pointed at his own chest with his index finger and opened his mouth, but no words came out. Then he walked to the exit, and Hatty stood by Jason's side.

Satch placed his hand on the door and hung his head. "It's tough being brothers," he finally said, his gravelly voice thick. Heavy. Tired.

Then he pushed through the opening and was gone.

———

Hatty walked with Jason back to the lobby. "Thank you for coming," Jason said.

She grabbed his arm. "I'm not here as a friend, Jason."

He looked away from her. "But you are my friend, aren't you, Hatty?"

"Yes. I am." Her words were stilted. "That's why this case . . . and especially what I've got to do right now . . . is so hard." She nodded to someone behind Jason.

"What are you talking about?" Jason asked, as he felt his hands being grabbed and then placed in handcuffs.

"What the hell is going on?" Shay asked, walking toward them. "You can't be serious, Hatty."

"Unfortunately, I am. Jason, you were involved in what can only be described as a gunfight tonight. Such behavior clearly violates the conditions of your bond. You were also required to stay in Marshall County, and you were twice seen in Jackson County yesterday. Such reckless disregard for the bond requirements can't be tolerated." She hesitated and touched his arm. "Jason, I *am* your friend, and this is for the best. Even if you were compliant with the bond, you are a danger to Marshall County right now. Since you've been arrested, there has been a shooting and a bombing on the square, one deputy is dead, and there are at least ten dead bodies in the wreckage of Shay's mom's ruined house on Gunter Mountain. And Captain Mickey Tonidandel has lost his life. Your bond must be revoked, you must be held in custody, or more people will get hurt."

"This is Wish talking," Jason said.

"It was his idea," Hatty said. "But I happen to agree with it."

Jason looked at Shay, and his partner said nothing. *Silence is acquiescence,* Jason thought, remembering the criminal law tenet and swallowing acid in his throat.

"Jason James Rich," Hatty said, her voice clear and firm, "you are under arrest for violating the terms of your bond. The court will set a revocation hearing, but until then, you'll remain in the custody of the Marshall County Sheriff's Office." She paused and took a card out of her purse. She looked at it and then read: "You have the right to remain silent . . ."

PART FIVE

80

In the war room of the Marshall County Sheriff's Office, Wish French and Hatty Daniels went over their witness and exhibit lists. "Pretty straightforward, really," Wish finally said.

"Very," Hatty agreed.

"Outside of the coroner and you, I only plan to call four other witnesses."

"Candy Atkinson, Dooby Darnell, the traffic controller to authenticate the stoplight video that shows Jason Rich leaving the scene." Hatty grimaced. "And Captain Chuck Tonidandel to prove up the Glock 17 purchase."

"Yep. Simple case, and we're ready to go."

"I'm ready for it to be over," Hatty said, standing and walking to the end of the table.

"Any developments on the search for Matty Dean?" Wish asked.

"No. But having Jason locked up the last month and a half has at least stopped the violence."

"Well, I'll rest a lot easier when Dean is in prison. I still tense up every time I start my car."

"I bet," Hatty said, not looking at him.

"Something wrong?"

Hatty gazed out the plexiglass window, where deputies were scurrying down the hallway chasing leads. Phones were ringing. Work was being done.

But Matty Dean is still out there. "You ever think we're on the wrong end of this?" she said.

"What do you mean?"

"I mean Tyson Cade was a drug dealer. An awful human being. If Jason Rich did kill him, he likely did the county a favor. Now, he's in a war with Matty Dean, who obviously wants revenge for Tyson's death. Dean doesn't care about justice. The law." She snickered. "I doubt it will end for Matty Dean when we get a conviction. Jason will be sent to prison for the rest of his life, but he won't die of natural causes there. He'll . . . *have an accident.*"

"All we can do is our job, Hatty. Jason Rich has made his bed by the company he keeps and the choices he's made."

She bristled. "Doesn't seem right. We tracked Tyson Cade for years and made no progress. And now we're searching for Matty Dean. And so is the FBI." She flung up her hands. "And we got nothing. *Nothing.* I mean, how is that possible? No one's that smart."

"The Sand Mountain thing is real," Wish said.

"What do you mean?" Hatty turned toward him, frustration boiling over.

"I mean they take care of their own. They doted over Cade and treated him like Robin Hood. Now they do the same for Dean."

"I don't think so. Maybe with Cade . . . but something else is in play with Matty. He's not the charismatic demigod that Cade was."

"Charisma is overrated," Wish said. "Relationships and contacts are what really matter in that business. And Matty Dean . . ."

"What?"

". . . must be very connected."

They locked eyes, and Hatty finally nodded her agreement. "Must be."

Wish walked to the door. "What do you think Rich is going to do on Monday?"

Hatty sighed and shook her head. "I have no idea."

81

The holding cell was hot. The heat in the building turned up.

Jason's shirt was off, his chest and face covered with sweat. He'd just done a hundred push-ups. Now he was balancing himself on his forearms, doing planks until his abdominals cried for mercy.

He heard the clanging of metal and footsteps approaching. "Lawyer's here, Rich."

The guard opened the door as Jason slipped on the green T-shirt he'd been assigned. Even though it had been washed, the fabric had the perpetual stale fragrance that permeated every part of the building. The smell of rotting life.

Jason followed the man down the corridor. For the last month and a half, he'd embraced routine and habit. The mornings were for working out. Push-ups, planks, crunches, jumping jacks, burpees, and even running in place. Shay would normally come by midmorning for a check-in. Not every day, but at least three times a week. The afternoons were for naps, and the nights . . .

Jason didn't like to think of the nights.

When he walked into the attorney consultation room, he smiled, as Shay had brought goodies.

"Sausage, egg, and cheese McGriddle," Shay said, pushing the sack over to Jason. "And black coffee."

"Thank you," Jason said, then opened the package and took a bite of the mouthwatering goodness. "This really ought to be illegal," Jason said, talking with his mouth full.

Shay frowned.

"That's not a happy face."

"We're three days from trial, Jason. And I'm not feeling good about it."

"Oh, why not?" Jason asked. "Is it because we can't possibly win?"

"Actually, yeah. That's it."

Jason chewed his food, trying not to think about his impending conviction. Or anything about the case.

"Have you been working on your opening statement?" Shay asked.

Jason continued to eat, pointing at his forehead. "All right here."

"Can you be serious for a few seconds?"

"No," Jason said. "When I get serious, I start thinking about Mickey. And Chuck at that god-awful injury rehab place. And Satch . . ." Jason looked away.

"Still haven't heard from him?"

Jason shook his head. "Have you?"

"No. I'm sorry I haven't gone out to see him. I've been meaning to . . . it's just . . . it's been rough since that night. I didn't think about it much when it was going on. There wasn't time to think. But . . . we were so lucky. And now . . . when I'm not working on the case, I'm trying to get Mom situated in our rental house." She paused. "Jason, I'm sure if we filed a motion to continue—"

"No," he interrupted. He gave his head a jerk. "No," he repeated. "I want this over." He looked at the last bite of the McGriddle, no longer hungry. He could eat when he didn't think. When he did think . . . he could barely do anything.

That's why the nights were so bad.

"Jason, what do you want me to do on Monday?"

He studied her. "Help me pick the jury. Younger folks tend to be more liberal, so I'm hoping for a millennial-laced jury of mostly women. I doubt the pool will be that diverse, but Black people also tend to lean left. A diverse millennial-laced jury of mostly women. Can you do that for me?"

Shay snorted. "In your dreams. This is Marshall County. The odds are strong that you will end up with twelve old white guys on the jury."

Jason looked down at the table. "Well, that's what I want you to do."

"I'm a lawyer, Jason. Not a magician."

"Shay Lankford, you are incredibly talented. You managed to rig the accelerator on a Ford Raptor with a crowbar and fired an AR15 pretty damn well for having only shot one a half dozen times. Picking a young, diverse jury ought to be a cinch."

"It'll be a miracle if that happens, and you know it."

"Well, that's what we'll need, right? A miracle. Might as well start with the jury."

Silence for a few seconds, and then Shay reached across the table for his hand. "What else, Jason? I want to help you."

He looked at her. "Any word from Hooper?"

"He's still working an angle with Matty Dean. He's had a hard time getting the records because they go back past Alacourt. It's all paper in a warehouse a block from the courthouse, and none of it is organized. He's there now and has been going through them for weeks. He just hasn't found what he's looking for. I'm going to go over there when I'm done here and help him." She paused. "Again, a motion to continue—"

"Would probably be denied."

"After all that's happened? No way. I'm sure we'd get several more months."

Jason shook his head. "I'm not going to stay in this dungeon another three months. I just can't do that. Look . . . let's move on. What about Darnell's mother?"

"We went through the records last week. She's been at Marshall Manor for three years. Invoices were originally satisfied by checks from Dooby . . . but, in the past year, all of them have been paid in cash.

Since Cade's death, the cash payments have continued. I've met with the administrator, and she says the payments typically come in an unmarked envelope with no return address." She paused. "Nothing has changed since Cade's death."

"Any luck getting Darnell to meet with you again?"

"No. She's still in police custody but unwilling to sit for another interview."

"OK," Jason said. "Sounds like you're doing all you can do."

"Jason, have you decided whether you're going to testify or not?"

He nodded. "I am."

She crossed her arms. "It's a mistake. He'll eat you alive."

"I'm trying this case pro se. I have to tell the jury that I didn't do it."

"It's not worth all the admissions you'll have to make."

"It's my case. It's my life. If I'm going down, I'm going down swinging."

"Then we need to practice my direct examination of you. And get you ready for Wish's cross."

"Yep." Jason was now staring at his hands. Depression was beginning to seep in. "So all we really have is the state's failure to link me to Darnell . . . and our theory that Darnell was in on it because she stopped Cade for his change."

When there was no response, he finally looked at her.

"I'm sorry, Jason. I wish there was something else. Some other angle. Maybe Hooper . . ."

Jason stood and walked to the door. "Does your mom still pray for me?"

"She does," Shay said, still sitting. "Every night." She paused. "So do I."

Jason knocked three times on the door to alert the guard. "Thank you."

82

Matty Dean sat in a rocking chair on the dock of the boathouse in Langston. He held a rod and reel in his hand, but he had stopped fishing for a moment to enjoy the sunshine.

The house was shielded on both sides by trees, and there wasn't another boathouse within a half a mile. There was a fisherman about a hundred yards away, but otherwise no one in the vicinity. The view of the main channel was tremendous, and Matty soaked it in.

Maybe I should live here forever. He snickered, knowing that his time at this hideaway was in short supply. He'd stay through the trial, and then he wasn't sure.

It was hard to run his operation as a fugitive, and things had really been dialed up since the ambush at Beth Lankford's home on Gunter Mountain.

But the only people Rich and the colonel could identify were already dead, and Matty was a chameleon. He'd manage somehow, even if he had to hide out in the cabin in Mentone. The business would go on.

Just as Tyson would want it.

He thought of his friend often. Matty still missed him and pined for the times they had together in the boat when it was just the two of them. He closed his eyes.

He'd gone to Birmingham three times in the last month, meeting the banker in a different hotel each time. And though Matty liked Sam and enjoyed their interludes, they were a means to an end. They weren't near as intense as his encounters with Ben Raggendorf. The attraction not as strong as it had been with Tyson.

But Matty needed the contact. The escape. And when this was over . . . when he had done what he'd set out to do . . . he might very well walk away from the business. He had enough money stashed away. He could disappear. Maybe head to the Keys. Live out his life fishing blue water and living outside of the closet.

He smiled. Could he really do that? Leave his home. Leave Sand Mountain.

Yeah, he thought he could. He knew there were whispers afloat. His plan to take down the Tonidandels had been partially successful, but they'd lost Chief and nearly all his team. Ten people had been killed. Too many casualties.

Revenge had been Matty's primary motivator. Revenge for Tyson and his people had gone along with it. If Jason Rich killed Tyson Cade, then the attorney deserved the same fate.

But now Rich was responsible for ten more deaths.

Matty's smile faded. *No . . . I'm responsible.*

He knew if he had that thought, then others did as well. Lu Stephens had been particularly quiet as of late. He wondered if Lu was planning what Reg and Tanner had tried nearly four months ago.

Bring it, Matty thought, but he had to admit he was worried. And tired.

But regardless of whether Jason Rich won or lost next week, Matty had a plan. He cast his line and began to reel it in.

He'd wait in the weeds like the copperhead snake he was. And when the time was right, he'd strike without warning.

He'd figure the future out afterward.

83

It was strange the way life worked.

There were so many characteristics that a person on the run might have that would allow someone else to find them.

Ambitions. Goals. Strengths. Weaknesses. Impulses. Addictions. Vices.

But there was one undeniable trait that almost always gave someone away in the end.

Habits . . .

Richard Griffith had worked stakeout a lot in his early years in the department, and he'd rather enjoyed the mundaneness of it. He liked tracking people until he found them and watching them until they made a mistake.

And while Matty Dean was more unpredictable than most of his targets over the years, the experienced drug lord wasn't without his vices, as his dalliance with Ben Raggendorf had shown. Griff had made quite a few contacts over his years in law enforcement, and several still owed him favors. One of those was a man named Jacob Hall. Griff had dismissed a first-offense DUI on Hall ten years ago after the man had gotten drunk at a lake party in Goose Pond and tried to drive home. Hall had been the husband of one of Griff's wife's friends, and he'd let him go through a pretrial diversion program. Hall completed the program, and the charges were dismissed. Then he'd gone to rehab, come out as gay, and moved to Birmingham.

But he never forgot his pal Richard Griffith, and Griff didn't forget him. About a month ago, Griff reached out to Hall about the LGBTQ+ bars in the Birmingham area, sent a picture of Matty Dean to him, and asked him to look around.

A week ago, Hall hit pay dirt, sending Griff a pic of a man sitting in a booth. It was Matty Dean. Griff drove straight to the bar, getting there in just over an hour and a half. Matty was still there.

Griff watched the drug dealer finish off another round and his dinner. Then he and a man wearing a suit walked down the street to a hotel.

Dean didn't leave until three in the morning. Griff kept a good distance behind him but followed him all the way to the house in Langston.

He could hardly believe his eyes when Matty Dean drove up the driveway and parked in the garage.

Unbelievable.

Griff had been in that house before.

He'd watched the home for twenty-four hours straight, and Matty hadn't left. Since then, Griff had staked the property out from the water, as it was an easier cover. Some of the best fishing on Lake Guntersville was in Langston.

Today was the closest he'd gotten to the drug lord. He held his fishing pole tight and gazed into the bottom of the boat. His rifle was out of its case and loaded. Griff was an excellent shot. Over the past hour, he had drifted to within fifty yards, and Dean appeared to be lost in his thoughts.

I could put an end to him right now.

But he didn't go for his weapon. His curiosity had been piqued.

What in the hell is going on here? he thought, looking at Matty and then back at the beautiful home that Griff and Cheryl had attended parties at years ago.

Griff had thought only of revenge for so long that it was hard to harbor other ideas. But he was having them nonetheless. Was there a chance here to do something good?

He doubted it, but as he eyed the rifle and then again stared at Matty Dean, he decided that discretion was the better part of valor. He could jump off this wave . . .

. . . or he could ride it all the way to shore.

Griff put his craft in gear and motored past the boathouse.

Let's ride it out.

84

On Saturdays, visitation at the Marshall County Jail was from 10:00 a.m. to noon. These times also applied to pretrial detainees. Jason was surprised when the guard said there was someone here to see him.

In the last six weeks, he hadn't had any visitors except his consults with Shay. Satch hadn't come, but that didn't surprise him. The colonel was devastated from his brother's death and dealing with getting Chuck the right doctors. And he wasn't much for talking when it wouldn't do any good. He was also sick, and God knows what the encounter with Matty Dean on Gunter Mountain had done to him physically, mentally, and emotionally. Just thinking about Satch made him sad. Jason had gotten several letters and cards from Izzy, encouraging him to keep his head up and stay positive, but she hadn't come, and he didn't blame her. She'd even said in her last letter that while she was with him in spirit, she couldn't go back there again. In similar fashion, both of his nieces had sent him cards of encouragement, but he'd written back asking them to stay well clear of Guntersville until after the trial. Perhaps they could visit him in prison one day. Finally, he'd gotten a few letters from clients, wishing him well and telling him that they were pulling for him.

As he followed the deputy out into an open area with picnic tables, he was glad to see that it was a sunny day. Breathing natural air was a blessing when you'd been locked up for over a month. Especially when outside breaks were stunted due to the cold.

When he saw her, his legs gave a little, but he managed to keep his balance as the officer unlocked his cuffs. Now that he was free to move, he found that he couldn't. He tried to speak, but he was not able to do that either. Jason wasn't an overly emotional person, but his lips shook at the sight of her.

Nola Frances Waters had long strawberry-blonde hair and wore dark jeans, a white turtleneck, and a brown vest. Her eyes were her mother's crystal blue.

"Hey," Nola said, her voice tentative.

Jason hadn't seen his youngest niece since she'd left home on the eve of the Cowan trial.

"Hey."

For a moment, they just stared at each other. Nola had a fierce look on her face. "I can't stay long."

He nodded his agreement. "Too dangerous."

Nola blinked back tears and stuck out her jaw. "I . . . wanted to tell you something."

"OK."

"You're going to think I'm crazy."

Jason snorted. "I think you've forgotten that my only friends are the Tonidandels."

Nola's face broke into a grin. "I miss them. Especially Colonel Satch." Her smile faded. "I'm sorry about Mickey. He was the silly one."

Jason tried to say something, but the words wouldn't come.

"Sometimes I hear my mom in my thoughts," Nola said. "And in my dreams."

Jason's stomach tightened into a knot as he tried to maintain some sense of composure. *That makes two of us.*

"Most of the time it's her saying that I shouldn't wear something because it makes me look trashy. Or that I shouldn't kiss a boy." She giggled. "Or that I should kiss a boy. I know it sounds crazy, but it's like she's right in my head, speaking to me. A lot of times I don't know if she's trying to help or hurt me. Do you know what I mean?"

"Yes, I do," Jason said, peering down at the ground. *More than you know.*

"My psychologist says that it's not uncommon to hear a loved one's voice in your mind. It doesn't actually mean that they're a ghost. Just that you miss them. That they were important to you. He also said it could just be my own thoughts and self-talk, and that I'm interpreting them as Mom's." She sighed. "I guess I don't know what to believe. I only know that I hear Mom sometimes. A lot actually."

Jason stared at his niece. He felt the sun on his face as the heat dried the moisture on his cheeks. "Nola, what did—?"

"Don't quit." Nola's voice had cracked, and the dam on her tears had finally broken. "Last night before bed, I was looking at some old photographs on my phone from last year . . . of you and me and Chase and the Tonidandels . . . and I heard her voice in my mind. That's what she said. Tell his ass not to quit." Nola paused, blushing. "I thought you might want to know that before your trial begins."

Jason wiped his now steadily flowing tears. All he could muster was a nod.

"I have to go now," Nola said. She strode forward and threw her arms around him, squeezing his back hard. Then she kissed his cheek and spoke directly into his ear. *"Don't quit."*

Before he could respond, she stepped backward several paces and put her hands on her hips. In that moment, she was the mirror image of her mother. "There was one other message she wanted me to give you."

"Yeah?"

When Nola spoke, her voice was firm and harsh. "Don't be a pussy."

85

The warehouse on Blount Avenue had a lake view from one of its windows, but the only sight Shay had was of at least a thousand manila file jackets. And that might have been an underestimation.

There was no air-conditioning or heat in the building, and with temperatures a balmy seventy-five degrees, which was warm for early March, Shay was sweating profusely. She wished she'd worn shorts and a tank top instead of jeans and a T-shirt. Her companion, Albert Hooper, wore khaki shorts and a crimson #2 Derrick Henry jersey. His brown hair was matted down with sweat, but he seemed to be enjoying himself.

"Remind me again what we're looking for," Shay said.

"Outside of his arrest last year for drug possession and not registering his boat, Matty Dean's criminal record is remarkably clean for a career drug dealer. His only conviction was a misdemeanor controlled-substance conviction in Jackson County. Nothing in Marshall."

"So he's slippery?"

"I said no convictions. On Alacourt, there were five charges. All dismissed by the prosecutor. In other words, the district attorney abandoned the case. I'm sure you know who that must have been."

"Wish French," Shay said. "But so what? I've done that myself on numerous occasions when I realize that the facts or circumstances don't justify the effort."

"Five times? With the same defendant."

"It's possible."

"I looked at the computer files, and there's not much in them. But one thing is consistent with each case. Dean had the same attorney."

"Who? Barry Martino."

"No," Hooper looked at her above one of the files. "Terrence Jerome Barber." He smiled. "Now . . . the Honorable Terry Barber. Back then, he must have—"

"Been a criminal defense attorney," Shay finished the thought. "Damn, really?"

"See for yourself. My own file that I printed off the computer is in my briefcase in that chair over there."

Shay put a pen in the manila folder she was reviewing to hold her place and walked over to the briefcase. Sure enough, Hooper was right.

Terry Barber had been Matty Dean's lawyer. Not exactly incriminating or anything. Every defendant was entitled to counsel, and she guessed that Judge Barber took a lot of court appointments back during that time frame. If he got appointed to one case, he might get all of them.

There was another printout in the briefcase that didn't match the quality of the others. The words were more faded, the font dimmer. She squinted at it, and her eyes widened. "What's this?" She turned and held it up for him to see.

"That, my dear, is the holy grail. As you know, Alacourt only goes back to 2003. All of the files before then are stored in this warehouse." He paused. "However, while the actual files are kept here, a catalog of the cases prior to Alacourt going live is preserved on microfiche and filed on the second floor of the courthouse. What you are holding is the summary of all of the charges against one Matthew Jefferson Dean prior to 2003."

"I'll be damned," Shay said.

"Sixteen charges. Every single one of them dismissed. All during Wish French's long reign as district attorney and most during the 2000 to 2002 time frame."

"Is Barber—"

"That's what I'm looking for in these files. To see if Barber was Dean's attorney on all of these cases. I'm also looking for something else. Something really juicy."

"What?"

"Did you know that the Honorable Judge Barber had a troubled son who was charged with marijuana and cocaine possession on multiple occasions?"

"No."

"Terrence Jerome Barber Jr. Goes by Jerome. Three different charges when he was nineteen years old. All dismissed by Wish French." Hooper paused. "Eighteen months before Barber ran for circuit court judge the first time."

"Hooper, this is all rather interesting, but where does it leave us?"

"Matty Dean had a confidential attorney-client relationship with the judge presiding over this case. He also managed to have the district attorney prosecuting this case dismiss charges against him *on twenty-one separate occasions.*" He paused. "And he is your best alternative theory, right?"

Shay felt it coming together. "Yes. Probably."

"Then shouldn't Judge Barber recuse himself?"

"Maybe. It would be stronger if there was still an existing relationship or some kind of pull one had over the other now. But even if we can prove a link like that, what does it give us?"

"Grounds for a mistrial?" Hooper asked.

"Possibly. I guess that's good, but I really want something we can use to help Jason win the trial."

"If the district attorney and the presiding circuit court judge are both beholden to a known fugitive, then that type of scandal will take the roof off the courthouse. At worst case, Wish would have to go. Perhaps a new district attorney might feel differently about these charges . . ."

"So what do we need to find?"

"I want the sixteen old case files on Matty Dean. They may not show anything, but there might be a gold nugget in them. Paper files used to contain more than the computer.

"I also want the files on Terrence Barber Jr."

Shay sucked air between her teeth and looked around the huge warehouse. "You think they're in here?"

"They have to be," Hooper said.

Shay wiped sweat from her forehead. "Is there anything else you're working on?"

Hooper grinned. "Oh, yeah."

"What?"

"I got a damn Tua to Smitty–style connection I'm developing that could blow it all to hell."

"What's that?"

Hooper's eyes blazed. "For two career bureaucrats, Barber and French both owned property on the lake in addition to their homes in downtown Guntersville."

"So what. Maybe they're good investors."

"No. I said *owned*. In the early 2000s, both of their lake homes were heavily mortgaged, and Barber had to sell his."

"That's weird," Shay said, scratching her nose. "The judge has a Fourth of July barbecue every year at his lake house. I've gone to the last three."

Hooper held out his palms. "Maybe he sold the place and rented it back. Lease records wouldn't be public."

Shay stuck out her chin. "A status seeker like Barber wouldn't want the world to know he'd lost his pride and joy, and he damn sure wouldn't disclose such a sell-and-rent-back arrangement."

"So . . . maybe not so weird," Hooper offered.

"Maybe not," Shay said. "What about Wish?"

The investigator snapped his fingers. "Ah, but Wish French's lake home is free and clear. Paid off in cash. Right around the time these sixteen cases against Matty Dean went away . . ."

"Holy shit."

"I just need to find these damn folders."

"I'm sure there's no way to prove that Dean or the Sand Mountain drug trade paid him off."

"No, probably not, but it stinks to high heaven. And it might be an indicator of why Matty Dean hasn't been found yet. Ever thought of that? All these folks looking for him, and he's . . ." Hooper snapped his fingers again. ". . . vanished."

Shay felt an ice-cold shiver run up her arms and dry the sweat on her neck. "Jason was right about you, Mr. Hooper. You're good."

"Roll Tide."

86

The courtroom was as quiet as a church during prayer.

It was Monday morning. Jason turned and glanced at the clock on the far wall. The time was 8:55 a.m. He moved his eyes to the empty benches on both sides of the large space.

Judge Barber had banned the press and any spectators. Only the families of the defendant and the victim were allowed to be present. And on this one point, Jason appeared to have something in common with Tyson Kennesaw Cade. He had asked his nieces not to come, but he knew that neither of them would have voluntarily been here.

And Cade had no family.

Jason wore a charcoal suit, white shirt, and blue tie. He'd lost about ten pounds since his bond was revoked, and the fabric felt loose on him. He observed the empty jury box, which would be full by the end of the day with the twelve men and women who would decide his fate. *Surreal,* he thought, to be both lawyer and defendant in the same case. He glanced at Shay, who was all-business in a black suit. They'd spoken briefly when he was escorted to the table. The tension was palpable.

This is it.

Adrenaline surged through Jason's veins, as he raised his eyes and met Wish French's gaze. The prosecutor looked distinguished in his light-gray ensemble. Next to him, Sheriff Hatty Daniels wore the khaki uniform of the Marshall County Sheriff's Office. Jason took in a breath and slowly exhaled, trying to focus on his breathing.

After his visit with Nola on Saturday, he'd woken on Sunday with an odd detachment from his situation. In the cramped confines of his holding cell, he worked on jury voir dire and his opening statement, outlining the key points and thinking about all he'd learned from his three trials in the past two years. The state's claims against him were based on a chain of powerful circumstantial evidence and Cade's dying declaration. It was a strong case. With only one potential chink in the armor.

Dooby Darnell . . .

But that wasn't the only advantage for the defense. As he paced his cell, Jason realized there was another angle he must explore. In most murder cases, putting the victim on trial was a huge risk. If not handled delicately, the tactic could inflame the jury. Here, though, the traditional line of thinking wasn't in play. The victim, Tyson Cade, was the scourge of Marshall County. A bad, evil person who had been investigated for years by the sheriff's office. Jason could use that. A jury that didn't feel sorry for the victim had to be a good thing, right? He and Shay had vetted all the state's discovery responses, and, while there was very little in the way of helpful information, the surveillance footage produced by the Alder Springs Grocery, which went back a month prior to the murder, was interesting. The outside camera showed people entering and exiting the store, while the inside lens was trained on the register. On November 13, 2019, the interior one showed Tyson Cade appearing to assault Darnell minutes before the shooting. *And neither camera ever shows me . . .*

Putting the victim on trial could work under these circumstances.

Along those same lines, Jason's best alternative suspect, Matty Dean, was a fugitive, wanted for numerous crimes including an attempted murder on the sheriff herself. Jason could use that too. He could shine the spotlight on the victim's bad acts and the sheriff's department's futility in finding Dean. He might even be able to inflame the jury against the prosecution. Twelve old white guys, if that's what they ended up with, were unlikely to be sympathetic to a murder defendant. But they were just as unlikely to sympathize with a dead drug dealer.

It was, as Jason liked to think, *something*.

Finally, there was perhaps the defense's greatest advantage. Exemplified by the crowd of reporters, including his old friend, Kisha Roe of the *Advertiser-Gleam*, that had circled the courthouse. The television news vans. The endless media coverage of the case that had been nonstop in the past week. They weren't here because a notorious drug lord had been murdered. Indeed, Cade's name, while mentioned in these stories, was almost an afterthought. They were here because of the billboards that once covered the entire Southeast. The commercials. The money. The brand.

They were here . . .

Judge Barber's bailiff exited His Honor's chambers and strode toward the bench. Next to him, Jason heard Shay whisper a short prayer.

. . . *because of me.*

"ALL RISE!"

87

Richard Griffith complied with the subpoena.

The order required him to report on Monday morning at nine, and he'd arrived with time to spare. He sat on a bench outside the circuit courtroom. He saw and felt their stares, but they didn't bother him as much as he thought.

He had other things on his mind.

He took out his phone and looked through the photographs he'd taken over the weekend. He'd gotten several shots of Matty Dean sitting on the dock of one of Guntersville's more prominent citizens' houses. If he showed his phone to Hatty Daniels, then perhaps there was a way back in for him?

Was redemption possible?

Did he even want that?

He'd never have his old life again. Before coming in this morning, he'd driven by the old house. He saw Cheryl taking Richard and Lida to school. Then he left. He'd made eye contact with all the key players since his arrival.

Shay.

Rich.

Wish.

Hatty.

No one had spoken to him, and, really, what was there to say? He knew the score. Was redemption possible? No.

He'd done too much.

But that didn't change the current situation. There was a statewide manhunt for Matthew Jefferson Dean.

Griff knew where he was. Knew where he was hiding.

And knew the truth would rock Marshall County to its core.

88

By 4:55 p.m., they had their jury, and Shay wasn't far off in her predic-
tion. Ten men. Two women. All white. All above the age of fifty.

Well . . . shit, Jason thought, sizing up the jury of his peers, which
looked like his father's 1987 Sunday school class at the First United
Methodist Church. He tried to focus on his plan to put Cade on trial.
How this makeup might help that endeavor. But all he could see was
disapproval and irritation in the jury's eyes.

"Head up, eyes forward," Shay said.

"At least they aren't claiming the death penalty," Jason whispered
back.

"True," his partner hissed.

Barber banged on the bench with his gavel. "Members of the jury,
we thank you for serving this week. Please arrive tomorrow no later than
eight forty-five a.m." After they were escorted out of the courtroom,
His Honor looked at Jason and then Wish. "We'll start with opening
statements at nine in the morning. We are adjourned."

———

Once back in the consultation room, Jason peered at Shay. "Are we any
closer to establishing a link between Darnell and Matty Dean?"

"No," Shay said. "In the past six weeks, I've met with almost every person that lives within a two-mile radius of that grocery store. None of them are able to shed any light on anything. Based on the surveillance footage produced from inside the Alder Springs Grocery, the four people she talked to the most were Tyson Cade, Trudy Cowan, Trey Cowan, and the current desk clerk, Frank Crutcher. I've had at least three meetings with Trudy in the last month, but they have produced nothing, and Trey and Crutcher won't talk to me."

Jason scratched his neck. "It doesn't hurt to try again." He paused. "Do we know anything about Crutcher?" He thought of his and Satch's tense encounter with the desk clerk the first and only time Jason had been around the man.

"No, and Hooper wasn't able to garner much either. Born in Alder Springs. Graduated from Albertville High. No college. Had several convictions for controlled-substance possession in his twenties. Then he enlisted in the army, where he served for approximately a decade. He spends most every day at the grocery now. Before Darnell's departure, he only worked the evening shift, but now he's there from daylight to closing time. Father is in Marshall Manor. No criminal background to speak of since his return. Seems like the only logical conclusion is that he and Darnell are coworkers."

Jason rose from his chair. He walked toward the exit, thinking it through. "That's probably correct, but it doesn't hurt to take another look." He rapped his knuckles on the steel door.

"He hangs the phone up every time I call and threatened to call the police the one time I tried to meet with him in person. Do you have any ideas on how to get to him?"

Jason stepped back as the guard opened the door. Then he stared down at his partner. "Send Satch."

89

The house was dark, and Shay wasn't sure if anyone was home. She knocked, and when there was no answer, she turned the knob. It opened.

She stepped inside, feeling her heart begin to race. "Colonel! It's me, Shay. Are you home?" Now that she was inside, she heard a sound coming from the back. A song that she thought she recognized. She frowned. *But that can't be right . . .*

Shay adjusted her eyes to the darkness and breathed in the scent of spoiled food. She turned toward the smell and saw a stack of unwashed dishes in the kitchen sink and several dirty plates on the counter. One of them had half a sandwich still on it. She saw light flickering in a room past the kitchen and walked toward it. When she stepped into the cozy den, the smell of sour mash whiskey hit her nostrils.

Satch Tonidandel sat in a La-Z-Boy recliner. His feet were up, and his hands were locked around his neck. On the coffee table next to him was a fifth of Jack Daniel's. The top was off.

The song was coming from the television, the volume so high that it hurt her ears. Shay looked at the screen and saw two motorcycle cops riding down a huge highway as the classic eighties instrumental theme song blared.

"*CHiPs*," she said, smiling. *I was right . . .*

Satch ignored her. He pointed at the couch, and Shay sat.

"Colonel, I—"

He held up his index finger, glared at her, and again pointed at the couch. "After," he said in a harsh whisper.

"OK." She took her seat.

———

For the next fifty-two minutes, Shay let herself travel back to 1981. When Francis "Ponch" Poncherello and John Baker guarded the freeways of Los Angeles. She knew she didn't have time for this respite, but she found herself enjoying the break from reality. In the episode, an old friend of Ponch's decided to start wrecking cars on purpose on the freeway, and Ponch had to decide whether loyalty to the job or his friend was more important.

The badge won out, and Ponch locked up his buddy.

They watched the show, complete with commercials. Satch never said a word and barely moved. When the credits played, he finally took the remote and clicked off the tube.

Now they sat in total darkness, and Satch didn't turn on a light. "How's your mother?" he growled.

"Better. Pretty much healed. I mean . . . physically."

"Good. She's a fine woman."

"Colonel, I'm sorry I haven't visited . . . it's just been . . ." She trailed off.

"You don't have to apologize to me." He coughed, bringing his fist to his mouth.

"How are you?"

"Making it," Satch said. He reached for the open whiskey bottle and took a swig, swallowing it down with a cough. "I'm hurting some. My back. Shoulder. Hell, everything."

The cancer's spreading, Shay thought.

"Jack Black helps, but not enough." He coughed again. "How did today go?"

"We picked the jury."

"Get what you want?"

"Not exactly, but not much of a surprise either."

"Twelve old white guys?" Satch coughed again.

"Ten," Shay said. "And two old white women."

"Marshall County diversity." He hacked out a laugh, and Shay joined him.

"I'm sorry about Mickey. I should have gone to the funeral, but—"

"Wasn't no funeral. Not yet."

"Oh. Well . . . how is Chuck doing?"

"He's making it. I'm picking him up in the morning. Been in rehab the last month. Trying to learn how to function with only one arm."

"I'm sorry."

He grunted. "It was my fault," Satch said. "Listen, you want to go outside? It gets a bit stuffy in here, and I need to walk off some of this whiskey."

"Sure."

She followed him through the dark house. The colonel wore an unbuttoned flannel shirt and jeans. He appeared to be thinner, but still walked with a strong gait. Once outside, Satch walked over to a wood pile. "Won't be long before we have to take out the trash again."

Shay wrinkled her face, confused, but decided not to press it. "Jason wants you to talk with Frank Crutcher. He's the—"

"I know who he is."

"His background is army. Ever heard of him?"

Satch gave his head a jerk. "Decent soldier, but a dipshit of the first order. Got out of the service and went straight to working for Cade. Now Dean."

"Outside of the Cowans and Cade, he had the most contact with Dooby Darnell prior to the murder. That's probably because they were coworkers."

"Probably," Satch agreed.

"Will you talk to him?"

He nodded.

"Colonel, why haven't you been to see Jason since his bond was revoked?"

Satch scratched his neck and peered at the tarred wood. "Because I don't believe in feeling sorry for myself or for any damn body else. No matter how close I am to them." He spat. "There ain't nothing I could do for him, and I've had my hands full with my brothers."

"That's what Jason said."

"He knows me pretty well."

"But there is something you can do now," Shay said. "Crutcher won't talk to me."

"He'll talk," Satch said. "But I doubt he knows anything."

"Let me know what he says." Shay took a step back, intending to leave, but she stopped. "Can I ask you something?"

"Shoot."

"Jason told me about your devotion to eighties television shows. I didn't quite believe him, but I do now." She paused. "What's up with that?"

Satch walked over to her, his gait slower. When he looked at her, his eyes were tired but determined. "November 19, 1982."

Shay wrinkled up her face.

"We didn't have much money. We lived on the other side of the water. Right there in that house." He cocked his head toward the plywood structure. "So, in the evenings, we watched television together. It was . . . the only thing we did as a family." He snorted. "*CHiPs* actually came on Sunday nights, but I don't remember much about Mondays, so I watch it twice now. Sunday and Monday." He guffawed and then coughed. "Anyways, Tuesdays was the sitcoms. *Happy Days*, *Laverne & Shirley*. That was OK, but things really got good on Wednesdays with *The Fall Guy*. Then Thursdays was *Magnum* fucking *P. I.*" His voice had intensified, eyes wider as he relived the memories. "And Fridays was the by God best of all. *The Incredible Hulk, The Dukes of Hazzard*, and the crème de la crème, *Dallas*. Then, we lost *The Hulk* but picked up *Falcon Crest*. Not an even trade, but that damn Angela Channing was a mean, sexy woman." Satch scratched at his face and picked up a stick, digging at the ashes.

"What happened on November 19, 1982, Colonel?"

Satch turned to her, and his eyes gleamed in the light from the full moon above. "Friday night, man. The *Dukes* that night was all about Deputy Enos getting in a fix. Then *Dallas* had J. R. and Bobby fighting for Ewing Oil a few episodes after Jock's will was read. And *Falcon Crest* was all about who was the father of that crazy Melissa's son."

"Colonel, that was almost forty years ago. How can you remember the episodes so clearly?"

"I was ten years old, Chuck was six, and Mick was just a baby. I remember it vividly. Dad would eat some old Orville Redenbacher popcorn and sit in his old recliner. Me and Chuck were on the same couch you sat on tonight. Mick was in the crib, and occasionally Mom had to go check on him." He was nodding to himself. "I can still smell the popcorn. That was . . . what we did." The gleam went out of his eyes. "And that was the last night we were all together."

"What are you saying, Colonel?"

"My dad had a heart attack that Saturday morning. He was dead before he hit the floor. Momma had to work nights from then on out, and it was up to me to take care of my brothers." His voice shook, and he coughed again. Shay felt tears forming in the corners of her eyes. "I did the best I could."

"Colonel, I—"

"Got them through high school, and then we all joined the army. I took care of them." He scratched at his neck. "But once we enlisted, I realized that I was good at only one thing." He peered back at her. "War. It came easy to me. I relished the strategy of it. The tough decisions.

The survival test. I tried to teach Chuck and Mickey, and they became good soldiers . . ." He peered up at the sky.

". . . but they ain't like me. They didn't see Daddy on the ground. Didn't feel Momma's nails pinching into their back, asking why God would take him so soon." He paused and stirred the unlit fire with his stick. "Something broke in me then. Made me hard. Mean. The army gave me an outlet for all that hurt. But when I watch those old shows, it takes me back to that time before I was broken. Like when you build up cards into a pyramid. And then, when the show is over . . ." He swung the stick through the air, creating a whoosh sound. "Gone. Back to being the ornery SOB that I am." He cleared his throat. "That make any sense?"

"Yes," Shay said, trying to keep her voice from cracking. "Thank you."

"Is that all you wanted?"

"No, there's one more thing. Jason is a good attorney. So am I. But he may still lose this week. And losing may not be the worst thing."

Satch squinted at her. "Dean?"

"Jason thinks he may take another shot."

Satch turned and dug his stick into the ashes.

"Colonel, I know you've been through hell since Mickey died, but Jason feels he has no one. They're only letting family in the courtroom, and there's nothing but an empty space behind him. He wouldn't let his nieces come because of the danger." Shay paused and took a couple of steps back. Satch had now knelt by the ashes.

"He needs you, Colonel." She let out a breath she'd been holding. "We all do."

90

The last Little League game at Optimist Field ended at 9:30 p.m. It had been a hard night for "Blue," as the fans liked to call the umpires. Trey Cowan had to eject one of the coaches for yelling that Trey needed to "get off his knees" because he was "blowing the game."

Nine years old, Trey thought, as he trudged to his truck. *And the coaches and parents act like it's game seven of the World Series.*

It was depressing, but Trey couldn't say that it was much of a change from his playing days. Most parents ruined the game for their kids. Ridiculous expectations. Yelling at them for making a mistake. Cursing the umpires.

That's why so many kids stopped playing sports once they were in middle school and had the slightest bit of independence. Trey had always thought he'd been unlucky having a drunk for a dad and a mom who was rarely home because she worked two jobs.

Hell, compared to what he witnessed tonight, he'd won the parent lottery, truth be known. He'd popped three delta-8 gummies during the game, but it was time for something stronger. By the time he reached his car, he could almost taste the bourbon. He reached toward his glove compartment, where he'd hidden the pint of Jim Beam.

Before he could open it, he heard three loud knuckle raps on his window.

Great, he thought, wondering which parent or coach wanted to pick a fight tonight. But when he saw who was waiting on him, his stomach clenched, and he felt a chilly breeze blow through the interior of the car. He clicked a button, and his window rolled down. "What's up, Crutch?" he asked.

Frank Crutcher wore a faded Atlanta Braves cap, a vintage powder blue #3 Dale Murphy jersey, and jeans. He leaned on the sill. "Your lawyer's trial started today," Frank said.

Trey looked away from him, staring at the steering wheel. "I know."

"I just wanted to remind you of our little arrangement."

"I don't need a reminder," Trey said, feeling sweat break out on his forehead.

"Good. Because we'd hate to have to take all that money back." He leaned closer to Trey's ear. "Or go for a ride on that sweet snatch you've shacked up with." He lowered his voice. "Or cut your momma's throat." He squeezed Trey's neck. "No attacks of conscience, you hear, Trey?"

Trey let out a ragged breath. "I hear."

91

The bathroom on the second floor of the Marshall County courthouse was a place Jason had spent quite a bit of time. As diarrhea ran with the territory . . . no pun intended . . . of any trial he handled, he'd already spent his fair share of minutes inside this sanctuary. Now, as Tuesday morning had dawned and he'd have to deliver his opening statement in a mere matter of minutes, he washed his hands and focused on the beginning of his opening statement, trying to decide whether to trust his gut or go conventional. His father would no doubt tell him to be professional, but . . .

. . . *I'm Jason motherfucking Rich.*

He walked with his head down as deputies escorted him from the hallway into the courtroom. When he reached the defense table, he saw two sets of dark boots, which didn't fit. He was expecting only Shay's high heels. He raised his head and swallowed back a gasp.

The colonel was in full uniform, just as he'd been when the Cowan case was dismissed. He was a tad thinner but looked no worse for wear. The last time Jason had seen him was walking out of the morgue of Marshall Medical Center South. Jason fought for his voice, but couldn't find it. Seeing Satch was hard enough, but it was the other uniformed man that shook him to the core.

Captain Chuck Tonidandel was also in uniform. His left sleeve hung limp, where his arm used to be. His bald head shone from a recent shaving, and his salt-and-pepper beard stretched down to his belt. Chuck leaned forward and put his right hand on Jason's shoulder. Satch grabbed Jason by the neck. "Bring it in, Shay." She followed his order, and the four formed a huddle.

"Dear Lord." Chuck spoke in a harsh whisper. "Be with our brother Jason and his partner, Shay. Give them strength. Show them the way . . ." Chuck paused. ". . . *to victory*. Amen."

"Amen," Jason managed, his cheeks streaked with fresh tears.

"Amen," Shay said.

"A-fucking-men," Satch growled.

Jason pulled back from them, but Chuck moved his one hand down to Jason's heart. "*Believe*," he whispered.

92

When Judge Barber caught sight of the two uniformed men sitting behind the defense table, he fumbled the gavel as he tried to bang it on the bench. "I thought I made it clear that there would be no spectators."

"Your Honor, you said no one . . . but family." Jason forced his voice not to shake. He gazed over his shoulder at Satch and Chuck. *That's my family.*

"I know you," Barber said, ignoring Jason. "You were here last fall. Dressed the same." His Honor glared at Satch, who rose from his seat. "Said you were going to protect this court. Said you had your two brothers with you. You were out of line then, and you're out of line now. And if you and the man next to you don't leave right now, at once, I'm going to hold you in contempt and have you forcibly removed from this courtroom. There are at least one hundred members of the National Guard outside more than capable of doing the job."

"Well, you'll need them all. We ain't leaving."

"Judge, I also object to the way he's dressed," Wish said. "I mean, it gives some air of authority about the defendant. I think that's an unfair advantage and will be a distraction to the jury."

"A distraction?" Jason said. "That's completely ridiculous, Your Honor. The jury will have to go through that entire army of National Guardsmen every day. I think they'll be plenty distracted without the colonel. At the first hearing in this courtroom, I was almost shot and killed. Sergeant Greta Martin was shot and killed. If it wasn't for the colonel and the captain here, others would have died."

Barber scowled at Jason. "It's still a violation of my order."

"Judge Barber." Hatty stood. "As the sheriff of this county who remembers full well Colonel and Captain Tonidandel's bravery in December, I have no objection to either of them being present in court."

Wish eyed her with exasperation and then turned back to Barber. "Well, I respectfully disagree with the sheriff," Wish said. "I want them removed right now."

"Then come and get some," Satch growled.

"This is an outrage," Wish cried. "Mr. Rich is once again turning this court into a circus, and we haven't even started yet." He grabbed the lapels on his coat, gathering himself. "Your Honor, Captain Chuck Tonidandel is a witness for the state. He's under subpoena, and we have invoked the rule. By law, he must wait outside."

"Counsel, please approach," Barber finally said, snatching his glasses off his face. "Wish, state your position for the record."

"I object to the Tonidandels' presence and move that they be escorted from this court. Chuck Tonidandel is a witness, and we have invoked the rule. Colonel Tonidandel is not a witness, but he has no business in this courtroom. As you correctly pointed out, Your Honor, he is not a family member of Mr. Rich's, and you excluded all patrons but family."

"Mr. Rich?" Barber said.

"We agree that Chuck should wait outside. But the sheriff has already consented to the colonel's presence, and she is the law in this county. And given the events that have happened since this case started, I would think everyone here would *want* Colonel Tonidandel around."

"Judge, this is *ridiculous*." Wish spoke through clenched teeth. "I want them both removed right now."

Barber gazed above Wish's head to the colonel. "I think I see Mr. Rich's point. I'm going to allow it. Look, it's foolish to be taking our time up with this."

"Judge, I can't believe—"

"Are you going to escort him out?" Barber snapped.

"But what about the guardsmen?"

"Do you think they'll come in here and remove a decorated full colonel of the United States Army?"

"They will if you tell them to."

Barber again looked past Wish to Satch. "I don't want it to go that far."

Jason winked at Satch as he took his seat while Barber spoke from the bench.

"Captain Tonidandel, you must leave the courtroom pursuant to the state's invocation of the general exclusionary rule. Colonel . . . you may stay. All right . . . bring in the jury pool."

———

Five minutes later, Wish French stood before the jury. Gone was the agitation he'd shown at the presence of the Tonidandels. He was the picture of cool confidence dressed in his navy suit, white shirt, and maroon tie. His voice and tone were deliberate as he meticulously outlined the state's case. He ended with his theme.

"Members of the jury, the evidence in this case is overwhelming. The defendant bought a new gun two weeks before Tyson Cade's death, which Emily Carton, our county coroner, who just so happens to also be a ballistics expert, will tell you was the exact type of weapon that killed the victim on November 13, 2019. That gun is now missing. We couldn't find it in the defendant's house, car, or any other property that he owns. The defendant was seen on Hustleville Road a few minutes after the murder in a dark-burgundy SUV, and an eyewitness remembers observing a dark SUV leaving the scene. You'll hear the sheriff herself testify that the defendant blamed the victim for the killing of his lead investigator and friend last year and had threatened to kill him just weeks before he did just that. Finally, you'll hear Tyson Cade's dying declaration spoken to an eyewitness seconds before his death. Cade identified his killer as the defendant." Wish paused. "The evidence against the defendant is overwhelming and irrefutable. When you hear all of it, I'm confident that you will render the only verdict that justice allows . . . *guilty*."

———

"Mr. Rich, are you ready to give your opening statement?"

Jason rose and buttoned his coat. He was wearing a charcoal gray suit, white shirt, and red tie. The same outfit he'd worn on a thousand billboards. *You are the brand,* Izzy used to tell him. He knew he had to seize on the familiar. Tug on who they thought he was. Most of all, he had to be himself.

"May it please the court," Jason said, feeling the strength in his voice and body. "Your Honor." Jason bowed to Judge Barber. "Counsel." He nodded to Wish French. Glancing behind him, he looked at his partner, Shay Lankford, who was killing it in a burgundy suit and heels. Jason could smell the competition in the air. The nerves. The electric current. Trying a case was so much like a sporting event. The way he'd feel in college when he'd putt before his round started in the roped-off practice green. The cold stares of the other golfers. The hopeful but intense eyes of his coach. Most of all, the inner struggle for control. For confidence and self-assurance.

To trust yourself, your swing, and your game.

Jason glanced behind Shay to the back of the courtroom, where Satch had taken a seat. The colonel's arms were at his side. He was ready to move if needed. His eyes like slits.

Jason's heart pounded as he turned back to the jury and strode to the well of the courtroom.

"Members of the jury," he finally said. He saw curiosity and interest in each of their eyes. *You'll never have them more engaged than when you start your opening,* Knox Rogers had advised him before Jana's trial. *Don't waste those first few precious seconds.*

Jason moved his eyes to each one of them and started with the simple, cold, hard truth.

"I didn't do it."

———

By the end, Jason felt a buzz. His four-word beginning had brought smiles from three jurors and an outright chuckle from a woman in the front. *A laughing jury doesn't convict,* he'd heard. He ended with the theme of his defense. The one connection that the state wouldn't be able to make. The tiny crack in their Death Star of a case.

"Members of the jury, the state cannot show any link between me and Marcia 'Dooby' Darnell. Ms. Darnell stopped Tyson Cade just before the shooting, offering the shooter a clean shot. Otherwise, the true killer would have had to hit a moving target walking away from him. I ask you to listen closely for any evidence of an association between me and Ms. Darnell. You won't see it. At the end of this case, I promise you that you'll have doubts about whether the state has proven its case. And, if you do, the only verdict that justice allows . . . is not guilty."

93

After a break for lunch, the first witness for the state was Dr. Emily Carton, the county coroner, whose testimony, Shay and Jason had both concluded, was almost impossible to attack. After covering her extensive background in ballistics analysis, Wish elicited the opinions he needed.

Dr. Carton testified that the cause of Tyson Cade's death was three gunshot wounds to the chest, and that time of death was approximately 10:30 a.m. Bullet fragments discovered in the victim's chest cavity were Winchester nine millimeter, which was a typical ammunition for all manner of nine-millimeter handguns, including the Glock 17. Based on her review of Marcia Darnell's witness statement and the condition of the wounds and fragments, Carton estimated a distance of at least sixty feet that the shots were fired from. In light of the length of the shot, she opined that the murder weapon was a longer-barrel nine-millimeter pistol and agreed a Glock 17 would be consistent with her finding. She relayed her testing of Jason Rich's Glock 43X pistol, and that ballistics analysis determined that the 43X was not the murder weapon. Wish ended with whether Carton had been able to test the defendant's other gun, a Glock 17.

"No, sir. We were not able to test that pistol, because it was not found."

On cross-examination, which Shay handled, Carton admitted that the bullet fragments, wounds, and distance of the shot would also be consistent with any number of other nine-millimeter handguns, including the SIG Sauer P320, the Smith & Wesson M&P, the Springfield Armory XD, and the Walther PPQ.

"All you are telling this jury is that the gun that killed Tyson Cade is consistent with a Glock 17," Shay said.

"Correct."

"Not that the murder weapon was, in fact, a Glock 17 and certainly not that it was Mr. Rich's Glock 17."

"Well, since the sheriff's department was unable to find Mr. Rich's Glock 17, we obviously couldn't test it."

It was a good comeback, and a warning to Shay that Emily wasn't afraid to spar with her.

"No further questions," Shay said.

Next up for the state was the traffic controller, Vann Sweeney. Sweeney was a thirty-year county employee. He testified that the stoplight at the Martling Road intersection of Hustleville Road had a video camera in it. Wish then introduced the footage from the morning of November 13, 2019.

Sweeney used a red pointer pen to identify the date and time at the top corner of the projector screen to the left of the jury. Then he pressed play.

The last image the jury would see on the first full day of trial was Jason Rich holding the steering wheel of his dark SUV and looking directly into the camera with blank eyes. The time on the screen was 10:43 a.m. on November 13, 2019. Six and a half miles from the Alder Springs Grocery. Ten minutes after the shooting.

"Nothing further," Wish said, with a happy pitch to his tone.

"Cross-examination," Barber asked, and Jason stood, shaking his head.

"None, Your Honor."

"The witness is excused." He lowered his spectacles. "OK, it's almost five o'clock. We are going to adjourn for the day."

———

As the jury filed out, the video screen still showed Jason's blank face. It was a smart tactic by Wish, burning the image into their minds.

Once back in the consultation room, Jason placed his forehead on the cold metal table.

"We knew the first day was going to be bad," Shay said. "And it was." She paused. "But your opening statement was outstanding."

"Thanks," Jason said, not lifting his head.

"They'll call Hatty first thing in the morning. Then Darnell, Chuck, and close with Atkinson."

"I hate that Chuck has to testify."

"That's where you bought the Glock 17. I doubt he'll be asked anything else, but I'm going to prepare him for some character-type questions."

"What do you mean?"

"I mean . . . about your drinking. Being a bit out of control in the days before the murder. Your hatred of Cade."

"You think Wish will get into all of that with Chuck?"

"He could."

Jason winced, hating to put the middle Tonidandel through any more trouble.

"Jason, have you thought any more about our witnesses? Are you still planning to call Griff?"

Jason lifted his head off the table. "I can't believe he showed up."

"Me neither. Are you going to call him?"

"I don't know. Any word on the Cowans? Or Crutcher?"

"Trudy finally agreed to another meeting tonight, but I'm not holding out much hope that she'll change her tune. Satch is going to handle Trey and Crutcher." She gave a tired smile and rose from her chair. "I've got to go."

94

Trudy Cowan met Shay at Wintzell's Oyster House. "Not in the Sprangs" was one of two parameters that Trudy had put on the meeting. The other being that the place served alcohol.

Trudy had already started a tab by the time that Shay arrived a little after nine. She was drinking bourbon and Coke, and by the looks of it, she'd already had at least two.

"Trudy, I'll make this brief. Jason thinks you're holding back on him. That you know something about Dooby Darnell . . . or your son, Trey, that might be useful."

She took a long sip of her drink and then shook the ice cubes in the almost-empty glass. "He's a smart man. And he did right by my son. That means something to me." She was fidgeting in her seat and rolling a napkin with her left hand, her nerves palpable. "I hate to see him go down for something he didn't do. Trey would've . . ." She trailed off, and her lip began to tremble.

". . . been put to death by lethal injection if Jason Rich hadn't saved his ass." Shay completed Trudy's thought, her tone edgy. "Please tell me, Trudy, what is it that you're holding back? We're running out of time."

"I can't," she whined, drinking the rest of her cocktail in one gulp, ice falling onto the table.

"*Why?*"

"Because Matty Dean will kill me." She was now speaking in a loud whisper. "I'm surprised he hasn't already. The only reason he hasn't killed Dooby is that the sheriff saved her. As soon as the trial is over and Dooby is out of the sheriff's protection, she's a dead duck." She pressed the empty glass to her forehead. "And so am I."

Shay felt adrenaline surge through her bloodstream. "Trudy, if what you're saying is true, and I believe wholeheartedly that it is . . . if Matty is going to kill you and Dooby regardless, then why won't you help Jason? We can offer protection. Security." Desperation had creeped into Shay's tone despite how badly she was trying to stay calm.

Trudy scoffed and glared at her. "Y'all can't even protect yourselves."

Shay peered around the mostly full restaurant. What was it about these Sand Mountain meth lords? She was so tired of the fear that they instilled in her home. That she saw in Trudy Cowan's eyes and so many others in Marshall County. Her frustration finally boiled over, and she brought her fist down on the table, causing the ice cubes in Trudy's glass to jiggle.

"*Goddamnit*, Trudy, what do you have to lose?" She glared at the other woman and wiped spittle from her chin. "Please, for the love of—"

"Dooby is close with a man named Frank Crutcher," Trudy interrupted, speaking fast and looking past Shay to the bar behind her. "He's the current clerk down at the Sprangs Grocery. I think . . . they may have a thing now. I'm not really sure. I know Crutch . . . a lot of us that know him well call him Crutch . . . has been sweet on her for a long time. When he enlisted, he lost touch, and by the time he came back, she was with Tyson."

"Does Frank Crutcher work in the Sand Mountain meth ring?"

"Probably. I know Crutch's dad was thick as thieves with King Hanson and Matty Dean, but I'm not sure about Crutch. He's always played things close to the vest." Trudy continued to gaze past Shay, as if not looking at her somehow absolved her of these admissions.

"You said he enlisted. Which service?" *Keep her talking . . .*

"Army. He was in for about ten years."

Shay thought it through while the waiter asked if they needed anything. Trudy ordered another bourbon and Shay a Diet Coke. As he walked away, Shay leaned her elbows on the table. "Trudy, explain to me why Matty would want to kill you?"

"Because I knew Dooby went to Gadsden. She told me she was scared he was going to kill her, and that's why she ran."

"Why would she be scared?"

"She didn't tell me, but . . . I figure it's one of two reasons. Either she was in on Tyson's murder and Matty wants revenge. Or she was in on Matty's plan to kill Tyson, and he wants to get rid of all the players."

Shay's mind buzzed with the possibilities. "But either way, she was in on it."

"Absolutely."

The waiter returned with their drinks. Shay pressed the glass of soda to her lips, taking a small sip. "How can you be so sure?"

Trudy took a long, slow swig from her glass. "Two things. One, Tyson Cade never got his change. Ever. He tipped Dooby and everyone else on Sand Mountain. That's a bullshit story if I've ever heard one." Confidence had risen in her voice, and she was now staring right at Shay.

"And two?"

"She hated Tyson and wanted him dead."

"Why?"

Trudy took another sip of her bourbon drink, saying nothing. Her hands shook, and she placed the glass down on the table. Her face had paled to a sickly white.

"Please, Trudy. *What's the truth?*"

"He raped her," Trudy said, her voice cracking. "Tyson raped Dooby repeatedly. He would hit her and . . . force her to have sex with him. Most of the time, right in the store."

"I thought their sexual relationship was consensual."

419

At this, Trudy turned up her drink and finished the rest. She slammed the glass down and glared at Shay, smacking her lips. "No relationship with Tyson Cade was . . . *consensual*. You did what Tyson said . . . or you paid the consequences."

"How do you know Dooby was raped by Tyson?"

"She told me."

Hearsay, Shay thought. *But she could be a rebuttal witness if Dooby lies about it.* "Do you have any other evidence?"

"No, but Crutch might. After the last time Tyson roughed her up, I know Dooby told him."

"Do you think Crutch could have killed him?"

Trudy stared at Shay with bleary eyes. "Truth?"

"Yes."

"That's exactly what I think happened."

95

The Alder Springs Grocery closed at 9:00 p.m. After Frank Crutcher locked up, he saw a silhouetted figure in the reflection of the glass door. "Thought I told you to stay away from here?"

"I don't follow orders," Satch said. "I give them."

Frank turned and looked at the colonel, who was holding a pistol against his side.

"Think it's time we had a little talk," Satch said.

96

Shay filled Jason in on the night's events at the defense table right before the start of the third day of trial.

"Oh my God," he said. "Are we going to subpoena Crutcher?"

She slid the return-service receipt across the table. "Already did."

Jason gazed at the signature on the process server. "Colonel Satchel S. Tonidandel." He turned and looked at the colonel, who was sitting in the same seat he had yesterday in the back of the courtroom. Satch nodded.

"What's he going to say when we call him?"

Shay also glanced at the colonel. "I don't know yet."

"Is the state ready to proceed?" Judge Barber asked from the bench.

"Yes, Your Honor."

"Very well. Call your next witness."

Wish French cleared his throat. "The state calls Sheriff Hatty Daniels."

I hate this case, Hatty thought as she walked with authority to the stand. She had prepared last night with Wish and felt ready, but she couldn't help but think that something was amiss. Perhaps it was seeing her old boss, Richard Griffith, out in the hallway during each break. Sitting on a bench, arms crossed, like any other subpoenaed witness. If that wasn't unsettling enough, the presence yesterday of the Tonidandels, especially one-armed Captain Chuck Tonidandel, had struck a nerve.

This is a war, she had thought several times over the past month as she'd investigated the gunfight and fire at Beth Lankford's house.

Matty Dean obviously didn't care about this trial. He wanted justice for Tyson Cade the Sand Mountain way.

Or maybe Dean killed Cade too.

It wasn't the first time that the thought had crossed her mind. As she took her seat in the witness chair, she peered at Jason and Shay. The former prosecutor, an old friend, and the billboard attorney . . . *A new friend . . . ?*

. . . yes.

And to the back of the courtroom, where Colonel Tonidandel was dressed in uniform again.

This is a war, Hatty thought again. It felt surreal to be on the opposite side of her friends.

I'm doing my job, Hatty told herself, gritting her teeth as Wish approached the jury railing to begin his direct of her. Her mind was a jumbled mess, but two questions kept popping in there.

Why can't we find Matty Dean?

"Sheriff Daniels, will you please introduce yourself to the jury?" Wish's voice boomed to the back of the nearly empty courtroom.

The other question that infiltrated Hatty's subconscious might bother her more.

"My name is Hatty Daniels," she said, looking right at the jury box.

Am I on the right side?

Jason watched as Wish French took the sheriff through her department's investigation, starting with the 911 call received from eyewitness

Candy Atkinson's cell phone at just after 10:30 a.m. on November 13, 2019. Hatty identified Marcia "Dooby" Darnell as the desk clerk who witnessed the shooting, after telling the victim that he had forgotten his change. Wish introduced two photographs of Tyson Cade's corpse, which he published to the jury over Jason's objection. Jason saw several of the jurors watching him with wary eyes as they examined the death photographs.

The prosecutor then focused his questions on the sheriff's personal interactions with Jason Rich. "Did the defendant ever tell you anything that made you suspect a motive for wanting the victim dead?"

"Yes, he did. After his investigator, Harry Davenport, was reported missing in Pulaski, Tennessee, Mr. Rich told me that he knew Cade was behind the murder. He also informed me that Cade was behind his young niece and his girlfriend's drug problems."

Last, Wish meticulously went over the department's search of Jason's house, office, and cars, introducing the inventory of everything that was found. Hatty testified that a Glock 43X was discovered in a drawer in Jason's bedroom. She testified that her office searched the Tonidandels' gun range and discovered an invoice showing the purchase by Jason of a Glock 17 handgun on November 1, almost two weeks prior to the murder.

The gun was Wish's closer, and he milked it for all it was worth. "Sheriff, in your department's extensive search of Mr. Rich's home, cars, and law office, did you find the Glock 17 pistol that he'd so recently purchased?"

"No, we did not."

Wish nodded and gazed at the jury. "No further questions."

———

"Cross-examination, Mr. Rich?"

"Yes, Your Honor," Jason said, sliding out of his chair and moving toward the witness stand with deliberate steps. He paused for a second, meeting Hatty's gaze. "Sheriff, we worked together last year, didn't we?"

She frowned. "I don't know what you mean."

"When Matty Dean tried to kill you in Pulaski, we worked together to try to bring him to justice, didn't we?"

She squirmed a bit in her chair. "Yes."

"And, because of our efforts, Mr. Dean was arrested last October, wasn't he?"

"Objection, Your Honor," Wish said, rising to his feet. "Relevance."

"Overruled," Barber said. "Get on with it, Mr. Rich."

"But he was let out by your predecessor, Richard Griffith, correct?"

"Yes."

"He's wanted in connection with several murders, including two members of your office, Detective George Mitchell and Sergeant Greta Martin, isn't that correct?"

"Yes, it is."

"Martin was killed when she stepped in front of a bullet meant for me after the first hearing in this case, correct?"

Hatty glanced at Wish and then to Jason. "We can't definitely say that for sure, but it is our working presumption."

"And why is that, Sheriff?"

"Because Mr. Dean is a dangerous man."

Jason looked at the jury. "A dangerous man who was also a fugitive on November 13, 2019, correct?"

"Yes."

"Who, despite your department's best efforts, is still on the loose."

"That's correct."

"Dean is from Alder Springs, isn't he?"

"I believe so."

"And yet he has never been investigated in connection with Tyson Cade's murder, has he?"

Hatty glared at Jason. "That's because all of the evidence we've found links you to the murder, and none suggests Dean did it."

"Really?" Jason asked, his tone reeking with sarcasm. "In all of your investigation, was there anyone that saw me at the Alder Springs Grocery at 10:30 a.m. on November 13, 2019?"

"No."

Jason was scratching the back of his neck in mock thought. "And in all of those interviews and meticulous detective work, did any witness ever say they had seen me talking with Marcia 'Dooby' Darnell?"

"No."

"Is there any evidence that I ever communicated with Dooby Darnell prior to Tyson Cade's murder?"

"No."

"Sheriff, how many years was Tyson Cade investigated by your department?"

She peered down at her feet. "Many."

"And that was in connection with his role as the leader of the Sand Mountain meth trade, correct?"

"Yes."

"In all of the years that the Marshall County Sheriff's Office investigated Tyson Cade's meth operation, was he ever arrested?"

"No."

"Ever charged with a crime?"

"No."

"Is it the belief of the Marshall County Sheriff's Office that Matty Dean succeeded Cade as leader of this meth empire?"

"That is . . . one angle of our investigation."

"And yet Dean, the fugitive, is still out there, correct?" Jason was walking back to the defense table.

"Yes."

"No further questions."

97

One of the things that Matty Dean did best was remember details. Little things that ended up making a big difference.

Sometimes all the difference.

As the trial of Jason Rich began, he had Lu watching for Dooby Darnell, but the witness was under police protection at a nearby apartment being rented by the state. "Three officers on her at all times."

It bugged him that his efforts to corner Dooby in Gadsden had failed. He knew that Frank Crutcher and Lu were probably right about retaliation. He could take out Trudy Cowan anytime. Killing her would be like euthanizing a sick dog.

And Trey . . . *same thing*.

There'd been a big body count on his watch already, and he didn't want to kill anyone who didn't have to go.

Besides, would Trudy or Trey be so stupid as to have warned Dooby of the ambush?

No.

So what in the hell happened? Matty had a hunch and figured there was a relatively simple way to find out.

He called Lu, and she answered on the first ring.

"Hey," she answered, her voice alert and hyper. "My source in the clerk's office says the sheriff just testified. She gets her info from the

bailiff, so her intel is spot on. Says Rich's whole cross-examination cen-
tered on you as a fugitive and being wanted for all these other murders."

Matty was clipping his nails and had his cell phone on speaker.
"Not surprising," he said. "Listen, has Dooby testified yet?"

"No, but Matty, like I told you, there's no way—"

"I have a different project for you." He used a file to smooth out
the rough edges around his thumb.

"Oh." Silence on the other end of the line while she waited.

"I need you to go to Gadsden."

98

"The state calls Marcia Darnell." Wish's voice had started to tire by one thirty in the afternoon, and Jason figured part of his fatigue had to do with preparing this witness for the cross-examination she was about to endure.

He's in for a surprise, Jason thought, forcing himself to keep his face blank.

Marcia "Dooby" Darnell walked to the stand with what seemed to be cautious trepidation. Her red locks were up in a ponytail, and she wore a sweater over a khaki blouse. She looked conservative and plain. Exactly as Wish had hoped.

"You sure about this?" Shay asked. "It's awful risky."

"I know, but . . . it's also sound."

Shay nodded her agreement.

On direct examination, Wish brought out Dooby's memory of November 13, 2019, which, not surprisingly, was a bit more descriptive and informative than Jason and Shay's stilted interview of her in January. According to Darnell, Tyson Cade came into the store a little before 10:30 a.m. Got his usual combo of a Twinkie and a Sun Drop. They did get into an argument where Cade threatened to stop paying for her mother's nursing home fees. She and Cade had been lovers for over a year and sometimes, like all couples, they would get into fights about money. He did grab her around the throat, but he didn't hurt her. Then he left and forgot his change. Dooby realized it. Walked outside and called after him.

"And then what happened, Ms. Darnell?"

"I heard gunshots. At least five of them, and Tyson fell to his knees and then onto his back." Her voice cracked and she stared down at the witness stand.

"No further questions."

"Cross-examination?" Judge Barber asked.

Jason stood. "Your Honor, we'd like to reserve our cross of this witness."

Barber cleared his throat, clearly surprised. A defendant could reserve cross-examination until his case in chief, but this tactic was rarely if ever employed.

This is a sound decision, Jason told himself again, hoping his instincts were correct.

"All right then, Mr. French, call your next witness."

Wish gazed across the courtroom at Shay and then Jason, his eyes curious and maybe a tad anxious. Then he peered up at the bench. "State calls Captain Chuck Tonidandel."

———

The direct examination of Chuck was hard to watch. Not so much for the testimony, which was expected and undisputed, but having to hear it from Chuck. Jason had only seen him briefly yesterday. Looking at him now, in his uniform but without his left arm, brought on a sense of depression. Would he ever be able to go kayaking again?

Everyone that gets close to me gets hurt, Jason couldn't help but think. He'd thought the Tonidandel brothers were immune to his jinx, but they weren't.

"Captain Tonidandel," Wish said, after he'd quickly had Chuck state his name and his role with the gun range. "Did Jason Rich frequent the shooting range you owned and operated with your brothers?"

"Yes, sir."

Wish grabbed a piece of paper from the prosecution table and put it in front of Chuck. "Captain, I'm showing you what I've marked as State's Exhibit 12. Can you identify it?"

"It's an invoice."

"Which shows a Glock 17 handgun being purchased at your range on November 1, 2019."

"That's correct."

"And, on the invoice, is the purchaser's name listed?"

"Yes it is," Chuck said.

Wish snapped his fingers, and a copy of the invoice appeared on the huge television screen between the witness and the jury. To the jury, the prosecutor's action might seem like a magic trick, but Jason saw a young man wearing a suit sitting behind the prosecution table with a laptop balanced on his knees, who was using the courtroom's Wi-Fi connection to broadcast exhibits onto the big screen. The image was enlarged to show the model of the gun—"GEN 5 G-17"—and the date of purchase. Wish hovered his red pointer over each item. Then he snapped his fingers again, and the screen zoomed in on the name of the buyer. The prosecutor's choreography with his IT assistant had obviously been rehearsed.

But it's effective as hell, Jason thought.

"Captain Tonidandel, is the purchaser of that handgun in this courtroom?"

"Yes."

"Can you point him out for the jury."

"He's right there at the defense table. My brother Jason Rich."

Wish raised his eyebrows at Chuck and then looked at the jury. "Let the record reflect that the witness identified the defendant.

"Also, for the record, Captain, the defendant is not your biological brother, is he?"

Chuck peered down at Jason. "No, he's not. But we been through a lot, and that's how I think of him. We lost our brother Mickey about six weeks ago, and we always been three. The colonel, me, and Mickey." Chuck turned to the jury. "Jason's our third now. And I know that's how Mickey would feel if he were here."

"Ohh . . . kay," Wish said, a tad bit of sarcasm in his voice. Jason looked away from the stand at the framed portraits of former judges that hung on the wall to the right of the bench. He bit his lip to keep it from shaking, and Shay passed him a Kleenex.

"Captain, did Mr. Rich practice with his new weapon after he purchased it?"

"Yes."

"And did you observe him shoot with the weapon?"

"Yes, I did."

"How would you describe his shooting?"

Chuck smirked. "For a lawyer? Not bad."

"Would you agree that he was fairly proficient from up to a distance of fifty to eighty feet?"

"What do you mean by that?"

"Did he hit the target most of the time from that distance?"

"Yes."

"Thank you, Captain." Wish peered up at Judge Barber. "No further questions."

"Mr. Rich? Cross-examination?"

Jason continued to gaze at the wall of judges. He felt his elbow being nudged by Shay, but he didn't look at her.

"Mr. Rich?" Judge Barber repeated, irritation in his tone.

"We have no questions of this witness, Your Honor," Shay said.

"Very well. The captain is excused."

As Chuck walked down the aisle, Jason turned and watched. In the back of the courtroom, Satch had stood for his brother. Before leaving, Chuck saluted the colonel, who returned the gesture.

"It's almost five, everyone," Barber said. "We are going to stop for the day." The judge's voice was as tired as Jason felt. As he gave his customary end-of-the-day instructions to the jury, Jason felt Shay's breath in his ear. "That didn't go as bad as you think," she whispered. "The two female jurors and three of the men seemed moved by him calling you his brother. They were watching you from that point on. That's good, Jason." She squeezed his elbow.

He nodded, thinking of Mickey Tonidandel and what Satch had said when he'd left the morgue.

It's tough being brothers . . .

99

Wish and Hatty regrouped back in the war room. The prosecutor seemed wired after the day's events, but Hatty was exhausted.

"What do you think?" Wish asked.

"I mean, it's gone pretty much like I expected," Hatty said, her voice thick, her throat dry. "Except for Jason reserving the right to cross Darnell."

Wish scratched his neck. "Yeah, that was surprising."

"She's the only chink in our armor."

"No, she's not," Wish said. "She went outside to give her boyfriend . . . lover . . . whatever you want to call him his change."

"And he turned around just in time to give his killer a clear shot at a stationary target."

"It's a coincidence and nothing more. It doesn't change the mountain of evidence against Rich."

Hatty said nothing. She didn't feel like arguing.

"Good grief, Hatty. It's like you're expecting this bastard to pull a rabbit out of his hat."

"I've seen him do it twice."

Wish snorted and walked to the door. "That wasn't against me."

"See you tomorrow," Hatty said.

Wish shut the door behind him without a word.

100

As he pulled into Colleen's driveway after another miserable night of being yelled at by the parents of nine-year-old baseball players, Trey Cowan wanted a cold beer and a shower.

And sex, Trey thought, taking a pull from the pint of Jim Beam. But as he hopped out of his car and began to trudge toward the door, a gritty voice stopped him.

"I'm curious."

Trey turned toward the sound and squinted into the darkness. He saw a man approaching and, for a second, thought it had to be Matty Dean. But this man was wearing a uniform.

"Curious about what?" Trey asked.

Satch Tonidandel stuck an envelope into Trey's hand. "Whether you'll show tomorrow."

The man started to walk away.

"I don't know anything," Trey whined.

"I don't believe you, Trey," Satch growled, looking over his shoulder at him. "Neither does Jason Rich." The colonel glared at him. "Not even your momma."

For a second there was silence, and Satch turned to face him. "Are you really going to commit perjury for Matty Dean?"

Trey glanced at the house and then back at Satch. "I don't know what you're talking about."

"Right," Satch said. "See you tomorrow."

101

Shay had fallen asleep in the library when she heard knocking on the door. "I'm coming," she said, taking out a pistol from her purse and striding to the door. She checked her phone. The time read 8:47 p.m.

When she saw the familiar face staring at her from behind the glass door, her heart rate sped up.

She opened the door and looked at him. "Well."

Albert Hooper hummed the first bars of "Yea, Alabama."

"What?" She escorted him in and relocked the door.

Once in the library, he opened his briefcase and pulled out the files. He held up his briefcase. "I've got all sixteen. Terry Barber represented Matty Dean in every case. All dismissed by Wish French." He licked his lips. "Counting what's on Alacourt, that's twenty-one total cases. All dismissed. All with the judge on Jason's case representing Matty Dean."

"When was the last charge?"

"2008."

"Twelve years," Shay whispered to herself. "Barber might argue that over a decade is too long to show any prejudice. Besides, Dean isn't the defendant. Jason is."

"But Dean is the defense's alternative theory. He's also a known fugitive who's wanted for several murders that are connected to this case, including Greta Martin and Mickey Tonidandel."

"Agreed. Still not sure it will be enough. A lot of smoke, though."

Hooper's eyes were dancing, and he took another document out of the case. He mimicked a quarterback and took three steps back. "Tua drops back. He's looking for it all." He flung the document at Shay, who caught it.

"What's this?" She scanned it.

"I dug deeper into property owned by Wish and Barber. I'd already checked their individual status, but I thought men of their rank and status might try to hide assets in a corporation for tax purposes." He gestured at the document. "According to the Alabama secretary of state's database on corporations, Jerome Barber is the president of a corporation called TBE Inc." A devilish grin came to his face. "Look who the vice president is."

Shay sucked air between her teeth. "Aloysius French." She stuck her index finger on the page. "This says the company is still in operation. Holy . . . shit."

"Oh, it gets better," the investigator said, his voice manic. Hooper reached into his briefcase and pulled out three sets of stapled papers. He laid them out carefully on the table.

"What's this?"

"Let's call it a puzzle. Remember how I said that Barber sold his lake property in late 2003, and you said that was weird because Barber had thrown parties at that lake house as late as last year."

"Yes."

He grabbed the first document. "Well, here is the deed, which was filed on December 22, 2003, from His Honor to a company called King LLC." He moved his hands to the next document. Hooper grabbed the second set of papers and mimicked a quarterback's throwing motion. *"DeVonta Smith is open down the sideline."* He slammed the pages down on the table. "And here . . . is a deed of that same lake property on January 26, 2004, from King LLC . . . to TBE Inc."

"Oh . . . my . . . God." Shay couldn't believe her eyes. "That means that the prosecutor and the judge own property together." She was bouncing on her toes. "That should've been disclosed! Barber should've recused."

"But he didn't. I doubt Terry Barber or Wish French ever thought anyone in Marshall County would look into this . . . and my suspicion is that French lent Barber money so that the judge could stay as co-owner through this corporation of a lake house. On the surface, Barber wouldn't have lost any status. He could still have his parties and look like the big shot he wanted everyone to think he was. And . . . in return . . ."

"Wish owns Barber." Shay's voice was a low whisper. "Forever." She forced herself to take a breath. "That lake house . . . it's nice, but it's kind of far out. Secluded, if I remember." Shay's voice had risen.

"It's in Langston," Hooper said. Then he grinned so wide that Shay suspected that his face might hurt. "Oh . . . but I haven't even told you the best part." Hooper grabbed the third document, which consisted of one page. "Here is the secretary of state's information for King LLC. The company dissolved on February 12, 2004, about two weeks after it deeded the lake land to French and Barber's corporation. That meant the corporate records for it were archived, so I had to drive down to Montgomery yesterday afternoon." He dangled the page in front of her. "Their warehouse was a bit more organized than the one here."

Shay snatched the document and placed it on the table.

Hooper spoke the pertinent parts as Shay read them. "Date of organization. November 5, 2003. Date of dissolution, February 12, 2004." He put his index finger on the names of the two members. "President, Jonathan Hanson." He tapped the page. "I believe the Sand Mountain meth folks called him by another name."

"King," Shay croaked. "King . . . Hanson." She ran both hands through her hair. "Sweet and merciful Jesus."

"See what he did there," Hooper teased, pointing from the name of the company to the president's line. Then he eased his finger down the page to the line for secretary.

There was a momentary pause, and then they both spoke the name out loud.

"Matthew Jefferson Dean."

Shay looked up from the page and into the investigator's round face.

"Touchdown," Hooper said, but his tone was no longer goofy or joyous.

"Holy Mary, mother of God." Shay stepped back from the archived corporate record like it might be a poisonous snake that had just bitten her. "He owns them both."

102

The boat docked a quarter mile from Polecat Hollow.

Lu hopped on board first and undid the rope from the hook. Then Matty followed and pressed his feet to the wooden dock, giving them a few feet of push-off.

Frank Crutcher, wearing his faded Atlanta Braves cap, was in the captain's chair, and once the boat was a few feet from the dock, he cranked the ignition. As they sped away, the air was thick with the rotten-egg scent of the Pilgrim's Pride chicken plant.

Matty Dean felt a warmth come over him despite the chill in the air. Polecat Hollow was a cove on the water near the Highway 227 overpass. For twenty years, Matty had lived in a log cabin on the water. *Home,* he thought. When was the last time he'd been here?

The Friday before I was arrested.

Almost five months ago.

At 9:30 p.m. on a Wednesday night, the main channel was deserted. Matty couldn't see any other boats as they headed toward Scottsboro, while the only lights came from the town of Guntersville behind them and a few flickers from shorefront houses.

After they had been cruising for an hour, Matty was ready.

"Stop here, Crutch," he said, reaching inside his pocket for his pistol.

But the younger man was fast and turned with two pistols drawn, one aimed at Lu and the other at Matty. "I wouldn't," he said.

Lu fired her sawed-off shotgun from its place on her hip and hit Frank in the right kneecap. The blast sounded like a stick of dynamite in the close confines of the watercraft. Frank screamed in pain and fired his pistol at Lu as he fell over on his back, but the shot sailed high.

"Neither would I," Lu said.

Matty stood and placed his foot on Frank's neck as the boat floated on the dark water. Above them, the clouds had cleared, and the waning full moon draped a sheen of light on the water about a hundred yards away.

"You know, for almost two months, I've wondered how Dooby Darnell could have gotten out of our spiderweb in Gadsden." Matty spoke in a calm tone as he kept pressure applied to Frank's neck. "I mean, she had to have been warned."

"Trudy . . . Cowan . . . did that," Frank managed, his voice hoarse and raspy from the tightening around his larynx.

Matty eased off him and took a step back, as Crutch took in a ragged breath and wrapped his arms around his ruined right knee. "Once . . . we're past this trial and Rich and the Tonidandels had been handled . . . I was going to take her and her shitleg son out. That *was* the plan, right?"

Matty scoffed. Crutch was a good liar. Even under duress. "Tell him, Lu."

"Had an interesting conversation with the bartender at the Old Mexico Cantina off I-59 in Gadsden. Name's Mandy and she remembered Dooby Darnell coming in almost every night for a month to get a margarita." Lu pursed her lips. "The only person she saw with Dooby was a man. She didn't remember much about him other than his Atlanta Braves cap." She cleared her throat. "I showed her your picture anyway, just to confirm, and she said it was you."

"I seem to recall asking you if you'd seen Dooby pretty soon before we tried to corral her," Matty said.

Frank had crawled back into his seat. "Matty—"

The crack of the pistol sounded like a firecracker going off, and Frank screamed as he crumpled to the ground, now holding his left knee. He gasped for air and struggled to raise his head. "Matty, it's not what you think."

"You mean, you weren't hiding your girlfriend in Gadsden, knowing full well that I might want to clean up this mess? Fucking her on the sly and telling me to my face that you didn't know where she was?"

"That's . . . not it," Frank spoke through clenched teeth, pulling himself up to the boat's railing. He grimaced. "She was an emotional wreck and needed . . . space."

"Why did you lie to me, Crutch?"

"Dooby was scared." Frank's voice was weak. "She said you told her to do something to stop Tyson out by the pumps. She said you gave her money. Sh-sh-she didn't know you were planning to kill him." Frank glanced at Lu, who now had her sawed-off shotgun pointed at his chest. "N-n-none of us did."

"That lying bitch," Matty said, training his Glock 17 on Frank's head.

"Did you do it?" Frank asked, his hands shaking as he clutched his ruined kneecaps, again glancing at Lu. His voice now seemed distant. Resigned to his fate. He snickered. "Or did you have your whore here pull the trigger?"

The shotgun thundered like a cannon, and the force of the blast sent Frank Crutcher flying off the side of the boat.

Lu lunged toward the railing and fired another shot into the water. Matty joined her, and they both stared into the dark lake, where the ripples of the splash had dissipated.

"Well . . . shit," Matty said. "I'd hoped to talk to him a little more."

"He was spewing nonsense," Lu said, glancing down at the long-barrel pistol in Matty's hand and then into his eyes. "Right?"

Matty said nothing for several seconds as they both watched the water for any movement, but saw none.

Frank Crutcher's corpse was probably sinking to the bottom of the Tennessee River. How many bodies had Matty Dean planted on that same silty surface over the years?

"Right, Matty?" Lu whispered, but he was already moving to the rear of the boat again.

"Drive us back, would you, Lu? I need to think." He didn't answer the questions. Tyson Cade had never answered his inquiries, and he'd be damned if he was going to answer to Lu or any damn body else.

Once he was seated again and the boat was moving toward Marshall County, Matty's thoughts turned to the next task. The trial was about over.

The district attorney was either going to give Jason Rich his justice . . .

Matty Dean glared back at the spot where they'd left Frank Crutcher.

. . . or I will.

103

"The state calls Ms. Cassandra Atkinson."

As the attractive English teacher from New Hope High School walked to the stand on Thursday morning, Jason leaned toward Shay. His heart was still pounding with the information she had just shared. "Are you *sure?*"

"I saw the documents myself. I think you can have a mistrial whenever you want one."

Jason gazed across the courtroom at Wish French, who was leaning against the jury railing with his arms folded. His thick white hair didn't have a strand out of place. Black pinstripe suit and red-striped power tie. Then he glanced to the bench, where Terry Barber sat with his elbows in front of him. His black robe flowing behind him. Spectacles resting a few inches down his nose.

Two of the most powerful people in Marshall County, Jason thought. *In bed with each other . . .*

. . . and Matty Dean.

It was hard to believe. *Hooper did it again,* Jason thought.

"What do you want to do?" Shay whispered.

He turned and looked into her brown eyes. He could smell her perfume, a watermelon-type fragrance. "A mistrial isn't a win, and we are talking about ancient history. The transactions all happened more than sixteen years ago. They smell bad . . . but they aren't necessarily illegal."

"Barber has a clear conflict of interest, and he should never be the judge on a case prosecuted by Wish French," Shay snapped. "Jason, a mistrial may be as close as we can get to a win."

Jason wondered if Shay was thinking beyond his case to what might happen if it became public knowledge that the district attorney had an ongoing business relationship with a circuit court judge and had conducted land transactions with two of the most powerful figures in the Sand Mountain meth trade, including someone who was now a known fugitive.

Wish will be out . . . and someone will have to be appointed . . .

That might be good for Shay. *And it might not have any impact.*

"I don't want a technical win," Jason said. "I want . . ." Jason thought of what Chuck had prayed for at the beginning of trial. ". . . a victory."

"Jason—"

"We're going the distance," he said, feeling a deep resolve. "To verdict."

———

"Ms. Atkinson, tell the jury what happened next?" Wish had spent the first few minutes of his direct establishing Candy Atkinson's unquestioned credibility. She was a schoolteacher from New Hope. An innocent bystander who did not know Tyson Cade and was only aware of Jason Rich through seeing his billboards.

"After I heard the shots, I was in shock for a couple of seconds. I saw a man on the ground, and a dark-colored SUV pulling out of the parking lot. I dialed 911 and then ran toward the man and knelt beside him. He looked at me and was mumbling some things."

"Did you hear what he said?"

"Yes, sir."

"Tell the jury."

"He said 'I can't believe the bastard got me.'"

"Then what happened?"

"He was kind of chuckling and looking at the highway. I asked him 'Who?'"

"What did he say?"

Atkinson, who clearly had been coached, paused and looked directly at the jury. "Jason Rich."

Wish gazed at the jury and then up at Barber. "No further questions."

———

Shay's cross was short but effective. "Ms. Atkinson, at any time while you were at the Alder Springs Grocery on November 13, 2019, did you see Mr. Jason Rich?" She put her hand on Jason's shoulder.

"No, ma'am."

"And you testified on direct examination that you were familiar with Mr. Rich. In fact, when we met at my office a couple of months ago, you said you recognized him from his billboards, correct?"

"That's right."

"But you didn't see him on the day of the murder, did you?"

"No, ma'am."

"When you were at my office, we also let you look and walk around Mr. Rich's SUV." Shay went over to her laptop and clicked a few buttons, and a photograph appeared on the screen behind the witness. It was from the inventory taken by the prosecution and introduced during the sheriff's testimony. "I'm showing you what's been previously marked as State's Exhibit 4. Have you ever seen this SUV before?"

"Well, I remember coming by your office in January and seeing that Explorer."

"Ms. Atkinson, is this the SUV you saw leaving the Alder Springs Grocery seconds after the shooting of Tyson Cade?"

"I don't know. I can't be certain."

"No further—"

"I thought the car I saw was darker," Candy added.

Shay glanced at Jason and then to the jury. "No further questions."

———

As Candy Atkinson left the stand, Jason looked behind him to the far wall. It was 10:00 a.m. Then he lowered his eyes to the colonel, who was in his customary spot in the back, dressed again in full regalia.

"Any more witnesses, Wish?" Barber asked.

"No, Your Honor," the district attorney said, glaring across the room at Jason. "The state rests."

104

In the hallway outside the circuit courtroom, Jason stood with two deputies on either side of him. He'd give anything to be able to take a walk outside, but that wasn't in the cards. The recess Barber had granted was for only fifteen minutes, and there was no way any of these officers would grant him a request for fresh air in light of the shooting that happened in November.

"How you holding up?" Satch asked.

Jason exhaled. "I'm OK. My brain's a little scrambled. I'm about to testify."

Satch brought his right palm to Jason's face and patted him twice on the cheek. "Take it right here. Head on. Eyes straight. No apologies."

Jason peered at him.

"That's an order."

"Yes, sir," Jason said, nodding at him as he turned away.

"Looks like you have company," Satch said.

Jason watched as the colonel stepped back and Richard Griffith came into view.

"Sheriff," Jason said. "Enjoying your week?"

"Are you going to call me?" Griff asked. His eyes were bloodshot red. He also had an odd earthy scent to him.

"You all right, Sheriff?" Jason asked.

"I'm peachy. Are you going to call me or not?"

Jason held his gaze. "I haven't decided yet." It was the truth. Depending on how his testimony and Dooby's went, he might still throw the Hail Mary and put the former lawman on the stand.

"You prick," Griff said, his voice just above a whisper. "I . . ." He looked toward the double doors leading into the courthouse.

"What?"

Griff glared back at him. "Fuck off." Then he walked away.

Satch chuckled. "You have a way with people, don't you?"

"Colonel, did you get a whiff of him?"

"Yeah."

"What was that?"

Satch took a deep breath and exhaled. "The lake."

———

Griff took his seat on the bench outside the courtroom and crossed his arms, rocking back and forth. He was going on over twenty-four hours without any sleep, and he was exhausted from what he'd done last night.

And what he'd seen.

There'd been no time for a shower this morning, and he could smell the mud that was still caked on his legs.

Did last night really happen? he asked himself. He'd almost said something to Hatty three times, but he had stayed quiet. A good man would have already come forward, but Griff felt paralyzed.

He pulled up his pantlegs and saw the remnants of mud and eel grass. *Yes,* he thought. *It did happen . . .*

Griff had followed Matty Dean to Polecat Hollow yesterday evening. The drug lord had been picked up at sunset in Langston by a woman operating a ski boat, and they'd made the trek by water into Marshall County. Griff had been watching from his fishing rental craft, and followed from a safe distance behind with his lights off. He watched through binoculars as they docked near an abandoned pier less than a mile from the Pilgrim's Pride chicken plant.

There, they hopped into a runabout boat and headed back out into the channel. Another man was behind the wheel of this vessel.

With their faces in closeup, Griff had recognized the two people taking this evening ride with Matty Dean. Marshall County wasn't a big place, and Griff knew all the players in the Sand Mountain meth trade.

When he saw the sparks from the barrel and heard the shotgun blast, he'd almost dropped his binoculars into the lake. He'd grabbed them and strained against the darkness to see. Frank Crutcher's anguished face was barely visible. Griff watched as Matty shot Frank with a pistol in the kneecap.

Finally, he saw Lu fire another shot that sent Frank head over heels into the dark water.

Griff had waited until Matty's boat was safely away before he tried to find Frank Crutcher. He yelled, flashed his lights, and finally jumped into the water. It was useless, but he felt compelled to try. He found a mesh Atlanta Braves cap floating on the surface of the lake.

But he didn't find Frank.

When he'd finally worn himself out, he climbed back into his boat. He was freezing and in shock. Luckily, the trek Matty had taken was back into Jackson County and only a few miles from the ramp where Griff had left the pickup and trailer he'd rented a few weeks ago.

He'd spent the rest of the night in the cab of the truck, trying to figure out his next move. The situation was completely off the rails, and he didn't know what to do. Part of him wanted to take his newfound knowledge and get his revenge on all the people who'd ruined his life.

But the lawman that was left in him wanted something else.

Justice?

He scoffed. Richard Griffith wasn't even sure he knew what the word meant anymore. And even if he did . . .

. . . *this is Marshall County and Sand by God Mountain.* He'd seen justice delivered the Sand Mountain way last night.

Griff closed his eyes. And waited.

105

"Mr. Rich, you may call your first witness."

Shay stood and spoke in a clear, firm voice. "Your Honor, the defendant calls Mr. Jason James Rich."

Jason walked to the witness stand as if he were in a dream. When he sat down, he peered at the jury, seeing all their eyes on him. Then to Hatty at the prosecution table, who had folded her hands together and was leaning her chin on them. And finally to the back, where the colonel took his hand and patted his own cheek twice.

"Would you please introduce yourself to the jury?" Shay said, walking to the left-hand edge of the jury railing, the farthest distance that she could get away from him. Direct examination was about the witness. The lawyer was just a facilitator.

"My name is Jason James Rich."

"Mr. Rich . . ." Shay paused and glanced at the jury. ". . . did you kill Tyson Kennesaw Cade?"

Jason tried to make eye contact with as many of the jurors as possible. "No."

———

For the next forty-five minutes, Shay took Jason through his background and education in Guntersville to his time at Davidson and then the University of Alabama Law School. And finally to his career as a personal injury plaintiff's attorney. He admitted to being an alcoholic, to receiving discipline from the Alabama State Bar twice, and that he was currently under a two-year suspension. Finally, he described the weeks after his suspension and his falling off the wagon. Then Shay got to the heart of the case.

"Jason, why did you buy a Glock 17 handgun on November 1, 2019?"

"Because I wanted a weapon with a little more distance. I had a Glock 43X that I liked a lot, but the Glock 17 is very well thought of, and Captain Chuck Tonidandel said it was the natural next step for me."

"Why did you want a next step with respect to shooting guns?"

"Shooting is something I've gotten into in the last couple of years. A stress reliever. It kept me away from drinking."

"But you were drinking when you bought the Glock 17, isn't that right?"

"Yes."

"Then why, again, did you buy it?"

"I'm not exactly sure. I was bored, and I wanted another gun to shoot. I was spending a couple hours a day up there. I wanted something else to shoot."

"Had you gotten pretty good with the 17?"

"Yes. Like Chuck said, I normally hit the target."

Shay paused and gazed at the jury. "Walk us through the events of November 13, 2019?"

"I got up around seven or so. I drank a little Jack Daniel's."

"How much is 'a little'?"

"Half of a fifth," Jason said.

"Then what?"

"I got in my Explorer and took a drive."

"Where did you plan to go?"

Jason shrugged. "I had no plan. Just wanted to get out of the house."

"Where did you go?"

"Drove past my office, which I had to abandon after my suspension. Took a left on Lusk Street . . . Highway 227 . . . and then hung a right on Hustleville Road."

"Why did you go to Hustleville Road?"

"I'm not really sure. I wasn't thinking lucid."

"What did you do?"

Jason took a deep breath. He could feel the heat on his cheeks and forehead. "I had my gun . . . my Glock 17 . . . it was in the seat next to me. I rolled down my windows, and I put the barrel of the gun against my temple . . ." His lips and voice started to shake. ". . . I really felt like I wanted to do it."

Shay's expression was shock. Jason hadn't told her this part. He'd wanted the jury to see the real Shay Lankford.

"You felt like . . ." She approached closer to him. ". . . you wanted to take your own life?" Her voice was just above a whisper.

"Yes, but . . . I couldn't do it. Instead I fired two or three shots out the window. Then I turned around and headed home."

Shay pulled up the footage of Jason sitting at the intersection of Hustleville Road and Martling Road. "Jason, the following video was marked as State's Exhibit 3. Why were you at this intersection at 10:43 a.m. on November 13, 2019?"

"I was heading home. I'd almost just killed myself."

"It wasn't because you were fleeing the scene of the Alder Springs Grocery after killing Tyson Cade?"

He gave his head a jerk. "No."

"After leaving this intersection," Shay began, pointing at the screen, "what happened next?"

"I drove home to Mill Creek and went down to the dock. I drank some more whiskey and went to sleep."

"Then what happened?"

"I woke up to sirens coming up my street."

"When you woke up, did you still have the Glock 17?"

"Yes."

"What did you do with it?"

Jason looked directly at juror number eleven, Mary McCoy. She had short brown hair and a kind face. "I threw it into the lake."

Mary flinched, and Jason saw several similar expressions from the other jurors. In some ways, getting rid of the gun was the most damning evidence of all.

"Why did you do that?" Shay asked, purposely letting exasperation seep into her tone.

"I panicked. I thought someone might have seen me shooting the gun out the window of my car. I . . . panicked."

"Then what happened?"

"The sheriff took me into town for questioning."

Shay walked to the defense table as if she might be through. Then she turned back to Jason. "Mr. Rich, you indicated that you almost took your own life on Hustleville Road?"

He cleared his throat. "That's right."

"Why?"

"Because I thought I was a failure. I'd lost my job. My nieces had moved away. My sister, Jana, was dead. Everyone I cared about . . . except the Tonidandel brothers . . . had been hurt by my actions. I just . . ." His voice shook. ". . . didn't see a light at the end of the tunnel."

Another pause and Shay took several steps toward him. "What made you stop?" She was violating the rules of direct examination by standing so close to Jason that she could touch him.

Jason wiped tears from his eyes as he let himself relive those awful moments. He saw an image of Jana and then Nola in his mind as he finally let himself feel what he'd been feeling that morning.

"Why, Jason?"

"I know this is going to sound crazy," he said, looking to the jury and using the same words his niece had used. "But sometimes I hear my sister's voice in my head." He nodded back his emotions.

"Your Honor, I object," Wish said. "I think we've gone well beyond the ridiculous."

"Overruled," Barber snapped.

"Why, Jason?" Shay asked again.

Jason wiped his eyes. "Because I heard something in my thoughts . . . in Jana's voice."

"What did you hear?"

"Don't be a pussy."

There was a pause, and then two of the male jurors burst into nervous laughter. But, in the front row, juror number eleven, Mrs. Mary McCoy, had a tear in her eye.

"Mr. Rich, did you kill Tyson Cade?" Shay asked again.

"No, ma'am."

Shay walked to the end of the jury railing, gazing at the jurors. "No further questions."

———

Wish asked his first two questions from the table. "Mr. Rich, you think this jury is stupid?"

"No, sir. You, on the other hand . . ."

More laughs from the jury.

"You like getting people to laugh, don't you, Mr. Rich?"

"I don't dislike it."

"You enjoy creating a carnival with your billboards and catchphrases and outlandish behavior, don't you?"

"Objection, Your Honor," Shay said. "This is argumentative and borders on badgering the witness."

"Sustained," Barber said. "Move it along, Wish."

Wish rose from his seat and took a stance close to Jason where he could easily glance at the jury too. "You admit to being on Hustleville Road on November 13, 2019, at approximately ten thirty a.m."

"Yes."

"You admit you had your Glock 17 handgun with you."

"Yes."

"You had been drinking, correct?"

"Correct."

"You even admit to firing your Glock?"

"I do."

"And then, when you got home, when you saw the cops pulling up your drive, you disposed of the gun, isn't that right?"

"Yes."

Wish shook his head. "No further questions."

106

The hallway was getting crowded.

Jason pushed through the double doors with his deputy escort and stopped before going into the restroom. He glanced to his right and saw Trey Cowan and his mother, Trudy, sitting on one bench. Dooby Darnell was standing with a couple of officers guarding her. And behind them, the former sheriff, Richard Griffith, remained on his bench.

One missing, Jason thought. He looked for Satch, and the colonel was right behind him. "Where's Crutcher?"

"Not here," Satch confirmed the obvious. "I've sent Chuck to the Alder Springs Grocery, but he's not there either. Were you planning to call him?"

"No. I just wanted him here for effect. Same role as the Cowans. I want Darnell to at least think about it before she commits perjury." He sighed, knowing that time was winding down. "She's our only hope."

———

Dooby Darnell's mind was a scrambled mess. She rocked on her heels and tried to make eye contact with Trudy or Trey, but they didn't look at her.

Crutch is dead, she thought. She got a text message from a burner phone last night saying that he'd been called out for a lake assignment with Matty and Lu. Said he'd text today but hadn't done so. Dooby knew there were other explanations for his failure to reach out, but she didn't buy them. She'd lived on Sand Mountain her whole life. She'd seen what happened to people who tried to walk a double line.

They ended up like Kelly Flowers, who'd been a good kid when he joined the sheriff's department and was seduced into being Tyson Cade's inside source.

Now he's dead . . . just like Crutch . . .

. . . just like me if I tell the truth.

Dooby sighed and bit her lip, remembering how Tyson had abused her. She'd hoped that the nightmare would end with his death.

But it had only gotten worse. She was trapped.

"It's time, Ms. Darnell," one of the officers said. As she walked toward the courtroom, she felt a firm hand grab her by the arm.

"Trudy." She looked down at the older woman, whose eyes burned into her. "You're hurting me," Dooby said.

"Ma'am, let go," a deputy said.

"It ends today," Trudy said. "You hear? *Today.*" She stood from the bench and leaned close to Dooby's ear. *"Tell the fucking truth . . . or I will."*

Dooby started to say something but was then whisked into the courtroom as she heard Jason Rich call her name. *Who am I kidding?* she thought.

I'm dead either way.

107

There were moments in a trial . . . like a sporting event . . . that defined everything. Jason knew that he'd held his own on the stand with Wish, but the damage was done. There was a mountain of evidence against him, and the only weakness in the state's case was walking to the stand and being sworn in right now.

He thought about all he'd learned about trying a case, and his backup plan if his attempts to turn Dooby Darnell failed. Trudy could help, but she wasn't enough. And Trey . . . *Isn't going to talk.* Crutcher and Griff were both Hail Marys.

This is it, Jason thought, gazing into the eyes of the one person who could set him free.

The courtroom was silent as a morgue. So quiet that Jason could hear the hum of the heater that warmed the vast space. He glanced at the jury and saw anticipation in many of their eyes. Jason had reserved his cross-examination. This was something they were waiting on. As he peered around the large courtroom and its familiar furniture, Jason knew he must be on his game.

"State your name again for the record," Jason said.

"Marcia Darnell."

"Ms. Darnell, you've been in the protective custody of the sheriff's department for two months, isn't that correct?"

"Yes."

"That's because the sheriff's office believes your life is in danger, correct?"

"I guess so."

"Because Matty Dean is still out there . . . and they are worried that he might try to hurt you."

"I don't know why they're so worried."

"Play the video," Jason said, and Shay pulled up the interaction between Tyson Cade and Dooby on November 13, 2019, just before the shooting. "Freeze it there.

"See where Mr. Cade has his hand, Ms. Darnell."

She swallowed. "My throat." She glanced down at her hands.

"He was choking you, wasn't he?"

"Not exactly. I could still breathe." Her voice had gone a tad monotone. Gone was the energy that she'd brought to Wish French's direct examination of her. As he waited to fire his next questions, Jason felt sweat rolling down his back and percolating under his armpits. The heater continued to hum.

"He was squeezing your throat, correct?"

"Yes."

"Because he was upset with you."

"Yes, we'd had an argument."

"About what?"

"I can't remember."

"Did you have arguments often with Mr. Cade?"

"Sometimes. Not often."

"He paid for your mother to be in a nursing home?"

"Yes."

"And you and he engaged in a sexual relationship, correct?"

"Yes."

"He expected sex in return for his goodwill, didn't he?"

"No." She squirmed in her seat. "But I did sometimes give him information."

461

Jason noticed perspiration on Dooby's forehead, and he looked at the jury. "In exchange for him paying off your mom's nursing home bill, right?"

"We never signed a contract or anything."

"You knew that if you stopped giving him information or refused to do so, you'd run the risk of not having your mom's care paid for anymore."

"I guess."

"And that goes the same for his sexual advances, right? If you didn't give in to him, then you worried he'd pull his funds."

She shook her head and clasped her hands together. "No."

"Did you ever talk with Trudy Cowan about your relationship with Tyson?"

"I may have."

Jason walked to the edge of the jury railing, biting down hard on his lip as if he did not want to ask the next question. "Ms. Darnell, did you ever tell Trudy that Tyson had raped you?"

Dooby crossed her arms, but Jason could see that her hands were trembling. "I don't know."

Weak, Jason thought. *She's breaking.* "He did rape you, though, didn't he?"

She gazed past him to the back of the courtroom. "Tyson could be rough . . . and demanding . . . but no. No, he didn't."

"You left town almost immediately after Tyson's murder. Why?"

"I was scared."

"Of what?"

"I don't know. I was right there when it happened."

"You were scared, because you had a role in the shooting, right?"

She shook her head. "No."

"You yelled after him. Said he'd forgotten his change, and he stopped dead still, didn't he?"

"Yes. But he left his change."

"Tyson Cade never expected change from you, did he? He tipped you every time. For sex. For information."

"No, not every time."

"Most every time?"

"Maybe," she admitted, but her voice was now shaky. Weaker.

"You left because you thought someone might think you were involved in the shooting, isn't that correct?"

She wrung her hands. "I was scared. I don't know. Matty Dean was still out there."

Jason could have kissed her. "That's right, and you were scared of him, weren't you?"

She rubbed her arms as if she were cold despite the stifling heat of the courtroom. "Everyone on Sand Mountain is scared of Matty."

Jason wanted to ask whether Matty Dean or Frank Crutcher or Trey Cowan had given her instructions to stop Tyson, but he knew she could simply deny those charges. He looked at Shay, and she nodded. "No further questions."

"Wish, do you have anything else?" Barber asked.

"No, Your Honor."

"All right then, the witness is excused. Call your next witness."

Jason stood. "Your Honor, may we have a brief recess?"

Barber grunted and then sighed. "Very brief, Counselor."

108

Jason knelt in front of Trudy Cowan. Trey sat next to her, his face stoic.

"I need you to rebut some of what Dooby said, Trudy. I'm sorry."

"All right then. Let's get on with it." Trudy rose, but Trey touched her shoulder and kept her from moving. Instead, he stood.

"No, Momma. I . . . can't let you do it."

"What the hell you talking about?" Trudy snapped.

"You were right," he said. He moved his eyes to Jason, who had risen to a standing position. "So were you, Mr. Rich."

"About what?" Jason asked.

He stuck his jaw out. "Everything."

109

Trey Cowan took the stand, and Jason could see the surprise register on Wish's face. Jason looked at Shay. "I need you here, partner. He was my client. I can't be the one who asks him questions. Can you wing this one?"

"What's he going to say?"

"I'm not exactly sure. But he said I was right, and all I've ever asked him about is some connection with Dooby Darnell."

Shay rose to her feet. "OK."

The former prosecutor walked toward the stand, the picture of confidence. "Please state your name for the record."

"Trey Cowan."

"Mr. Cowan, do you have information concerning the murder of Tyson Kennesaw Cade?"

"Yes, ma'am, I do."

"Your Honor," Wish said, his tone nervous. "I object. That's too broad."

"There's nothing objectionable about that question," Shay fired back. "And the district attorney was late on the draw. The witness already answered."

"Judge—?"

"Overruled," Barber interrupted. "Continue, Ms. Lankford."

"What information do you have, Mr. Cowan?"

"About five days before Tyson Cade was shot and killed, a man came to me and gave me money if I would approach Dooby Darnell with a proposition."

My God, Jason thought, as he watched from the table.

"How much money?"

"Ten thousand dollars."

Shay peered at the jury. "And what was the proposition?"

"Objection, Your Honor. Hearsay." Wish's voice sounded desperate, and Jason saw several scowls directed his way from the jury box.

"Overruled," Barber said.

"Mr. Cowan, what was the proposition?" Shay repeated the question and looked at the jury.

Trey gazed at Jason. The former quarterback of the Guntersville Wildcats had flat eyes, and his words so far had carried little inflection. He appeared resigned to his fate.

Come on, Trey . . .

"Mr. Cowan?" Shay was standing next to him. Close enough to touch. "What did this man ask you to do?"

Trey moved his eyes to the jury box. "Tyson Cade liked to drop by the Alder Springs Grocery around midmorning, about ten o'clock or so every day." Trey's mouth twisted into a lifeless half grin. "Always ordered either a Twinkie or an oatmeal creme pie and a Sun Drop. The Sprangs is a small place, and Tyson was a powerful person. That was common knowledge." Trey cleared his throat and again stared at Jason. "My job was to convince Dooby to distract Tyson Cade outside the store on the morning of November 13, 2019."

"To *distract* him? What do you mean?"

Trey looked at Shay. "To hold him up in some way so that he would stop."

"Was the plan for someone to shoot him?"

"I wasn't sure what was going to happen. I just followed instructions." He peered down at the floor. "I needed the money."

"Why you?" Shay snapped, gazing at the jury and walking to the end of the railing.

"The man offering the deal knew that Dooby and I were close. She was like an older sister to me, and he figured she'd listen if I asked her to do it. If someone she trusted was also in on it."

"And did she listen?"

"Yes."

"What was in it for Dooby?"

"She was also paid ten thousand dollars."

"How do you know?"

"Because I gave it to her. She got hers before I got mine."

Shay let the answers hang in the air. *Time to bring it home,* Jason thought as adrenaline poured through his veins.

"Mr. Cowan, who approached you with this deal?"

Trey peered back at her. "A man named Frank Crutcher."

Jason felt gooseflesh break out on his arms, remembering that Trudy Cowan had predicted Crutcher's involvement.

"And who is Frank Crutcher?"

"He's a Sprangs lifer, just like me and Dooby. Worked at the store with Dooby. I think he was also sweet on her."

"And, to your knowledge, did Frank Crutcher have any involvement in the Sand Mountain methamphetamine trade?"

"Objection, Judge." Wish's voice was dry as sandpaper. "Lack of foundation."

"Shay?" Barber squinted down at her from the bench.

"Your Honor, the witness just testified to growing up in Alder Springs with Frank Crutcher. Since he knows the man, we've laid all the foundation we need."

"That's not enough, Your Honor," Wish said. "There's been no predicate laid that this witness has any knowledge of the Sand Mountain meth business."

Silence filled the courtroom for several seconds. "I'm going to sustain the objection," Barber finally said. "Unless Ms. Lankford can establish such knowledge." He glanced at Shay, his voice hoarse.

Shay peered at Jason from across the room. *Do it,* Jason tried to convey with his eyes. *Ask him.*

"Mr. Cowan, do you have any knowledge of the Sand Mountain meth trade?"

Trey squirmed in his seat and looked out over the courtroom toward the clock on the far wall. "Unfortunately . . . yes. I did a few deliveries over the years for Tyson to make money. I hated doing it."

"Did you ever work with Frank Crutcher on these deliveries?"

"Yes, ma'am, I did. Crutch . . . was pretty high up in the organization. He was close to someone near the top."

There was an audible sigh from the jury box, and Jason squeezed his hands into fists. *Boom,* he thought, staring hard at Wish French across the courtroom. The old prosecutor had his arms folded tight across his chest. He looked like a playground kid who'd had his beloved football taken away from him.

"Mr. Cowan, did Frank Crutcher ever convey to you his motivation for this deal?"

"Objection. Hearsay." Wish's voice was weak, but Jason was impressed that he hadn't given up.

"We are not offering this testimony for the truth, Your Honor," Shay said. "The question goes to Frank Crutcher's state of mind."

"Overruled," Barber said. "The witness may answer."

"Mr. Cowan?" Shay nudged.

"Crutch said that Tyson was sexually abusing Dooby. He thought it had gone too far. That . . . was part of it."

"What was the other part?" Shay asked.

"He said his powerful friend was fed up with Tyson too."

Shay had her fist under her chin, watching Trey. "And who was this friend?"

Trey looked at the jury. "Matty Dean."

110

We've got a massive problem.

Matty looked down at the text message. Before he could ask about the problem, there was another one.

Trey Cowan just testified that Frank Crutcher paid him and Dooby $10,000 each to make sure Tyson was held up outside of the Alder Springs Grocery just before he was killed. Rich's partner proved a link between Crutch and us and said that you were fed up with Tyson.

Matty Dean was on the dock of the house in Langston. He dropped his fishing rod. Then he ran his hands through his hair and beard. He moved his eyes out over the lake and saw a bass boat two hundred or so yards away.

No, he thought, walking down the dock, soon beginning to trot.

This can't be happening . . .

———

Albert Hooper snapped three pictures from the bass boat. There was no good way to get to Langston by car, and he thought he might have better luck by boat.

He'd been correct. He looked at the photographs he'd snapped. Then he looked at the mug shot of Matty Dean.

Then he hummed the first bar of "Yea, Alabama."

He sent Shay Lankford a text.

Is this the infamous Matty Dean?

111

"Closing argument, Mr. Rich?"

"Yes, Your Honor." Jason stood and buttoned his coat. Adrenaline raced through his veins like a dog chasing a squirrel. He strode to the well of the courtroom, trying to control his breathing. The steady hum of the heating unit was the only sound he could hear, and even it was faint.

The last half hour had been a whirlwind. About all Wish French had established during his brief cross-examination of Trey Cowan was Trey's potential bias due to being represented by Jason last year. It was all Wish had, and it wasn't near strong enough to damage Trey's devastating testimony on direct examination. As soon as Trey left the witness stand, Jason and Shay rested their case.

After a very brief recess, Judge Barber called for closing arguments. Wish French, never one to quit, had focused his summation on all the circumstantial evidence the state had proved against Jason over the course of the past four days.

But he made the mistake of leaving out what was emblazoned on the jury's mind.

Jason peered at the twelve people who would decide his fate, knowing that this might be the last time he ever acted as a trial lawyer in a courtroom. *Focus,* he told himself. *Trust your instincts and believe . . .*

"Members of the jury, when I was on the stand, the prosecutor asked me if I thought you were stupid." He paused. "I don't." He looked at Wish. "But Mr. French apparently feels like you all were in the bathroom when Trey Cowan testified."

Two jurors in the back row laughed, and several others appeared to be holding in a chuckle.

Jason took a step toward the railing and spoke with deliberate intensity. "Trey and Dooby Darnell were paid $10,000 each by a known associate of the Sand Mountain meth trade, Mr. Frank Crutcher, to make sure that Dooby held up Tyson Cade on November 13, 2019. Dooby followed instructions, yelling after Cade that morning that he'd forgotten his change. Cade stopped, turned, and was shot three times in the chest. The plan worked."

Jason made eye contact with as many of the jurors as he could. "The only way that you can convict me of murder is if you feel that the state has established its case beyond a reasonable doubt." He glared at Wish French. "And the state has failed miserably."

He ended with the dagger.

"The state has shown no connection between me and Marcia 'Dooby' Darnell. They've proven that I'm an alcoholic, and I'll admit to that. They've demonstrated that I'm incredibly unlucky, and I'll agree to that as well. But they haven't put forth any evidence that I killed anyone. Trey Cowan's testimony, by itself, provides a truckload of reasonable doubt." He took two steps back and held his arms out wide. "Like I told you to begin this trial four days ago . . ." Jason again gazed at each member of the jury, holding on the kind face of Mary McCoy.

". . . *I didn't do it.*"

112

While the jury deliberated, Sheriff Hatty Daniels hoped to check her email and return some calls. But an old colleague stepped in front of her as soon as she exited the courtroom.

"I know where he is."

Richard Griffith reeked of a lake-y, muddy smell. "Griff, are you . . . OK?"

"Matty Dean," he hissed. He fumbled for his phone and showed her several photographs of a boat dock and a house.

And several closeups of a man with gray hair and a beard.

"Oh my God," she whispered under her breath. She turned for the double doors and almost ran into Shay Lankford, who was holding her phone up.

"You're not going to believe this, Hatty," Shay yelled, showing her a picture of the same boathouse.

And the same man.

"Matty Dean," Hatty gasped.

"Our investigator took these pictures thirty minutes ago," Shay said, intensity resonating from her tone. "I had my phone turned off for closing arguments."

"*Thirty minutes*," Hatty whispered.

She pushed past Shay and Griff and headed for the stairs, taking out her own phone as if on autopilot. Her chest was about to explode.

When the dispatcher answered, Hatty's voice thundered. "We need every available officer to converge on a lake house in Langston, Alabama. The address is—"

"2122 Bonaveer Lane," Griff said. He'd caught up to her and was walking in step.

Hatty repeated the address to the dispatcher.

"OK, Sheriff, I'm sending out an all points."

Hatty ended the call and began to run.

"Be careful," Griff said.

But Hatty ignored him, racing down the steps and subconsciously rubbing the shoulder that Matty Dean and his team of thugs had shot to hell last year.

You're mine, she thought. *Finally . . .*

113

The jury was out for eight whole minutes.

When Jason saw the bailiff barrel out of the double doors and announce that a verdict was in, he froze in his chair. He couldn't believe it. He'd barely had time to use the bathroom and wash his hands. He hadn't been able to ask Shay what she'd told Hatty that had made the sheriff hustle out of the courtroom. *What the hell is going on?* Jason's hands were clammy, and his stomach felt queasy.

What could such a quick decision mean? In civil cases, the general rule of thumb was that a quick verdict meant a defense win.

But in criminal cases, it normally indicates the opposite. Which means . . . He stared at Shay for encouragement, but his partner's face was white as a sheet.

. . . I'm screwed.

———

Five minutes later, Shay and Jason stood together as the jurors returned to their seats. Once they were all in place, Judge Terry Barber banged his gavel twice.

"Probably the last time he ever does that," Shay said under his breath, and Jason shot her a confused glance.

"Has the jury reached its verdict?" Judge Barber asked.

"Yes, we have, Your Honor." The jury foreman, Mrs. Mary McCoy, spoke in a clear voice. She stood and gripped a single sheet of paper with both hands.

Jason Rich closed his eyes and held his breath, hoping that Mrs. McCoy's presence as a leader in the jury room was the positive development that it seemed like. He felt his right hand being gripped by both of Shay's. The heating unit hummed, and Jason could feel the rapid rhythm of his heart as it struggled for control. He heard his partner's shallow breaths . . .

And his sister's voice in his head.

My brother ain't no pussy.

"And what is the jury's verdict?" Barber asked.

The foreman cleared her throat. "We, the jury, find that the defendant, Jason James Rich, on the charge of first-degree murder, is . . .

". . . not guilty."

———

The world felt like it was moving in slow motion.

Jason sank into his chair. He felt Shay's hands on his neck and then her lips on his cheek. "Congratulations."

Jason wiped his eyes and managed to stand. He looked over at the state's table and noticed it was empty. Hatty hadn't been there for the reading, but Wish had.

The prosecutor was already gone.

"What a sore loser," Jason said to Shay.

She shook her head. "Something's going on." Her eyes were dancing. "Something *big*."

Before Jason could ask what, he felt his legs being lifted off the ground. Satch had bear-hugged him. "You did it, you sonofabitch." The colonel set Jason down. Then Satch craned his neck toward the ceiling. "Hoo-rah!" he yelled.

Jason squeezed the colonel's neck and then looked at Chuck, who pointed upward with his good arm.

Jason knew the captain was reaching not to the ceiling, but to the sky and beyond.

To God . . .

. . . *and Mickey.*

"Victory," Chuck said, his voice thick with emotion.

"Victory," Jason repeated.

114

At least twenty sheriff's department cruisers surrounded the lake house at Langston. The National Guard was also there.

Sheriff Hatty Daniels spoke into a walkie-talkie. "I want the house converged on from the back and front. I also want officers on that boathouse." Beyond the dock, she saw police vessels with lights flashing and sirens blaring heading their way. "Wait for the team leader's signal."

You're mine, she thought, seeing a vision of Matty Dean in her mind and grinding her teeth. It was dusk. Not quite dark. *We need to move . . .*

"Sheriff, I'm in the house," a deep male voice blared from her handheld. His name was Richard Gosberg, but everyone in the department called him Goose. Hatty had made him team leader on the drive. Since Greta Martin's death, Goose had stepped up and handled several felonies while Hatty focused on the Rich case.

If anyone in her department was up to the task, it was him.

"About to give my team and the one in the flank the go signal," Goose said. "I don't see anything y—" His voice cut off, and then it was back. "Oh sh—!" But then his voice was gone.

Drowned out by the force and sound of an explosion.

Hatty felt her feet being lifted off the ground, and she fell backward onto the concrete driveway. She scrambled up to stand and saw fire and smoke billowing from what remained of the lake house. Goose was running toward her, waving his arm in the air. He'd gotten out.

Thank God . . .

Hatty's ears rang as she turned to a deputy who was saying something that she couldn't hear. She moved her eyes to the boathouse, feeling her heart constricting. Hatty felt like she was in a dream where she couldn't move. "Get off the dock!" She couldn't tell if her voice was working or not, but at least the officers were moving, scrambling back toward the shore. The boats beyond had also stopped.

"Get off the—"

The second explosion was louder than the first.

Hatty sank to her knees and watched in horror as the boathouse became engulfed in flames.

"Lord Jesus," she said.

The home . . . the boathouse . . . everything . . . was covered in fire and smoke, and Hatty's nostrils burned and her eardrums throbbed. She couldn't see but a few feet in front of her, and she could barely breathe without coughing.

He couldn't have left by car . . .

She was thinking on autopilot, subconsciously using every ounce of experience and police knowledge she had. There were no good ways to get to Langston by road. She grabbed her handheld and spoke into it. "He's on the water," she spoke, again wondering if any sound was coming from her mouth, her hearing gone. "I repeat, the fugitive, Matty Dean, is on the lake."

Hatty was running. Reacting on instinct and lighting out toward the nearest boathouse a half mile away. Smoke filled her lungs, but she coughed it out. Her abdomen stitched up, but she ignored the pain. *"Marshall County One."* She bellowed the name of the sheriff's department's largest vessel as the smog cleared and the neighbor's pier burst into view. "Meet me at the next dock over right now. I want all watercraft turning around and moving back toward Guntersville. Our officers on the ground here will handle the cleanup and rescue efforts."

Three minutes later, Hatty leaped onto the hull of *Marshall County One*. A deputy said something to her, his eyes wide. Hatty's hearing was beginning to return, but she brushed past him to the helmsman.

"Where to, Sheriff?" the captain asked, and Hatty could barely make out the words.

"Mill Creek!" she screamed.

115

At 6:55 p.m., the Raptor pulled into Jason's driveway. Satch and Jason sat in the front seat. Both men were exhausted, and neither had spoken on the way home.

Chuck was giving Shay an escort to the rental home in Grant. Any celebration of their victory would have to wait.

The excitement of the jury's verdict had been muted as soon as they'd heard the news that Sheriff Daniels had dispatched an army of officers to a lake house in Langston. A home most people in Marshall County thought was owned by the Honorable Terry Barber.

And which was now the refuge of Matthew Jefferson Dean.

As Satch opened the door to the truck, Jason's phone began to ring. "Yeah," he answered, putting the device on speaker.

"Jason, it's Hatty! We've got a problem!" She was screaming into the phone.

The colonel slammed his door shut. "What's wrong, Sheriff?" Satch asked.

"Matty Dean got away. He blew up the lake house, the boathouse, and the dock in Langston."

Satch grunted but said nothing.

"He left by water," Hatty continued. "I don't know where he's going or how long he's been gone, but my gut tells me that—"

"He's headed here," Satch said, then ended the call and drew his gun. "Damnit," he said, putting the Raptor in gear and driving a few feet into the grass so he had a view of the lake.

"What are you—?" Jason started, but Satch cut him off.

"Damnit," the colonel repeated. "Not enough light."

Darkness had descended on the cove. If Matty Dean was out there, they probably wouldn't be able to see him. "Let's go to my house," Satch ordered. "We'll have better cover in there, and I'll arm you with a piece. The cavalry will be here in no time."

"All right," Jason said.

Satch backed out of the driveway and onto Mill Creek Road. Then he pulled into his own driveway and handed Jason the key to the house. "I'll cover you while you open the door, got it?"

"Yes, sir," Jason said. He could hear the edge in his voice. Fatigue replaced by adrenaline and fear.

It's still not over, Jason thought.

"All right, don't lollygag," the colonel barked, opening the door and then holding his gun with both hands. Without hesitating, Jason ran toward the home and inserted the key into the lock. The ancient latch clicked open, and the two men entered the house. Satch pushed past Jason into the kitchen, breathing hard, while Jason tried to focus.

"Lock it back," Satch ordered, and Jason did as he was told. The colonel had now stridden from the kitchen into the den.

Jason followed after him, noticing that Satch hadn't turned any lights on. *But don't the boys always leave at least one lamp on?* "Colonel, is there something—?"

"Get down!" Satch screamed, pointing his gun into the darkness.

Then the sound of machine gun fire lit up the plywood house.

———

For the second time in the last two hours, Jason felt the earth moving in slow motion. As the automatic weapon pattered away, breaking the windows behind him, Jason dropped to his knees and then his belly, crawling forward and trying not to scrape his stomach on broken glass.

In the glow of the sparks flying from the barrel end of the gun, Jason saw Matty Dean holding an assault rifle and standing in front of the television set. The drug dealer's eyes were wild with rage. Jason sensed a presence to his left and crawled toward it. Then he felt hot breath in his ear. "Cover me, Jason," Satch spoke in a rasp as he placed the pistol in Jason's hand. "Whatever happens, don't stop shooting. You hear me?"

Jason's eyes had adjusted to the darkness, and he saw blood pouring from the colonel's neck.

"Satch, no." Jason's voice shook along with the house as the AR15 continued to destroy everything around them.

"It's the only way," the colonel gasped.

No. Jason opened his mouth, wanting to tell this man that he loved him.

But no words would come.

"Me, too, brother," the colonel whispered. Then he slammed his fist into his own chest and leaned his back against the wall, sliding his shoulders up the barrier until he was standing. His breath came in shallow rasps as blood pooled on the floor below him.

When the rifle fire finally stopped, Satch didn't hesitate.

The big man crouched low and sprang around the wall toward Matty Dean. He dropped, hitting the floor with his right shoulder and rolling as Jason fired at the drug lord from behind him.

Jason saw Dean rock backward as a bullet penetrated his chest, but he didn't go down.

The sound of the rifle exploded again as Satch came out of his roll, using his legs to lurch off the ground toward Dean. The colonel howled as machine gun bullets ripped into his upper body.

But the big man didn't stop. He plowed into the drug dealer, knocking him into the wall. Dean spun out of his grasp and struck Satch with the barrel of the rifle, and the colonel fell hard into the back wall. Dean then began to turn his weapon toward Jason, who had stopped firing when Satch and Dean were in each other's grasp.

Now Jason acted on pure instinct. He knew his pistol was no match for the assault rifle, so he threw it at Matty Dean's face. The meth king ducked, and Jason lunged toward him, then grabbed the barrel of the AR15 and pushed it toward the ceiling as it went off in Matty Dean's hand.

The two men rolled across the floor as Sheetrock from the ceiling and walls covered the tiny room. They scratched and clawed at each other, battling for the rifle. Jason had almost wriggled it out of Matty's grasp . . .

Jason felt his lower back explode in pain as Matty released his grip on the gun and punched Jason hard in the kidney. Once. Twice. Three times.

The air went out of Jason's lungs as the automatic weapon slipped from his fingers. He tried to get up, but the meth dealer was already on his feet, reaching for the weapon.

Matty Dean stood in the smoke-filled den and cackled. He pointed the rifle at Jason's head. "I win, motherfucker."

Jason held up his hands in a futile attempt to block the shots. Then a guttural growl rang out that sent gooseflesh up his spine.

Bullets covered Matty Dean's body, hitting him from every direction.

116

Matty was still alive.

Not by much. And not for much longer. He gasped for breath and looked up at the three people who stood in front of him. The lights were on in the house now.

But about to go out on me.

"I can't believe it," he gasped, staring up at Sheriff Hatty Daniels.

"I can," Hatty said. "I knew I'd get you . . . but I had help." She gave an uneasy glance to the man standing to her left.

Matty squinted up at him. "You?"

"Me," Richard Griffith said. The former sheriff stared down at Matty. "You and Tyson Cade ruined my life," Griff said. "Now you can rot in hell with him."

Matty's eyes rolled back in his head. "I'll save you a spot," he said.

"Do that," Griff said.

"Who else? I know it wasn't you, Rich." Matty glared at the man standing to the sheriff's right, but the billboard lawyer said nothing. "I had you dead to rights, and I'd already killed the colonel." Matty spat the words.

Hatty pursed her lips and took a step back. She turned and peered behind her, and Matty followed her gaze.

Chuck Tonidandel knelt over his brother and applied pressure to the colonel's chest wound. He was repeating Philippians 4:13, over and over. *"I can do all things through Christ which strengtheneth me."* Tears streamed down Chuck's cheeks.

"The ambulance is on its way," Hatty told the middle brother.

"Jesus . . . ain't goin' help your brother, Chuckie," Matty said, struggling to talk. His breathing had shallowed. "And neither . . . will the paramedics." He touched his chest and brought his hand to his face, staring at the blood that covered his fingers and palm. His whole body felt like it was on fire. He swallowed and tasted iron in his throat. *"I killed . . . that sumbitch."*

Matty ground his teeth. The room had begun to spin, and he couldn't feel his feet or legs. The world went black for a second, and then, blinking up, he saw that Griff was kneeling beside him. The former sheriff's eyes gleamed.

"How does it feel?" Griff asked.

"How . . . does . . . *what* feel?" Matty's fingertips felt cold.

"Justice."

———

Jason was in shock. He hadn't said a word since Hatty, Chuck, and Griff arrived.

He had won the trial . . . but the jury's verdict felt like it was rendered a million years ago.

He was going to lose again.

Not Satch . . . please, God, not Satch.

Chuck and Hatty were reciting Psalm 23 behind him, but Jason couldn't move. Couldn't open his mouth. Could barely breathe.

"Thou preparest a table before me in the presence of mine enemies."

"You killed . . . my best friend." Matty's voice was flat, but his eyes were clear as he glared up at Jason.

Jason was still far away. Watching the meth king through a lens or a screen. *Not Satch . . .* He heard the Bible verses like they were being broadcast on a distant radio channel.

"Thou anointest my head with oil; my cup runneth over."

Matty coughed blood and tried to spit, but his mouth was too dry. Saliva ran down his cheek. "Did you hear me?"

Snap out of it, J. J.

The voice in his head startled Jason. It was loud. Agitated. Impatient. And unmistakable. His sister was the only person in the world who'd ever called him J. J.

More to do, baby brother.

Jason staggered backward and breathed in the gunpowder. He heard Chuck's sobs and felt them in his bones . . . and his heart. He was lightheaded. Dizzy.

Furious.

"Did you hear me?" Matty asked again.

"I heard you," Jason finally said, his voice hoarse and dry.

The two men glared at each other, and Jason could feel the hate in the air.

"I . . . loved . . . Tyson Cade." Matty coughed more blood. "*And you . . .* killed him."

Jason could hardly believe his ears. Matty Dean was dying . . .

. . . and he still thinks I did it.

Jason turned and looked at Satch Tonidandel, who lay unconscious in Chuck's arms. Next to him, Chuck, Hatty, and Griff brought home the finale of Psalm 23.

"Surely goodness and mercy shall follow me all the days of my life . . ."

Jason remembered how Matty Dean had described Mickey's death.

". . . and I will dwell in the house of the Lord forever."

Through the broken windows, Jason saw an ambulance and a fire truck pull into the driveway. Then he looked down at Matty Dean's bullet-ridden body—shot up just like Sonny Corleone—and another passage from the Bible came to him.

An eye for an eye . . .

PART SIX

117

Arlington, Virginia, November 13, 2020

The sky was gunmetal gray.

The air cold, the wind chilly and brisk as it whipped Jason in the face. He tried to be strong. He knew the deceased would urge him to be so.

Jason and Chuck walked side by side behind the horse-drawn caisson. Chuck was in full uniform. Jason wore a charcoal suit and red tie. The military band played "Taps," and Chuck hummed along, gripping tight to the worn leather Bible he held in his hand.

Jason had thought this day would never come. Because of the COVID-19 global pandemic, which began soon after his trial, full honors military funerals had been delayed for months.

But here we are, he thought.

Gooseflesh covered Jason's arms, and he looked over his shoulder. Sheriff Hatty Daniels gazed at him with kind eyes. Next to her, Shay Lankford did the same.

Jason had never been to Arlington National Cemetery. He'd never walked along the massive expanse of white graves that honored the men and women who died fighting for our country. The experience was overwhelming.

Next to the band, an escort platoon from the One Hundred and First Airborne marched in formation. *The Screaming Eagles,* Jason thought, remembering how Satch Tonidandel had introduced himself to Tyson Cade over the phone just after Jason had first asked the brothers for help.

He predicted this . . .

When they reached the gravesite, there was a moment of silence.

Then the escort platoon raised their rifles. Seven officers, each of whom fired three shots. The twenty-one-gun salute was immediately followed by the roar of four fighter jets as they flew directly overhead.

Tears streamed down Jason Rich's cheeks, and he didn't wipe them. He felt an immense combination of pride and grief. *It's tough being brothers . . .*

Then Chuck Tonidandel strode forward to the gravesite and turned to face the gathering. There were two rows of white chairs, but most of the attendees were standing.

Jason stood next to Shay, and they clasped hands.

"We're here to celebrate the life of my brother . . ." Chuck's voice boomed out over the historic burial ground. ". . . Michael Christopher Tonidandel." He wiped his eyes. "We called him Mickey."

———

Chuck's eulogy was brief and respectful. He recounted a couple stories from the boys' youth and ended with Matthew 25:23. *"Well done, good and faithful servant."* Chuck took a deep breath and exhaled. "Before we adjourn, there is one other person who'd like to speak on Mickey's behalf." Chuck's lip trembled. "His . . . and my . . . commanding officer in the Screaming Eagles . . .

". . . our brother . . . Colonel Satchel Shames Tonidandel."

Jason turned and looked over his shoulder as Satch walked toward them. He carried a cane, and his weight was now just under two hundred pounds. His uniform hung loose on his body. Jason still couldn't believe he was alive.

After the shock from Matty Dean's ambush had passed, Hatty Daniels had explained to Jason what happened. Before passing out from blood loss, Satch had emptied his chamber into the drug dealer's chest at almost the same time that Hatty, Chuck, and Richard Griffith had arrived at the house.

"I'll hear the colonel's growl forever," Hatty had said. "I've never seen . . . or heard . . . anything like it."

But the bullet wounds from Matty Dean's AR15 had healed, and the colonel had finally taken Jason's advice and seen an oncologist. He'd gone through several months of radiation and chemotherapy, and he was scheduled for a thoracotomy next month. If the procedure went well, he'd be in remission.

Unbelievable, Jason thought, but then he remembered what Mickey had said about Satch.

He's a special man . . . I just don't see how anything could kill him.

The colonel had refused a wheelchair, and he'd watched Chuck's presentation from a respectful distance behind the crowd.

Satch hugged Chuck and then faced the gathering. He cleared his throat and spoke in a voice that had gotten even gruffer with the treatments he'd undergone. "My brother Mickey was a good man and an excellent soldier. I think . . . he was just beginning to find himself when he was taken from us." Satch hesitated, and Jason followed the colonel's gaze, seeing Mickey's girlfriend, Tiffany Shrout, crying in the first row of chairs.

"Life's not fair," Satch continued. "Sometimes it seems like heaven gets all the good ones." Satch bowed his head. "We lost our parents when we were kids. I was the oldest, and I've . . . always felt responsible for my brothers. When we were young . . . and into the army . . . and I guess forever." He leaned against his cane and struggled for the words.

Next to him, Jason heard Shay's sniffles. He wiped his own eyes and tried to keep it together. A gentle breeze drifted through the trees, and Jason looked past the colonel to the spectacular array of brown, orange, and yellow autumn colors.

So much pain, he thought. *And yet so beautiful . . .*

"I never got to say goodbye to him," Satch continued, facing the caisson that held the coffin. "So I'm going to do that now."

Jason gripped Shay's hand tight, and she squeezed his palm.

"I'm proud of you, Mick. And I'm sorry for letting you down. Tell Mom and Dad I miss them." He let out a ragged breath and then stared out at Chuck. Then Jason. And finally back to the caisson carrying the body of Mickey Tonidandel. "I love you, brother." The colonel arched his neck, and the anguished battle cry burrowed deep into Jason's soul.

"Hoo-rah!"

118

After the service, Jason and Shay took a long walk through the cemetery. They made stops at the Tomb of the Unknown Soldier and the John F. Kennedy Eternal Flame. Finally, they took a seat under the shade of a huge oak tree.

"I'm sorry, Jason," Shay said. "I know you loved him. And, God, do those brothers love you."

Jason winced, and his chin trembled. Finally, he wiped his eyes and nudged her elbow. "So, I have to ask, how are you enjoying being back in power?"

In the days and weeks after Jason's trial, both Wish French and Judge Terry Barber were arrested in connection with harboring Matty Dean. Though Barber swore his innocence and said he had no idea that Dean was staying at the house, he couldn't get past the fact that he was a part of the corporation that owned the land where Dean had camped out for months. He pled guilty and was now serving out a three-year prison sentence at Pell City Correctional.

Wish French, on the other hand, hadn't gotten off so easy. Not only was he alleged to have harbored a fugitive, but the prosecutor was also charged with conspiracy to commit murder and attempted murder, as it was determined that the same type of explosives that were used to bomb his vehicle after the first hearing in Jason's case were discovered in a storage unit that Wish rented in Albertville. Once the grand jury handed down its indictment, Wish decided that he wouldn't be dying in prison.

Out on bond, he put his best black pinstripe suit on, drove into downtown Scottsboro, and shot himself on Hamlin Street in basically the exact spot that Loy Campbell's car exploded on the first Monday of December 1972.

A note was found in his pocket that was short and to the point.

I failed my family. I failed my profession. I failed in every way possible. God forgive me.

In the aftermath of these events, Shay Lankford was appointed by the State of Alabama to serve out Wish French's term as the district attorney of Marshall County.

"It's crazy," she said, replying to Jason. "I love being a prosecutor, so I'm thrilled to be back doing a job I'm passionate about. But . . . I am a little sad about Wish. I couldn't stand him, don't get me wrong. But he taught me a lot too. And I tried many cases in front of Barber." She ran her hands through her long brown hair. "I tend to believe Barber was a patsy in all of it, and Wish was pulling the strings, but I guess we'll never know." She gave her head a jerk. "And then there's Griff. I hear he's living on his farm in Boaz and has started exercising his visitation rights. Cheryl and the kids have moved to Huntsville, and Griff drives up and sees them on the weekend. I guess I'm happy for him, but . . . it doesn't change what he did."

Jason said nothing. He wasn't sure how he felt about anything.

"How about you?" Shay asked. "How are things, Jason?"

He gazed off in the distance, looking at the white headstones and then upward to the dark-gray cloud-filled sky. "I'm really not sure," he finally said.

"You should be proud," she offered, now nudging his elbow. "This is your one-year-sober anniversary. Congratulations."

"How'd you know that?" Jason asked, turning to her, finding it hard to believe himself. For the past eight months, he'd remained on the wagon by staying busy. Most of his time was spent caring for Satch in the aftermath of the shootout in the Tonidandel den. Doctor's visits. Consultations with specialists. Oncology appointments. He'd continued his morning kayak rides whenever the weather permitted. He'd made it this far, but he knew the battle against alcohol addiction wasn't over.

It would never be over . . .

"Because this is also the one-year anniversary of Tyson Cade's murder," Shay said, her answer breaking through his thoughts. "And I'm assuming that you haven't had a drink since."

"Right you are. And . . . thank you." He stood, stretching his arms over his head.

"When will the bar make its decision?" Shay asked.

"Any day now," Jason said.

"I hope our letters helped." Shay and Hatty had written notes to the Alabama State Bar in support of the reinstatement of Jason's license.

"I'm sure they did," Jason said.

"Regardless of what happens, I'm pulling for you. And . . . I miss seeing you."

"I miss seeing you too."

"Why haven't you called or texted?"

For a long few seconds, Jason peered down at her. "Because you deserve better than what I am."

She stood and took his hands, gripping them firmly. *"I like who you are."*

"Thank you, Shay. I like you too." He gazed into her brown eyes.

The prosecutor held eye contact and then frowned. "What's bothering you? I mean, I know Mickey's funeral was incredibly emotional and heartbreaking, but there's something else, isn't there?"

Jason took a few steps forward and put his hands on his hips. "I told you what Matty Dean said right before he died."

She had followed him and put her arm around him. "He was crazy, Jason. Out of his mind. You have to let that go."

"He still thought I did it. He was dying, and *he still blamed me* for killing Cade."

"And Cade's dying declaration blamed you too. He was wrong. Dean was too. They were crazy. And who knows? Maybe Crutcher truly acted alone. I interviewed Dooby Darnell and Trey Cowan once I was appointed DA. Both swore they didn't know Cade was going to be shot. That's probably bullshit, but Hatty and I agreed we didn't have enough evidence to prosecute them. And Crutcher is dead. Griff gave a full statement of what he saw the Wednesday night of your trial. Dean and Luann Stephens shot and killed Crutcher and threw him into the river. Don't those actions seem consistent with someone trying to cover up a killing?" She stopped and took a breath. As she exhaled, she moved her hand to his neck and rubbed it. "Matty Dean killed Tyson Cade. It was an inside job. There is no other logical explanation."

Jason gave his head a jerk. "Maybe." *But I don't think so . . .*

For a long moment, there was silence. Finally, he felt her breath in his ear. "When you get back home . . . call me, OK?" She gave him a peck on the cheek and brushed past him. But after ten feet, she turned and looked at him over her shoulder. "Let it go, Jason. It's over."

119

At 10:30 a.m. on November 14, 2020, approximately twenty-four hours after the funeral of Captain Mickey Tonidandel, Jason Rich walked through the doors of the Alder Springs Grocery. He'd draped a duffel bag over his right shoulder. He didn't look at the clerk as he heard the jingle that announced his presence. He strode to the cooler in the back and pulled out a soda. Then he perused the aisle until he found the snack cake he wanted. He inhaled a slow breath and exhaled, his eyes moving along the rows of conveniences.

Fishing tackle. Rods and reels. Candy bars and toiletries. Bread and milk.

He took it all in, his thoughts turning to Tyson Kennesaw Cade.

The demigod drug lord. Who died right outside this store 366 days ago.

He was here. In this very spot minutes . . . seconds . . . before a nine-millimeter pistol ended his life. Jason's heart rate picked up, but he forced himself to walk with deliberation to the front.

He placed the Sun Drop and Twinkie on the counter.

Cute, baby brother. Jana in his mind. Forever Jana.

Next to the items, Jason placed two rolls of ten one-hundred-dollar bills each. "Keep the change," he said.

"What's this about?" Dooby Darnell had crossed her arms. Her red hair was up in a ponytail, and her jaw worked on a piece of gum. The convenience store smelled of floor cleaner and Juicy Fruit. A Christmas song, "Have a Holly Jolly Christmas," played on the radio. Jason's breathing slowed.

"There's no reason to lie anymore," he said.

"What the hell are you talking about?"

"Tyson Cade is dead." Jason chose his words carefully, just as he'd rehearsed on the plane ride home. *I have to know* . . .

"Matty Dean is dead too," Jason continued. "You have your job back, and the money you made off Tyson Cade's murder will pay for your mom's nursing home bills for a few months." Jason took a few steps backward until he knew he was out of range of the video camera. He dropped the duffel bag to the ground. He unzipped the satchel so that Dooby could see the stacks of green. "And there's enough in here to pay for your momma's care for the foreseeable future." He licked his lips. "Maybe you can take some of it and visit your sister in Fort Walton. I hear Hightide has great clam strips."

"What *the fuck* do you want?" Dooby's lip was trembling.

"Frank Crutcher is also dead. My sources tell me that Lu Stephens is now running the Sand Mountain meth cartel. Apparently, there wasn't enough credible evidence to charge Lu with Frank's murder, but that hasn't stopped the sheriff and the district attorney from watching the new meth queen like a hawk." Jason felt emotion rolling within him. "The war is over, Dooby. You're safe now, and I have to know. Trey and Trudy Cowan are safe, too, and I appreciated Trey laying it on the line for me at trial. But Trey has more courage than brains. He's not street smart like you. Frank told him a story." Jason left the bag of cash on the floor and approached the counter. "I'm betting he told you the truth."

Dooby looked away, keeping her arms crossed. The radio was now playing Elvis's version of "Blue Christmas." Jason felt sweat pooling on his lower back under his button-down.

"Dooby, I didn't kill Tyson Cade, and I don't think Matty Dean did either. I have to know," he repeated.

"What?" she finally asked, pursing her lips. "What do you *have* to know?"

Jason had the ridiculous thought that he was now Tom Cruise's Lieutenant Daniel Kaffee in one of his favorite movies, *A Few Good Men*, cross-examining Jack Nicholson's iconic Colonel Jessup in the seminal scene.

He knew what he wanted . . .

. . . *but can I handle it?*

"The truth," Jason whispered, letting out a raspy breath he'd been holding. "Did Frank Crutcher act alone . . . or was someone else behind it?"

Dooby looked past Jason to the drink coolers. She opened her mouth, then closed it.

"Please—" But Jason's words were interrupted by the clerk's despondent sob.

"Crutch was double dealing." Dooby spoke through her tears. "He'd been close to Matty his whole life . . . but . . . ." Her face wrinkled in anguish. "I've had a hard life, Mr. Rich. I'm sorry for lying on the witness stand, but I was scared. Terrified. I knew Matty had killed Crutch." She shook her head. "Tyson did rape me. He used me for information and sex, and I wanted him dead. When Crutch and Trey both came at me with their plan, I finally caved. I knew Crutch liked me. I wanted a better life. Is that so wrong?"

"No," Jason said, his tone soft. "It's not wrong at all. I'm so sorry for all that's happened to you. I . . . can't imagine." He stared at the Twinkie and Sun Drop, thinking of all the lives that Tyson Cade had shattered. Then, licking his lips, he forced himself to go on. "You said that Frank Crutcher had been close to Matty his whole life, *but . . . but what?* Who was he working with?"

Dooby wiped tears from her face and looked at Jason with sad eyes.

"You have nothing to be afraid of anymore." Jason pointed behind him to the duffel bag. "I know you've been through hell, and I'd like to help you."

"I don't want your money, Mr. Rich," Dooby said. "I'll tell you."

"Who?"

Dooby leaned her elbows on the table. "Like I said, Crutch and Matty were tight . . . but the army changed Crutch. When he returned to Alder Springs, he went back to the meth business, but only for the money. He had to pay for his daddy's care, same as me. But when he found out what Tyson was doing to me, he went after some help."

Jason's whole body began to shake.

"Crutch said we were in a war," Dooby continued. "And there was only one person in the world he could trust."

"Who?" Jason cried the words and felt Dooby's cold hand touch his own.

"Crutch was a member of the One Hundred and First Airborne."

Jason was shaking his head. *I can't handle it . . .*

"They go by a nickname," Dooby said. "I think you know it."

Jason staggered back from the counter and out of the grasp of Dooby Darnell, his eyes moving around the store, a sob escaping his chest. He couldn't talk. He could barely breathe.

"I'm sorry, Mr. Rich."

120

The fire was raging full tilt when Jason walked across Mill Creek Road.

The smell of burning embers made him think of his first trek here for help. He was being bullied by Tyson Cade, and he'd been desperate. So far gone that he'd sought assistance from three men he'd feared his whole life.

The by God Tonidandels, his father had called them.

Jason had only wanted protection. But instead, he'd gained three brothers.

As Jason rounded the corner of the house, he took it in. Since the shootout with Matty Dean in March, the windows, doors, and exterior siding had been replaced and a fresh coat of light-blue paint applied. The home looked good as new, but it retained its understated charm.

The colonel was sitting in a lawn chair, stoking the flames with a stick. There was an empty chair next to him, and Jason collapsed into it, folding his hands into a tent to keep them from shaking. "When were you going to tell me?"

Jason had driven the streets and roads of Marshall County all day. Until well past sundown, thinking it all through. He'd been so shocked at the Alder Springs Grocery that he'd left the duffel bag of money.

But that was OK. Dooby Darnell had been through hell and back. He had plenty of money, and perhaps the funds would provide her a fresh start. Jason again looked at the painted home of the Tonidandels.

But is that even possible?

Satch grunted. "What are you talking about?"

Jason scratched his chin and stared at the blaze. "Matty Dean still thought I killed Cade. Even as he lay dying. That's bothered me for eight months."

The colonel continued to work the stick over the fire. "Jason, the important thing is that you didn't do it. You were tried and acquitted. It's up to the sheriff's department to make an arrest. Or the new district attorney, our lovely friend Ms. Lankford, to come up with a new theory."

"I had to know, Satch." He licked his chapped lips. "So I made a visit to the Alder Springs Grocery this morning." Jason had been holding a plastic sack in his hand. He took out the untouched Twinkie and Sun Drop and threw them into the fire along with the sack.

"You did *what?*"

"She told me the truth. About Frank Crutcher being in the Screaming Eagles and how he sought out the only man he could trust when he wanted to bring down Tyson Cade."

Satch glanced at the fire and rose to his feet. He took his cane and walked around the blaze. Leaning against the device, he gazed out over the road to the dark waters of Lake Guntersville. "We have a rendezvous with destiny." The colonel growled the words. Then he turned to Jason, and his eyes shone bright in the light from the blaze. "That was our motto. 'We have a rendezvous with destiny. Our strength and courage strike the spark that will always make men free. Assault right down through the skies of blue; keep your eyes on the job to be done.'" The colonel's voice rose, and he spoke through clenched teeth, his voice shaking. "'*We're the soldiers of the Hundred First; we'll fight till the battle's won.*'"

Jason walked over to Satch and stood beside him. He was emotionally drained. Unable to comprehend what he'd learned. *I can't handle it,* he thought again. He moved his eyes to Satch, who was now looking right at him.

The colonel's face was pale and gaunt. His eyes had a haunting bloodshot hue to them. "Crutch served under me. I was his commanding officer. Just like Chuck and Mickey. He was in our unit." Satch turned back to the fire. "He was one of us."

"Tell me." Jason croaked the words. His legs felt like jelly, but he had to hear it all.

"After Sergeant George Mitchell's murder, Crutch had seen enough." Satch spoke while looking at the lake. "And so had I. We were in a war with Tyson Cade and Matty Dean, and they weren't coming after us anymore because it was good for business. They wanted revenge." Satch cleared his throat. "It was kill or be killed, and something had to be done."

Jason felt sick to his stomach. "So Crutcher approached you with a plan to kill Tyson Cade by using Dooby Darnell?"

For a long moment, the only sound was the rustling of the kindling. "No, Jason," the colonel finally said, peering down at the grass. "Crutch did come to me . . . but the plan was mine." He stared at Jason with slit-like eyes. "I told Crutch to use Trey Cowan to get to Dooby. I instructed him to tell Trey that Matty Dean was calling the shots. Crutch followed orders and put everything in motion." He stopped for a moment and stared at the sky. "I guess Crutch must have finally broken and told Dooby about me during one of those nights in Gadsden while she was hiding out."

As the fire crackled behind them, Jason didn't want to ask, but he heard the words coming out of his mouth anyway. "Colonel, who shot and killed Tyson Cade?"

Satch turned his head toward Jason. When he spoke, his voice was gruff and unapologetic. "I did."

Jason swallowed, but his mouth was so dry he started to cough. "No," he croaked.

"Yes," Satch said.

"I don't believe it," Jason said. "Colonel, how could you do that? Think of all the people who got hurt afterward. Sergeant Greta Martin was killed. Mickey, your own brother, lost his life. And I was charged with a crime that I didn't commit . . . *and that you did*. You could have prevented all of that pain if you'd have just come forward with the truth."

"If it were that simple, Jason, I would have confessed."

"What's complicated about it? You killed him. I was charged with the crime. If you disclose the truth, it all plays out different."

Satch turned away from him and tossed another log on the fire. "You're right about that, Jason. *But different don't mean better.* I knew that if I confessed to the murder, then Matty Dean wasn't going to stop trying to kill Chuck, Mickey, and you." He lifted his cane and pointed it at Jason. "I was no good to any of you locked up."

"And I was?"

"You're a lawyer, Jason. And you admitted that you needed to represent yourself to get your career and life back and to stay off alcohol." He shook the walking stick at Jason. "And if you hadn't've been so stupid to throw your gun in the lake, you'd have been exonerated long before trial, but you still won."

"What did you do with your gun?" Jason asked. "Was it a Glock 17?"

"Yes, it was. A loaner from Crutch that he'd bought illegally and was untraceable. It's long gone now."

"In the lake?"

"That's not something you need to know."

"Just like I didn't know the truth until now and had to find out from Dooby Darnell. Not my . . ." His lower lip shook, and his voice caught in his throat.

"I didn't tell Chuck and Mickey either," Satch said.

"People died because of what you did, Colonel. How can that be OK?"

"Casualties of war," Satch said, his tone grim. "More would have died if I'd confessed. Do you really think you, Chuck, and Mickey could have held Matty Dean and the entire Sand Mountain meth cartel at bay with me in jail? They were coming after us, don't you understand? Cade and Dean and the people that followed them don't play by the rules, Jason." He coughed and spat on the ground. "Justice was never going to be delivered in a courtroom."

Jason didn't answer. His brain was scrambled.

"I know you're upset, Jason, but I'd do it all again in a heartbeat. This ain't Mayberry. This is Sand Mountain. The line separating good and evil is pretty damn blurry. I did the best I could to protect my family . . . and that includes you. I miscalculated the night Mickey died. I got lazy, and my brother paid for my mistake with his life. I'll have to live with that forever. I wish Sergeant Martin hadn't been killed, but who's to say the same thing wouldn't have happened if I'd been in your place? Cade and Dean wanted us all dead. They were after their pound of flesh, and they weren't going to stop. It was them or us . . . I chose us."

Satch trudged toward Jason and then around him. He stopped and once again stared out at the lake. The wind blew through the leafless trees, and a whip-poor-will sang a song in the distance. Jason forced his feet forward until he was standing beside the colonel.

"I'm sorry for a lot of things in my life, Jason." He bit his lip and gave his head a jerk. "But I'll never apologize for killing Tyson Cade. Or Matty Dean. If I hadn't done it—"

"They'd have killed us." Jason finally admitted the harsh truth. "All of us." Now that he was away from the fire, the bitter cold enveloped every fiber of his being.

For a few seconds, neither man spoke. The whip-poor-will continued its sad song. Then, leaning on his cane, the colonel looked at Jason with a glint in his eye. "You remember, a long time ago, what I said about Sand Mountain?"

Jason swallowed. Finally, he gazed at the best friend he'd ever had. "There is only one kind of justice on Sand Mountain."

Colonel Satch Tonidandel lowered his voice to just above a whisper. "That's damn right."

EPILOGUE

January 4, 2021

On the first Monday of the new year, Jason Rich started the morning off with a chilly but life-affirming kayak ride to the back of the cove with Chuck Tonidandel, who had learned how to maneuver his craft with one arm. When they'd finished the trek, Chuck offered breakfast, but Jason declined. He had a nervous stomach and wanted to get going.

"How's the colonel?" Jason asked as they parted ways at the dock.

"Cranky as hell, but better." Satch had undergone a thoracotomy three weeks ago. He was still hurting but in remission.

"Good deal," Jason said. He tried to slip away, but Chuck grabbed him by the arm. The captain said a silent prayer, ending with a barely audible "Amen."

"Amen," Jason replied.

Thirty minutes later, after showering and getting dressed, Jason clicked the garage door open. He peered at the midnight-black Porsche with the personalized license plate that still advertised the brand.

GETRICH.

He'd received his reinstatement letter from the Alabama State Bar in early December, but it almost hadn't felt real. He'd wanted to get past Satch's surgery before doing anything. Besides, the holidays were always a slow time for litigators.

January, though, as his friend Bo Haynes liked to say, was "wide ass open."

As he hopped inside the sports car, the reality of his return to the law finally hit him. He forced back tears and cranked the ignition. Then he pulled out of the driveway.

Seconds later, he was on Highway 79.

He'd called Izzy on Christmas Day. There were some tears and a tiny bit of argument. But, in the end, she'd understood, and they agreed to partner up if she ever had business in Marshall County.

"I love you, Jason Rich," Izzy had said, ending the call before Jason could respond.

"*I love you, too, Iz,*" he'd whispered into the phone.

As he turned onto Highway 431 and passed by a billboard advertising another lawyer's services, Jason rolled down his windows. Then he clicked a button, and the top of the Porsche lowered.

His new beginning wouldn't include any fancy advertising campaign.

Am I a new man? Have I grown up? Do I have my oxygen mask on?

Jason didn't have all the answers, but he thought, perhaps for the first time in his life, that he was moving in the right direction. He had finally called Shay, and they had gone on their first date. Nine holes of twilight golf at Goose Pond followed by dinner at the Docks.

So romantic . . .

It was Mickey's voice, which now permeated his thoughts just as Jana's still did. Jason had texted back and forth for a while with Ashley Sullivan, but their moment had passed. Jason hoped that there might be a future with Shay, but he wasn't going to press it.

He was just grateful to have hope again.

You need people in your life, Mickey had said. *People you care about . . .*

Jason passed by the turnoff for Gunter's Landing and thought, as he often did, of his nieces. They'd called at Thanksgiving and Christmas, but neither had come home. *Maybe one day,* Jason thought. Again, he wouldn't press it.

There were some things you couldn't force.

As the Porsche ascended the Veterans Memorial Bridge, Jason knew he wouldn't be able to help himself. There were some traditions that had to carry on.

"WOOOOOOOOOOOOOOOOO!" he screamed, tilting his head back and thinking the Nature Boy himself would have appreciated that one.

It was an unseasonably warm and balmy day for January, and Jason relished the sun on his face and the wind in his hair. As he started to tell Siri to play his theme music, he decided that his mood called for something mellower.

"Siri, play, 'Black Water,' by the Doobie Brothers."

As the classic tune poured out of the speakers, Jason peered to his left and then his right at Lake Guntersville. A fog was lifting, a bass boat visible on the horizon.

It was beautiful. Yet dangerous . . . and mysterious.

Sounds kinda like . . . me. Jana's singsong tease. For better or worse, his sister lived forever in his soul.

As his car sped down the bridge into downtown Guntersville, Jason let off the accelerator. He passed Bakers on Main, the Old Town Stock House, and the courthouse. Finally, he peered up ahead at the law office and stared at the humble sign.

THE RICH LAW FIRM

Jason felt something inside him that a thousand billboards hadn't produced. He may have never gained Lucas Rich's acceptance or pride, but now he had something more important.

He was proud of himself.

Jason parked in front of the old brick building. He rolled up the windows and put the top back on the Porsche. He sat in the cozy front seat and thought of Mickey, who was gone but never forgotten. Then Chuck, a true believer if there ever was one.

And, finally, the colonel.

Satch by God Tonidandel. The strongest human being Jason had ever known. The colonel had made decisions that Jason still wrestled with and probably always would.

It's tough being brothers . . .

Again, he thought of the dark waters of the lake. Of Jana and Chase. Of Izzy Montaigne. Nola and Niecy. Harry Davenport and Mickey. Hatty and Shay. His father . . .

Of all that had been lost . . . and everything found.

As the southern anthem reached its close, Jason gazed at the sign and then the building where three generations of his family had practiced law. His mind drifted to the motto of the Screaming Eagles.

Jason Rich had never loved the lake, but his journey had somehow brought him back to where it all began. *Is this my destiny?*

He grinned and opened the door.

It was time to go to work.

THE END

ACKNOWLEDGMENTS

My wife, Dixie, has listened to every crazy book idea I've ever had. This incredible journey doesn't happen without her encouragement, love, and support.

Our children—Jimmy, Bobby, and Allie—continue to grow and delight us with their adventures. They are easily our greatest creations, and I love them so much.

My mom, Beth Bailey, is my biggest fan and always my first reader, and there's no telling how many books she has sold for me over the years at Sunday school, at the beauty shop, or in the grocery store.

My agent, Liza Fleissig, continues to drive our boat forward, and I am incredibly grateful for her persistence and friendship.

My developmental editor, Clarence Haynes, once again made suggestions and gave advice that made this story much better. I love bouncing ideas off him and enjoy our annual telephone call so much. As always, excelsior, Clarence!

To Megha Parekh, Gracie Doyle, Sarah Shaw, and my entire editing and marketing team at Thomas & Mercer, thank you so much for your support. I am so grateful to have you as my publisher.

My friend and law school classmate, Judge Will Powell, continues to be my go-to source for criminal law and trial research questions, and as always, he came through again. Randy Travis sang about "heroes and friends," and Powell is both for me.

Thank you once again to my friends Bill Fowler, Rick Onkey, Mark Wittschen, and Steve Shames for their early reads and for continuing to support my storytelling journey.

My brother, Bo Bailey, is a constant source of steady advice and support. I couldn't have written the scenes between Jason and the Tonidandels in this story without Bo's inspiration. *It's tough being brothers* . . .

My friend Jonathan Lusk continues to be a fantastic source for Guntersville and Marshall County local flavor and history. Jonathan's father, Louis Lusk, passed away during the writing of this novel. Louis Lusk was an icon of Marshall County law and will be sorely missed.

My friends Joe and Foncie Bullard from Point Clear, Alabama, have been with me since the beginning. I feel privileged to know them and look forward to our annual get-togethers in Fairhope so very much.

My friend Richi Reynolds has been incredibly supportive of my career, and, through her blog posts, has helped Marshall and Jackson County get to know me and my stories.

To Gary Baker, the Grammy Award–winning songwriter of "I Swear" and so many other number one hits, thank you for your support and friendship.

To Beth Ridgeway of the Sheffield Public Library, thank you for the wonderful events you've hosted for me over the years and for all you do to promote reading and local authors. You are a treasure!

To Cindy Nesbitt of the Giles County Public Library, thank you for your support since the beginning of this journey. I love my annual trips to Pulaski so much.

To the Page & Palette bookstore in Fairhope, thank you for hosting so many wonderful signings and for promoting my stories.

To Lady Smith of the Snail on the Wall bookstore, thank you for helping me launch my last five novels and for making it so easy for readers and fans to order signed copies of my stories.

To Melinda Jones of the Athens-Limestone Public Library, thank you for your continued support and for all the great events you've hosted for me.

My father-in-law, Dr. Jim Davis, to whom I dedicated this novel, has been an early reader of all my novels. Doc is my go-to source for firearms, and, since he is a voracious reader, his opinion holds a lot of weight to me. I am so grateful for his infectious positive energy and his unwavering support of my career. During the darkest days of my life, after my dad had died and while Dixie was still going through her cancer battle, Doc was the calm in the storm. Always available for a call no matter how late at night, even if all I wanted to do was vent. It is hard to put into words how much that meant to me. Thank you, Doc. I love you, man.

ABOUT THE AUTHOR

Photo © 2019 Erin Cobb

Robert Bailey is the *Wall Street Journal* bestselling author of *Rich Waters*; *Rich Blood*; the Bocephus Haynes series, which includes *The Wrong Side* and *Legacy of Lies*; and the award-winning McMurtrie and Drake series, which includes *The Final Reckoning*, *The Last Trial*, *Between Black and White*, and *The Professor*. He is also the author of the inspirational novel *The Golfer's Carol*. *Rich Justice* is Bailey's tenth novel. For the past twenty-four years, Bailey has been an attorney in Huntsville, Alabama, where he lives with his wife and three children. For more information, please visit www.robertbaileybooks.com.